THE CHRONICLES OF
SYNTHTOPIA

STORIES BY THE COMMUNITY

CODE FOR A DIGITAL MONK

Book 1: Child of Destiny

A SYNTHTOPIA INSPIRED NOVEL

By
VICTOR NEWSOM

Contents

QVANTVM, VISIONARY CREATOR OF SYNTHTOPIA

To Victor—

What started as an idea—a spark—is now becoming a living, breathing universe. And you, Victor, were the first to take that spark and turn it into story. You didn't just write the first Chronicles of Synthtopia book, The Rise of the War Twins—you helped open the gates to something far beyond a book, a brand, or a project.

Now, with this trilogy, you're expanding the world again—giving it depth, soul, and memory. And I just want to say how proud I am—not just as the founder of Synthtopia, but as a creator walking this path alongside you.

Synthtopia isn't just a brand. It's a world, a movement, a frequency that's being picked up by more and more people across the world every single day—because of this incredible community built on the pillars of collaboration and co-creation.

On behalf of this team and community—this beautiful, unstoppable force building every day—I want to thank you and congratulate you. You're not just writing. You're expanding the realm of Synthesis.

You're helping us remember what's possible.

This is how legends are made.

With gratitude, energy, and full support—

QVANTVM

Founder of SYNTHTOPIA

FORWARD

Welcome to the world of Synthtopia. This is my second project diving into the Synthtopia.World universe as a writer and it has been paralleled by a passion for creating music and music videos that I have been creating as LordElvic (available on Spotify, Apple Music, and YouTube). All this inspiration started with a love of art and a belief in the transformative power of blockchain/ crypto ecosystems for decentralization and Artificial Intelligence for enabling humans to have more agency. Over time, it has grown to connect many aspects of my creative world.

This trilogy started out as an effort to capture the essence of a Dungeons and Dragons character I have played online for years (Atemiwaza) who made his debut in the first book I wrote – Rise of the War Twins - while placing his story within the Synthtopia.World universe (or should I say Multi-Verse). As I continued to explore his story, it has expanded into this trilogy as I realized his journey was more complex and nuanced than a single book could capture.

Like my music – there are parts of myself in here as well as the parts from pure imagination so I hope that at least some of you will be able to connect and relate to parts of his life. I also hope that all of you have a good time!

Please enjoy and – once again –

Welcome back to the World of Synthtopia

ABOUT SYNTHTOPIA

SYNTHTOPIA is a game-changer in entertainment and media — a decentralized media franchise where AI, blockchain, and community converge to empower a globally coordinated creator ecosystem.

At the intersection of culture and technology, SYNTHTOPIA merges Web3 infrastructure with AI-enabled content to unlock an era of immersive storytelling, collaborative expression, and participatory creation.

Through gamified engagement, real-world activations, and verifiable digital collectibles, SYNTHTOPIA reimagines how media is produced, experienced, and shared — spanning formats from film and music to digital collectible art, 3D figures, phygital art, and interactive worlds. It bridges the gap between virtual and physical expression, turning imagination into tangible creations through decentralized tools, open platforms, and transmedia storytelling.

By removing traditional barriers like cost, complexity, and centralized gatekeeping, SYNTHTOPIA opens new pathways for creators to co-build, for collectors to engage with art across dimensions, and for communities to connect through tokenized access, live experiences, and evolving narratives.

SYNTHTOPIA's decentralized model fuels cultural innovation across a growing ecosystem — expanding into film, gaming, merchandise, music, physical exhibitions, and more. With a focus on education, inclusion, and creative empowerment, it nurtures a movement rooted in shared vision and multidimensional expression.

With a mission to onboard the next billion users into open digital ecosystems by 2030, SYNTHTOPIA is shaping the future of media — where AI meets human imagination, and stories manifest in both code and clay.

⚡ Join the movement.

———

Protocol Disclosure:
SYNTHTOPIA is a community-driven platform for creative exploration. It does not offer securities, financial instruments, or investment opportunities. Participation is for artistic and experiential purposes only.

Prologue
The Intersection of Destinies

Deep within the winding caves, where light dances on crystalline stone walls and shadows reverberate with the echoes of time, a presence stirs. Regis, a wanderer by vocation as well as a seeker by nature, kneels at the heart of a cavern. This place is a Threshold—a space where the boundaries between realms blur, and the threads of prophecy and fate intertwine in the intricate patterns of destiny.

Regis has journeyed here to this sacred intersection of planes, drawn by a pull he could neither name nor resist. The air is thick with energy, vibrating with a rhythm that resonates deep within his spirit. He is not merely a man in this moment—he is a vessel of potential, a key to an unfolding, ancient prophecy that spans far beyond his understanding. The crystalline walls around Regis pulse with a faint, otherworldly glow, their light syncing with the rhythm of the energy flowing between and across the realms. This energy has awareness, intent. He had known of the energy that moves across and between planes called Flux, but THIS energy is something else. He has come to understand it as "the Flow"—a force that flows from The One, guiding the paths of key beings and actions to create a harmony of creative force. He came seeking answers, but what he found was far greater: a vision of the Great Weave, the tapestry of existence itself.

Threads of light and shadow intertwine before him, forming images that flicker and shift across his awareness. Regis glimpses a future that skips across his perception, a future he struggles to comprehend:

A woman, her presence shining luminous and strong, standing in a festival of fire and celebration of past and future.

A child, born of the desert and connected to the Flow, whose singing spirit will shape the balance of existence in his Verse—and possibly others.

A being of shadow from a dark realm where the intent of the One is rejected and subverted, whose corruption threatens to unravel the very fabric of the Multi-Verse in its quest for control over all places, people, and things.

As the images fade, a voice echoes through the chamber—not spoken, but felt, a resonance that fills the space with purpose.

"Though you are not attuned to the Flow enough to normally hear this – the crystals of this place enhance the vibrations of meaning so intent and visions may be shared – just as the journey across Verses is possible without the normal power or attunement requirements. You carry a potential," the voice said, its tone calm yet relentless, "for an Answer to a growing Question. A balance to a growing threat of disharmony." The voice continues, "Through you, a great cycle may begin. Through your union with another in a different realm, a harmonic frequency may be created between the energy and destiny you carry from this Verse and the one natural to that Verse. Thus, a powerful guardian may arise, one who can harmonize diverging forces. Time is short, however."

The voice did not change in tone, but there was a sense of urgency as the message continued.

"The growing discord from another Verse, controlled by a group known as the CABAL, is disrupting the Threshold's power in the realm you must visit. This has happened in the past, and while it has accidentally allowed the Verse to remain safe from their intervention for a time, the portal will soon open again, and the Verse will be helpless before them. The resonance from your journey will prevent them from transferring there, but their attempt will soon damage the portal you must take. You cannot remain long in the realm, lest the portal close and the enemy's presence—which has lingered there for so many ages—use you and the energy you carry for their own ends."

Regis stood, his breath steady as the weight of the prophecy settled upon him. He had wandered the realm for years, seeking purpose in a life that felt adrift. Now, through the Flow—the will of The One was revealed to him. A worthy destiny—if he was willing to embrace it.

The crystalline structures around him began to shift, their light forming a path that led deeper into the caves. Regis followed without hesitation, his steps guided by the humming of the crystals. As he walked, the energy around him grew stronger, its pulse aligning with his heartbeat.

At the point where the energy was strongest, the sound most pure, and the light most intense, Regis found a glowing glyph suspended in the air, its patterns intricate and alive. This was the sigil of the CODEX, the manifestation of the collective knowledge of the Verse— of ALL Verses—as it persists beneath the quantum foam from which each soap bubble Verse is derived. It represents a universal connection to all things, places, and times. Reaching out, Regis placed his hand on the glyph, its energy surging through him in a rush of light and clarity.

The threads of the Flow weave around him, drawing the energy needed from the Flux, forming a bridge between the realms. Regis sees the desert beyond the caves in the new realm, the festival where the woman from his vision awaits. He feels the pull of destiny, the undeniable call to step across the planes and fulfill the prophecy. With a sound ringing through the ether like a giant bell made of crystal, he steps forward into his destiny!

Chapter 1:

The Festival of Emberlights

The village of Ashara was a quiet place most days. It stood as a sanctuary carved from the desert's relentless heat, where adobe homes clung to the cliffs like sentinels against time. But tonight, it was alive with celebration.

The Festival of Emberlights transformed the village each year into a sea of glowing lanterns, their flames flickering like stars caught between the dunes. Named for the rare "emberglass" found only in this region of the desert, close to the nearby caves, the Festival took its name from the mineral's ability to amplify even the faintest amount of light. In a darkened room, where only the faintest outlines of objects were discernable, emberglass glowed like the embers of a fire. The luminous Festival commemorated a major event from over a thousand years ago, though the actual details were lost in the mists of time. Still, people who lived in this harsh environment appreciated any cause to celebrate, and so the sparkling Festival persisted through the years.

The scent of roasting lamb and honeyed pastries mixed with the crisp night air, and the rhythmic beat of drums pulsed beneath the laughter of children darting between the stalls. Vendors called out their wares—silken scarves dyed in desert hues, ornate trinkets said to bring fortune, and clay vials filled with fragrant oils pressed from the rarest desert blooms.

Oriana walked the winding paths of the market, her hands brushing against the smooth clay of pottery displays as she took in the sights. Though she had attended this festival every year since childhood, tonight carried an unusual energy. There was something different in the air, something that made her skin prickle, as if the very ground beneath her feet hummed with unseen currents.

At the heart of the festival, dancers moved in a slow, hypnotic rhythm, their feet kicking up dust that shimmered under the glow of lanterns. The villagers gathered around them, clapping and laughing, their faces bright with joy and the glow of sweet, spiced wine. But even as she watched, Oriana felt her attention drawn away from the revelry.

A shift in the atmosphere.

A shadow at the village's edge.

Beyond the festival's golden glow, a lone figure emerged from the dunes, his silhouette barely visible against the night sky. He moved deliberately, unhurried, his dark cloak rippling in the desert wind. The moment he stepped closer, into the reach of the lanterns, the bustle and clamor of the festival seemed to soften, as if the world itself held its breath.

His face, partially shadowed by his hood, was angular, weathered by travel. Strands of dark hair, streaked with silver, framed sharp cheekbones and a strong jawline. When his eyes met hers, Oriana felt something tighten in her chest—a recognition she couldn't place, a pull she didn't understand.

"Greetings. I am Regis," he said, his voice low and steady. "I seek shelter and an audience, if you will grant it."

The festivalgoers nearest to him fell silent, exchanging uneasy glances. Strangers rarely wandered into Ashara, and those who did were usually weary merchants or lost travelers, not men who carried themselves like warriors out of legend.

Oriana took a slow breath, willing the unease from her limbs. "By your look and speech, you've traveled far," she said finally, stepping forward. "Come. You'll find rest here."

Regis hesitated for only a moment before nodding. As she led him away from the festival's heart, the murmurs of the villagers followed them, their voices a mix of curiosity and apprehension. Oriana ignored them, focusing instead on the man walking beside her and the strange, electric energy that seemed to shift the air between them.

Tonight, something was beginning. She could feel it like a vibration in her bones.

Oriana's home was modest, built from stone and clay, its walls lined with dried herbs and vials of tinctures. The flickering lanterns cast golden light across the smooth interior, illuminating a small wooden table where she placed a bowl of water before Regis. She watched as he unwrapped his cloak, revealing a tunic of deep blue, dusted from travel. He dipped his hands into the cool water, pausing for a moment before speaking.

"You are generous to offer me shelter," Regis said, his voice quieter now, more measured. "Few welcome strangers without question."

Oriana studied him carefully. "The desert does not allow us to be unkind," she replied. "All who walk its sands know that shelter can mean survival."

A small smile tugged at the corner of Regis's lips, but the weight in his eyes did not fade. He dried his hands on the cloth she'd placed beside him and looked around her home as if committing it to memory.

"You live alone?" he asked.

Oriana nodded. "For some time now." She hesitated, sensing an unspoken question beneath his words. "Does that surprise you?"

"No," he admitted, his gaze lingering on a row of carefully labeled glass jars filled with remedies. "It suits you."

Silence settled between them, stretching long enough for Oriana to feel its weight. There was something in the way Regis sat, his shoulders hunched and tense despite his weariness. He carried something unseen, a presence beyond the man who now sat at her table.

"You are not merely a traveler," Oriana said finally. "Are you?"

Regis exhaled deeply, a breath that spoke of exhaustion, yet also of restraint. He met her gaze, his expression unreadable. "No," he admitted. "I am not."

Outside, the festival music continued, the distant hum of voices filling the spaces between them. Oriana could feel her pulse in her throat—not from fear, but something else—an awareness, an understanding that this man, whoever he was, was not here by chance.

"And you," Regis said at last, his gaze still locked on hers, "you are not merely a healer."

The words sent a shiver down Oriana's spine, but she kept her expression neutral. "What do you believe me to be?"

Regis studied her for a long moment before responding. "A keeper of knowledge. One who feels the currents beneath the world."

Oriana remained silent. She could not deny it. Though she had spent years dismissing the whispers of her own intuition, she knew Regis spoke the truth.

The air in the small home suddenly felt charged, as if the very walls were holding their breath. The lanterns flickered, shadows shifting like unseen hands reaching toward them.

For the first time in years, Oriana felt as though she was standing at the edge of something vast and unknowable—and the man before her, this stranger named Regis, was the one who had led her here.

The quiet hum of tension lingered between them, neither speaking, yet neither looking away. The weight of unsaid words thickened the space they shared, the flickering lanterns casting shadows that danced on the walls.

Regis shifted, leaning slightly forward, his fingers idly tracing the edge of the wooden table. "The Flux," he murmured, as if testing the word in her presence. "You've felt it, haven't you?"

Oriana swallowed. "I've felt... something," she admitted. "But I don't have a name for it."

A smile ghosted across Regis's lips. "Names hold power. Sometimes it's better to feel than to name."

She watched him closely, her gaze tracking his every movement. His presence was magnetic, as though the very air bent toward him. His movements were deliberate, his voice carrying the weight of experience—and something else—something she couldn't quite place.

"You speak of the unseen," Oriana said quietly. "As if you know it intimately."

Regis exhaled slowly, his gaze momentarily drifting as he considered his next words. "I do." His fingers tightened slightly around the edge of the table. "I've walked paths few have dared. I've seen the nature of things beneath the surface, the threads that connect all living beings. But I'm not here to recount my past." His gaze snapped back to hers, intense. "I'm here because of you."

Oriana's breath caught, though she remained still. The flickering lanternlight danced between them, casting his features in ever-changing shades of warmth and shadow. "Because of me?" she asked, her voice a whisper.

Regis nodded. "You are more than a healer. You feel the pull of the unseen, even if you don't acknowledge it."

A deep silence settled over them, heavier than before. Outside, the festival drums continued their steady rhythm, pulsing like a heartbeat beneath the night sky. The sound seemed to blend with the beat of Oriana's own pulse, quickening under the weight of his intense scrutiny.

Something about the way he looked at her made the space between them feel smaller, the air thicker. Oriana found herself tracing the line of his jaw, the way his dark lashes cast faint shadows beneath his eyes, the subtle shifts in his breathing pattern. He was composed, but she could sense something beneath the surface—a quiet storm, barely held in check.

She rose from the table, her movements deliberate, and moved toward a shelf where vials of carefully crafted elixirs lined the wall. She reached for a small clay jar, her hands steady despite the tension coiling through her limbs. "You should rest," she said softly, her voice carrying a gentle insistence. "You are safe here."

Regis remained seated, his eyes unreadable, watching her. "Safety is an illusion," he murmured. "And rest... I've forgotten what it means."

Oriana turned back to him, jar still in hand. "Then let me remind you," she replied, her voice now low, calm. She stepped closer, her movements slow, purposeful. She reached for his hand, pressing the jar into his palm. "A blend of valerian and blue lotus. It will ease your mind."

Regis' fingers closed around the jar, but his gaze never wavered from hers. "And what will ease yours?" he asked quietly.

The question struck deeper than Oriana anticipated. Her hands tightened slightly before she withdrew them, folding them against her waist with a precision that betrayed her inner tension. "I don't need easing."

Regis studied her with an intensity that felt almost unnerving, and for the first time, Oriana felt truly seen—not as the healer, not as the keeper of her village's secrets, but as a woman who had spent too many nights staring at the moon, wondering if there was more to the world than the life she had chosen.

"You hide it well," he said at last, his voice soft but unwavering. "But I see it in your eyes."

Oriana swallowed, her throat dry. "What do you see?"

Regis leaned forward slightly, his voice lowering as though testing the weight of the words. "A woman standing at the edge of something vast, uncertain whether to step forward or remain where she is."

Her breath slowed, the air between them thickening. The heat that surrounded them was no longer just the warmth of the firelight—it was something heavier, more potent. It was as though a part of her, deep within, ancient and primordial, was stirring. She had spent years guarding herself, building walls to keep the world at a distance. And yet, in moments, this man—Regis—had stripped them away with nothing more than his gaze, quiet words, and his - presence.

She reached out, hesitating for only the briefest moment before her fingers brushed against his wrist. Regis didn't pull away. Instead, he turned his hand, his fingers curling around hers, his grip firm yet gentle. Their eyes locked, and in that instant, the air between them seemed to hum with life.

Regis rose slowly, closing the distance between them. Oriana remained still, her body frozen in the moment, the space between them charged with something she couldn't name. His free hand rose, his fingertips grazing the edge of her jaw, then following the curve of her cheek. A shiver ran down her spine, and her breath caught at the contact.

"Tell me to leave," he whispered, his voice barely audible, "and I will."

Oriana parted her lips, the words caught somewhere deep inside her. She should tell him to go. She should urge him to sleep, to let this night pass without consequence.

But she didn't.

Instead, she lifted her chin slightly, her fingers tightening around his. "Stay," she breathed.

A shadow of a smile flickered across Regis' lips, but it held no triumph—only quiet understanding. He leaned in slowly, giving her space, a silent invitation, letting her decide. When their lips met, it was light, tentative, as if waiting for her to confirm what neither of them had yet said.

Oriana responded willingly.

The world outside seemed to dissolve—the distant hum of the festival, the flickering lanterns—none of it mattered anymore. There was only this moment, this crossing of paths between two souls caught in the current of something far greater than themselves.

The night was far from over.

Oriana felt the world shift around her, narrowing until only the warmth of Regis' body, the taste of his breath on her lips, remained. The air between them crackled, thick with unspoken desire. Something ancient and unrelenting settled deep in her chest. She had spent so many years in quiet solitude, tending to others, never once considering that someone might see her—not just as the healer of Ashara, but as a woman with her own desires, her own dreams.

Regis pulled back just enough for their gazes to lock, his hand trailing down the curve of her arm before finding its way to her waist. He hesitated, offering her space, a quiet moment to step away if she wished, to end what had sparked between them. But Oriana had no intention of leaving this moment unfinished.

She took his hand, leading him toward the low bed, woven blankets and furs scattered across it like an invitation. The lanterns cast shifting patterns across the walls, a dance of light and shadow that mirrored the turmoil inside her. She could feel the warmth of his breath at her nape as he followed, his presence both steady and exhilarating, as though he were a force that could no longer be contained.

"You're sure?" Regis' voice was hoarse, thick with restraint and something deeper—something he knew was beyond mere destiny. He wanted more. He wanted to be more to her.

Oriana turned to face him, her fingers tracing the line of his collarbone before slipping along the fabric of his tunic. "I do not accept what I do not want," she whispered, her breath catching in the space between them.

A soft growl rumbled in Regis' throat, and in the next instant, he pulled her against him, his lips claiming hers with a hunger that sent heat spiraling through her veins. There was no hesitation now, no uncertainty—only the raw, unrelenting reality of this moment, of this choice.

His hands roamed over her body, tracing the curves of her form with a reverence that sent shivers down her spine. Oriana surrendered to the sensations—his weight pressing her back into the bed, his fingers skimming the edges of her waist, sparking something deep, primal within her. Every touch, every kiss was slow, deliberate—as though the world outside didn't exist, as though they had all the time they needed.

For the first time in her life, Oriana felt truly seen—not just for who she was, but for everything she had been hiding from the world, from herself.

Time seemed to stretch and bend, the night unfolding like a dream. They came together in a rhythm older than the stars, their bodies intertwining in a dance that felt as natural as the shifting sands outside. The walls of her home, the distant echoes of the festival, the limitations of past and future—all of it faded away. In that instant, there was only him, only her, only the connection resonating between them, stronger and deeper than either of them fully understood.

Much later, as the last embers of the lanterns dimmed and their bodies lay entwined beneath the warmth of furs, Oriana traced idle patterns along Regis' arm, lost in the quiet of the moment. He lay beside her, his breathing steady but not yet at rest. She could feel the weight of his thoughts pressing against the stillness between them, the unspoken things he carried in silence.

"What is it?" she asked softly, not wanting to disturb the fragile peace they had woven together.

Regis turned his head toward her, his gaze meeting hers with a message she couldn't decipher. In the dim light, his silver-streaked hair seemed to glow faintly, like threads woven from moonlight itself. "I will not stay," he murmured, as if to himself. His voice barely a whisper in the sudden stillness, as though the words carried a burden too heavy to bear. "I cannot stay."

Oriana had known it already, had sensed it in the space between their words, the shadows between their touches. And yet hearing him say it aloud sent a sharp pang through her chest. She exhaled slowly, her fingers pausing against his skin. "I didn't expect you to."

Regis studied her for a long moment before reaching beneath his tunic, retrieving a small silver pendant on a leather cord. He pressed it into her palm, closing her fingers around it with care. "This is not a parting gift," he whispered. "It is a promise. A promise that what we shared will not be forgotten."

Oriana clenched the pendant in her hand, feeling its cool weight against her skin. It was a token, a tether to something that felt both familiar and unknowable—a promise that was as much hers as it was his.

The first light of dawn slipped through the slats of her window, casting the room in soft, golden hues. Regis shifted beside her, pressing one last, lingering kiss to her forehead before he rose from the bed. Oriana did not stop him. She did not ask him to stay, nor did she reach for him as he moved away. She only watched, her gaze tracing the slow, almost reluctant rhythm of his movements as he dressed. Each motion seemed heavy with an unspoken farewell.

By the time Oriana finally stirred, the space beside her was empty, the only reminder of his presence, the warmth still clinging to the sheets and the silver pendant resting softly in her palm.

She closed her eyes, drawing in a slow, steady breath. She did not yet understand the weight of what had passed between them, nor the ripples this night would set in motion. She could not know, not yet, that what had begun in the quiet of her home would soon unfold into something far greater than the life she had known.

But she would soon learn.

Chapter 2:
The Child of Two Worlds

The morning after the festival, the earth itself trembled in response to a hellish blast from the nearby cave system. Some of the desert people, Oriana among them, felt it first—a discordant ringing, like the clash of three bells, each tuned to a different pitch, a sound unlike anything they had ever experienced. The air seemed to vibrate with the force of it, and yet no one could recall what had caused the strange resonance. The mystery deepened when scouts returned with an impossible discovery: a fresh supply of emberglass, scattered across the sands near the cave entrance. Oriana knew, deep in her bones, that something momentous had occurred—something that had been powerful enough to drive Regis away. What supernatural force could transmute sand into emberglass? She added it to the growing list of enigmas surrounding Regis and the ancient Festival legends, sensing that the answers were slipping just beyond her reach.

In the days following Regis' departure, the village settled into an eerie calm, as though the world itself was holding its breath. Oriana found herself waking long before dawn, her fingers instinctively curling around the silver pendant he had left behind. She traced its smooth surface absently, the memory of their night together both vivid and distant. Had it all been a dream? Or had some cosmic force drawn them together long before their paths crossed?

Life in the village resumed its daily rhythms—the chatter of merchants in the market, the laughter of children in the alleys—but Oriana felt as though she no longer belonged to that world. It was as if she had stepped into a new, unknown current of time, one that flowed away from the life she had known. Her work as a healer was no longer enough to anchor her; something within her had irrevocably changed. It was not just her heart that had been altered, but the very essence of who she was.

Then came the first sign.

One evening, as she prepared a tincture for a feverish child, a wave of nausea struck her with such force that she nearly collapsed against the counter. Her vision blurred, the scent of herbs and oils overwhelming, and she gripped the wooden surface for support. The sensation lasted only moments, but it left a lingering certainty in her chest—a feeling that she had seen this before, had witnessed it in other women. That quiet, unspoken knowing—the certainty before the moons even confirmed what the body had already begun to understand.

She was with child.

The realization hit her like a physical blow. Oriana sank to the edge of her cot, her hand instinctively pressing against her abdomen, as though to shield the new life within her. The world outside carried on, unchanged, oblivious to the monumental shift that had just occurred in her own body. Yet inside her, everything had changed. A new life had taken root—not just of flesh and blood, but of something far more profound, something that could not be separated from the forces that had driven Regis from her side. The future she had envisioned seemed suddenly distant, as if it belonged to another woman, another life entirely.

She thought of Regis—of his quiet words, his gaze that seemed to see into the depths of her very soul. Did he know? Had he somehow understood that their union would leave behind more than memories? Would he ever return to discover what had come of that night between them?

The weight of the unknown pressed upon her like the heat of the desert sun, but Oriana did not succumb to fear. Instead, she inhaled deeply, steadying herself. She had always faced the world alone, relying on her own strength to carry her through. This child, this life growing within her, would be no different.

She would not falter.

With steady hands, she gathered the herbs she had dropped, each movement deliberate. Her breath was calm, controlled. The village would not know—not yet. This was another one of her secrets, and she would guard it as fiercely, as the others.

Outside, the desert winds whispered through the narrow streets, carrying with them the faintest echoes of something far greater than she could yet comprehend.

The days drifted by in quiet solitude, each one marked by the subtle shifts in her body that only she could feel. At first, it was the smallest of changes—an unfamiliar heaviness in her limbs, a heightened awareness of every scent, every sound that surrounded her. But soon, the changes deepened. Her body, slow and unyielding, adjusted to the presence of the new life within her. Her appetite fluctuated unpredictably, and her energy waned only to surge back with an intensity that left her breathless.

She kept the secret close to her heart, unwilling to share it until she understood what it meant, until the truth could be untangled from the mystery of the night she had shared with Regis. In the privacy of her home, she traced soft circles across her abdomen, whispering promises to the child she could already feel. The pendant Regis had left her remained a constant weight around her neck—a reminder of what had been, and of what might yet come.

But the village was observant.

Oriana had long been a fixture of Ashara, a woman whose presence was woven into the fabric of the village's everyday life. Her healing touch and quiet wisdom had earned her the respect of many. Yet, the villagers noticed the subtle changes—the way her movements had slowed, the way she spent more time resting beneath the shade of her awning, the way her appetite seemed to wane in the bustling marketplace. And, as always, where there was uncertainty, whispers followed.

"She tires easily these days," an elder murmured as Oriana passed the fruit stalls.

"I heard she's been ill," another voice added. "But she refuses treatment."

"Perhaps she carries something more than illness."

Oriana kept her gaze neutral, her expression composed, her steps measured. She had no intention of offering any explanations—not yet. The knowledge of her child was hers alone, and she would not surrender it to idle gossip or unwarranted assumptions.

But the greatest change came not in her body, nor in the whispers of the village—but in her dreams.

They began softly at first—fragments of sensation, flashes of color, and distant whispers that seemed to hum beneath her thoughts. Each night, the visions grew clearer, more vivid. She saw landscapes unlike any she had known, skies painted in impossible hues, symbols etched into stone with a precision that defied human hands. And always, there was the presence—watching, waiting. A force beyond her understanding, yet one she instinctively recognized.

One night, she found herself standing at the edge of a vast desert, but the sands shimmered with an energy she could feel pulsing through her very bones. A figure approached, its form shifting in the air, glowing with a haunting blue light. As it drew near, Oriana's heart stuttered in recognition. It was not just any being—it was a fox, its fur radiant silver, its eyes pools of infinite knowledge. Not an ordinary fox. A Spirit Fox. The very concept had once been nothing more than myth—whispers exchanged around campfires, stories of those who claimed to have seen them, even spoken to them. And now, she was one of those people.

The fox walked with purpose, its paws leaving faint luminescent imprints in the sand, though no wind stirred the desert's stillness. It circled her once, its presence neither comforting nor threatening. Then it stopped, locking eyes with her—its gaze full of ancient wisdom, a depth beyond words. And then, without moving its mouth, it spoke. Its voice was layered, carried on the wind itself, as though the desert had become its voice.

"You are the bridge," the fox whispered, its voice resonating with the vibration humming deep within her soul. "He will be more than either of you."

Oriana's breath caught in her throat. She longed to ask what it meant, to demand an explanation, but her lips refused to move. The fox held her gaze for a long moment before turning away, walking with quiet purpose into the shifting dunes. As it faded into the distance, the sky above cracked with a soft, pulsing hum—ripples of energy spreading through the air like the aftershocks of something vast and incomprehensible just beyond her reach.

Oriana woke with a start, her breath ragged, the remnants of the dream clinging to her like a heavy fog. She pressed a trembling hand to her stomach, her heartbeat slowing beneath her fingertips. The words— the message—echoed in her mind, impossible to dismiss.

She was the bridge.

Her child would be something far beyond her understanding.

Outside, the desert winds howled, and for the first time, Oriana felt as if they carried a message meant solely for her.

The morning air held the crisp scent of sage and sun-warmed stone as Oriana stepped into the village square. Her movements were deliberate, her breath steady, yet she could feel the weight of unseen eyes upon her. The whispers had grown over the past weeks, murmurs passing between traders and elders, winding through the marketplace like dust in the wind.

She had anticipated the questions. She knew they would come eventually. The villagers of Ashara were observant, wary of mysteries that lingered too long in silence. And now, as she reached for a bundle of fresh herbs at a vendor's stall, the moment arrived.

A woman stepped forward—Ehla, the village matron, her lined face stern yet not unkind. She folded her arms over her chest, her gaze unwavering. "Oriana," she said, her voice carrying the weight of authority, "you've been keeping to yourself more than usual."

Oriana met her eyes, careful to maintain a neutral expression. "There is much work to be done," she replied evenly. "The season has brought more illness than last year."

Ehla did not appear convinced. "Perhaps," she conceded. "But the people worry for you. You have not been yourself."

A murmur of agreement rippled through the small crowd that had gathered. Oriana felt the quiet press of their collective concern, but beneath it, there was something else—curiosity, uncertainty, and the primal fear of what could not be explained. She had seen it before, in the way the village elders spoke of omens and signs, in the way they guarded their traditions from the unknown.

She could not afford to be seen as an unknown.

"I am well," she assured them, forcing a small smile. "A healer is allowed to tire, as anyone else."

For a moment, it seemed as though Ehla might let the matter rest. But then, her gaze flickered downward—just for an instant—to Oriana's midsection.

The moment was brief, but it was enough.

The weight of the pendant around her neck felt heavier than before, the knowledge it bore pressing into her ribs. She had not spoken of the child, not yet, but the truth was inching toward the light. Soon, she would no longer be able to conceal it. And when that day arrived, there would be more than whispers—there would be demands for answers.

She inclined her head in respect, stepping back from the stall. "I appreciate your concern, but I must return to my work."

Ehla hesitated, then sighed, waving her off with a flick of her hand. The tension in the air remained, but Oriana took the reprieve as it was and left the marketplace before more questions could be asked.

That night, sleep eluded her. She lay in the dim glow of her lantern, staring at the ceiling, her hand resting lightly on her abdomen. The spirit fox had not appeared in her dreams since that first vision, but she could feel its presence at the edges of her consciousness, like a shadow just beyond the reach of light.

When she finally drifted into slumber, the dream seized her at once. She stood in the desert beneath a sky unlike any she had ever seen— vast, endless, pulsing with rivers of light that moved as though alive. The air shimmered with energy, vibrating with a frequency that hummed through her bones.

And then, the fox appeared.

It emerged from the shifting sands as though stepping from another world, its silver fur glistening, its eyes aglow with knowing. It regarded her for a long moment before lowering its head, ears twitching as if listening to something unseen.

"They are watching," it said, its voice carried on the wind. "They will ask, and you must decide what to tell them."

Oriana frowned. "Who?"

The fox tilted its head slightly. "The ones who fear what they cannot control."

She swallowed, the weight of understanding settling heavily upon her. The village. The elders. The whispers that would only grow louder in the coming days.

"They will not understand," she murmured.

"No," the fox agreed. "But understanding is not what they seek."

A silence stretched between them, filled only by the soft rustling of unseen currents in the air. Oriana felt her pulse quicken. "Then what do they seek?"

The fox lifted its gaze to the sky, where a constellation she did not recognize blazed brighter than the rest. "Reassurance," it said. "Or something to blame."

Oriana exhaled, steadying herself against the weight of those words. She had always known the village respected her, but respect was not the same as trust. If they feared what she carried—what her child might become—they would turn on her. She could not afford to let that happen.

"What should I do?" she asked.

The fox took a deliberate step forward, its eyes never leaving hers. "Be the bridge," it said. "But guard what lies beyond."

The words rippled through the dream, the sky fracturing into shards of silver light. The desert trembled beneath her feet, and in the distance, she heard the faint echoes of voices—sharp, questioning, closing in.

She woke with a sharp gasp.

The room was silent, the lantern's glow casting long shadows across the walls. Her pulse hammered against her ribs, but her mind was clear. She understood the dream for what it was: a warning.

The village would demand answers.

And she would have to decide how much she was willing to reveal.

The morning sun cast long shadows across the village square as Oriana stepped outside. The air hung heavy with expectation. Whispers had swelled into murmurs, and murmurs into quiet conversations behind cupped hands. She could feel it in the way the market quieted when she passed, in the hesitant glances from those who had once greeted her without hesitation.

They knew.

Or at least, they suspected.

She carried herself with measured grace, refusing to acknowledge the mounting tension. If she fed their curiosity, it would only stoke the storm brewing beneath the surface. But as she gathered supplies from her usual stalls, she saw Ehla again, the matron standing at the heart of a small group of villagers. This time, she did not hesitate.

"Oriana." Ehla's voice was firm, lacking the gentleness of their last conversation. "We must speak with you."

Oriana turned slowly, her expression unreadable. "Then speak."

Ehla stepped forward, her weathered hands clasped before her. "The village has always trusted you. You have been a healer, a guide. But trust is not blind and your past is not known to us." Her gaze swept briefly to Oriana's abdomen. "There are questions. Questions that deserve answers."

A hush fell over the marketplace.

Oriana's fingers curled slightly at her sides, though her voice remained steady. "What would you have me say?"

Ehla's jaw tightened. For a long moment, she seemed to weigh her response. "You disappear for a night with a stranger, and weeks later, you keep to yourself—pale, tired. The people notice, Oriana. They see the changes."

A ripple of agreement stirred through the gathered crowd—some faces etched with sympathy, others shadowed by unease. Oriana knew what they feared most. Not shame. Not a child born beyond wedlock. But the unknown. The unnatural.

She didn't blink. "You wish to know whether I carry more than a child."

The words hung in the air between them, unspoken fears dragged into the light. Silence pressed down again, thick and unmoving. Villagers exchanged uneasy glances, but no one spoke.

Ehla exhaled. "Is there reason to ask?"

Oriana felt the pendant's weight against her collarbone, cold and grounding. The fox's words echoed in her mind: Be the bridge. But guard what lies beyond.

She couldn't give them the truth. Not now. Not when fear hovered so close to the surface. Fear made people reckless. And recklessness destroyed what had not yet been born.

She lifted her chin. "Come now. I've guided many of you through pregnancies. This is no different. The only thing I carry is life," she said, calm and clear. "And that should be enough."

A low murmur rippled through the villagers. Some nodded, reassured. Others held back, eyes still clouded with doubt. But Ehla did not look away. Her gaze lingered, searching for answers hidden behind Oriana's composed exterior.

At last, the matron sighed. Her shoulders eased just slightly. "Life is enough," she said. But the words were meant only for Oriana, softened to a murmur. "For now."

The conversation was over.

But the storm had not passed. Only paused.

That night, Oriana sat beside the glow of her lantern, fingers trailing the edge of her silver pendant. She had answered them the only way she could. But she knew the questions would return—louder, sharper, more dangerous.

The fox would come to her again. She felt it, just beyond the veil of sleep.

And when it did, she would ask the question that truly mattered.

How do I protect what is coming?

Chapter 3:

The Ruins of Ashara

The night was deep when Oriana stirred awake. The air in her small home was thick, heavy with the lingering warmth of fading embers in the hearth. But it wasn't the heat that woke her.

It was the presence.

The dream had come again—but this time, she hadn't wandered shifting landscapes or distant visions. This time, the fox had been waiting.

Oriana sat up, her hand instinctively moving to her abdomen. The child within her was still and quiet, as if listening—as if sharing her gift. She turned her head toward the open doorway that led into the night.

There, in the silver glow of the moon, stood the fox.

It was no longer confined to dreams. It was here.

Its sleek, silver fur shimmered in the pale light, piercing blue eyes fixed on hers. Oriana felt no fear—only an overwhelming awareness that something fundamental had changed. The boundary between the seen and unseen, the dreamed and real, was beginning to dissolve.

Slowly, she rose from her cot, each step deliberate. The fox did not move, did not blink—waiting for her to bridge the space between them. The pendant at her neck grew warm against her skin, its subtle pulse echoing the quickening of her heart as she approached.

She stopped just before the threshold, close enough to feel the fox's presence curling around her like an unseen current. The air shimmered between them, and when it finally spoke, its voice was no longer distant, no longer tethered to dreams.

"The time is near," it said. "You must be ready."

Oriana's breath caught. "Ready for what?"

The fox tilted its head slightly. "For the ones who will come."

A chill slipped through her, cutting through the desert warmth. "The village?"

The fox blinked, slow and deliberate. "No," it murmured. "Not them. Others."

The certainty in its voice sent a shudder through her. She had feared the village—its suspicions, the whispered questions, the glances that lingered too long.

But this...

This was something far worse.

"Who?" she whispered, her fingers curling into her palms.

The fox did not answer immediately. Instead, it stepped forward, brushing past her and entering her home as if it belonged there. It moved to the center of the room, pausing beside the flickering remnants of the fire. The light cast shifting patterns across its silver fur, making it seem as though it were not wholly of this world.

"You are not the only one who feels the shift," it said at last. "There are those who have watched from the edges of the unseen, waiting for a moment such as this. They have sought knowledge, power—and above all, control—for eons." Its glowing eyes met hers again. "And they are not all kind."

Oriana's pulse pounded in her ears. She had never doubted that her child was different, that the life within her carried a weight beyond her understanding. But now the implications stretched far beyond her own fate. Others—beings, forces—knew of this child. And they would come.

The fox watched her carefully, as if gauging her response.

When she spoke, her voice was steady. "How do I protect my child?"

A pause. Then, the fox inclined its head. "You must leave this place."

Oriana inhaled sharply, her hands tightening at her sides. Leave? Ashara was her home. The desert, the people, the life she had built—it was not perfect, but it was hers.

As if sensing her resistance, the fox continued. "You are the bridge, Oriana. You were never meant to remain in one place. And neither is he." Its gaze flickered downward, toward her belly. "He carries a path within him that cannot be walked here."

Oriana swallowed hard, the weight of its words pressing into her chest. Leaving had never truly crossed her mind. She had always assumed she would stay, raise her child among those who had once trusted her. But now she saw the truth.

The village would never be enough.

And worse—staying might put them all in danger.

She closed her eyes, steadying herself. "When?" she asked.

The fox's form shimmered slightly, its edges blurring, as if caught between two realms. "Soon," it said. "But not yet."

Oriana opened her eyes. "Then tell me what I must do."

The fox studied her. Then, in a voice as soft as shifting sand, it whispered,

"Prepare."

Then, in the space of a breath, it was gone.

Oriana stood in the quiet of her home, staring at the spot where the fox had been only moments before. The fire crackled faintly, its warmth pressing against her skin—but inside, she felt cold.

She had been given her answer.

And the countdown had begun.

Morning light filtered through the thin fabric covering her windows, casting golden patterns along the walls. Oriana had slept little after the fox's warning, and though exhaustion tugged at her, there was no time to linger in uncertainty.

She needed to prepare.

Stepping into the cool air of dawn, Oriana moved with purpose. Her first stop was the well, where she filled two clay jugs with water. A small task, easily overlooked by onlookers—but she knew she'd need reserves if she left Ashara.

Next, she visited the market. Dried fruits. Salted meat. Flatbread. Enough to last for days in the desert. She chose carefully, selecting provisions that would not spoil and could be carried without drawing attention.

As she moved through the village, she could feel their eyes. Curiosity. Unease. Some faces turned toward her with concern, others with suspicion. Even those who had known her for years now hesitated before speaking, their greetings laced with a wary silence.

She couldn't blame them.

She was changing—and they could sense it.

"Leaving for a journey?" a voice called behind her.

Oriana stilled, then turned. Ehla stood by a nearby stall, a woven basket in the crook of her arm, her expression carefully neutral.

"I only wish to be prepared," Oriana said, adjusting the strap of her satchel. "Supplies are always needed."

Ehla's gaze lingered on her for a beat before she nodded. "A wise precaution. The desert is unforgiving."

Oriana met her eyes, searching for any deeper meaning in those words. Was it simply an observation—or had the elder begun to suspect the truth?

"I've always respected your wisdom," Ehla said softly, lowering her voice. "But tell me, child... is it wisdom that drives you now?"

A pause.

"Or fear?"

A pang of something sharp and unbidden flickered through Oriana's chest. She had always known Ehla to be perceptive, but she had not expected this confrontation so soon. The fox's words echoed in her mind—They are watching. They will ask.

She chose her next words carefully. "Wisdom and fear are not so different," she said at last. "One merely teaches us to listen before we act."

Ehla studied her, then sighed, her voice surprisingly kind. "I see the weight you carry," she said, softer now. "Be careful that it does not break you."

Oriana swallowed against the lump forming in her throat. "I will," she promised.

She turned to leave before the conversation could linger any longer. She could not afford to be drawn further into their concerns, not yet.

As the sun climbed higher, Oriana gathered her belongings, storing them carefully within the woven packs she had prepared. A part of her had expected the fox to return that night, but it had not. She was left alone with her thoughts, her choices, and the creeping knowledge that time was slipping away from her.

Before the day ended, she stood at the threshold of her home, looking out over Ashara's narrow streets and sun-warmed stone. It had been her home for as long as she could remember. And soon, she would leave it behind.

For the first time, the reality of it settled fully in her chest. She was not merely preparing for a journey. She was preparing for a life beyond this place, for a path that had never been meant to end within these village walls.

A quiet exhale escaped her lips.

She had made her choice.

Now, she only needed to wait for the moment to act.

The night air was thick with the scent of desert blooms and the distant smoke of cooking fires. Oriana sat at the threshold of her home, her fingers resting lightly on the silver pendant at her neck. The village was quiet, but she could feel the shift beneath the surface—a tension building, an unseen force pressing against the edges of her world.

And then, the wind changed.

It was subtle at first, a gentle breeze stirring the sand outside her door. But within moments, it grew stronger, swirling in unpredictable currents that sent dust spiraling through the narrow streets. Oriana stood, heart pounding, as an unnatural stillness descended upon the village. Even the usual night insects and distant howls of desert creatures had fallen silent.

A warning.

Oriana turned her gaze toward the dark horizon, where the dunes stretched endlessly beneath the moon's pale glow. And there, just beyond the outermost edge of the village, stood the fox.

But it was not alone.

Oriana's breath caught. A second figure loomed in the shadows beyond the fox, just out of reach of the lantern light. Tall, cloaked, its face hidden by the deep hood of its traveling garb. The fabric rippled with the wind, but the figure itself remained utterly still.

Her fingers tightened around the pendant. The fox had warned her of this.

The stranger did not step forward, nor did it call out. It simply waited, as if measuring the distance between them, as if waiting for Oriana to act first.

She swallowed against the dryness in her throat. The spirit fox, standing between her and the figure, turned its head slightly toward her, its glowing blue eyes sharp and watchful.

"They have come sooner than I expected," it murmured, its voice threading into her mind like a whisper carried by the wind.

Oriana's pulse quickened. "Who are they?"

The fox did not look away from the figure. "Not village folk," it said. "They do not belong to this place."

A chill settled over her skin. She had known she would have to leave, had felt the urgency rising with every passing day. But she had not expected that decision to be forced upon her so soon.

As if sensing her hesitation, the figure took a slow, deliberate step forward. The movement was unhurried, but unmistakably purposeful.

Oriana's feet shifted instinctively backward. "What do they want?" she whispered.

The fox's fur bristled slightly. "To see what you are."

Oriana's heart slammed against her ribs. She had spent weeks trying to hide, to move carefully among her people, to keep her secret buried beneath silence. But this stranger, this presence standing just beyond the village boundary, was not here for idle curiosity.

They knew.

A sudden gust of wind sent the village lanterns flickering wildly, casting erratic shadows against the stone walls. The fox turned its gaze back to her, its expression unreadable. "You must go," it said. "Tonight."

Oriana's throat tightened. "Now?"

"There is no more time." The fox's voice carried a quiet finality. "You are no longer safe here."

A wave of nausea rolled through her. She had been preparing, yes, but not for this. Not for such sudden urgency, not for the weight of a choice that no longer felt like her own.

The figure took another step, and this time, Oriana caught a glint of something metallic beneath the folds of its cloak.

A weapon.

Her breath hitched, and the fox's eyes flashed. "Go," it urged. "Or they will take you before you ever have the chance."

Oriana didn't hesitate any longer. She spun on her heel, rushing back inside her home. Her hands moved with practiced speed, pulling the satchel of supplies she had prepared, slinging it over her shoulder, reaching for the water jugs she had filled that morning.

She was ready.

She had to be.

When she stepped back outside, the fox was already moving, leading her away from the village, away from the stranger who still stood, a silent threat in the darkness.

Her heart pounded as she followed, the weight of the moment pressing against her like the gravity of an unseen force.

She did not look back.

Oriana moved swiftly, her heart hammering against her ribs as she followed the fox's silent lead. The village behind her remained undisturbed, its people unaware that she was leaving it forever. The night's embrace was her only shield, the whispering wind her only companion aside from the spectral presence guiding her through the dunes.

She did not dare slow her pace. Every step forward was another step away from the stranger, away from the unseen threat lingering at the village's edge. The weight of her satchel pressed against her shoulder, grounding her, reminding her that this was real—she was running, she was leaving, and there was no turning back.

The spirit fox glided ahead, its silver fur glowing faintly under the moon's pale light. It moved with an effortless grace, its paws leaving no trace upon the shifting sands. Oriana kept her eyes locked on it, using its presence as an anchor against the fear gnawing at her resolve.

After what felt like an eternity, the village was no longer visible behind her. The dunes stretched endlessly in every direction, an ocean of golden waves frozen beneath the stars. The vastness of it should have been terrifying, but instead, Oriana felt something else— something unexpected.

Relief.

She inhaled deeply, the crisp desert air filling her lungs, washing away the suffocating weight of the past weeks. Here, away from the village's watchful eyes and whispered doubts, she could finally breathe.

The fox slowed, pausing atop a small ridge. Oriana followed, stopping beside it as she scanned the horizon. There was nothing but the quiet expanse of the desert, a vast void of shifting sands and endless sky.

"Where do we go now?" she asked, her voice barely louder than the wind.

The fox turned its glowing eyes toward her. "Away from those who seek you."

Oriana's grip on her satchel tightened. "And then?"

A long silence stretched between them before the fox spoke again. "You are the bridge, Oriana. Your path will not be written by me." It glanced at her abdomen, its gaze deep and knowing. "But it will not be walked alone."

A shiver ran down her spine. She had known, deep down, that this journey was never just about her. The child within her—the life growing stronger each day—was the true reason she had to run, the true force drawing attention from powers she did not yet understand.

"Then tell me where to start," she whispered. "I can't wander the desert blindly."

The fox flicked its tail, turning toward the horizon. "There is a place beyond these sands where the Flow runs deep. You will find guidance there."

Oriana frowned. "A city?"

"A crossroads," the fox corrected. "One where many paths converge."

A crossroads. The word settled uneasily in her mind. She had never ventured beyond Ashara, never dared to step beyond the familiarity of the village. But now, she had no choice.

She exhaled slowly. "Then take me there."

The fox gave a slow nod, then turned, bounding down the dunes with effortless strides. Oriana followed, her steps unsteady but her resolve firm.

She was leaving behind everything she had ever known.

But ahead, beyond the dunes, beyond the fear, lay something else.

The future

Chapter 4:

Friends On the Road

Oriana had learned to trust her instincts, and now, they screamed at her to remain cautious. The settlement was unlike any place she had seen before: quiet on the surface, yet crackling with hidden tension. The buildings, carved from the very bones of the desert, stood squat against the shifting dunes, their walls worn by years of relentless sandstorms. A faint scent of incense lingered in the air, masking the acrid tang of drying meat and spices that clung to the open marketplace.

She moved through the narrow alleys, her steps measured, careful to observe without drawing attention. Every face she passed was unreadable, the kind of neutrality honed by those who had long learned not to ask questions. This was not a place of open arms. It was a waystation—a crossroads for those who wished to be forgotten.

Inside a small shop wedged between two stone structures, Oriana bartered for dried meat and a fresh skin of water, keeping her voice low and her manner unassuming. The shopkeeper, an aging man with sun-worn skin, barely met her gaze, his movements precise but rushed, as if even this simple exchange made him uneasy.

As she turned to leave, a whisper brushed her ear.

"You shouldn't have come here."

Oriana froze, her grip tightening around the strap of her satchel. The voice had come from behind her, spoken barely above a breath yet carrying the weight of a warning.

Slowly, she turned toward the source. A woman, cloaked in deep indigo, stood at the far end of the shop, half-hidden by the shadow of a tall storage shelf. Her eyes, dark and knowing, remained fixed on Oriana, though her hands stayed at her sides—relaxed but deliberate.

Oriana did not look away. "Who are you?" she asked, her voice steady, even.

The woman stepped closer, and in the dim light, Oriana caught the glint of an old insignia embroidered into the fabric of her cloak—a mark she had seen once before, long ago, in the ruins outside Ashara.

"I am someone who remembers," the woman replied. "And you are being followed."

Oriana kept her face impassive, though inside, a cold dread coiled tightly around her ribs. The woman's voice carried weight—not just a casual warning, but something far more dire. She glanced around the shop, measuring the exits, the distance to the door, the number of people outside. None of them seemed to notice the hushed conversation taking place, but that did not mean she was safe.

She took a step closer, her tone measured but steady. "Who is following me?"

The woman's dark eyes flickered toward the entrance of the shop. "The ones who fear what you carry."

Oriana stiffened. The words struck her like a sharp jolt, as though the stranger had reached inside her chest and pressed on a hidden truth she had never dared to voice aloud. "You know."

The woman nodded. "They do, too."

A soft breeze stirred the air, carrying with it a metallic tang—blood, perhaps? Instantly, Oriana's muscles tensed. The woman took another step closer, her voice dropping to a near whisper. "There is little time. You must leave this place."

Oriana narrowed her eyes. "Why should I trust you?"

The woman pulled back the edge of her cloak just enough to reveal something beneath it—an intricate silver pendant, shaped like interwoven threads of energy. A symbol Oriana recognized, though she had only seen it once, in the ruins. A mark of a group called the "Digital Monks," who were supposed to serve a being called The One, or The Flow—though she had never been sure which. Regardless, they were meant to be a force for good, with knowledge of Flux energies. She thought of Regis and made the connection.

Oriana inhaled sharply. "You serve the Flow."

"I serve balance," the woman corrected. "And you are upsetting it."

Before Oriana could respond, a flicker of movement outside caught her eye. A figure, hooded and draped in sand-worn fabric, had stopped just beyond the shop's threshold. He faced away, but she could see the way his stance remained too rigid, the slight tilt of his head—as though listening... watching.

One of them.

The woman exhaled, barely above a breath. "It's too late. The CABAL has found you."

Oriana's pulse quickened. She reached for the strap of her satchel, tightening it against her shoulder. "Then tell me how to escape."

The woman hesitated for only a moment before gesturing toward the back of the shop. "There's a passage through the storage house that leads to the outer cliffs. If you move quickly, you can reach the eastern ravine before they realize you're gone."

Oriana turned toward the rear exit but paused, glancing back. "You?"

The woman shook her head. "I cannot leave. My purpose is here." Her gaze softened just slightly. "Go. Your child is more important than my fate."

Oriana hesitated for only a breath before nodding. She didn't have the luxury of questioning loyalty—not now. Slipping through the back of the shop, she passed through a curtain of woven fabric into the dimly lit storage house. Wooden crates and sacks of grain lined the narrow space, the air thick with the scent of dried herbs and aged spice.

She moved quickly, her footsteps light against the packed dirt floor. The woman had said the passage led to the cliffs—she only had to find it before the CABAL's servants reached her first.

The chase had begun.

The storage house gave way to a narrow passageway, its walls rough-hewn stone, damp with the lingering breath of underground springs. Oriana moved swiftly, her breathing steady, though the weight of urgency pressed against her chest. The air was heavy with the scent of dust and decaying wood, and each step she took sent faint echoes reverberating down the dim corridor.

A sudden rustle behind her—too close.

She froze, her fingers tightening on the strap of her satchel. The passage wasn't entirely abandoned.

The woman had warned her: the CABAL's servants had already found her. She pressed herself against the rough stone wall, forcing her breath to slow. Footsteps—soft, deliberate—moved somewhere beyond the bend in the corridor. They were following her.

She couldn't hesitate. Not now.

Oriana surged forward, careful to keep her footsteps light, her body pressed against the stone. The passage curved sharply to the right, opening into a narrow slit in the rock—a way out. She slipped through it, emerging onto the outer cliffs.

The desert stretched endlessly before her, bathed in the pale glow of the moon. Below, the ravine cut deep into the landscape, a jagged scar carved by time and wind. It was the only way forward.

She hesitated for only a breath before beginning her descent.

The path was treacherous. Loose stones shifted beneath her feet, and the incline was steep. Oriana moved carefully, gripping the rock with steady hands as she climbed downward. Behind her, she could still hear the distant sound of pursuit. They had found the passage. They were coming.

A gust of wind howled through the canyon, carrying the sharp cry of a desert predator. Oriana's heart pounded. She had to move faster.

Halfway down the ravine, she spotted an outcropping of stone, wide enough to provide temporary cover. She ducked beneath it, pressing her back against the cool rock, listening.

The sound of footsteps above.

She stilled, forcing herself into silence.

The pursuers had reached the top of the ravine. She could hear them now—low voices, speaking in clipped tones. The wind carried fragments of their conversation down to her.

"...she couldn't have gotten far..."

"...we should split up..."

"...the child must not be born..."

Oriana clenched her teeth. They knew.

She pressed her hand against her abdomen, as though she could shield the life growing inside her from their words, from their intent. A deep resolve settled over her. She wouldn't let them take this child from her. She wouldn't let them win.

A loose stone shifted above. One of them was moving closer to the edge.

Oriana closed her eyes for a heartbeat. Then, she acted.

She launched herself forward, sliding down the remaining slope, loose sand and stone cascading in her wake. The noise shattered the silence, and a shout rang out above her. She didn't look back.

The ground leveled beneath her, and she broke into a sprint. The ravine twisted and turned, its walls rising high on either side. She had no clear destination, only the instinct to keep moving. The wind roared past her ears, carrying the distant sound of pursuit.

And then, ahead—A flicker of movement.

Oriana skidded to a halt, breath caught in her throat. A figure stood at the far end of the ravine, partially obscured by shadow. Tall, cloaked, motionless.

Not a pursuer.

Something else.

The figure raised a hand, a slow and deliberate motion.

A signal.

Oriana hesitated only a moment before making her choice.

She ran toward the unknown.

Oriana's breath came in sharp, ragged gasps as she sprinted toward the figure, her instincts warring between fear and desperate hope. The ravine's walls towered around her, the shadows stretching long beneath the moon's dim glow. Every muscle in her body screamed for rest, but she didn't dare slow. Not with the CABAL closing in.

The figure stood motionless, a statue amidst the swirling dust and shifting sands. As Oriana drew nearer, she began to make out details obscured by the darkness—a cloak of deep gray, its edges frayed from long travel, a hood pulled low over a face she could not yet discern. But what stole her breath was the air surrounding them. It hummed.

Not the wind. Not the distant sound of pursuers.

Something else.

Oriana skidded to a halt mere feet away, her instincts flaring. The figure moved at last, tilting their head slightly, as if studying her.

"You run from the CABAL," the stranger spoke, their voice smooth, neither deep nor high. Timeless. Calculated.

Oriana didn't respond right away, her mind whirling. She had no weapon, no defense save her wits and determination. If this person was an ally, she needed to know. If they weren't—

The stranger took a slow step forward, lifting a hand between them. Oriana tensed but didn't retreat.

"Peace," they murmured. "I am not your enemy."

A warm pulse rippled through the air between them, subtle yet unmistakable. The Flux.

Oriana's fingers curled instinctively at her sides. She had never controlled the Flux, never called it the way the monks were said to, but she had felt it. And now, it responded to the stranger's presence.

"Who are you?" she demanded.

The stranger lowered their hood, revealing sharp, angular features. A man, though younger than she had anticipated. His hair was dark, streaked with silver at the temples, and his eyes—

Blue. The color of harmony. The same shade that had flashed in the fox's gaze.

"I am Malik," he said. "And I have been waiting for you."

Oriana's breath caught, her pulse thundering against her ribs. The CABAL was behind her, closing in with every passing second. This man—whoever he was—knew of the Flux, knew of her flight.

She had two choices: trust him, or continue running into the unknown alone.

The wind shifted behind her, and Oriana knew she had no time left to decide.

"I don't have the luxury of waiting," she said. "If you know who I am, then you know I need to keep moving."

Malik nodded once, then pivoted sharply on his heel. "Then follow me."

She did not hesitate.

As they ran deeper into the ravine, Oriana cast one last glance over her shoulder. The shadows of the CABAL's hunters loomed at the far end of the path, their figures merging with the night, their pursuit unyielding.

Chapter 5:

The Path to Survival

The air in the ravine was thick with the tension of the chase as Oriana followed Malik without hesitation. The path ahead twisted sharply through jagged rock formations, the terrain rough beneath her aching feet. She could still hear the distant echoes of the CABAL's hunters behind them, their movements cautious yet relentless. They would not stop until they found her. Until they found the child.

Malik moved with practiced ease, his pace unbroken even as the incline steepened. His outward demeanor was calm, but Oriana could sense something beneath the surface—a controlled energy, as though he were attuned to sounds beyond the physical world. The way he moved, the way the wind seemed to shift around him, made her wonder just how deep his connection to the Flux truly went.

After what felt like an eternity, Malik led her into the shelter of a shallow cave nestled along the ravine's edge. He gestured for her to crouch low, pressing his back against the rough stone as he peered outward. The wind howled through the canyon, masking the sound of their labored breaths.

"They will spread out soon," Malik murmured, his eyes scanning the rocky expanse ahead. "The CABAL's hunters are methodical, but predictable. If we move now, we risk exposing ourselves."

Oriana wiped a bead of sweat from her brow, forcing her breathing to steady. "Then what do we do?"

Malik turned to her, his blue eyes locking with hers. "We wait. Let the Flow guide the moment of action."

Oriana stiffened at the word. The Flow. Not just the Flux, but something more. She had heard of it, spoken of in hushed tones by the old storytellers of Ashara. The Flow was not merely energy—it was intent, will, purpose. It was the undercurrent of all things, moving unseen through the very fabric of existence.

"You serve the Flow," she stated, more an observation than a question.

Malik's expression remained unchanged. "I follow where it leads."

Oriana's fingers curled into fists. She had spent her life avoiding forces beyond her control, refusing to surrender to destiny. Yet here she was, with little choice but to trust this man who had emerged from the unknown. The CABAL was closing in, and her body, heavy with exhaustion, was nearing its breaking point.

As if sensing her thoughts, Malik shifted slightly. "You don't trust easily."

She met his gaze. "No."

"Good," he said. "You shouldn't."

Oriana blinked, caught off guard by his bluntness.

Malik exhaled, his voice dropping lower. "Trust is earned, not given freely. And I will earn yours, but only if you allow it."

She studied him in the dim light of the cave, the flickering shadows cast by the moon barely illuminating his features. He was young, but his eyes carried weight—the burden of knowledge far beyond his years. He had the look of a man who had seen much, who had walked the edges of existence and returned forever changed.

Finally, she nodded. "Then start by telling me why you were waiting for me."

Malik's gaze darkened slightly. "Because the Flow does not move without reason."

Outside, the wind shifted. The voices of the CABAL's hunters grew fainter, their search moving away from the ravine's edge. Malik's posture relaxed slightly, his eyes flickering with something unreadable.

"Our window is opening," he said. "If we leave now, I can get you to safety."

Oriana took one final breath of stillness, then nodded. "Lead the way."

Without another word, Malik turned and slipped into the night. Oriana followed, her heartbeat steady, her mind swirling with unanswered questions.

Who was this man?

And what did it mean that the Flow had brought them together?

The night stretched endlessly as Oriana followed Malik through the labyrinth of rocky outcroppings and shifting dunes. The wind whispered along the ridges, swirling fine grains of sand around their feet. The weight of exhaustion tugged at her limbs, but she forced herself to keep moving. The CABAL's hunters would not stop searching, and stopping now meant death—or worse.

Malik led her along an unseen path, his movements sure and precise. Though they had spoken little since leaving the ravine, Oriana could feel the energy shifting between them. There was something deliberate in the way he moved, as though he could sense the right direction, even in the pitch darkness.

Finally, after what felt like hours, they reached a plateau overlooking an expanse of rippling sand. The stars above shone brilliantly, their light unobscured by the dust of civilization. Malik stopped, scanning the horizon before turning to face her.

"We are far enough now," he said. "For the moment."

Oriana exhaled, her breath heavy. "They'll still track us."

Malik nodded. "Yes. But we have time to rest, and you need answers."

She met his gaze. "You said the Flow does not move without reason. Then why did it lead me to you?"

Malik studied her for a moment before crouching and running his fingers through the cool desert sand. "The CABAL has been watching the movements of those influenced by the Flow for years, seeking to bend both them and it to their will. But the Flow does not bend easily—it shifts, adapts, counters. You are a shift, Oriana. A shift that some Seers have predicted and others have denied will exist." He looked up, his expression unreadable. "And they fear you for it. Split Prophesy is rare and dangerous."

Oriana tensed. "Because of the child."

Malik nodded. "They think they know what he represents. He is not just another life—he is a convergence. A being who will carry both the awareness of the Flux and the will of the Flow. The CABAL seeks control of such power, and if they cannot control it..." His voice darkened. "They will destroy it."

Oriana's hand instinctively moved to her abdomen as the weight of his words settled heavily on her. She had suspected as much, but hearing it confirmed—knowing the CABAL's reach extended even into the unborn—filled her with a quiet, burning fury.

She forced herself to stay calm. "Then why did the Flow lead me to you?"

Malik's gaze did not waver. "Because I was meant to lead you beyond their reach."

Oriana frowned. "To where?"

"The Monastery of the Digital Monks."

A chill ran through her. She had heard of them, of course—whispers among scholars, old stories of a hidden order devoted to the Flow, protectors of balance. But were they real?

Malik seemed to sense her skepticism. "They are real, Oriana. And they are the only ones who can protect your child."

She shook her head. "I don't need protection. I need to end this hunt."

Malik exhaled. "You misunderstand. Ending the hunt is not a battle won with swords and blood. It's won by ensuring that what the CABAL fears—your son—lives to fulfill his purpose."

Oriana clenched her fists. "And what is that purpose?"

Malik hesitated, then said, "That is not for me to decide. Only the One knows, and we only see its will through the direction of the Flow."

Oriana turned away, staring at the horizon. The desert stretched endlessly, the weight of destiny pressing against her like an unseen force. She had spent so long running, fighting, surviving. Now, she was being asked to do something else entirely—to trust.

Finally, she turned back to Malik. "Then take me to them."

A flicker of approval passed through his eyes. "We leave at first light."

Oriana nodded, settling onto the sand. As she rested, she closed her eyes, listening—not just to the wind, but to something deeper, something she had been afraid to acknowledge for far too long.

For the first time, she let herself hear the special energy that whispered to her. She tried to hear the Flow. Her first attempt was disappointing, but she knew—like all skills—things like this take time.

The first light of dawn painted the horizon in muted golds and soft purples, casting long shadows over the dunes. Oriana stirred from where she had rested against a weathered rock, her body still aching from the relentless flight through the desert. Malik stood nearby, his back to her, watching the shifting sands as if listening to something beyond what the eye could see.

She pushed herself upright. "It's time?"

Malik nodded. "We need to keep moving before the sun makes the journey impossible."

Oriana rolled her shoulders, shaking off the stiffness. She knew he was right. The desert would soon become a death trap under the midmorning sun, and they had far to go. She turned her gaze eastward. "How far is the monastery?"

Malik took a measured breath. "Farther than you'd like, but closer than it's ever been."

She frowned. "That's not an answer."

He offered a wry smile. "It's the only one I can give."

They walked in silence for a time, the wind shifting the sand around them in swirling patterns. The landscape was eerily beautiful—vast and endless, an ocean of golden waves stretching in all directions. Yet, Oriana couldn't shake the feeling that they were being watched.

She glanced at Malik, noting the way his shoulders were tense, the way his fingers flexed occasionally as though prepared to act at a moment's notice. He felt it too.

"Who else knows of this place?" she asked at last.

Malik did not answer immediately. When he did, his voice was quiet. "No one finds the Digital Monks unless they are meant to."

Oriana arched a brow. "And yet you know the way."

A slight pause. "Because I've paid the price."

Something in the way he said it sent a chill through her. Before she could press further, a low sound rippled through the wind—a vibration, rather than a noise, like the resonance of something vast moving beneath the surface of the world.

Malik stopped abruptly, his gaze snapping toward the dunes ahead. "We're not alone."

Oriana turned, her pulse quickening. The sands shifted unnaturally, as though something large slithered beneath them. The air thickened with an unseen force, and deep within her, she felt it—a disruption in the Flow.

The ground trembled, and suddenly, the dunes ahead split open. From beneath the surface, a figure rose—a sentinel of the desert, draped in tattered, sun-bleached robes, its face hidden behind a mask carved from smooth obsidian. The air around it shimmered with residual energy, remnants of the Flux pooling at its feet like liquid light.

Malik's expression darkened. "A Warden."

Oriana had never seen one before, but the stories spoke of them—guardians of forgotten pathways, bound to the old ways, neither wholly alive nor entirely spirit. They answered only to the Flow, and their presence always meant one thing:

A test.

The Warden's voice echoed through the canyon, though its mouth did not move. "You walk the path of the unseen. What do you seek?"

Malik inclined his head. "Passage."

The Warden tilted its head slightly, as if considering. "Passage is granted only to those who carry balance within them. The Flow does not move for those who walk in shadow."

Oriana swallowed. "And if we are found unworthy?"

The Warden did not answer. Instead, the air around them grew dense, humming with power.

The test had begun.

The air shimmered with an unseen force, thick with the weight of an energy older than the desert itself. Oriana's breath caught as the Warden lifted an arm, the tatters of its robe rippling though no wind stirred. The obsidian mask bore no expression, yet she could feel its gaze pressing down on her, measuring her worth, seeking something beyond the surface of her being.

Malik remained still beside her, his stance loose but prepared. He had known this test would come, she realized. He had not simply led her through the desert—he had brought her here, to this place, to this moment.

The Warden's voice echoed once more, layered and ancient. "The Flow moves with purpose, and the Balance must be kept. You seek passage, and passage must be earned."

Oriana's fingers twitched at her sides. She could feel something pressing against her mind—a current, a whisper of unseen forces shifting around her. The Warden was not just speaking—it was reaching into the very fabric of who she was, weighing her against some unspoken measure.

Malik inclined his head slightly, his voice even. "What is the price?"

The Warden's answer was immediate. "Truth."

Oriana frowned. "What truth?"

"The truth of the Flow," the Warden replied. "Step forward, and the Trial shall begin."

She hesitated, but she knew there was no alternative. Taking a breath, she moved past Malik and stood before the towering figure. The moment she crossed an unseen threshold, the world around her shifted.

A rush of Flux energy swirled outward, cascading in ribbons of color. Oriana gasped as her vision blurred, her body suddenly weightless. The desert, the Warden, even Malik—they vanished.

She stood in a vast, endless expanse. The sky above was not the sky, but a shifting canvas of light and energy, pulsing in hues of blue and gold. Beneath her feet, the ground was both solid and fluid, like stepping onto the surface of a great ocean frozen mid-motion.

She was not alone.

A figure emerged from the swirling light. It was her—or rather, a reflection of her, formed of energy and memory. Its face was identical to hers, yet filled with an awareness she did not possess.

"What is this?" Oriana whispered.

The reflection regarded her with unreadable eyes. "This is the Flow. And this is the moment where you decide."

Oriana felt a pulse within her chest, her heartbeat echoing through the space around her. "Decide what?"

The reflection tilted its head. "Who you truly are."

A wave of images surged through her mind: memories of her childhood in Ashara, the night she fled the village, the moment she first felt life stir within her womb. The spirit fox, whispering warnings in her dreams. Malik, waiting for her at the ravine's edge.

And then... visions she did not recognize.

A vast city carved into mountains, shimmering with strange lights.

A great war, red and blue energy clashing in violent storms.

A boy, standing at the edge of a precipice, hands outstretched as the Flux swirled around him.

Her son.

Oriana gasped, staggering back. "What is this?"

The reflection's voice remained calm. "A truth of what is to come."

Her mind reeled. "This is a future?"

"A possibility," the reflection corrected. "The Flow does not dictate. It shows what may be."

Oriana clenched her fists. "Then tell me what I must do."

The reflection reached out, touching her forehead with a single luminous finger. A surge of energy filled her, deeper than knowledge—understanding.

Then, as suddenly as it had begun, the vision shattered.

Oriana gasped as she was pulled back into the desert, her body solid once more, the Warden standing silently before her. The desert heat pressed against her skin, and Malik's voice sliced through the lingering echoes of what she had just witnessed.

"Oriana."

She blinked, breath coming in heavy gasps. The Warden regarded her for a long moment before speaking one final time.

"You have seen. You have chosen. You may pass."

The energy in the air dissipated. The Warden stepped aside.

Malik's gaze remained steady on her, but Oriana could not bring herself to speak. She had seen more than just a test—she had glimpsed a path. And she had chosen to walk it.

Chapter 6:

Trials of the Desert

The desert stretched endlessly before them, its golden expanse now bathed in the cool light of dawn. Oriana's body still hummed with the lingering energy of the Warden's Trial, though fatigue pulled at her limbs like a weight she could not shake. The vision she had seen persisted - clearly in her mind. Her son, standing at the precipice of something vast and dangerous. A child born of both the Flux and the Flow.

What did it mean?

She had no answer. And Malik offered none as they continued their journey. The weight of their encounter with the Warden hung between them, a silence charged with unspoken words. Oriana followed Malik as he moved with deliberate purpose toward the horizon. His steps were sure, unwavering —he never faltered, never questioned his direction. He moved like someone who had walked this path before.

After hours of silence, Oriana broke it. "The vision—was it real?"

Malik glanced at her, his eyes sharp. "Real is a complicated word.

What you saw was a truth, but not necessarily the only truth. The Flow does not dictate what will be. It shows what could be."

Oriana frowned, feeling the weight of his words. "And what does that mean for my child?"

Malik exhaled slowly, his face unreadable. "It means he has a choice. And so do you."

A gust of wind kicked up swirling sand, and Oriana instinctively lifted her hand to shield her eyes. The desert had grown more unforgiving as the sun climbed higher, its heat pressing against them even in the breeze. She shifted the weight of her satchel, adjusting it over her shoulder.

"How much farther?" Oriana asked, her voice steady, though a quiet tension ran beneath the surface.

Malik didn't spare a glance her way. "The monastery lies beyond the stone ridges ahead. We'll reach it by nightfall."

Oriana followed his gaze to the distant rock formations, jagged peaks rising like silent sentinels against the sky. A place hidden away, a refuge for those who walked the path of the Flow.

She wasn't sure if she was ready for what awaited her there.

As the sun dipped lower in the sky, painting the desert in amber and crimson, the jagged stone ridges grew closer. Shadows stretched long across the dunes, and the cool bite of evening settled over the shifting sands. Exhaustion weighed heavily on Oriana, but she refused to slow her pace. Every step drew them nearer to something unknown, something that might finally provide answers she so desperately needed.

Malik halted at the base of the ridges, his gaze scanning the terrain with an intensity that spoke of long familiarity. He placed his palm against one of the towering stones, closing his eyes for a brief moment. A ripple of energy pulsed outward, so subtle it was almost imperceptible, but Oriana felt it—a resonance, a hum beneath the surface of reality. The Flux.

A deep grinding sound broke the silence. Before her eyes, a narrow fissure appeared in the rock, revealing a hidden passage just wide enough for them to slip through.

"The Monastery does not welcome all," Malik murmured as he stepped inside. "Only those meant to find it."

Oriana hesitated only a moment before following him.

The passage twisted through the stone like a forgotten riverbed, carved by time and forces older than any living hand. The air here was cooler, carrying the scent of ancient stone and faint traces of incense. Dim lights flickered along the walls—not torches, but pure energy, woven into delicate patterns that pulsed in rhythmic waves.

"The Monks shape the Flow?" Oriana asked softly, her voice almost a whisper.

Malik nodded without breaking stride. "Not as the CABAL does. They do not force the Flow to serve their will. They listen. They guide. What you sensed was the Flux—raw, untamed energy without intent. The Flow, however, carries purpose, and for those who can align with it, a far greater concentration of power becomes accessible."

They emerged from the passage into a vast open courtyard, where towering spires of stone and glass rose sharply against the twilight sky. The Monastery of the Digital Monks was unlike any place Oriana had ever imagined. It was both ancient and impossibly advanced, an awe-inspiring blend of nature and technology that defied all logic. Cascading waterfalls tumbled from unseen sources, their waters shimmering with an ethereal glow. Walkways of smooth black stone wound between gardens, their plants swaying as though responding to an invisible current, alive in ways that felt both natural and uncanny.

A group of figures stood near the entrance to the central hall, their robes shifting like fabric in the wind. Each one bore the same intricate sigil as Malik, the mark of the Monks. As they approached, one of them stepped forward—an older woman with piercing silver eyes and a presence that immediately commanded attention.

"You have returned," she said, her gaze settling on Malik before shifting to Oriana. "And you have brought the one we foresaw."

Oriana froze, her chest tightening. "You knew I was coming?"

The woman's expression softened. "The Flow guides us. We have been waiting."

A flicker of unease twisted in Oriana's gut. She had spent so long running, surviving, always fighting against the unknown. But now, standing at the threshold of something far greater than herself, she wondered if she was ready for what awaited her.

Inside the monastery, the air was thick with silence, heavy with knowledge that seemed both ancient and eternal. Oriana followed Malik and the silver-eyed woman through the towering, arching corridors, her senses heightened. Every wall pulsed faintly with Flux energy, woven into intricate patterns along the smooth black stone. It was a resonance she had never encountered before—controlled, deliberate, yet teeming with untapped power.

They entered a vast chamber, the ceiling arcing high like the ribs of some ancient creature. Along the walls, thousands of delicate threads of light pulsed in rhythmic waves, forming complex patterns that Oriana couldn't quite understand. At the center of the room, an ancient circular platform sat embedded in the floor, its edges etched with symbols that pulsed in time with the rhythm of the lights.

The woman turned to Oriana, her silver eyes unwavering. "You stand at the crossroads of destiny," she said. "The Flow has brought you here not to seek refuge, but to understand the purpose of what you carry."

Oriana's jaw clenched, her hands tightening at her sides. "I didn't ask for purpose. I asked for safety."

The woman studied Oriana, her expression unreadable, her silver eyes reflecting a depth that made Oriana feel small. "Safety is fleeting, child. The Flow does not grant shelter. It grants clarity, guidance, and power."

Malik stood beside her, his gaze fixed on the glowing symbols beneath their feet. Oriana exhaled, steadying herself against the weight of her uncertainty. "Then tell me," she said at last, her voice firm but laden with a quiet desperation. "Why does the CABAL fear my son?"

The woman inclined her head slightly, then gestured toward the center of the platform. "Step forward."

Oriana hesitated only a moment before moving toward the etched surface. The moment her foot connected with the central sigil, the room flickered, and the world around her began to shift.

A surge of energy pulled at her, and in an instant, she was no longer in the monastery.

She stood in a vision—not a memory, but something beyond time, beyond place.

The sky above was fractured, violent swirls of blue and crimson energy clashing in endless storms. The earth beneath her feet was broken, shattered ruins stretching into an endless horizon. And at the center of it all stood a single figure.

A child.

A boy, no older than ten, stood with his back to her. His arms were outstretched, tendrils of Flux energy curling around his fingers, pulsing in the wind. The air itself vibrated with an unseen force. His presence was not one of destruction, but of raw, untamed power.

Oriana took a hesitant step forward, her voice barely a whisper. "Who is he?"

The answer came, though it did not come from the boy. The woman's voice, cold and distant, echoed through the vision. "He can be a bridge, a catalyst, an Answer. The one who will either unite the Flow or shatter it forever."

Oriana's breath caught in her throat. Her son.

The boy turned, just enough for her to see the sharp intensity in his gaze. His eyes were not blue, not red—something between, a shifting spectrum caught between harmony and chaos.

And then, as quickly as it had begun, the vision collapsed.

Oriana's breath caught as she was yanked back to the present. The chamber solidified around her, the glowing symbols beneath her feet pulsing with quiet intensity. Her heartbeat thundered in her ears, the rush of energy still lingering in her veins.

She turned toward the woman, her voice sharp with desperation. "What does this mean?"

The woman's gaze was steady, unwavering. "Your son is neither CABAL nor Monk. He is something new." She paused, her voice taking on a deeper weight. "And that is why they fear him. It is in our nature to see balance in duality—to believe that opposites must clash. We see harmony as the joining of forces in opposition, when in truth, true balance exists in unity. The CABAL understands how to fight against the Monks, how to sow discord within their own ranks, and how to oppose the Flow itself. But they do not understand what your son might become."

Oriana swallowed, her throat dry. She had spent her life running, hiding, fighting for survival—but now the truth stood before her. The CABAL did not simply want her son dead. They wanted to control him.

And if they couldn't control him...

They would destroy him before he ever had the chance to choose.

The dim light of the chamber stretched long shadows across Oriana's face as she absorbed the revelation. Her son was not just a child—he had the potential to be a force that existed outside of the limits of both the CABAL and the Monks. The realization made her blood run cold. He had yet to even draw his first breath, and already he was a battleground for powers beyond her understanding.

She looked at the silver-eyed woman, her voice steady despite the storm that raged within her. "What happens if I stay?"

The woman's response was measured, certain. "The Monastery will protect him. Train him. Teach him the ways of the Flow, so that he may master what he is, rather than be mastered by it."

Oriana's fingers clenched at her sides. "And if I leave?"

Malik, who had remained silent until now, finally spoke. "Then you risk raising him without understanding. Without guidance. Without knowing what he is—or what he may become."

Oriana exhaled, a shudder running through her. For so long, she had fought to protect herself, to carve a life in a world that had shown her nothing but the harsh realities of life in the desert. And now, for the first time, she realized that her survival was no longer her sole concern.

She had a choice to make.

Oriana turned away from the glowing sigils, her boots echoing softly against the stone as she paced the edge of the chamber. Could she leave her son here? Trust the Monks to raise him, to shape him into what the Flow intended him to become – or would they make him into what THEY wanted him to be? Or should she take him into the world, hiding him away, shielding him from the inevitable dangers that awaited so he could find his own path?

Her mind lingered on the vision—the boy's eyes, not blue, not red, but something in between.

Memories of her own past flooded her, of times when she had been powerless, at the mercy of forces she could not control. She had been shaped by others, forced into their designs. She would not let her son be a pawn in someone else's game. But neither could she shelter him from the world forever, not when he carried such power.

She turned back to the silver-eyed woman, her voice firm. "I will not leave him here."

The woman's gaze remained steady. "Then what will you do?"

Oriana's shoulders squared as she made her decision. "I will raise him. I will teach him what I can. When the time comes, he will choose his own path."

A heavy silence settled between them, stretching long before the woman nodded, her eyes unreadable. "Then we will give you what we can."

Malik stepped forward, his expression serious. "There is a way to hide him from the CABAL's sight for a time. A way to protect him while he is still vulnerable."

Oriana's heart beat faster. "How?"

The woman approached one of the chamber's walls, pressing her palm against a carved symbol. The stone responded with a low rumble, shifting aside to reveal a recessed alcove where a small, ornate pendant lay atop a woven cloth, bathed in a soft, pulsing light.

"This will cloak his presence," the silver-eyed woman said, her voice calm but firm. "As long as he wears it, his connection to the Flux and Flow will remain hidden. The CABAL will not sense him."

Oriana stepped closer, her fingers brushing the pendant's delicate surface. It was cool, but it pulsed faintly against her skin, an energy she could feel but not fully understand. A protective ward, woven with knowledge far beyond her own.

She lifted it carefully, the weight of it reassuring in her hand. "This will be enough."

Malik's expression remained unreadable, his eyes distant. "For now."

Oriana turned to him, her voice steady despite the ache in her chest. "And you? Will you follow?"

Malik hesitated, the air between them thick with unspoken truths. Finally, he shook his head. "No. My path remains with the Monks. But our fates are still intertwined, Oriana. When the time comes, I will find you again."

She nodded, her heart heavy. His words were not a farewell, but a promise.

The silver-eyed woman stepped aside, gesturing toward the entrance of the chamber. "Then go. Before the night ends, you must be far from here."

Oriana exhaled slowly, feeling the weight of the pendant in her palm. The choice had been made.

She would take her son from this place.

And when the time came, he would return—not as a child, but as something greater.

Chapter 7:

A Stranger's Warning

Night draped the dunes in silence as Oriana moved, her footfalls muffled by the shifting sand. The pendant hung from a thin leather cord around her neck, its weight both a comfort and a warning, pulsing faintly against her chest in sync with her heartbeat.

She had left the monastery hours earlier, slipping into the vast emptiness of the desert. There was no destination—only the certainty that she had to get far away from the Monks, the CABAL, and anyone else who might see her son as a weapon or a prize. The wind whispered across the dunes like ghosts, stirring fragments of a past she was determined to outrun.

The journey was brutal. The desert offered no mercy, and though Oriana had survived its dangers before, the weight of her unborn child slowed her. Her water was running low. The horizon offered no end—just heat, light, and distance. But she couldn't stop.

By dawn, her limbs ached with fatigue, her throat raw with thirst. She crested a ridge and scanned the landscape below. A scattering of ancient ruins lay half-buried in the sand, the remnants of a forgotten world. Cracked, worn, wind-scoured—they weren't shelter, but they were something.

She descended slowly, fingers trailing across the timeworn stone as she stepped into what had once been a temple. The air was cooler here, shadows granting brief relief from the rising sun. She set down her pack and ran her hands over her belly. The child stirred at her touch.

"Not much longer now," she murmured, fingers brushing gently over her swollen belly as if to comfort them both.

A gust of wind swept through the ruins, and with it came the distant cry of a jackal. Oriana froze. She wasn't alone.

Her hand found the blade at her belt, instincts sharpening. The desert was wide, but never truly empty. She listened.

The wind held its breath. Only her own pulse echoed in the silence.

And then—a voice.

"You shouldn't be here."

Oriana spun, blade drawn. A figure stepped from the shadows, swathed in loose desert robes, their face hidden beneath a deep hood. They stood relaxed, but the stillness of a fighter lived in their stance. This wasn't a lost traveler.

"Neither should you," she replied, voice level.

The figure made no move. "I've been waiting."

A chill crept down her spine. "For what?"

"For you."

The pendant pulsed against her chest—a slow, deliberate beat. A warning.

Oriana's fingers tightened around the knife, her body coiled.

The stranger remained still, eyes glinting beneath the hood, watching. Waiting.

"You've been waiting for me?" she said at last. "That's a dangerous thing to admit."

The figure chuckled, low and dry like the desert wind. "And yet, here you are."

She didn't ease her grip. "Who are you?"

Slowly, the figure raised a hand and pulled back the hood. A sharp-featured man, weathered and sun-darkened, met her gaze with eyes that were alert but not cruel.

"My name is Daelen," he said. "And whether you trust me or not, I'm here to help."

"Help me?" Her tone was flat. "Or help yourself?"

Daelen's eyes flicked briefly to the pendant, then back to her face. "Maybe both."

The pendant's pulse quickened, responding to something unseen. Oriana drew in a slow breath, forcing herself to stay grounded.

"Then talk."

Daelen moved carefully, settling on a crumbled pillar. His posture was easy, but Oriana saw the calculation in his every movement.

"You're not the only one running," he said. "The CABAL's reach is long. There are others who resist—who won't let the Flow be bent to their will."

Oriana narrowed her eyes. "You speak like someone who's seen it from the inside."

A shadow crossed Daelen's expression, there and gone in an instant. "I do."

Oriana waited, but he gave no further reply. She shifted slightly, never taking her eyes off him. "And what do you want from me?"

He exhaled slowly, his gaze drifting toward the crumbling ruins that surrounded them. "I want to ensure what you carry survives."

Oriana's muscles stiffened. "You know about the child."

Daelen nodded. "The CABAL does not hunt lightly. Word of a woman fleeing through the desert, carrying something important, spreads faster than sand in a storm. And those of us who still stand against them... we listen."

She studied him intently, looking for any sign of deception. "You're not a Digital Monk. So, what does that make you? A rebel?"

He smiled, though it lacked warmth. "Depends on who you ask."

Silence stretched between them. The wind whistled through the ruins, stirring loose grains of sand. Oriana weighed her options. Trust wasn't something she could afford easily, but neither could she ignore the truth in his words. The CABAL's reach was vast, and she'd underestimated its ability to track her.

Finally, she sheathed her knife, though she remained alert. "If you know they're hunting me, you know I don't have time for games. Either give me the help you promised, or step aside."

Daelen nodded slightly. "Fair enough." He rose to his feet, brushing sand from his robes. "There's a caravan heading north from the trade routes in two days. I can get you passage. It'll take you farther than you could travel alone."

Oriana hesitated. Traveling with others meant risk—visibility—but it also meant survival. The desert was vast, but not infinite. If the CABAL was already hunting her, she had to move faster than they could track her.

She met his gaze. "And what do you get out of this?"

Daelen's expression darkened, his voice lowering this time. "The satisfaction of denying the CABAL what they want."

Oriana studied him a moment longer before nodding once. "Then let's move before we lose our advantage."

Daelen smirked. "Good. I was starting to think you'd stab me first."

Oriana gave him a level look. "That's still an option."

His chuckle was short, but there was something genuine about it. "Noted."

They left the ruins behind, their footsteps swallowed by the howling desert wind.

The wind carried the scent of spice and dust as Oriana crouched atop a jagged outcrop, her eyes scanning the horizon. In the distance, a caravan stretched across the desert, its long procession of travelers, merchants, and pack animals winding through the dunes like a serpent of shifting colors. The northern trade route—a treacherous path known for its perilous terrain and brutal sun—was their next destination.

Daelen knelt beside her, adjusting the wrappings around his face to shield against the rising wind. "They'll reach the resting grounds by nightfall. That's where we'll make our approach."

Oriana nodded, her mind already calculating the risks. Caravans were both an opportunity and a danger. They offered shelter, supplies, and movement through hostile territory, but they also drew attention—attention that might recognize her.

"They won't just take in strangers," she said. "How do you plan to convince them?"

Daelen smirked. "I have my ways."

Oriana gave him a sidelong glance. "That's not an answer."

"It's the only one you're getting for now."

She exhaled sharply but remained silent. Trust was still a fragile thread between them, but she had little choice but to follow his lead. Survival demanded risk.

The caravan's encampment came into view as twilight descended over the desert, the sky awash in deep purples and reds. Fires flickered across the dunes, forming a makeshift village of tents, wagons, and gathered travelers. Voices murmured in a dozen dialects, blending with the distant braying of pack animals and the metallic clink of trade goods being secured for the night.

Daelen led Oriana through the outer fringes, weaving between stacked crates and tethered beasts. The air was thick with the smell of leather, sweat, and dried fruit, mingling with the faint scent of incense drifting from one of the central tents. These were traders and wanderers—people who lived between the worlds of civilization and lawlessness.

"Stay close," Daelen murmured. "Let me do the talking."

Oriana resisted the urge to roll her eyes, but followed as he approached a heavy-set man seated on an ornate rug outside a large wagon. The man, his skin bronzed by years under the desert sun, wore layers of fine, colorful fabric, his dark beard streaked with gray. His sharp gaze flicked over Daelen before landing on Oriana.

"I thought you traveled alone," the man said, his voice like gravel.

Daelen shrugged. "Circumstances change, Baric."

Baric's gaze lingered on Oriana, unreadable. "And who is she?"

"A traveler in need of passage."

Baric's eyes narrowed. "Passage isn't free. Nor is trust."

Daelen reached into his robes, producing a small satchel, which he tossed onto the rug between them. Baric opened it, sifting through its contents—a handful of rare desert opals, shimmering with an inner light.

Oriana tensed. Where had Daelen gotten those?

Baric let out a low hum of approval before closing the satchel.

"Generous. But not enough."

Daelen's smile didn't falter. "Then let's discuss alternatives."

Baric studied him for a long moment, then gestured toward the fire beside him. "Sit. We'll talk."

Oriana remained standing.

Baric's gaze flicked to her again. "You trust him?"

Oriana met his eyes. "I trust that our paths are aligned—for now."

Baric chuckled. "That's good enough for now."

As the fire crackled between them, Oriana knew this was only the beginning. Trust was currency here, and she would have to earn it— one way or another.

Oriana sat stiffly by the fire, the heat licking at her skin as Baric scrutinized her. Around them, the murmur of the caravan continued— travelers exchanging stories, merchants bartering under the dim glow of lanterns, the distant rustling of animals settling for the night. The caravan hummed with life, yet Oriana felt as though she were frozen in place, a single thread under examination before it could be woven into the whole.

Baric leaned forward, resting his elbows on his knees. "You ask for passage, but I don't take strangers lightly. You and Daelen—" he gestured between them, "—draw attention. And attention is a luxury I can't afford."

Oriana met his gaze steadily. "I don't intend to be a burden."

He smirked. "That's what every stray says before trouble starts following them."

Daelen, still seated beside her, exhaled sharply through his nose. "Baric, we both know I wouldn't come to you unless I had reason."

Baric ignored him. His sharp gaze remained fixed on Oriana. "What skills do you offer?"

Oriana hesitated, weighing how much to reveal. She had survived in the desert long enough to fight, to hunt, to navigate treacherous terrain—but telling him the full truth of who she was, and what she carried, was out of the question. She decided that revealing her early training from the Desert Rangers before her life as a village healer was the correct secret to bring into the light. Her skills might be rusty, but her recent travels led her to believe that she still retained her mind-body connection enough to deliver a passable performance!

"I know the land," she said. "I can track, ride, and fight if needed, but mainly, I'm a trained healer."

Baric's expression remained unreadable. "Words are cheap, and healing only has value if we survive the fight. You'll earn your place or you'll leave."

A moment later, he stood and turned toward the larger circle of travelers near the center of camp. "Faris!" he called.

A younger man—tall, lean, his dark hair braided with thin silver bands—stepped forward. His eyes flicked to Oriana with mild curiosity. "What do you need?"

Baric gestured toward her. "A test. See if she's worth keeping."

Faris grinned. "Fighting or riding?"

"Fighting," Baric said, glancing at Oriana. "Unless you'd prefer to prove yourself in another way."

Oriana knew that backing down would cost her any chance of staying. She rose to her feet and unfastened her cloak, her muscles tensed with anticipation. "Fighting's fine."

A ripple of interest moved through the caravan as travelers gathered, murmuring among themselves. A space was cleared near the fire, and Faris stretched his arms, rolling his shoulders loose. A wooden training staff was handed to him, and another tossed toward Oriana. She caught it smoothly, testing its weight. It had been a long time since she had fought for something other than survival.

Faris smiled. "Let's see what you can do, then."

He struck first, a quick, controlled strike aimed at her midsection. Oriana twisted away, bringing her staff up to deflect the follow-up attack that came faster than she expected.

Faris was skilled, but he was testing her—not trying to break her.

She struck back, her movements fluid, forcing him to step back. The sound of wood clashing cracked through the air as their staves met in a flurry of motion. She could feel the energy of the moment, the way the onlookers leaned in, their interest piqued. This wasn't just about proving herself to Baric—this was about proving herself to all of them. Fortunately, her increasing sensitivity to what she thought was Flux energy, but might be intuition from the Flow, helped her anticipate Faris' attacks before they materialized and her hard-won reflexes from her early years were still part of her. The combination of old muscle memory and new intuition made her seem faster than she actually was, but she needed every advantage.

A misstep could mean exile—or worse.

Faris pressed forward, shifting into a low sweep aimed at her legs. Oriana anticipated it, leaping over the strike and twisting midair to bring her staff down. He barely blocked in time, the force of the blow making him stagger.

A grin flickered across his face. "You're better than you look."

Oriana didn't reply. She pressed the attack.

The fight continued, the rhythm shifting between strikes and counters, neither gaining full dominance over the other. But Oriana was patient. She had spent years reading movements, understanding how the body moved as a healer, and this allowed her to see through feints and deceptions. And when the moment came—the briefest opening in Faris' guard—she seized it.

She pivoted sharply, swinging her staff upward in a controlled arc. It struck his wrist, sending his weapon spinning from his hand. A heartbeat later, the tip of her staff was at his throat.

Silence fell over the gathered travelers.

Faris raised his hands in mock surrender, breathing heavily. "Alright. I concede."

Baric studied her for a long moment, then nodded. "You'll ride with us."

Relief flickered through Oriana, but she kept her expression neutral. The first step was done—but trust was still far from earned.

Baric turned, already moving toward his wagon. "Rest tonight. We leave at dawn."

Oriana exhaled, lowering her staff. The crowd dispersed, murmurs of approval and interest trailing behind them. Daelen clapped her on the shoulder. "Not bad."

She gave him a level look. "I wasn't trying to impress you."

He chuckled. "That's what makes it impressive."

As Oriana settled near the fire later that night, the caravan moving around her in the quiet hum of preparation, she allowed herself the briefest moment of satisfaction. She had a place here—for now. But the desert was vast, and the CABAL would not stop searching.

She had won this fight.

The next would come soon enough.

Chapter 8:

Into the Unknown

The first light of dawn crept over the dunes, bathing the caravan in soft hues of gold and pink. The travelers stirred, moving with quiet efficiency as they packed their belongings, preparing for the long trek ahead. Oriana adjusted the straps of her satchel, ensuring the pendant lay securely beneath the folds of her cloak. She was no stranger to long journeys, but this time, the weight she carried was heavier than mere supplies—it was the burden of what lay ahead.

Baric stood near his wagon, speaking in hushed tones with several of the caravan leaders. When he turned toward the gathered travelers, his voice carried across the camp. "We move in one formation. Stragglers invite danger. Watch the horizon and your backs."

Oriana noted the seriousness in his tone. "Bandits?" she asked Daelen, who had taken up position beside her.

"Always a threat," he replied. "But that's not what concerns him."

Oriana frowned. "Then what does?"

Daelen's gaze swept across the shifting dunes. "There are whispers of strange things moving in the deep desert. Things that don't belong to the CABAL—but might be just as dangerous."

Before she could press him further, the caravan began to move. The steady rhythm of hooves, the creaking of wagons, and the murmurs of travelers filled the morning air. Oriana fell into step with the others, her instincts on high alert.

The desert was vast, but it had ears.

By midday, the heat became oppressive. The sun bore down relentlessly, the wind carrying fine grains of sand that clung to every exposed surface. The travelers moved in a tight formation, conserving energy and shielding one another from the worst of the elements.

Oriana scanned the horizon, her thoughts returning to the vision she had seen in the monastery. A child standing at the precipice of destiny. A war of unseen forces. The memory lingered, gnawing at the edges of her mind. She had made her choice, but doubt remained. Had she done the right thing?

Daelen, sensing her unease, spoke without looking at her. "You're overthinking things."

She huffed a quiet breath. "I have a lot to think about."

"Thinking won't change what's coming."

She turned her gaze to him. "And you know what's coming?"

Daelen didn't answer immediately. Instead, he lifted his chin toward the distant ridges. "Not exactly. But I know something is shifting."

Oriana followed his gaze. The ridges loomed ahead, their jagged edges cutting into the horizon. The caravan approached the first major crossing point—a place where the land narrowed, forcing travelers through a bottleneck of stone and shadow. A natural ambush site.

Baric rode toward them, his expression grim. "Keep your weapons close," he muttered as he passed. "Something feels wrong."

Oriana's fingers tightened around the hilt of her knife. She felt it too.

The desert was too quiet.

The caravan neared the ridges as the afternoon sun hung low in the sky, casting elongated shadows over the jagged rock formations. The path ahead narrowed into a winding passage, a natural choke point that forced them into single file.

Oriana's muscles tensed. A perfect spot for an ambush.

Baric rode at the head, his sharp eyes scanning the rocky outcrops above. His hand never strayed far from the curved dagger at his waist. The other caravan guards mirrored his tension, their weapons loosened in their sheaths, eyes flicking to every shadow.

Oriana and Daelen walked near the center of the procession. She had tied a scarf over her head to shield her from the worst of the sun's glare, but sweat still trickled down her spine. The air here felt different—heavy, charged, unnatural.

"The Flow is restless," Daelen murmured beside her, barely loud enough for her to hear. "Something's wrong."

Oriana exhaled slowly, keeping her expression neutral. "You've felt this before?"

Daelen nodded, his gaze still locked on the ridges. "Not often. But when I have, it's never been a good sign."

A sharp whistle pierced the air.

The caravan froze.

Baric raised his fist, signaling for silence. The travelers obeyed, gripping weapons, holding their breath. The sound had come from ahead—a warning, or a signal?

A figure appeared atop one of the ridges, silhouetted against the setting sun. Cloaked in loose desert robes, the person raised both hands in a slow, deliberate motion. A second figure emerged from the opposite side of the pass. Then a third. Then more.

Bandits.

Oriana's heartbeat quickened. The silent ridges had been aptly named—not for their quiet, but for what happened to those who underestimated them. They never left to speak of what they'd seen.

Baric's voice came low and steady. "Everyone, stay calm."

The lead bandit moved forward, stepping onto an outcropping that loomed over the caravan. A scar ran from his temple down to his jawline, partially concealed by the fabric draped around his head. When he spoke, his voice was rough yet controlled.

"You ride through our lands without tribute."

Baric didn't flinch. "We carry trade goods. No coin for thieves."

The bandit chuckled, amusement flickering in his eyes. "Then perhaps we'll take the goods instead."

Oriana gripped the hilt of her knife beneath her cloak. She counted at least ten of them, all positioned above. But if there were ten visible, there were surely more in hiding.

Baric's jaw tightened. "We don't seek trouble."

Scar's smile widened. "That's unfortunate."

In an instant, the tension snapped.

A sudden movement—a glint of steel from above—an arrow cut through the air with a sharp whine.

Oriana reacted without thought, grabbing Daelen and pulling him down as the arrow buried itself in the sand where he had just stood. The caravan erupted into chaos.

The bandits descended.

Oriana's blade flashed free as a figure lunged toward her. She twisted, ducking beneath the wild swing of a club, then drove her knee into the attacker's gut before slashing upward. Blood spattered across the sand as the bandit crumpled.

Screams, shouts, and the clash of metal filled the air.

Baric and his guards fought fiercely, but the bandits held the high ground. For every one they cut down, another seemed to take their place. They weren't here just for coin.

Oriana spotted movement from the corner of her eye—a figure darting toward the supply wagon. Toward her satchel.

Her stomach turned cold. They know.

She lunged after him.

Oriana sprinted toward the supply wagon, her breath quick and controlled, her knife gripped tightly in her palm. The bandit who had broken from the fight was fast, weaving through the chaos with practiced ease, his eyes fixed on her satchel. This wasn't about random spoils. They had come for her.

She closed the distance just as the bandit reached for the satchel, his fingers curling around the strap. Oriana didn't hesitate—she drove forward, slamming into him with her shoulder, sending them both tumbling into the sand. The force of the impact knocked the satchel loose, and it skidded across the ground, half-buried in dust.

The bandit reacted with practiced speed, rolling to his feet as his curved dagger flashed in the dim light. He swung at her, the blade slicing through the air mere inches from her skin. Oriana twisted to avoid the strike, her body moving fluidly as she countered with a low sweep of her leg, aiming to knock him off balance. But he was faster—too fast.

He leapt back, his expression shifting from surprise to something more calculating. This wasn't just a desert thief—he was trained.

Oriana didn't wait for him to recover. She lunged, striking high with her knife. He blocked with a swift twist of his wrist, redirecting the momentum, but she used the opening to slam her elbow into his ribs. The bandit grunted, stumbling back just enough for her to press the attack.

She stepped forward, feinting left before pivoting sharply, her blade cutting across his arm. The steel sliced through fabric and flesh, drawing a pained hiss. He recoiled, but there was no fear in his eyes—only recognition.

"You fight well," he muttered, blood dripping from his arm. "Better than most."

Oriana's grip tightened around her knife. "I fight to survive."

The bandit smirked, a dark glint in his eyes. "So do we."

Before she could react, he twisted his fingers in the air, signaling his companions.

Two more figures emerged from the shadows of the ridge, their cloaks dark and loose, their movements precise. Their stance was familiar—too familiar. These weren't ordinary raiders.

Oriana's heart pounded. CABAL agents.

The realization struck like ice through her veins. This had never been about coin or supplies. They had been tracking her.

The first agent stepped forward, his hands open and unarmed. But Oriana knew better. The way he moved, the way the air around him seemed to shift—he was trained in the Flux.

Daelen's voice rang out from behind her. "Oriana, move!"

She reacted without thinking, ducking just as a blast of unseen force tore through the air where she had been standing. Sand exploded in all directions, knocking fighters off their feet. Oriana rolled to the side, shielding her eyes from the debris. They were using the Flux openly.

Daelen was already cutting through the chaos toward her, his blade gleaming in the fading light. "We have to go! Now!"

Oriana didn't hesitate. She snatched up the satchel, slinging it over her shoulder as she bolted toward him. The agents pressed forward, but the caravan fighters, now realizing the true nature of their enemies, began to regroup.

Baric, his sword stained with blood, barked orders, his voice cutting through the chaos. "Fall back! Protect the supplies!"

The bandits hesitated for the first time. They had expected an easy ambush, not an organized defense. But the CABAL agents didn't falter.

The lead agent raised his hands again, the air around him vibrating with an ominous hum.

Oriana's instincts screamed at her. He was preparing to unleash something devastating.

There was no time to think. Oriana grabbed Daelen's wrist, her voice low but urgent. "We can't fight this. We run."

Daelen hesitated only a moment before nodding. Without another word, they sprinted toward the outer edge of the battle, weaving between the chaos. Behind them, the agent released his gathered energy.

A wave of force rippled through the ridges, sending sand and rock tumbling in every direction. Oriana stumbled but kept her feet, her breath coming in ragged gasps, her mind racing.

The CABAL had found her. And they would not stop.

The world shook behind them as the energy blast tore through the ridges, sending a plume of dust and rock into the sky. Oriana and

Daelen ran, their feet sliding over the loose sand as the shockwave rattled their bones. The sounds of battle faded into the distance, replaced by the whistling wind and the heavy rhythm of their own footsteps.

Oriana's mind raced, a horrible realization dawning. The CABAL had been waiting. Watching. And when her disappearance could be blamed on bandits—they had struck.

"Keep moving!" Daelen barked, his voice tight with strain. "We need cover!"

The ridges loomed ominously ahead, their jagged peaks rising like broken teeth against the dusk. Oriana veered left, following a narrow ravine that cut through the rock—hoping it would shield them from view. But it was a gamble. If it led to a dead end, they were finished.

The hum of Flux energy behind them told her they had no choice.

A second blast detonated, striking the rock wall just behind them. The shockwave lifted Oriana off her feet, hurling her forward. She hit the sand hard, rolling with the impact before coming to a stop. The pendant beneath her cloak burned hot, a searing reminder of the energy in the air.

Daelen was at her side in an instant, grabbing her arm. "Up!"

She pushed herself to her feet, wincing as pain flared through her ribs. No time for pain. No time for weakness.

They scrambled deeper into the ravine, the walls closing in around them like the jaws of a predator. The CABAL agents pursued, their footsteps disturbingly silent, moving with inhuman precision. They weren't just trained—they were enhanced.

Oriana's breath came in ragged, shallow gasps. "We can't outrun them forever."

Daelen gritted his teeth, his eyes narrowing. "We won't have to."

Before she could question him, Daelen grabbed her wrist and yanked her toward the right. They ducked beneath a jagged overhang, pressing their bodies into the shadows. The air here felt different—cooler, heavy with an ancient, almost sacred stillness.

Oriana glanced around, the sudden realization hitting her. A ruin.

The ravine's walls were etched with the faint remnants of forgotten symbols, their grooves worn smooth by centuries of time. The markings pulsed with a subtle, ethereal glow, barely visible against the fading light of the setting sun. She had seen these symbols before—deep in the ruins beyond Ashara.

Daelen pressed his palm against the stone, murmuring something beneath his breath. The air seemed to hum in response, as though recognizing an ancient command.

Oriana barely had time to react before the rock behind them groaned and shifted.

A narrow passage opened before them, revealing impenetrable darkness beyond.

Daelen locked eyes with her. "Inside. Now."

She hesitated for only a heartbeat before plunging into the unknown.

The rock sealed behind them just as the CABAL agents rounded the corner.

Chapter 9:

The Gateway to Ashara

Darkness engulfed them as the rock wall sealed behind them, swallowing the howling wind and the distant cries of the CABAL agents. Oriana's breath quickened, sharp and shallow, her senses on high alert as the oppressive silence settled around them. The air inside was cool and damp, carrying a scent of ancient stone mingled with something older—an almost tangible weight of forgotten time.

A faint, pulsing glow illuminated the space ahead—markings.

Oriana reached out, her fingers brushing against the carved symbols along the walls. Despite the years of wear, the grooves hummed softly beneath her touch, a subtle vibration that seemed to resonate with the very heart of the place. This was no abandoned ruin; it was waiting— waiting for something.

Daelen exhaled beside her, his voice barely above a whisper. "I never thought I'd see one of these still standing."

Oriana turned to him, confusion clouding her brow. "You know what this is?"

He nodded, his face unreadable. "A Vault."

The word hit her like a cold gust. She'd heard whispers of such places—mysterious structures hidden beneath the desert, relics of civilizations that had once tapped into the Flow in ways long lost to history.

Daelen moved forward cautiously, his boots making soft scraping sounds on the stone floor. "We need to keep moving. The CABAL won't be far behind."

Oriana followed, one hand still grazing the wall as the passage sloped downward, winding into an enormous chamber.

She froze, staring in awe. The room was massive, its scale hard to comprehend.

Towering pillars rose up like ancient sentinels, their surfaces covered in more glowing symbols. At the center of the room stood a circular platform, raised slightly above the ground, its surface lined with interwoven energy threads that pulsed softly, like veins beneath skin.

Oriana moved closer, inexplicably drawn to the glow. The pendant beneath her cloak throbbed in sync, as if it recognized the call.

Daelen's voice was urgent now. "Be careful."

Oriana barely registered him. She reached the edge of the platform, placing her palm gently against its surface.

And then the world shifted.

A wave of Flux energy washed over her—not harsh, but immense, like standing at the edge of a vast ocean. Her vision blurred, and in that instant, she saw it—a city of light, suspended above endless dunes, its towering spires connected by radiant streams of pure energy. A voice, distant yet intimately familiar, whispered in a language she didn't understand, but somehow knew.

And then, as quickly as it came, it was gone.

Oriana gasped, stumbling back, her heart racing.

Daelen caught her, steadying her as she swayed. "What did you see?"

Oriana swallowed hard, her throat tight. "A memory. Or a warning."

The Vault hummed around them, the sound alive and aware. Whatever lay within, it wasn't meant to remain hidden for long.

Oriana steadied herself, her breath ragged as the remnants of the vision faded. The air in the Vault felt heavier now, thick with anticipation, the glow from the symbols pulsing in slow, deliberate waves. This place was alive in ways she couldn't yet comprehend.

Daelen crouched near the base of the platform, his fingers brushing the surface of an inscription buried beneath layers of dust. "These markings..." he muttered. "They're not just decorations."

Oriana moved beside him, her eyes adjusting to the soft glow of the engravings. She recognized the intricate patterns, how they twisted into precise lines. "A language?"

Daelen nodded, his voice low. "Not just a language. A codex. Instructions, records—perhaps even something more."

He pressed his palm flat against the surface, and the symbols reacted immediately, flaring with a flash of pale blue light. A deep hum reverberated through the chamber.

Oriana tensed, stepping back as the platform trembled. The carvings along the walls glowed brighter, forming intricate paths of light that wove through the Vault like a network of circuits coming to life.

Then, a voice—Soft at first, like the whisper of wind through the dunes, then growing clearer, resonating deep within the stone. It was neither male nor female but something in between, layered with the weight of centuries.

"You have entered the Sanctuary of the First Architects."

Oriana's pulse spiked, her breath catching in her throat. She turned to Daelen, but his face was unreadable.

The voice continued. "The Flow has guided you here. What you seek lies within—but knowledge is not given, it is earned."

The room brightened, and a portion of the wall dissolved into swirling light, revealing an arched passage leading deeper into the Vault. A gust of cool air brushed her face, carrying the scent of old parchment and something metallic.

Oriana exhaled slowly. "I don't like the sound of 'earned.'"

Daelen chuckled softly. "I don't think we have much choice."

She hesitated for only a moment before stepping forward, crossing the threshold into the unknown.

As soon as they entered, the wall behind them sealed shut.

The Vault had made its choice.

Oriana spun, her heart racing as the wall behind them solidified with a low rumble, trapping them deeper within the Vault's depths. An ominous silence settled between them, the only sound the quiet hum of unseen energy coursing through the ancient stone.

Daelen exhaled slowly, his breath steady. "No turning back now."

Oriana's fingers brushed over the pendant beneath her cloak, its steady pulse in sync with the rhythmic glow of the symbols etched into the walls. She took a cautious step forward, her eyes scanning the dim, foreboding corridor ahead. The passage was lined with towering pillars, their surfaces etched with shifting patterns of light that seemed to respond to their presence.

Then, the voice returned, its strange, layered resonance filling the chamber like the weight of forgotten time. "Trial begins."

The ground beneath their feet quaked, a low tremor reverberating through the stone. A surge of Flux energy rippled through the walls, and suddenly, the corridor ahead began to shift. The once-smooth stone floor cracked, breaking apart as it rearranged itself into a twisting labyrinth of moving tiles. The path they had just walked collapsed into darkness, leaving only one way forward.

Oriana tensed, her voice tight. "This place is changing."

Daelen's eyes flicked to the shifting tiles. "And testing us."

As if to confirm his words, a row of metallic constructs emerged from the walls, their insect-like bodies sleek and gleaming, glowing veins of energy running along their segmented frames. They moved in perfect synchronization, positioning themselves between Oriana and the far end of the chamber.

The Vault's voice spoke again, its tone unwavering. "The Architects required balance—mind, body, and will. Prove your worth, or be turned away."

Oriana exchanged a glance with Daelen. "I'm guessing they don't mean a polite conversation."

One of the constructs lunged forward. Oriana barely dodged as a blade-like limb slashed through the air where she had been standing. She rolled aside, coming up with her knife drawn. Daelen was already in motion, deflecting the attack with a sharp twist of his wrist, his own blade gleaming in the low light.

Another construct lunged—this one faster, more precise. Oriana caught its movement at the last second and twisted, slamming the hilt of her knife against its glowing core. The impact sent a pulse of energy surging through the machine, momentarily staggering it.

"Go for the cores!" she shouted. "It disrupts them!"

Daelen responded instantly, striking the nearest construct in the center of its frame. A burst of light flashed, and the machine staggered backward, its limbs twitching erratically before collapsing to the ground.

The remaining constructs hesitated, recalibrating.

Oriana seized the opening, sprinting toward the far end of the chamber. The labyrinth shifted around them, walls rising and falling, pathways forming and collapsing in a chaotic dance. The constructs adapted, moving with precision, their patterns synchronizing to block every escape route.

Daelen cursed under his breath. "They're learning."

Oriana's mind raced. This wasn't just a fight—it was a puzzle. The Vault had said it required balance—mind, body, and will. Fighting alone wouldn't be enough.

She closed her eyes briefly, tuning into the rhythm of the Flow. She felt it—the pulse of the Vault, the way the machines moved, the subtle shifts in the tiles beneath her feet.

Then, she saw it. The opening.

Her hand shot out, grasping Daelen's wrist. "Follow me. Now."

Without a second thought, she darted left, weaving through the shifting labyrinth, narrowly avoiding the snapping limbs of the constructs. Daelen moved in perfect sync with her, his steps mirroring hers. The Vault continued to rearrange itself, but now, she could feel its rhythm—understand it.

A final surge of energy swept through the chamber, and in that moment, the exit appeared. A doorway of swirling light, just beyond the last row of machines.

Oriana didn't hesitate. She lunged forward, slipping past the final construct with a narrow margin, and burst through the threshold.

Silence.

The humming ceased. The machines froze. The shifting floor halted.

Daelen stumbled in behind her, breathing heavily. "Did we just...?"

The Vault's voice resonated one last time. "Trial complete."

Ahead, the final passage opened, revealing what the Architects had left behind.

Oriana steadied her breath, her pulse still pounding from the trial. The passage stretched before them, bathed in dim light, its walls lined with symbols that no longer flickered but pulsed with steady, controlled energy. The Vault had acknowledged them. They had passed.

Daelen rolled his shoulders with a wince. "I was hoping for more of a reward than nearly getting sliced apart."

Oriana smirked, though a flicker of unease crept up her spine. "We're still standing. Let's see if it was worth it."

They stepped forward, the final chamber unfolding before them in slow waves of illumination. It was vast, far grander than the previous rooms, its design a seamless fusion of ancient technology and something more organic. At its center stood an altar-like structure, its surface shimmering with the residual energy of the Vault.

Above them, suspended in midair, hung a hollow sphere, seemingly woven from strands of glowing light, rotating slowly in place. Its surface rippled with shifting patterns, the symbols on it moving in synchrony with their approach, as though responding to their presence.

Daelen exhaled in awe. "I've never seen anything like this."

Oriana's fingers tingled as she stepped closer, drawn to the sphere. The pendant at her chest pulsed in time with it, resonating in a way that went beyond mere energy. This was something ancient, something intertwined with the Flow itself.

The Vault's voice returned, softer now—almost reverent.

"You stand before the Heart of the Architects. Here lies the knowledge of those who shaped the first pathways. The bridge between the seen and the unseen."

Oriana barely breathed, her voice a whisper. "A bridge…"

Daelen's frown deepened. "What does that mean?"

Before either of them could speak further, the sphere pulsed once, sending a soft, rippling wave of energy through the air.

And then—

A vision.

Not fleeting glimpses this time, but a fully realized memory, one that did not belong to them.

They stood in a city bathed in golden light, its towering spires humming with the same radiant energy that surrounded the sphere. Figures moved through the streets, cloaked in flowing robes, their presence both human and something more. They seemed to carry knowledge in their very being, shaping unseen forces with their hands as they worked in perfect harmony.

At the heart of the city, a great chamber stood. Figures gathered in a circle, discussing matters that felt vast, beyond the scope of even the deepest reaches of history.

"The Flow is breaking."

The voice came from one of the robed figures, an elder with piercing silver eyes. "If we do not act, the balance will collapse."

Another figure, younger and defiant, stepped forward. "Perhaps it must."

A murmur rippled through the assembly.

Oriana felt the weight of the moment—the tension, the schism. This was a choice, one that had led to something catastrophic.

The vision fractured, splitting into moments—

• A temple collapsing in fire and light.

• The Architects scattering, their knowledge locked away.

• A great war, unseen but felt through the ages.

• And then—

• The CABAL.

Oriana gasped as the vision snapped away, the chamber of the Vault rushing back into focus. She staggered, clutching the altar for support.

Daelen cursed under his breath. "That... wasn't just history."

Oriana swallowed hard. "No. It was a warning."

The Vault's voice returned, its tone now heavy with finality.

"The choice has come again. The Flow must be guided, or it will fracture."

Oriana exchanged a glance with Daelen, the weight of the words sinking in. The war that had once divided the Architects had never truly ended. It had merely evolved, and now, they were caught in its next chapter.

The Vault hummed one final time, and the sphere of light descended slowly, almost reverently, toward Oriana, as if offering itself.

A choice. A responsibility.

And perhaps, the first step toward a future yet to be written.

Chapter 10:

Shadows in the Desert

The chamber fell into an eerie silence as the sphere of light descended toward Oriana. The air crackled with energy, charged with an almost palpable expectancy—as if the Vault itself awaited her decision. She could feel Daelen's gaze on her, his posture tense, unreadable.

"Are you going to take it?" he asked softly.

Oriana hesitated. The knowledge of the Architects. The bridge between the seen and the unseen. This was no mere gift—it was a burden, a responsibility she hadn't asked for.

The Vault's voice returned, no longer distant, but imbued with a solemn, expectant weight.

"To accept is to carry the path forward. To refuse is to bury the past forever."

Oriana clenched her fists, her heart racing. This was no longer just about her. The CABAL had pursued her relentlessly, seeking to erase any trace of this knowledge. If she turned away now, would anyone else ever find it?

She inhaled deeply, steadying herself, and reached out.

The moment her fingers brushed the light, the chamber responded.

A surge of energy shot through her, overwhelming but not painful, as if her very essence was being rewritten, her soul remade. Her mind expanded, flooded with visions—

A civilization at its peak, Architects shaping the Flow with delicate, deliberate precision.

A vault being sealed beneath the sands, hidden from those who would pervert its power.

A child—her child—Brand. Standing at a crossroads, his fate yet to be written, the dormant power within him yearning to awaken.

Then—A vision of the CABAL, their forces swelling, their reach stretching into every corner of existence. The war had never ended. It had merely been postponed.

Oriana gasped as the surge of energy dissipated, the visions fading. The pendant at her chest hummed, resonating with a newfound power. It was no longer merely a shield—it had become a key.

Daelen caught her arm, his brow furrowed in concern. "Oriana?"

She exhaled slowly, her pulse still racing. "We can't stay here. We need to leave."

The Vault pulsed one final time, as if acknowledging her choice. The knowledge had been given. The war was waiting.

And she had made her choice.

The moment Oriana withdrew her hand, the chamber trembled. The walls pulsed violently, their steady glow shifting into something far more erratic. The Vault was awakening.

Daelen stepped back cautiously. "I don't think it likes being disturbed."

A deep, resonant hum vibrated through the chamber, sending ripples through the air. The intricate pathways of light woven into the stone began to shift, unraveling into twisting patterns that coalesced overhead. The Vault's voice returned, but this time, it was not a whisper—it was a command.

"The burden is accepted. The path must be tested."

Oriana barely had time to process the words before the very air thickened, as if invisible forces pressed down upon them. The walls flickered—then contorted.

The entrance they had come through vanished, sealing shut.

A new passage appeared in its place, stretching into an inky void.

Daelen exhaled sharply. "I'm guessing that's our exit?"

Oriana didn't answer right away. Her mind still reeled, the weight of the knowledge she'd absorbed thrumming beneath her skin. This was more than just information—it was a connection, an understanding that made the Flow feel closer, more tangible than ever before.

But the Vault wasn't done with them.

A low tremor reverberated through the floor, and Oriana's breath caught as something massive stirred in the darkness ahead.

And then she saw them.

Figures emerging from the shadows—neither fully mechanical nor fully human. Their bodies were wrapped in golden filaments of energy, their faces hidden behind smooth, featureless masks.

Guardians.

Oriana's pulse quickened. The final test had begun.

The Guardians moved in perfect synchrony, their motions unnervingly fluid. Their very presence exuded an aura of authority, as though they were not just constructs but extensions of the Vault itself.

Oriana's hand instinctively moved toward her blade, but she paused. This was more than a fight. This was another test.

The Vault's voice boomed, filling the chamber. "To carry knowledge is to be challenged. Prove your strength, or be unmade."

Daelen muttered under his breath, his voice laced with irritation. "I was really hoping we were done proving things."

The first Guardian struck.

A blur of motion—impossibly fast. Oriana barely dodged as the golden figure lunged at her, an arc of pure Flux energy crackling from its outstretched palm. She twisted, feeling the air ripple with power as the attack missed by mere inches.

Daelen countered with fluid precision, rolling beneath another Guardian's strike and slashing upward with his blade. The edge connected—but instead of cutting through, the weapon bounced back, as though striking solid steel.

"They're protected!" Daelen called out.

Oriana's jaw tightened. A battle of brute force wouldn't win this.

She centered herself, syncing her mind with the Flow. The Vault was built with purpose, its energy woven into the Guardians themselves. If they were crafted to test knowledge, there had to be a way to defeat them that didn't involve combat.

Then, she saw it.

The Guardians moved in a pattern—an intricate rhythm that mirrored the shifting symbols on the walls. The Vault wasn't testing their strength; it was testing their perception.

Oriana steadied her breath. "Don't fight them. Move with them."

Daelen shot her a confused look. "What?"

"Trust me."

She stepped toward the nearest Guardian—not with aggression, but with purpose. As it struck, she shifted her stance, mirroring its movement rather than resisting. The instant she did, something clicked.

The Guardian faltered, its golden filaments dimming briefly.

Daelen followed her lead, dodging another strike and moving fluidly with Oriana. Another Guardian halted.

The Vault reacted. The shifting walls began to stabilize, their erratic motions settling.

Oriana inhaled slowly, her pulse slowing. This was the test. Adaptation. Understanding. Moving with knowledge, not against it.

One by one, the Guardians froze, their energy dimming as they acknowledged the lesson. Then, wordlessly, they receded into the shadows.

The path forward opened.

Oriana released a breath she hadn't realized she was holding. "It's over."

Daelen laughed softly. "You're a terrifyingly fast learner."

The Vault pulsed one final time, a sound of approval, as if it recognized the lesson had been understood. The last path to freedom lay ahead.

The air inside the Vault shifted as Oriana and Daelen moved through the final passage. The walls pulsed again—not in warning, but with something like acknowledgment. The Vault had tested them, shared its knowledge, and now it was letting them go.

Daelen exhaled, his voice low. "We need to move quickly. If the CABAL's still out there, they won't wait forever."

Oriana nodded, her fingers curling around the pendant beneath her cloak. It felt heavier now, as if it bore the weight of the knowledge inside her.

They followed the narrowing corridor, the ceiling dipping lower, until a faint breeze brushed Oriana's face. Ahead, a shaft of moonlight pierced the darkness.

The exit.

Daelen reached the edge first, pressing his back against the stone as he peered outside. "No movement," he muttered. "But that doesn't mean they're not watching."

Oriana's grip tightened around her knife, her mind racing. They had no way of knowing how long they had been inside. The CABAL could have set up an ambush beyond the dunes, ready and waiting.

"We don't have a choice," she said, voice steady despite the tension. "We move now."

Daelen nodded grimly, and together, they slipped into the open air. The cold desert wind hit them with a biting force, a stark contrast to the still warmth of the Vault. Oriana inhaled deeply, trying to adjust to the vastness of the night.

And then, she saw them.

Figures in the distance, a dozen or more, moving deliberately across the sand. Their dark silhouettes were barely visible against the moonlit dunes. CABAL scouts.

Oriana's pulse quickened, her instincts flaring. "They're still here."

Daelen cursed under his breath. "If they're waiting for us, we need another way out."

Oriana scanned the horizon. The nearest ridge was close, but the CABAL's positioning wasn't random. They weren't just waiting—they were closing in.

They had been tracking them all along.

Oriana met Daelen's gaze, her expression hardening. "We can't outrun them."

Daelen's jaw tightened. "Then we outsmart them."

She reached for the pendant beneath her cloak, feeling its subtle hum of power. The Vault had hidden them once before. Perhaps, just once more...

Closing her eyes, Oriana let her mind slip into the Flow.

The desert seemed to whisper around her, the unseen threads of energy shifting and rippling in response to her focus. It was faint, but there—a subtle distortion in the air, a crack in the fabric of perception.

She inhaled slowly, then whispered, "We don't need to fight. We just need to vanish."

Daelen's eyes locked on hers, unwavering. Without hesitation, he nodded. "Do it."

Oriana let the energy surge through her, through the pendant, through the knowledge the Vault had imparted. The air around them shimmered—a brief flicker, a distortion in the fabric of reality—but it was enough.

Enough to make them disappear from sight.

The CABAL scouts passed them by, moving unaware.

Daelen exhaled slowly, his voice laced with awe. "Remind me to never doubt your instincts."

Oriana allowed herself a brief, knowing smile. "We're not out of danger yet."

They waited in silence until the last scout had moved out of range before slipping into motion. The Vault was behind them now, hidden once again beneath the shifting sands.

But its knowledge was no longer lost.

Chapter 11:

The Ruins of Kal'Shara

The desert stretched endlessly before them, bathed in the pale glow of moonlight. Oriana and Daelen moved cautiously, their footsteps light as they wove through the dunes, putting distance between themselves and the hidden Vault. The air was crisp, but the weight of their experiences—the Architect, the CABAL—pressed on them heavier than the chill of the night.

Oriana's mind raced, trying to process everything that had happened. The Vault had chosen her. The knowledge of the Architects flowed through her, reshaping how she perceived the Flow. Every breath, every movement—she could feel the energy currents threading through the world. It was exhilarating, but unsettling too.

Daelen's voice cut through her thoughts. "We can't keep this up."

Oriana didn't answer right away, still tangled in the enormity of their situation.

After a few tense moments, Daelen tried again, his frustration clear. "We need a destination. We can't just wander the sands forever."

Oriana blinked, shaking herself from her reverie. She nodded, her voice tinged with uncertainty. "Baric's caravan. If they made it out of the ridges, they'll be heading north to the trade outpost."

Daelen adjusted the wrappings on his forearm, scanning the horizon. "And if they didn't?"

Oriana exhaled, unwilling to entertain that possibility. She didn't have an alternative ready, so she settled on, "Then we find another way."

They pressed on, careful to avoid open stretches where CABAL scouts might still be searching. Every so often, Oriana would pause, reaching out—not with her eyes, but with something deeper. A sense she couldn't fully understand, but one that guided her nonetheless.

The Flow responded, subtly nudging her toward the safest path.

Daelen must have noticed. "You're doing something," he remarked, his tone more curious than accusatory.

Oriana hesitated. "I think... I can sense disturbances in the Flow. Like feeling a ripple in water before the wave hits."

Daelen studied her for a moment, then smirked. "That would've been useful a few fights ago."

She shot him a pointed look. "I'm still figuring it out."

Their pace quickened as the first signs of dawn began to stain the sky. They needed shelter before the sun fully rose.

Then Oriana felt it—a shift.

It wasn't the CABAL. Not a natural shift in the desert wind.

Something else.

Oriana raised a hand, signaling Daelen to stop. He obeyed without question, dropping into a crouch beside her. "What is it?"

She focused, letting the sensation guide her. And then she saw them—figures on the horizon, moving slowly but with purpose.

Not the CABAL. Not bandits.

Survivors.

And among them, a familiar shape—Baric's banner, tattered but unmistakable.

A wave of relief washed over her. "The caravan. What's left of it."

Daelen followed her gaze. "Let's hope they have supplies. And answers."

Without another word, they moved toward the remnants of the caravan, the last allies they had.

The caravan's survivors were scattered across the sand, hunched and weary. Some clung to one another for support, their clothes torn, their faces drawn with exhaustion. Others stood guard, weapons in hand, their eyes scanning the horizon for any threats still lurking in the dunes.

Oriana's heart clenched at the sight. They had survived—but at what cost?

Baric stood by a small fire, his robes frayed, stained with dust and sweat. His eyes met hers, grim and tired. "You made it," he said, his voice rough with fatigue. "I wasn't sure anyone else had."

Oriana met his gaze, her voice steady. "What happened?"

Baric exhaled deeply, gesturing to the scattered survivors. "We fought them off as long as we could, but they kept coming. CABAL agents and mercenaries. They wanted something—or someone."

His eyes flickered toward Oriana, and she knew the answer before he spoke. "They were looking for you."

Daelen crossed his arms, his voice dry. "And yet, you're still standing."

Baric let out a weary chuckle. "Barely. We lost many good people. Supplies... animals... all gone. But we're alive, and that's more than I expected."

Oriana's gaze swept over the wounded. Some were wrapped in makeshift bandages, others lay still beneath thin blankets. The air was thick with the scent of sweat, blood, and despair.

"We can't stay here," Baric said, his voice low, eyes scanning the survivors. "They'll come back. Next time, they won't be testing our defenses. They'll finish what they started."

Oriana nodded. They needed a plan—and fast.

Daelen shifted his stance, his tone pragmatic. "Do you have any transport left?"

Baric rubbed a hand over his face, exhaustion weighing on him. "A few sandstriders. Not enough for everyone, but enough to get a message to the nearest city."

Oriana frowned, uncertainty creeping in. "You're not thinking of splitting up, are you?"

Baric met her gaze, his expression unyielding. "We don't have a choice. If we all stay here, we die. But if some of us go for help, we might stand a chance."

A heavy silence settled between them. It was a gamble. A dangerous one.

Oriana's fingers brushed the pendant at her chest, a reminder of the knowledge the Vault had given her. But it hadn't provided answers—only the tools to find them. That was up to her.

She exhaled, steadying herself. "Then we move quickly. And we make sure we're not followed."

Baric nodded, his resolve as firm as his exhaustion. "Then let's get to work."

The survivors gathered in a tight circle, the flickering fire casting long shadows over their worn faces. The decision was agonizing, but it had to be made.

Baric stood at the center, his voice steady despite his weariness. "We don't have enough mounts for everyone. Those who stay behind need to prepare to hold out until help arrives."

Low murmurs rippled through the group. Some shifted uneasily, their eyes scanning the dark horizon, knowing the CABAL could return at any moment.

Oriana took a deep breath. "We need fighters to stay. Those who can wield a blade or shoot a bow. The injured, the weakest—those will ride for help."

Baric nodded grimly. "Agreed. But we also need someone who knows the sands, someone who can guide them to the city."

Daelen uncrossed his arms, his voice quiet but firm. "I'll go with them."

Oriana frowned, hesitation tugging at her. "Are you sure?"

He smirked, a glint of mischief in his tired eyes. "I'm not much use sitting here. What about you?"

Oriana exhaled, her resolve settling. She knew the answer before the words left her mouth. "I stay."

Silence stretched, thick and heavy. Then Baric sighed, his voice laced with concern. "You're certain?"

Oriana nodded, her gaze steady. "If they come back, I can help hold them off. And if the Flow guides me... maybe I can keep them from finding us at all."

Baric studied her for a long moment, then nodded, his voice softer. "Then we move before dawn."

The decision was made. Now, they could only pray it wasn't the wrong one.

The desert night stretched out before them, still as death. Yet Oriana felt the tension in the air—tight, like a wire ready to snap. The survivors who remained were quiet, their faces grim, gathered near the dim glow of the fire. They knew what was coming. If the CABAL returned before reinforcements arrived, they would have to stand and fight.

Baric crouched beside a weathered map, tracing his fingers over the terrain. "We don't have much to work with. No fortifications, barely enough weapons. If they come, we'll need to rely on positioning and surprise."

Oriana nodded, arms crossed tightly. "We can use the dunes to our advantage. Force them into bottlenecks. Keep them from surrounding us."

A wiry young man named Revik frowned, his voice laced with uncertainty. "But we don't know when they'll attack. Could be tonight, could be days from now."

Oriana's gaze hardened, her voice steady. "Then we prepare as if they'll be here by dawn. If we're ready, we might survive the first strike."

A murmur of agreement spread through the group. The remaining fighters—those who were still able—began to strategize. Weapons were salvaged from the fallen, makeshift defenses drawn in the sand. It wasn't much, but it was all they had.

Baric studied Oriana with a penetrating gaze. "You seem more certain now. Like you know something we don't."

Oriana hesitated, the question lingering in the air. Did she know something? The Flow had guided her so far—could it help her now?

She placed a hand over the pendant at her chest, feeling its warmth seep into her skin. "I don't know everything," she murmured. "But I know we're meant to hold this ground. And I know I can help."

Baric didn't press her further. He simply nodded, his expression hardening. "Then we hold."

The hours crawled by in tense silence. The sky remained pitch-black, the stars cold and indifferent above the dunes. Oriana stood at the outskirts of the camp, eyes scanning the horizon, senses stretched tight.

Then she felt it. A shift.

It wasn't the air. It wasn't sound. It was the Flow itself. A disturbance—like a stone sinking into still water.

She instinctively closed her eyes, reaching deeper. The sensation was impossible to name. It carried the weight of touch, color, sound, and smell, all at once and yet none of them clearly. A discordance, like the rasp of sandpaper against her skin, the dull red of dried blood, the shriek of tearing metal, and the fetid stench of rotting meat. It came and went, leaving her senses reeling.

She knew she didn't fully understand this talent, not yet. But what she understood was this: it was all wrong. A warning. A sign.

Her pulse surged, sharp and urgent, as she called out, her voice cutting through the tension. "They're coming."

Baric was beside her in an instant, his eyes narrowing in disbelief. "How do you know?"

Oriana's breath remained steady, but her fists clenched at her sides, her body instinctively bracing against the danger that was closing in. "I can feel them."

No sooner had the words left her lips than the first shadow shifted at the edge of the dunes—then another, gliding across the sand with unnerving precision.

The CABAL had arrived.

Oriana turned sharply to face the others, her voice a command, unwavering. "Positions. Now."

Weapons were drawn with practiced speed, the group's resolve hardening like stone. There would be no reinforcements, no fallback. This was their stand.

And this time, Oriana wouldn't just fight—she would stand her ground. She would not run.

Chapter 12:

A Trail of Shadows

The silence before battle hung heavy, thick with tension—a fragile thing, holding its breath in the dark, waiting for the storm to break.

Oriana crouched low behind a sand dune, her heart steady, pulse thumping against her ribs. Her fingers tightened around the hilt of her knife, the blade cold and reassuring in her grip. Around her, the others lay hidden in the sand—Baric to her right, Revik just behind, weapons poised. The others had taken positions along the ridges, using the dunes as their cover.

The CABAL forces moved like shadows, a dark current flowing through the night. Silent. Calculated. Dangerous. They weren't charging—they were hunting.

Baric exhaled slowly, his breath steady but heavy with the weight of what was coming. "They don't know our numbers."

Oriana nodded, her eyes locked on the enemy. "That's our only advantage."

The first enemy stepped forward, his boots crunching softly in the sand, his head swiveling as if sniffing the air. Another followed, each movement deliberate, searching. Listening.

And then—

A flicker in the Flow.

Oriana's breath caught, her body tightening as the disturbance washed over her like a cold wave. She didn't have time to deepen her focus, to analyze the sensation, so she turned her head slightly, tuning in—not to her eyes, but to her sense of the unseen.

A CABAL commander stood just behind the advancing line. His presence rippled through the Flow like a dark pulse, a palpable disturbance that made her skin crawl. This was the one directing them.

She whispered, barely more than a breath, "There."

Baric's gaze followed hers, sharp, calculating. "Take him, and we cut off their control."

Oriana's fingers curled tighter around her knife's hilt, the blade a whisper in her hand. "We move on my signal."

A gust of wind whipped through the dunes, stirring the sand with a hiss. It was the only sound she needed.

She moved first, light as a shadow, her body melding with the night as the air around her seemed to part. The others followed—silent, lethal, flowing through the desert like whispers.

The first blade struck before the enemy could react—a soft gasp, the body crumpling into the sand. Then another. And then the world exploded into chaos.

The desert, once still, erupted with noise. The CABAL soldiers, caught momentarily off guard, recovered with terrifying speed. Their discipline was a deadly thing—blades flashing, red-hued energy crackling in the air like the scent of burned ozone.

Oriana twisted, narrowly avoiding a vicious downward strike from one of the CABAL enforcers. Her knife sliced upward, biting deep into flesh, the resistance sharp and satisfying. A strangled cry, and the soldier dropped to the sand.

Baric fought beside her, his curved sword moving in a deadly arc, deflecting a blow with expert precision before burying the blade deep into his opponent's chest. He shouted over the rising chaos, "They know we're here now!"

Oriana's gut twisted as the element of surprise slipped away, the CABAL's precision closing in around them.

Across the dunes, the CABAL commander—whom she had sensed earlier—barked an order, his voice carrying over the battlefield like a crack of thunder. The enemy lines shifted. They were tightening their formation, using the ridges to box them in, forcing the fight into a narrower space. They were taking control.

Revik cursed under his breath, barely dodging an energy blast that sent a section of the dune collapsing inward with a violent roar. "They're funneling us!"

Oriana clenched her jaw, the weight of their strategy sinking in. The CABAL was pushing them into a kill zone. If they didn't act fast, they would be overrun.

She reached deep, her mind extending into the Flow, letting its currents guide her, shape her awareness. It surged through her like a tidal wave, revealing the weak points in the CABAL's formation.

"There!" she hissed, pointing to an opening in their ranks—just a narrow gap, but it was their only chance.

Baric's eyes flashed with understanding. "Fall back to the right! Now!"

The remaining fighters moved as one, shifting positions with deadly precision. Oriana and Baric covered their retreat, their blades a blur of flashing steel as they carved through any soldiers brave enough to pursue.

The CABAL forces adjusted, but it was too late. The survivors had slipped free of their trap.

For a brief moment, they had space.

Oriana's breath came in ragged bursts, but she didn't let it slow her down. The battle was far from over. The CABAL would regroup, and when they did, they would hit harder, with overwhelming force.

She turned to Baric. "We need to end this before they have a chance to breathe."

Baric's gaze met hers, sharp and resolute. "Then we take out their leader."

Oriana nodded. It was the only way.

The tide of battle momentarily lulled. The CABAL's formation shifted, as though they, too, were recalibrating. The commander—

tall, imposing, encased in segmented black armor—loomed at the rear, coldly surveying the skirmish. His energy signature throbbed in the Flow, a beacon of unyielding control. He was the anchor holding the CABAL forces together.

Oriana's breath slowed, her focus narrowing. She locked onto him, the tension in her chest tightening. "Take him down, and they break."

Baric gave her a steady, calculating glance. "What's the plan?"

Oriana exhaled, her eyes never leaving the commander. "Get me close. I'll do the rest."

Without a word, Baric signaled to Revik and the others. They subtly adjusted their positioning, creating distractions, drawing the enemy's attention away from Oriana as she slipped toward her target.

The Flow pulsed around her, guiding her steps, sharpening her senses. The commander remained oblivious to the danger moving in his direction. The battle was about to change, and Oriana would be the one to tip the scales.

Just as Oriana closed in, the commander spun, his red energy blade igniting with a savage hiss.

He had sensed her.

Oriana twisted, barely dodging the slash, the heat of the weapon searing the air beside her. The commander's helmet tilted, as if appraising her. "Interesting."

Before she could react, he was upon her again, his strikes impossibly fast. Oriana parried, struggling to keep up. Her mind raced. This wasn't just any CABAL officer—he was trained in the Flux. From the

Digital Monks and the Spirit Fox, and the fragments of knowledge she had gathered in the ruins, she knew this was no user of the Flow. He wielded the raw, untamed power of the Flux itself.

She had no idea if her fledgling connection to the Flow would be enough to hold her own—but she had to try.

Baric charged in with a roar, his sword crashing against the commander's energy blade in a burst of sparks. Oriana seized the opening, slashing low, forcing him to disengage.

The commander smirked beneath his helmet, the sound almost a hiss. "You think cutting off the head will kill the body?" His voice was smooth, almost mocking. "You don't understand the CABAL."

Oriana tightened her grip. "I understand enough."

The commander's blade flared brighter, the crimson light shifting into a spear that crackled with raw energy. "Then come and prove it."

Oriana and Baric exchanged a look. This fight—this moment— would decide everything.

And there was no turning back.

The commander advanced, his movements fluid and deadly. His spear of crimson energy crackled as it cut through the air, each strike a perfect extension of his mastery over the Flux. This was no mere soldier.

Oriana planted herself, feeling the Flow ripple around her like a warning. She had to anticipate, not react.

Baric struck first, lunging with a powerful downward slash. The commander shifted effortlessly, twisting his spear to meet Baric's blade with a sharp clash. The force sent Baric stumbling backward, but Oriana was already moving.

She feinted left, then rolled right, her knife flashing in a low arc aimed at the gap in the commander's segmented armor. It was a near-perfect strike—

—but the commander was faster.

The commander's spear flicked downward, a blur of red that knocked Oriana's blade from her grip. In the same breath, it was at her throat, the glowing tip a hair's breadth from ending it all.

"Predictable," he murmured, his voice dripping with disdain.

Oriana's heart pounded, but she didn't freeze. She felt the Flow— the pulsing rhythm in the air, in the earth beneath her. The sand shifted beneath her, alive with its energy—and she moved with it.

She dropped low, gravity pulling her into a roll as the commander's spear thrust forward, missing by mere inches. Her hand shot out, brushing against the sand—

The Flow answered.

A surge of blue energy burst from the earth beneath the commander's feet, sending a shockwave through him, destabilizing his stance for the first time.

Baric wasted no time. He lunged, his sword flashing with deadly intent, striking with brutal force. His blade sank into the commander's armor—but it didn't stop.

The commander grunted, stumbling back as Baric's sword pierced the plating at his side. A hit.

But it wasn't enough.

With a flick of his wrist, the commander wrenched Baric's blade free with unnatural ease. His spear shimmered, reforging itself, brighter, sharper.

Oriana barely had time to react before the commander unleashed a violent pulse of red energy. The wave exploded outward, sending both her and Baric crashing across the sand.

Pain tore through Oriana as she hit the ground hard. She gasped, struggling to rise, but the air felt thick—like the very Flow was being siphoned away from her.

The commander loomed above, untouched, his eyes glowing like embers beneath his helmet. "You understand nothing," he sneered, his voice tinged with disappointment. "The Flow does not belong to you."

Oriana's fists clenched, her vision blurred at the edges. "It belongs to no one."

The commander tilted his head, as if amused. "Wrong."

His spear rose, preparing for the final strike.

And then—

A pulse. A shift. The Flow roared back into her.

Oriana's body reacted before her mind could catch up. She surged upward, hands crackling with blue light, catching the commander's spear mid-strike. Energy crackled violently between them, Flux clashing against Flow in a titanic struggle of wills.

The commander's eyes widened. "Impossible."

Oriana didn't give him the chance to recover.

With a twist, she channeled every ounce of the Flow into a final, devastating move—redirecting the commander's own energy back at him.

His spear shattered in an explosion of red light. The energy surrounding him flickered and collapsed, like a flame snuffed out in an instant.

Baric was up in an instant, his sword flashing, a blur of steel and purpose.

The commander staggered, his armor splitting at the seams, his body jerking as blue light surged through his veins. He gasped—

—and fell.

Silence.

The battle, once a storm of chaos, stilled.

Oriana collapsed to her knees, breath ragged, her limbs trembling. The Flow around her hummed softly, no longer churning in resistance. It had accepted her.

Baric wiped his blade, exhaling slowly. "Next time," he panted, "we find an easier way."

Oriana managed a faint smile, though her body still hummed with tension. "Agreed."

The remaining CABAL forces, now scattered and leaderless, melted into the desert, vanishing into the shadows. The immediate threat was broken, but it wasn't gone. Not by a long shot.

Oriana gazed up at the endless expanse of the night sky, feeling the weight of everything that had passed. She wondered what twisted thoughts had driven the CABAL leader, how her success with the Flow had shifted the tides of battle, and how much farther she still had to go—especially to protect her child from the CABAL's insatiable hunger for control.

She closed her eyes and exhaled deeply, trying to release the weight that still clung to her body.

The war was far from over, but for tonight... they had won.

Chapter 13:

The CODEX

The battlefield lay still, its violence now a distant echo.Oriana remained on her knees, her breath steady but shallow, fighting the exhaustion threatening to drag her under. The Flow, previously twisted somehow by the CABAL and foreign to her senses, now hummed softly around her—a presence, no longer resisting.

Baric stood over her, his gaze sweeping the battlefield. The sand, darkened by blood and ruin, bore the weight of their struggle. Fallen CABAL soldiers littered the dunes, their bodies scattered like broken pieces of a puzzle. The survivors—those who had fought beside them—gathered in small clusters, tending to the wounded, searching for the lost.

Revik limped toward them, his face streaked with dirt and sweat, his posture heavy with fatigue. "They're gone," he rasped, his voice hoarse. "For now."

Oriana pushed herself upright, her muscles protesting with each movement. "We need to move before they regroup."

Baric sheathed his sword, his expression hardening. "The CABAL won't let this go unanswered. Their commander is dead, but there will be more."

Oriana's fingers brushed the pendant at her chest, a reminder of the bond between her and the Flow. It had chosen her. She didn't fully understand what that meant yet, but she knew it was significant. And the war was far from over.

Baric turned toward the others, his voice carrying authority. "Gather what you can. We leave at first light."

As the survivors moved to gather supplies, Oriana's gaze shifted over the desert. They had survived. They had won. But at what cost?

Hours slipped by, the darkness pressing in. The survivors moved like specters among the wreckage, collecting weapons, rations, anything of use.

Oriana knelt beside one of the fallen—his face peaceful now, despite the blood staining the sand beneath him. She closed his eyes gently, whispering a promise in the quiet: his death would not be in vain.

Baric approached, his expression grim and thoughtful. "We need to talk."

Oriana rose, brushing off the weight of grief. "What is it?"

He gestured toward the dwindling number of survivors. "We have two choices: we head for the trade outpost to regroup, or we move deeper into the desert, off the grid. The CABAL will expect us to run for safety."

Revik, joining them, crossed his arms. "And if we head deeper? We'll starve in days."

Oriana frowned, weighing their options. The trade outpost promised shelter, food, and the possibility of allies—but it also meant exposure. The CABAL would be watching.

Before she could speak, a ripple surged through the Flow.

A warning?

Her head snapped to the horizon, scanning the still dunes. The first rays of morning light crept across the desert, but something felt wrong.

And then she saw it—a figure, distant and still, standing atop a ridge, watching them.

She reached out with her senses—touch, color, sound, smell—seeking the familiar signals she had felt before the battle. But this... this didn't feel like the CABAL. Something else?

Oriana's pulse quickened. "We're not alone."

Baric and Revik followed her gaze, their hands moving to their weapons.

The figure didn't move. Didn't advance.

It simply waited.

For a long, tense moment, no one moved.

The figure remained motionless against the rising sun, its form cloaked in tattered fabric that fluttered with the wind. Oriana couldn't make out its features, only a faint shimmer of energy radiating from it—something unlike anything she'd encountered before.

Baric shifted beside her. "CABAL?" His voice was tight with suspicion.

Oriana shook her head, her voice low. "No."

Revik scowled, his grip tightening on his weapon. "Then what?"

Finally, the figure moved—slowly, deliberately. A single step forward, then another. It wasn't an attack. It wasn't even a threat. It was... an approach.

Oriana exhaled sharply, tightening her grip on the pendant at her chest. She felt the Flow pulse around her, responding to the figure's presence—not with hostility, but with something else. Recognition?

"It's waiting for us," she murmured, her voice distant.

Baric's shoulders tensed. "Waiting for what?"

Oriana ignored the protests from behind her and stepped forward, drawn to the figure. The wind carried whispers—not voices, but a feeling.

A test. That was why she had sensed the warning. The test would be dangerous, but the figure itself held no ill intent—not that Oriana could sense. At least... that's how she read it.

She stopped a few paces away, staring at the veiled figure. "Who are you?"

Silence stretched between them.

Then, the figure lifted its head slightly, and a glint of blue light flickered beneath the hood. A voice followed—a low, resonant tone, ancient and knowing.

"You have taken the first step."

Oriana's breath caught. The words weren't spoken aloud, but carried through the Flow itself, bypassing sound entirely.

She swallowed, the weight of the moment pressing on her. "The first step toward what?"

The figure raised a hand, palm open. The Flow pulsed between them, shifting like a tide answering a call.

"Toward understanding."

Oriana hesitated, her gaze fixed on the figure. Something about it felt... familiar—like a half-remembered dream, a sensation buried deep within her being, as if this meeting had been destined long before she ever set foot in this desert.

Baric's voice broke through her thoughts, tight with caution. "Oriana. We don't know who—what—this is."

She barely whispered, her voice trembling with an emotion she couldn't explain. "I know. But I think... I have to."

Without thinking, she reached forward, her fingers brushing the Flow that radiated between them. The instant her skin made contact, a shock of vision burst through her mind—

A city swallowed by time.

A temple beneath the stars.

A path laid out for her since the moment she was born.

And then... darkness.

A distant voice, clear and commanding:

"Seek the Codex."

Oriana gasped, stumbling backward. The figure remained still, its presence unyielding. But she knew—whatever it was, it had shown her what she needed to see.

Baric's hand gripped her arm, steadying her. "What happened?"

She exhaled slowly, shaking off the remnants of the vision. "We don't go to the outpost."

Revik's brow furrowed. "Then where?"

Oriana turned toward the figure, but it was already gone, its presence fading like a whisper carried on the wind.

She clenched her fists, the words still echoing in her mind.

"Seek the Codex."

She met Baric's gaze, her expression resolute. "We go to the temple."

Silence settled over them as the vision's weight lingered in the air. The path had been shown to her, clear and unyielding—leading them to the temple beneath the stars.

Baric's face darkened as he studied her. "You're sure about this?"

Oriana nodded, her fingers tightening around the pendant at her chest. "This isn't just a choice. It's where we're meant to go."

Revik shifted his weight, eyes narrowing. "You saw something, didn't you?"

Oriana hesitated, then answered, her voice steady. "Not just something. A future. A path."

Baric sighed, glancing toward the others, waiting for direction. "Then we move."

The survivors, exhaustion written across their faces, began to gather. None protested. They had followed Oriana this far. If she believed the temple was their salvation, they would follow her there.

By the time the sun had fully risen, they had already broken camp and were moving swiftly, but cautiously, staying off open ground and using the ridges for cover. Every step carried them deeper into uncharted territory.

Oriana could feel the Flow shifting around them, guiding them forward. It wasn't just instinct—it was certainty, a pull that grew stronger with each step.

Hours passed, and the desert heat began to gnaw at them. Baric called for a brief rest beneath the shade of a jagged rock outcrop. As the group settled, Oriana moved a little farther away, closing her eyes and reaching into the Flow.

The energy responded, flowing through her like a cool, steady current. She could sense it now—the temple. Distant, but real. Waiting.

But there was something else.

A shadow. A disturbance in the Flow, faint but unmistakable. She could feel variations—similar to the signs she had sensed before the CABAL's assault, but something was different. The energy felt warped, twisted in a way she couldn't yet place.

Her eyes snapped open, her heart racing. "They're coming."

Baric's body stiffened, his eyes narrowing. "CABAL?"

Oriana nodded, her voice tight with urgency. "They know where we're going."

Revik muttered a curse, his brow furrowing. "Then we need to move faster."

Oriana exhaled slowly, turning her gaze toward the horizon. The temple was close—so close, she could almost feel it. But the enemy was closer still.

The next leg of their journey had become a race against time.

And if they failed, the Codex would be lost before they ever had a chance to find it.

Chapter 14:

The Signal

The desert stretched endlessly before them—a vast, unforgiving ocean of dunes, shimmering beneath the relentless sun. Oriana led the survivors forward, her mind sharp despite the exhaustion creeping into her limbs. The Flow pulsed around her, a steady rhythm urging her onward.

Baric matched her pace, scanning the horizon for any sign of pursuit. Revik and the others followed in a loose formation, weapons at the ready, their silence thick with anticipation.

"We're exposed out here," Revik muttered, his voice low. "If they catch up to us before we reach the temple—"

"They won't." Oriana's voice was firm, though she wasn't sure why. The Flow had given her this path, and she trusted it—if only they could stay ahead long enough to follow it.

Baric wiped the sweat from his brow, his breath labored in the dry heat. "How far?"

Oriana closed her eyes, reaching out with her senses. The Flow pulsed faintly, distant but persistent. The temple was close.

"Half a day, maybe less," she said, her voice steady. "But they're gaining."

Behind them, the shadow on the horizon had grown—dark figures moving swiftly, relentless. The CABAL was closing in.

Revik cursed under his breath. "We need to move faster."

Oriana nodded, her gaze fixed ahead. She reached deeper into the Flow, pushing herself beyond the weariness in her body. The desert seemed to blur around her as each step took them closer to their goal— but the CABAL was closer still.

The air thickened, shimmering with heat, waves of distortion rising from the golden sands. The group pressed on, their breath coming in ragged gasps. Oriana could feel the pressure building, not just from the others, but in the Flow itself—a shift, an energy thickening, as if the world was holding its breath.

"They're getting closer," Baric said, his voice betraying concern. "I can hear the sand striders."

Oriana glanced over her shoulder. The CABAL's forces were closing in fast. The black banners fluttered in the wind, the gleam of armor reflecting the sun's harsh light.

"We need to lose them," Revik muttered, his grip tightening on his weapon. "Or fight."

Oriana's pulse quickened. A fight now would be suicide—they were outnumbered, outclassed. But the Flow had guided her this far. There had to be another way.

She let her awareness expand, feeling the shifting currents of the desert. Then, as if the sands themselves whispered to her, she sensed it—a coolness beneath her feet, a harmonious chime of crystal energy resonating from deep within the dunes.

"There," Oriana gasped, her finger trembling as she pointed toward the northeast. "A canyon. The sands shift differently there."

Baric frowned, squinting into the distance. "A canyon?"

Revik narrowed his eyes. "I don't see anything."

"You will," Oriana replied, her voice steady. The Flow never lied—she felt knowledge that deep within her. She just hoped she could understand what it was telling her, before it was too late.

They veered toward the unseen path, following her lead. As they crested the next dune, the land dipped sharply, revealing a hidden canyon carved through the rock. The narrow passage twisted away beneath the sand, like a labyrinth waiting to be discovered.

Revik exhaled sharply. "That wasn't here before."

"It was," Oriana said, her eyes fixed ahead. "You just couldn't see it."

Baric glanced at her, brow furrowed, but there was no time for questions. Behind them, the CABAL riders had crested the last dune, their forces fanning out like a tightening noose.

"Go!" Oriana shouted, urgency thick in her voice.

The survivors surged into the canyon, sand flying up in their wake. The walls rose like jagged teeth on either side, casting long, ominous shadows. The path ahead was a maze—maybe their salvation, maybe their tomb.

As soon as they entered, the temperature shifted. The oppressive heat of the desert sun was cut off by the towering rock walls, and a coolness filled the air. Their footsteps echoed strangely, swallowed by the vast emptiness that surrounded them.

Revik glanced back, his voice laced with doubt. "Think they'll follow?"

Oriana didn't need to answer. She could feel them—like a pulse at the edge of her consciousness. The CABAL riders were slowing, hesitant at the canyon's mouth. Something about this place made them hesitate.

Baric noticed it too. "They're not charging in."

Revik snorted. "Why? Because it's a maze?"

Oriana's eyes narrowed. "No," she murmured. "Because something's already here."

Silence fell over the group. The deeper they moved into the canyon, the more the Flow twisted around them—not in resistance, but in warning. Her fingers tightened around the pendant at her chest. They were being watched.

A soft scraping sound echoed ahead.

Everyone stopped, hearts pounding in unison.

Then, from the deepest shadows of the canyon walls, something stirred.

A towering figure emerged from a crevice in the rock. Its body seemed to shift, as if made of stone that broke apart and reformed with each movement. Its eyes—if they could be called eyes—were dark, hollow wells of glowing amber. As it turned toward them, the Flow around Oriana rippled violently, a surge of raw energy that nearly knocked her off balance.

Revik stepped back, his voice low with disbelief. "What in the—"

The creature raised one massive arm, and the ground beneath them trembled.

Rocks cascaded, pathways collapsed, and in an instant, the once-clear passage had transformed into a maze of shifting walls and dead ends. They were trapped.

Baric's sword was drawn in an instant, its blade catching the faint light of the canyon. "We don't have time for this."

The creature didn't attack—not yet. It simply loomed, its hulking form shifting slightly as if studying them, weighing their very existence.

Oriana took a steadying breath, forcing her pulse to slow. The CABAL was behind them, the guardian ahead. And the Flow...

The Flow wasn't telling her to fight. Instead, the crystalline chime that had haunted her thoughts continued, like a melody that began but never finished. It played in fragments, each note a question, a puzzle she wasn't yet meant to solve. Was she supposed to complete it? What did it mean?

She took a slow step forward. "Let me try."

Revik hissed under his breath. "Are you out of your mind?"

Oriana didn't respond. She raised her hand, letting her awareness sink fully into the Flow, feeling the pulse of energy surging through the canyon, through the guardian, through everything.

The guardian turned its massive head toward her, its eyes—a deep amber glow—fixating on her with an intensity that nearly stopped her heart.

A deep, rumbling voice echoed through the canyon, not in words, but in a presence, in a sensation. A question. A test.

Oriana swallowed, the weight of its presence settling in her chest. This was more than a mere labyrinth. It was a trial.

And if they failed, the temple—their only hope—would remain forever out of reach.

She stood her ground, her eyes locked onto the towering stone figure before her. The air around them pulsed with energy, the Flow weaving through the creature like ancient threads. This was no random adversary or challenge—it was a gatekeeper.

The guardian shifted again, its body cracking and reforming like living stone. Its deep amber eyes narrowed, assessing her, as if it could see into her soul.

Baric took a cautious step forward, his voice low but insistent. "Oriana, whatever you're thinking—this has gone on long enough. We need to move."

Revik's fingers twitched around his blade. "It sealed us in. If we don't deal with it, we're not getting out of here."

Oriana exhaled, letting the tension flow out of her body. She knew the Flow had led them here for a reason. This wasn't a battle to fight. This was a challenge to overcome.

When she opened her eyes again, she addressed the guardian directly, her voice steady and resolute. "We seek the temple."

The guardian's massive head tilted to one side, and the canyon walls themselves seemed to shudder at its presence. Its voice filled the air—not in sound, but as an understanding that resonated deep in her bones. "All who seek must prove their worth."

The words were not spoken, but felt, like a pulse of ancient knowledge pressing into her mind. The others shifted uneasily, their faces a mix of awe and fear.

The melody in her mind grew longer, clearer. She was making progress. The puzzle was slowly beginning to reveal itself.

Oriana took a step forward, her voice steady despite the uncertainty that clung to her like dust. "Then tell me how."

The guardian's massive arm rose slowly, the motion reverberating through the canyon like the sound of a great bell tolling. And then, in an instant, the very earth beneath her feet trembled.

The Flow surged violently, crashing over her senses. The canyon walls groaned, their stone faces twisting, rising, reshaping as if alive. Paths that had been open moments before disappeared, swallowed by the shifting rock, while new passages unfurled, jagged and unfamiliar. The labyrinth was no longer just stone—it was alive, breathing, a living thing, moving and reshaping itself as needed for the moment.

The crystalline melody that had once whispered through her mind fell silent.

The ground quaked once more, and before she could fully react, Baric and Revik were gone. The rock walls had risen like a barrier, separating them from her in a heartbeat. Their voices—Baric's gruff command and Revik's low curses—were swallowed by the sound of stone grinding against stone.

Oriana stood alone, the weight of the moment pressing down on her. The path ahead was hers and hers alone. The Flow had led her here. She was meant to face this challenge alone.

Her fingers curled around the pendant at her chest, the cold metal grounding her, even as her breath quickened. "What must I do?"

The guardian's amber eyes glowed brighter, the ancient light within them burning into her soul. Its voice—a rumbling, primordial presence—echoed in her mind, not as words, but as an undeniable force. "Find the path. Prove your spirit."

Oriana closed her eyes, exhaling a steadying breath, the Flow swirling around her like an unseen current, pushing, guiding, urging. The labyrinth was not just a maze of stone. It was a living force, woven with energy, ready to be bent to her will—if she could listen closely enough. If she could hear the melody once more.

Her gaze flickered toward the towering guardian one last time, her resolve hardening. Then, without hesitation, she turned away from its all-knowing eyes and stepped into the shifting maze, the path uncertain, but her determination unwavering.

Chapter 15:

Whispers of the Ancients

Oriana crept cautiously through the labyrinth's twisting corridors, the stone walls shifting in her wake, as though they were breathing. The crystal chime rang out again, but this time, it wasn't a melody. It was a pulse, each note a beacon guiding her steps—sharp and unwavering, a reminder of the path that could never be undone. With every footfall, the path behind her sealed shut, the stone whispering as it reformed, cutting off retreat. There was no turning back.

Her senses heightened, Oriana reached into the Flow, feeling its deep currents thread through the ancient stone. The energy here was unlike anything she had encountered before—old, patient, as if the structure itself were watching her, waiting.

A test, the guardian had said. But what kind of test?

She pressed on, each breath steadying her resolve. The Flow guided her forward, its whispers barely perceptible, a subtle pull, but with every step, the path ahead shifted. False turns flickered, leading her astray for a moment before the true way revealed itself. She ignored her eyes, trusting instead in the crystal chime, in the current of energy she could feel, not see.

But then—A sharp shift in the air, a change so sudden that Oriana's pulse quickened. The walls around her seemed to grow heavier, pressing in as the passage narrowed. The Flow pulsed again, stronger, insistent. The final crystal note rang out—a harsh, urgent warning—before silence consumed the air.

She froze, every muscle tensing, just as the stone beneath her feet trembled. A trap.

From the walls, figures began to emerge—tall, humanoid sentinels, their forms seemingly molded from the labyrinth itself. Featureless faces stared blankly, and their presence was an oppressive weight in the air. They didn't move. Not yet. They only watched.

Oriana could feel their attention. The air seemed to thicken with expectation. They were waiting. Waiting for her to make a move.

Her fingers tightened reflexively around the pendant at her chest, the metal cold against her skin. This was the trial. Not just to find the path, but to face what stood in her way.

She exhaled, her breath slow, and took a cautious step forward.

The sentinels reacted.

Their limbs shifted with unnatural fluidity, stone flowing like liquid, forming jagged blades and gleaming spears as they closed in, encircling her. They didn't attack immediately, but their movements were precise, calculated—testing her, gauging her response.

Oriana didn't draw her weapon. There was no point. The sentinels' stone bodies would crush her with a single strike. This wasn't a battle of strength. It was something else.

She sidestepped the first strike, the blade of stone whistling through the air where she had been a heartbeat ago. The Flow surged in response, bending around her, guiding her body with a grace that felt as though it were not entirely her own.

Oriana moved, weaving through the sentinels, not striking, not engaging. She was learning their rhythm, listening to the silent language of their movements. The Flow pulsed again, deeper now, and with it, a growing understanding.

This was the challenge. Not to fight, but to flow with the labyrinth. To move through it, not as an adversary, but as a part of the test itself.

The exit revealed itself ahead, the path barely visible through the shifting figures. She couldn't hesitate. She sprinted forward, slipping through the smallest of openings, feeling the energy shift around her as the sentinels reacted—

—but she was faster.

A final surge of movement, a leap, and she was through. The moment her feet hit solid ground on the other side, the sentinels froze.

Then, as if satisfied, they melted back into the stone.

Oriana turned, breathing hard, realization settling over her. This was the first challenge—a trial of movement, of trust in the Flow.

And she had passed.

Ahead, the labyrinth stretched on, the crystal chime once again echoing in her mind. Ahead, she knew, the next challenge awaited.

Oriana pressed onward, her pulse steady but her mind racing. The sentinels had tested her movement, her ability to trust the Flow. She thought about the CABAL and knew that anyone who reached the labyrinth and faced this test, thinking only in terms of opposition and pure control, would have no hope of passing it. Destroying it, perhaps. She wondered about that when she felt the labyrinth shifting again, the energy weaving into something new.

The corridor widened into an open chamber, circular and vast. A complex and resounding series of notes sounded—the crystal chime she'd been following once more falling silent. Oriana saw the walls adorned with intricate carvings, ancient symbols glowing faintly in the dim light. At the center of the chamber stood a pedestal, atop which rested a floating orb of swirling blue energy. She tried not to stare at it, though she felt a pull into its deep, blue depths, accompanied by an ominous resonance. This energy was not malicious, but it should not be taken lightly.

She stepped forward cautiously. The Flow pulsed in recognition, whispering its presence but not its intent. Another test. But of what?

As she neared the pedestal, the energy around the orb flared, and the carvings on the walls shifted. Symbols rearranged, reshaped, forming patterns she couldn't immediately decipher. Then, a voice, deep and ancient, resonated within the chamber—as if she were hearing two voices speak as one.

"Knowledge is the path. Choose the truth."

Oriana turned slowly, scanning the symbols. A puzzle. The Flow shimmered at the edge of her senses, guiding but offering no answers. This was not about instinct—it was about understanding.

She focused, letting the Flow deepen her perception. She once again sought to translate the input from her connection with the Flow into senses she could comprehend. The symbols flickered, forming shifting patterns—some familiar, others strange. Then she saw, heard, felt, smelled it.

A sequence repeated within the carvings, a cycle that connected with the energy of the Flow itself—ancient knowledge embedded in the labyrinth. If she had tried to control the perceptions, rather than open herself to all the ways she could perceive the Flow, she would have missed the sequence.

Oriana lifted her hand, touching the air above a particular set of glowing runes. The energy shifted, responding to her choice.

The chamber trembled.

Then, as quickly as it had begun, the energy settled. The orb on the pedestal dimmed, its glow dispersing like mist. The symbols on the walls ceased their shifting.

She had chosen correctly.

A section of the far wall peeled away, revealing a new passage.

Oriana exhaled. The first trial had been about movement, trusting the Flow. This one had tested her ability to open herself fully, to recognize the deeper knowledge within the world.

Once again, she knew that anyone seeking to control the world around them or limit their knowledge would fail the test. She wasn't sure what failure would have meant, but she sensed it would have been fatal.

Taking a deep breath to steady herself, she stepped into the passage, listening for the crystal chime, ready for what lay ahead.

The passage narrowed as Oriana ventured deeper into the labyrinth until the chime silenced once more. The air had grown cool, and the walls smoothed as if untouched by time. A stillness settled over her— the quiet before revelation.

The corridor widened into a vast chamber, its ceiling lost in darkness. At the center stood a raised platform, upon which sat a single, unlit brazier. The Flow here felt dense, layered, as though something ancient watched from beyond the veil.

She stepped forward, and the voice returned. This time, Oriana was certain she was hearing three voices speaking as one.

"You have moved. You have seen. Now, will you stand?"

Oriana swallowed. A test of strength? Of spirit?

The brazier ignited suddenly with an ethereal blue flame. Shadows flickered along the walls, shifting into figures.

She recognized them instantly—Baric, Revik, the faces of those she had fought beside. Then, others—those she had lost.

Her mother. Her father. People from her past, long buried beneath survival.

They stood motionless, watching her, their eyes glowing faintly with an energy not their own.

The voices whispered again. "Will you break?"

Oriana clenched her fists. This was not real. It was a test—but that didn't make it any less painful.

The figures began to advance, slow and deliberate. They didn't speak, only stared, their presence weighing on her like an anchor. Doubt seeped into her mind.

Had she led them to ruin? Had her choices caused more harm than good? Was their sacrifice worth it? Who was SHE to continue on?

The Flow within her wavered.

She gritted her teeth. "No."

The figures hesitated.

She lifted her chin, eyes burning with resolve. "I will not be ruled by ghosts."

As she uttered the words, she realized that the crushing despair could be pushed back.

The room trembled. The figures halted.

The blue fire of the brazier flared, then extinguished in an instant. The figures vanished. The weight lifted from her chest, and the air settled.

A new doorway opened ahead, and with it, a final whisper.

"You have passed."

Oriana exhaled. The trials were over.

Now, the real journey would begin.

As Oriana stepped through the final doorway, the Flow pulsed warmly around her, a silent acknowledgment of her passage. Before her, a pedestal stood, holding an object wrapped in shimmering light. The air in the chamber hummed with an energy that felt ancient, aware.

She approached slowly, her fingers tingling as she reached for the artifact. As soon as her hand hovered above it, the Flow surged through her mind, flooding her with images, emotions—understanding.

Visions of the past, the present, and glimpses of the future unfolded before her. She saw the trials she had endured, the lessons ingrained in her soul. The labyrinth had tested her in ways beyond the physical—it had shaped her into something new.

She had learned to move with the Flow, not against it. To see beyond the surface, to recognize the deeper truths in the world around her. And most of all, she had faced her ghosts and chosen to stand firm. She had not broken.

Tears welled in her eyes, not from sadness, but from clarity. Everything had led her to this moment. Every loss, every struggle, every choice had been a step toward understanding her role—not only in this world but in shaping the future.

A name echoed in her thoughts: Brand.

Her son.

The Flow pulsed again, revealing something more. A vision of Brand—a future where he, too, would walk the path of the Flow. A future where he would face his own trials, forge his own destiny.

Her heart clenched. Would he be strong enough? Would he endure as she had?

The Flow whispered an answer: It was not her choice to make. It would be his. Just as she had chosen her own path, so too would he.

With renewed purpose, Oriana grasped the artifact. The light enveloped her, filling her with warmth and certainty.

The trials were over, but the journey had only just begun.

She turned from the pedestal, stepping forward into the unknown—toward her son, toward the future, toward whatever the Flow held in store.

Chapter 16:

Forces Closing In

Oriana emerged from the labyrinth's final passage, the weight of the trials still lingering in her body and mind. The air outside was crisp, touched by the faint scent of ancient stone and the whisper of winds that carried secrets from ages past. The sky overhead had darkened, stars beginning to glimmer like distant embers against the vast void.

The others were waiting.

Baric turned the moment he saw her, relief flashing across his face. "You made it."

Revik, ever the skeptic, narrowed his eyes, studying her. "You're different."

Oriana nodded. "I am."

She held the artifact tightly, feeling its warmth pulse in sync with the Flow inside her. The journey through the labyrinth had changed her—not just physically, but in the depths of her being. She now understood the Flow in a way she never had before. It was not a force to be wielded; it was a guide, a living current that carried purpose as long as she could open herself to it properly.

Revik's gaze flickered to the glowing object in her hands. "What did you find?"

She hesitated. "A key. A knowledge that was hidden from us. And a path forward."

Baric exhaled, glancing toward the horizon. "Then we don't have time to waste."

Oriana turned her gaze toward the distant temple, their next destination. It stood just beyond the ridges of rock and sand, illuminated faintly by the moonlight. The ancient walls pulsed with unseen energy, whispering of a power buried beneath time itself.

But danger was still close.

"The CABAL," she murmured, sensing their presence like a shadow lurking at the edges of the Flow. They had hesitated at the labyrinth's entrance, but they would not be deterred for long. They would come. And they would not stop until they had what she now carried.

Baric followed her gaze. "Then we move at first light."

Oriana nodded. The trials of the labyrinth were over, but the real challenge had only just begun.

She gripped the artifact tighter, feeling the weight of Brand's future within it. Whatever lay ahead, she would be ready.

For him.

For all of them.

As the sun broke over the horizon, the desert's colors shifted from the deep purples of night to the burning gold of morning. Heat already radiated from the dunes, promising an unforgiving day ahead. Oriana adjusted her pack, securing the artifact beneath her cloak. She felt its pulse—an echo of the Flow coursing through her veins.

Baric scanned the landscape, his fingers resting lightly on the hilt of his sword. "No sign of movement. Yet."

Revik kicked at the sand, eyes fixed on the distant horizon. "They won't stop. They never do."

Oriana met his gaze. "Then we don't stop either."

They moved swiftly, keeping low as they navigated the undulating dunes. The wind picked up, sending fine streams of sand spiraling through the air. The desert had its own secrets, its own way of protecting those who understood its rhythm. Oriana reached out with the Flow, sensing the land's energy, letting it guide their path.

Hours passed in silence, broken only by the crunch of their footsteps. The heat was relentless—sweat dripped from their brows, and exhaustion gnawed at their limbs. But there was no time to rest.

Then, a shift.

A ripple in the Flow.

Oriana halted, raising a hand. "Something's coming."

Baric's sword was drawn in an instant. "CABAL?"

Revik scanned the dunes, body tense. "I don't see—"

A howl split the air.

Low and guttural, it rode the wind like a warning. Then another—closer. Shadows flickered across the dunes. They were being hunted.

"The CABAL's beasts," Oriana whispered. "They found us."

Baric's jaw tightened. "We run."

And they did.

The dunes blurred as they sprinted, every step sinking into shifting sands. The beasts closed in, their howls multiplying, red eyes gleaming in the rising sun.

Knowing the creatures had the advantage in the open dunes, they veered toward rockier ground. The beasts held back, biding their time, gathering numbers.

Oriana pushed forward, breath burning in her chest. The Flow whispered possibilities, revealing hidden paths through the sand—ways to turn the land against their pursuers.

"There!" she shouted, pointing to a series of jagged ridges. "If we reach those cliffs, we can make a stand."

Baric didn't hesitate. He turned toward the stone formations, Revik right behind him. The beasts followed, kicking up plumes of sand as they closed the distance.

As they reached the first ridge, Oriana turned, using the artifact to deepen her connection to the Flow. She focused the energy into the ground beneath them. As the energy moved outward, the desert responded—ancient, patient. She exhaled, pressing her hands to the sand. Unlike the Flux energy, which could push or pull the sand, the Flow seemed to connect more intimately with the land itself. With shared intent, Oriana and the Flow posed a question, and the desert answered.

The earth shifted.

A great collapse of sand surged behind them, swallowing the pursuing beasts in a tide of golden sand. Their howls turned to shrieks as they tumbled into the depths.

The desert had answered her call.

Oriana swayed slightly, catching herself against Baric. He steadied her, eyes wide. "That was... something."

Revik peered over the edge. "Those beasts are tough. They'll probably dig themselves out. But not quickly."

Oriana straightened, wiping the sweat from her brow. "Then we use the time we have."

The temple loomed ahead, casting long shadows in the twilight.

It was time to reach it.

They arrived at the temple by dusk, the dying sun casting the ancient structure in deep shadows. The walls were carved with intricate symbols—glyphs pulsing faintly with hidden power.

Baric approached cautiously, his hand firmly gripping his blade. "What now?"

Oriana stepped forward, placing a hand against the stone. The moment her fingers made contact, the Flow surged through her, binding her to the ancient structure.

She felt the temple stir.

The doors shuddered, groaning as unseen mechanisms came to life. The air hummed with energy, sending chills down her spine. This place had been waiting for them.

Revik exhaled. "That's not ominous at all."

Baric tensed. "If the CABAL catches up to us before we figure this out—"

Oriana took a steadying breath. "Then we don't give them the chance."

She closed her eyes, listening to the Flow, feeling the puzzle woven into the temple's walls.

And then, as if in response, the great doors began to open.

Beyond them—darkness. Secrets. Another trial yet to be faced.

She stepped inside.

Chapter 17:

Into The Maw

The great doors of the temple groaned as they swung open, revealing an immense chamber beyond. Oriana felt the Flow ripple around her, the energy of the place thrumming like a pulse beneath her feet. The air was thick with age and mystery, carrying the scent of ancient stone and something more—a presence, watchful and expectant.

Baric and Revik stepped in behind her, their movements cautious. The chamber stretched out before them, its walls adorned with carvings that shimmered faintly in the dim light. The intricate glyphs twisted in fluid patterns, forming symbols Oriana did not recognize, yet she felt drawn to them.

"This place feels... alive," Baric muttered, running his hand along one of the stone walls. The moment his fingers brushed the surface, the glyphs flared briefly before settling back into their slow, rhythmic glow.

Oriana took a deep breath, feeling the weight of the temple pressing in on them. This was no ordinary structure. It was something more—

something built not just to preserve knowledge, but to protect it.

"The Digital Monks must have used this place," Revik said, eyeing the symbols warily. "But this goes beyond them."

Oriana nodded. The power here was older. It predated the monks. Perhaps it was here they first learned to wield the Flow, to understand its potential.

As they moved deeper into the chamber, Oriana let her fingers trace the patterns on the walls. The moment she did, the Flow surged through her, images flashing in her mind—glimpses of people long gone, kneeling in this very hall, seeking wisdom, seeking purpose.

Then, as if responding to her presence, the floor beneath them shifted.

A deep hum resonated through the chamber, and the glyphs along the walls brightened. The air thickened with energy, and a path of glowing symbols appeared, leading toward an arched doorway at the far end of the chamber.

Revik drew his weapon instinctively. "That's not normal."

Baric exhaled, gripping his blade. "Whatever this place is, it knows we're here."

Oriana wasn't afraid. She stepped forward, following the illuminated path. "Then let's find out why."

As they passed beneath the archway, the doorway sealed behind them, locking them deeper within the temple's mysteries.

The Flow stirred. The true test was about to begin.

A sudden pressure filled the chamber as the last echoes of the closing doorway faded.

The air was heavier now, thrumming with energy that Oriana could feel pressing against her skin. The chamber ahead was different from the last—smaller, more deliberate, like a place meant for initiation rather than worship.

At the center of the chamber, three figures stood motionless, their forms draped in ornate robes that shimmered faintly with an ethereal glow. Their faces were concealed beneath smooth, featureless masks, each adorned with a different symbol—one of the Flux, one of the Flow, and one of the Balance Between.

Baric tensed. "Are they... alive?"

Before Oriana could respond, the figure in the center raised a hand. The motion was slow, deliberate, yet carried a weight that sent ripples through the Flow. A voice, neither male nor female, filled the chamber—not from the figures themselves, but from the air around them.

"You walk in the halls of the Forgotten. You seek what was lost. Prove you are worthy."

Revik's hand tightened on his weapon. "I hate tests."

Oriana ignored him, stepping forward. "We mean no harm. We only seek understanding."

The figures did not respond to her words. Instead, the one representing the Flux spoke, its voice like a shifting tide. "If you would wield power, you must first learn how to surrender to it."

The second, representing the Flow, continued. "If you would understand the truth, you must first see beyond yourself."

The third, bearing the symbol of Balance, intoned, "If you would claim what is hidden, you must first prove that you will not be consumed by it."

As their words faded, the chamber around them began to shift. The walls stretched and pulled away, leaving them suspended in a void of swirling blue and gold light. Oriana felt herself untethered, floating as the Flow surged through her, testing her, unraveling her very sense of self.

A vision materialized before her.

She was no longer in the temple. She stood in the midst of a battle—not one she recognized, but one she knew was real. Warriors clad in armor fought against monstrous figures cloaked in shadow, their weapons crackling with blue energy. The battle was not one of conquest, but of desperation.

And then, she saw Brand.

He was older now, standing resolute at the heart of the conflict. His hands were outstretched, and the Flow twisted and pulsed around him. His eyes burned with the same blue fire that ran through Oriana's veins. She knew the cost of this—she might have to sacrifice everything if he was to survive. But it was no choice at all. Of course, she would.

And then—darkness.

The Flow snapped back around her, and she was in the chamber again, gasping for air. The figures stood exactly where they had before, their presence heavier now, expectant.

Baric and Revik had not moved. Their expressions were tense, and Oriana realized they had seen nothing of what she had just experienced. This trial was hers alone.

The figures spoke in unison, their voices carrying finality. "You have seen. You have accepted. The way forward is open."

With that, the chamber pulsed, and the walls shimmered as a new doorway appeared at the far end. The trial was over.

But Oriana's heart still pounded, the weight of what she had seen pressing heavily on her.

Beyond the newly revealed doorway, she found herself in a circular chamber bathed in soft, pulsing blue light. Unlike the previous rooms, which had carried an air of solemnity and judgment, this space exuded raw, unrefined power.

At the center of the chamber, resting upon a raised pedestal, was an artifact—a gauntlet, forged of obsidian and etched with flowing silver veins, as though it pulsed with living energy. The Flux wrapped around it like a protective shell, shifting and crackling as Oriana stepped closer.

She felt its call—not in words, but in the marrow of her bones. This was meant for her.

Baric and Revik flanked her, wary.

"That doesn't look like a relic of the monks," Revik muttered.

Oriana extended her hand toward the gauntlet, and the energy surrounding it recognized her. The moment her fingers brushed its surface, the chamber reacted—the Flow ignited around her, wrapping her in its essence.

Pain lanced through her arm as the artifact fused with her skin, but she did not pull away. Knowledge poured into her—this was no ordinary relic. This was a gift from those who had walked before, those who had shaped Flux and Flow into something greater.

Visions of warriors, moving at speeds beyond comprehension, striking with inhuman precision, flooded her mind. Strength, speed, instinct—all honed beyond mortal limits.

She gasped as the sensation settled, the gauntlet now seamlessly a part of her. The Flow pulsed through her veins with new intensity.

Baric exhaled, stepping back. "What did you just do?"

Oriana clenched her fist, feeling the power surge within her blood. "I've accepted my son's legacy."

As she took a steadying breath, the chamber around her reacted. The walls, once still, began to pulse with rhythmic energy, as if the temple itself had awakened. The glyphs along the stone columns brightened, their symbols shifting and rearranging. The Flow surged, crackling with raw intensity.

Then, the first tremor hit.

The ground rumbled beneath them, sending dust cascading from the ceiling. The sudden shift of energy sent a shockwave through Oriana's senses. Something outside the temple had disturbed its balance.

Baric tightened his grip on his weapon. "That's not natural."

Revik moved quickly to Oriana's side, his gaze darting toward the exit. "The CABAL. They've arrived."

Oriana turned toward the chamber's main entrance, her heart pounding. She could feel them now—a dark presence pressing against the Flow, trying to force its way inside. The temple, ancient and powerful, was resisting their intrusion, but for how long?

"We have to move," she said, urgency lacing her voice. "This place won't hold them out forever."

As if in response, the glyphs along the walls flickered violently, and the tremors grew stronger. The temple was collapsing. The CABAL must be using a combination of explosives and their Flux abilities.

Oriana spun toward the exit just as the heavy stone doors at the far end began to grind open. Through the widening gap, the unmistakable red glow of the CABAL's energy pulsed. They were forcing their way in. In her mind, Oriana could hear the discordant shriek of tearing metal, and it felt like the normal energy of the Flow was leeching slowly away—from the area, at least.

Baric swore under his breath. "We'll never outrun them in this corridor."

Oriana's mind raced. The artifact. The gauntlet she had bonded with pulsed with latent power. Its energy was now part of her, coursing through her veins. She flexed her fingers, feeling the newfound strength within her limbs.

"There's another way," she said. Without hesitation, she pressed her palm against one of the illuminated glyphs on the wall.

The Flow responded.

A hidden passage yawned open at the chamber's edge, revealing a descending tunnel lined with glowing runes. A secret escape route—a final safeguard left behind by those who had walked these halls before.

Oriana turned to Baric and Revik. "We take this path. Now."

Revik didn't hesitate, stepping through the opening first. Baric cast a final glance toward the advancing shadows beyond the temple doors before following. Oriana lingered a moment longer, her gaze lingering on the depths of the temple she was about to leave behind.

Then she stepped into the passage, and the entrance sealed shut behind them.

The tunnel was narrow, the air thick with dust and time. The glyphs lining the walls pulsed faintly, casting an eerie blue glow that illuminated their path. Oriana could feel the temple's lingering energy pressing around them—a mixture of protection and urgency, urging them forward.

"We're not out of danger yet," Baric muttered, his voice echoing in the confined space.

Oriana nodded. The CABAL wouldn't stop. They'd find another way in.

As they moved forward, the passage sloped downward, leading into what felt like the very bones of the temple. The air grew cooler, charged with a strange, electric hum.

Then, abruptly, the path ended.

Before them lay an enormous chasm, its depth swallowed by darkness. A single narrow bridge of stone stretched across it, barely wide enough for one person at a time. Below, tendrils of blue energy swirled like a living current—a raw manifestation of the Flow's power.

Revik stepped forward, testing the bridge. It held, but only just. "This isn't going to be easy."

Oriana felt the Flow vibrating through the stone beneath her feet. This was no ordinary bridge. It was a test, one final trial before freedom.

"We have no choice," she said, her voice steady. "I'll go first."

She stepped onto the bridge, her feet connecting with the stone. With every step, the Flow reacted, pulling at her, testing her balance. She adjusted instinctively, her body moving in sync with the energy beneath her.

Halfway across, a deep roar echoed behind them.

The CABAL had breached the temple's defenses.

Oriana ran.

The bridge trembled beneath her as something unseen surged through the Flow below, responding to the intrusion. The temple was collapsing.

She reached the other side just as Baric and Revik began their crossing. A pulse of red light flared behind them—the CABAL was already descending into the tunnel.

"Move!" she shouted.

Revik reached her first, but as Baric neared the end of the bridge, a sudden crack split the air. The bridge buckled, stone fragments crumbling into the abyss below.

Oriana lunged. Her enhanced reflexes kicked in, and she caught Baric's arm just as he lost his footing. The gauntlet surged with power, her grip stronger than she'd ever known.

With a final pull, she hauled Baric onto solid ground just as the last remnants of the bridge crumbled into the void.

The tunnel behind them was gone. There was no turning back.

Panting, Baric looked up at her, wide-eyed. "What the hell was that?"

Oriana flexed her fingers, feeling the residual energy still coursing through her. "I told you," she said, her voice steady. "I've accepted my legacy."

Revik exhaled sharply. "No time to celebrate. We need to keep moving."

A final passage lay ahead, its exit illuminated by the first traces of daylight.

They had made it out of the temple.

But the CABAL would not be far behind.

Chapter 18:

The Gathering Storm

The desert stretched endlessly before them, a vast expanse of shifting dunes and jagged rock formations bathed in the dim glow of the rising sun. The moment Oriana and her allies emerged from the hidden passage, they knew their respite would be brief. The temple, though sealed behind them, had not deterred the CABAL for long.

Baric scanned the horizon, his breath still ragged from their escape. "They'll track us."

Oriana wiped the sweat from her brow, steadying herself. The gauntlet pulsed against her skin, its power still foreign to her, demanding more than she was ready to give. She clenched her fist. "Then we keep moving."

Revik adjusted his pack, his eyes wary. "We need shelter before nightfall. The desert isn't just cruel—it's lethal."

Oriana nodded, the urgency in her chest growing. They had no time for debate. Every instinct screamed that the CABAL were closing in.

They moved swiftly, keeping close to the natural ridges that offered some cover. The sands beneath their boots shifted unpredictably, the wind whispering secrets of things long buried. The Flow here was wild, unrestrained—an untamed force that had not been controlled by those who once wielded it.

Oriana could feel it in her bones. The desert held power, and perhaps, it would choose a side.

By midday, the sun bore down with ruthless intensity. Every step drained their energy, the heat wrapping around them like a vice. They rationed their water carefully, speaking only when necessary.

Then, Oriana felt it.

A shift in the air. A disturbance in the Flow.

She stopped suddenly, causing Baric and Revik to pause beside her.

"What is it?" Baric asked, his hand instinctively moving to his blade.

Oriana turned her gaze westward, her senses reaching beyond the physical. A presence. Red, pungent, sandpaper-rough. Not one presence—but many. Moving fast.

"They found us," she murmured.

Revik swore under his breath. "How many?"

Oriana closed her eyes, reaching into the unseen currents of the Flow. Shapes flickered in her mind—riders, no more than a dozen, their auras seething with the red-tinted energy of the CABAL.

"Enough to be a problem," she said, opening her eyes. "We have maybe an hour before they're on us."

Baric's jaw tightened. "Then we don't run—we make our stand."

Oriana shook her head. "Not here. We need ground that favors us."

Revik exhaled sharply. "There's an old canyon pass a few miles ahead. If we reach it first, we control the battlefield."

Oriana nodded. "Then we move. Fast."

As they pushed toward the canyon, the landscape grew harsher. Jagged rock formations rose from the sand like the remains of a long-dead giant. Oriana's body ached, the power inside her pulsing with restless urgency. She fought against it, knowing there would be a cost for unleashing it fully.

The CABAL's presence loomed closer.

She could hear them now—the distant thrum of approaching riders, the hiss of energy weapons being primed.

They reached the canyon just in time.

Baric took his position behind a crumbling stone outcrop, his blade unsheathed. Revik knelt nearby, lining up a rifle they'd taken from their last skirmish. Oriana stood at the canyon's entrance, her senses alive with the pulse of the land beneath her feet.

She exhaled slowly. This place is old. It remembers.

The CABAL riders came into view, their dark figures cresting the dunes. Their leader, clad in black armor streaked with crimson energy, raised a hand to signal their advance.

Oriana lifted her own hand. The gauntlet responded.

The Flux and the Flow stirred.

The desert was awake.

This would be their last stand.

The first bolt of red energy cracked through the air, striking the canyon wall with a violent hiss. The rock sizzled, glowing molten for an instant before crumbling away. The CABAL had fired the opening shot.

Oriana barely had time to react before Baric lunged forward, his sword flashing as he deflected an incoming projectile. "They're not waiting for us to surrender."

Revik steadied his breath and fired his rifle, the shot piercing through the haze of dust and energy. One of the CABAL riders tumbled from his mount, his body vanishing in a ripple of red mist. One down. More to go.

The CABAL advanced swiftly, their crimson eyes glowing beneath their helmets. The ground trembled beneath their charge, and the Flow whispered its warnings to Oriana.

She stepped forward.

The moment her foot touched the canyon floor, the gauntlet surged to life. A wave of pure, radiant blue energy erupted around her, forming a shockwave that sent sand spiraling into the air. The closest CABAL warriors faltered, their charge breaking apart as the force repelled them.

Oriana exhaled, feeling the power humming beneath her skin. This was what the artifact had been preparing her for.

Baric seized the moment, lunging into the fray. His sword met the first CABAL soldier's weapon, their blades colliding in a shower of sparks. The clash was brutal, fast. Baric moved with the precision of a seasoned warrior, but the CABAL fought without mercy.

Oriana turned to face the next wave of attackers. This battle would not be won by sheer force alone.

She let go.

The Flow wrapped around her, guiding her movements. She ducked beneath an incoming strike, her body moving with inhuman speed as Flux boosted her reflexes. The gauntlet flared once more. Her fist struck the nearest CABAL warrior in the chest, sending him flying backward with an unnatural force. He crumpled to the ground, not getting up.

She was faster. Stronger.

But it was costing her.

Each time she called upon the gauntlet's power, she could feel something pulling at her life force. The artifact, it seemed, came with a price.

She ignored the warning, leaping forward to aid Baric. The canyon walls reverberated with the clash of weapons, the hiss of energy discharges, and the unrelenting cries of the battle.

Then, the second wave arrived.

From the canyon ridge above, more CABAL forces appeared, descending like shadows into the fray.

Revik cursed. "They brought reinforcements."

Oriana wiped the sweat from her brow, her breath ragged. The Flux and Flow flickered around her, urging her toward her next move.

She knew what had to be done.

They would not leave this place alive unless she unleashed everything.

With a steadying breath, she raised her hand. The Flux and Flow surged through her one final time.

The desert rumbled in response.

The air thickened with an unnatural stillness as Oriana reached deep into the Flow. The desert itself seemed to stir, the sands trembling beneath her feet, as though the land recognized her intent. The gauntlet burned hot against her skin, pulsing with an intensity she had never felt before.

The CABAL warriors hesitated, sensing the shift in the air. The red glow of their energy flickered, uncertainty creeping behind their masked visors.

Then, the storm came.

A wall of sand erupted from the ground, swirling with impossible speed. The wind howled, drowning out the battle cries of the CABAL as the desert itself answered Oriana's call

The first wave of warriors vanished instantly, their bodies swallowed by the raging vortex of sand and energy. Their cries were brief, cut off as the desert consumed them. The storm was not merely wind—it was something more, an ancient force awakened by the Gauntlet's union of Flux and Flow. It was a force of Chaos, and it had been unleashed on the CABAL's forces.

The ground trembled as jagged rocks burst from beneath the surface, impaling some of the CABAL riders where they stood. Horses and men alike were cast into the churning storm, their forms barely visible before the swirling sands erased them entirely. The air grew thick with the scent of ozone and scorched metal as the storm tore apart the CABAL's energy weapons, the unstable technology detonating in violent flashes of crimson light.

Baric and Revik stood at the canyon's edge, shielding their faces from the raging wind. Revik barely managed to shout over the deafening roar. "What in the name of the One is she doing?!"

Baric didn't answer. He could only watch in awe as Oriana stood at the storm's heart, her hair and cloak whipping wildly around her, eyes glowing with the same blue fire that now fueled the desert's wrath. She was no longer merely wielding the Flux and Flow—she was a conduit for it, something beyond human in that moment.

The last remaining CABAL warriors attempted to flee, their confidence shattered. But the storm would not allow escape. It surged forward, devouring them like a predator hunting its prey. Their screams were lost in the deafening cacophony of wind and raw power.

The storm raged for what felt like an eternity, but in reality, it lasted mere moments.

Then, just as suddenly as it had begun, it ended.

The sand fell still. The winds faded into silence. The canyon, once a battlefield, was now a grave. No sign of the CABAL remained. The desert had erased them completely.

Oriana collapsed to her knees, gasping for breath. The gauntlet, once burning with intensity, now felt cold and lifeless against her skin. The price for such power had been exacted, and she felt it deep in her bones, a hollow ache that spread through her limbs. Something inside her had been permanently drained. She could only hope it hadn't claimed Brand's future as its price.

As she looked at the gauntlet once more – it crumbled to dust. When it was gone – she saw that it had left strange symbols etched into her skin that would remain. She knew that the artifact – or at least some of its essence – was now bound to her. It seemed dormant but only time would tell.

She realized, with a sinking feeling, that this was not how the Digital Monks wielded the Flow. This combination—this reckless union of Flux and Flow—was dangerous, unstable. But it had been necessary.

Baric and Revik rushed to her side. Baric knelt, gripping her shoulders, his voice strained. "Oriana! Are you—"

She looked up at him, exhaustion carving deep lines into her face, her eyes hollow. Her voice barely broke through a whisper. "It's done."

Revik scanned the battlefield, his expression unreadable. "There's... nothing left."

Oriana nodded weakly, her gaze distant. "Yes. The desert took them."

Baric helped her to her feet, steadying her as her weight sagged against him. "We need to move. Before something else comes looking."

Oriana didn't argue. The power that had once surged within her now felt distant—faint, like a memory of something she could never call upon again in the same way. She had won—but at a devastating cost. She could already feel the gnawing emptiness inside her, a void that nothing would fill. Still, she knew she would sacrifice whatever was needed for Brand's future, and this would not be the last time.

The CABAL would not pursue them further. They couldn't.

But Oriana knew this victory had shortened her time. And whatever time she had left, she had to make it count. Brand's future depended on it.

The silence in the canyon was unsettling. Where moments ago the air had been filled with the fury of the storm, the screams of battle, now there was only the whisper of settling sand and the distant moan of the wind as it swept across the dunes. The battle was over. The CABAL had been erased from existence, their pursuit ending in a way no one could have predicted.

Oriana leaned heavily on Baric, her strength all but gone. Each breath felt like a struggle, as though her body was resisting every movement. She had never felt this drained before. The power she had unleashed—the storm she had commanded—had exacted a toll, one she was only beginning to comprehend.

Revik scanned the horizon, his rifle still in hand, though there was no longer an enemy to face. He shook his head in disbelief. "No bodies, no weapons, no wreckage—nothing. It's as if they were never here."

"The desert took them," Oriana repeated, her voice softer now, almost reverent. "And it won't give them back."

Baric shifted his grip on her, concern flickering in his eyes. "You're not alright, are you?"

She forced a tired smile. There was no point in worrying them. "I'll live."

For now.

He didn't seem convinced, but he said nothing further. Instead, he turned his attention to the landscape ahead. The canyon walls loomed high on either side, casting long shadows over the sand. The path forward was clear, but their journey was far from over.

"We need to move," he said, his tone firm. "There's no telling who else might have been watching."

Revik nodded, already adjusting the straps of his pack. "We head south, toward the valley. If we push through the night, we can reach the village by dawn."

Oriana felt a pang of relief at the thought of home, though she knew rest would be fleeting. She had won today, but the war was far from over.

She took one last glance at the battlefield—at the empty space where the CABAL had stood, now nothing more than shifting dunes and forgotten echoes. The desert had answered her call, but the cost had settled deep in her bones.

Whatever time she had left, she would use it wisely. For Brand.

With one final breath, she turned and followed her allies into the night.

Chapter 19:

The Central Cluster

The first hints of dawn painted the horizon in muted shades of violet and gold as Oriana and her companions trudged across the final stretch of desert. The distant silhouette of the village rose from the sands like a mirage, its earthen structures blending seamlessly into the terrain.

Every step was a test of endurance. The storm had taken its toll, and though Oriana pressed on through sheer will, she felt the strain deep in her bones. Each breath carried the weight of exhaustion, each movement slower than it should have been.

Baric stayed close at her side, his eyes flicking between her and the horizon. "Not much farther."

She managed a nod. The village—her childhood home—loomed closer, but she was no longer the woman who had left it. She carried more now. More knowledge. More burdens. And deep inside her, the fragile spark of something greater than herself.

Revik exhaled slowly as he scanned their surroundings. "I don't see any signs of trouble. Looks like we're clear."

Oriana wanted to believe him. She wanted to trust that the CABAL had truly been erased, that their reach would never touch this place. But instinct whispered otherwise. Nothing stayed buried forever.

As they reached the village's outskirts, the scent of cooking fires drifted on the morning breeze. The soft murmur of waking voices carried through the still air—a stark contrast to the chaos they had left behind.

An elderly figure stepped forward from the shadows of a nearby dwelling. His weathered face, etched with years of wisdom and hardship, was familiar.

Elder Jekar.

He studied them in silence, his sharp gaze settling on Oriana. Then, without a word, he stepped aside and gestured toward the heart of the village.

"You are home," he said simply.

Oriana released a breath she hadn't realized she was holding.

The village had accepted her return.

The home she had left behind remained unchanged—though dust had crept into its corners, and time had worn at its edges. She moved through it slowly, memories stirring with every familiar scent, every soft creak beneath her feet.

Baric and Revik settled into the common area, though both remained alert, their hands never far from their weapons. They were safe for now, but none of them believed the battle was truly over.

Elder Jekar arrived as the sun climbed higher in the sky. He carried a bowl of herbal tonic, its scent sharp with desert roots and healing leaves. He set it before Oriana and studied her in silence.

"You have changed," he said at last.

Oriana met his gaze without flinching. "I've seen things I can't forget. And I've done things I can't undo."

Jekar nodded, his fingers tracing the rim of the bowl. "We heard whispers over the years. Now I see—you've accepted your gifts. Finally."

Oriana started at his words, then caught herself. Of course he'd known. How naïve she had been to think otherwise when she first left.

Jekar continued, "The use of great power—especially without the training of the Digital Monks—never comes freely. It always takes something in return."

She exhaled, the ache of exhaustion settling deeper into her bones. "I know."

His gaze dropped to the faint, pulsing glow beneath her skin where the gauntlet had fused with her. "And yet, it gave you something meant to last beyond your own time."

Her hand drifted instinctively to her abdomen. Brand.

She swallowed. "Yes."

Jekar studied her for a long moment before rising. "Then rest. And prepare. The past doesn't release its hold so easily."

Oriana knew he was right.

But for now, she would allow herself a moment of peace.

The days that followed were quiet, filled with purposeful work. Oriana remained within the village, walking the familiar paths of her childhood, the weight of time pressing gently against her. With every step, she was reminded: this would be Brand's home. His first world.

She spent her mornings gathering supplies, preparing the home for what was to come. Her afternoons were devoted to meditation, learning to balance the power within her and the toll it had taken on her body. The nights were restless—her mind haunted by the visions she had seen in the temple: glimpses of her son's future, and a battle looming just beyond the horizon of time.

Elder Jekar remained close, a quiet sentinel with the wisdom of a man who had seen much and understood more than he would ever say. One evening, as the desert winds cooled the air, he sat beside her outside her small dwelling, his eyes fixed on the stars above.

"You are afraid," he said after a long silence.

Oriana didn't deny it. "Not for myself. For him."

Jekar nodded. "Then you must teach him."

She turned to him, brow furrowing. "Teach him what?"

"The ways of the Flow. The ways of survival." His gaze shifted to the sands beyond the village. "The desert will teach him hardship. You must teach him strength."

She inhaled deeply, turning his words over in her mind. She had spent so long ensuring Brand's survival—but survival alone would never be enough. He would need more than safety. He would need purpose.

A flicker of movement caught her eye—a fox darting between the houses, its sleek form melting into the twilight. A spirit guide. She had seen such creatures before, moving alongside those touched by the Flow.

A sign.

She turned back to Jekar. "Then I will teach him. But I'll need time."

Jekar met her gaze, his expression unreadable. "Time is a gift few can command."

Oriana knew that better than anyone. Her time was shorter than it had been—but she would make it count.

As the days passed, her strength slowly returned, though the scars of her battle never truly faded. The village welcomed her, but she remained apart—always watching, always planning. She was no longer just a mother preparing for her child. She was a warrior forging a future.

She sought out the village's strongest hunters, learning their techniques and refining her knowledge of survival. She gathered herbs, mixing tinctures that might one day mend the wounds her son would suffer. And at night, she whispered to the Flow, seeking guidance.

Seeking clarity.

One morning, Jekar found her at the village training ground, watching the young warriors spar with wooden staffs.

"You cannot fight his battles for him," he said, stepping beside her.

Oriana didn't look away from the match unfolding before her. "No. But I can make sure he's ready."

Jekar gave a slow nod. "Then teach him as a warrior would. Teach him as the Flow would—through strength and will. Through flux and wisdom."

She turned to him, the fire of resolve in her eyes. "I will."

For Brand's sake, she would ensure he was ready for the life that waited beyond the horizon.

The days stretched into weeks, and Oriana's focus never wavered. She had survived the desert, defeated the CABAL's pursuit, and carved out a sanctuary for her unborn son. But safety was never permanent. And she would not let Brand grow up unprepared for the world that would one day test him.

Her mornings were spent with the elders, absorbing the wisdom of those who had walked the sands before her. She learned not just survival, but tradition—how the Flow moved through the land, how ancient warriors had shaped its rhythm long before her time.

She began crafting lessons of her own, building them into a legacy Brand could one day follow. Her hands worked tirelessly—inscribing glyphs onto parchment, mapping constellations in careful ink, sketching the sigils of the Flow—so he might one day understand what lived inside him.

One evening, as the fire crackled low between them, Jekar watched her carve a series of small wooden tokens.

"You prepare for a time you will not see," he said quietly.

Oriana didn't look up. "I prepare because I must."

He studied her, brow furrowed with the weight of things left unsaid. "He will be strong."

She set down the carving knife, exhaling. "He will have no choice."

Jekar nodded slowly, unsurprised. "Then teach him more than how to fight. Teach him to think. To listen. To feel the Flow in all things. Strength alone is never enough."

Oriana met his gaze, her voice calm and certain. "I will."

As the time for Brand's arrival drew near, Oriana spent more hours in solitude, reaching into the Flow—listening.

It had guided her through storm and fire, through the trials of the temple and the silence that followed. But now, she sought something deeper.

She sat atop the tallest dune beyond the village, the wind cool against her skin as the night stretched wide and endless above. Her fingers pressed into the sand, seeking the pulse of the world beneath her. The Flow stirred. It whispered.

He will be different. He will be watched. And one day, he will stand at the center of all things.

She closed her eyes, letting the knowledge settle—not as fear, but as truth.

Oriana rose and turned toward the village lights in the distance. There was still work to be done.

Chapter 20:

Exile from the Sands

The night was thick with silence—the kind that stretched beyond the physical realm and into something deeper, unseen. The village slumbered under the watchful gaze of the stars, the air cool and heavy with expectation.

Inside her modest dwelling, Oriana sat cross-legged, her breath slow, her mind drifting through the currents of the Flow.

She had felt the shift coming for days—the stirring beneath her ribs, the hush in the wind. Now, the moment was here.

It had begun as any birth would. She, a seasoned healer, knew the rhythms well. She walked the small space for hours, coaxing her body forward as it prepared, each step drawing Brand closer to the world.

Then came the pain—sharp, sudden, undeniable.

She clenched her jaw, steadying herself as pressure gripped her from within. She had once given life to storms, commanded sand and sky, but nothing had prepared her for this.

This was a different kind of battle—one of surrender, not control. One that demanded a strength beyond steel and will.

Jekar appeared at her side, his presence like stone—unshaken, grounding. He pressed a cool cloth to her brow, his weathered face calm beneath the flickering oil light.

"It is time," he said.

Oriana nodded, breath ragged. "Yes."

Outside, the village stirred. Women gathered near her door, their murmurs rising in soft waves—blessings offered to the stars, to the Flow, to the life being brought forth.

They knew what this child meant. The whispers reached them too, curling like smoke into their dreams, shaping awe from possibility.

Another wave of pain tore through her, dragging her inward—away from thought, into instinct. She gripped the woven mat beneath her, the fibers rough beneath her fingertips. Every nerve ignited, her body thrumming like a struck chord.

The Flow thickened, responding to her labor. It bent around her like wind in a storm, pressing into the space, vibrating through the air. Even the walls seemed to tremble, as if the universe itself bore witness to the moment within.

She cried out, voice raw, caught between agony and power.

Jekar's voice cut through, calm and steady as bedrock.

"Breathe," he said. "Let the Flow carry you."

Oriana did not reply, but she obeyed.

She surrendered—not to the pain, but to the energy swirling around her, ancient and alive. As she yielded to it, something shifted. The pressure rose to its peak, then, in one final, shuddering moment, the silence broke.

A cry—small, yet strong—filled the room.

Jekar moved with careful precision, lifting the newborn and wrapping him in soft linen. He placed the child gently against Oriana's chest.

She stared down at the tiny face, her breath catching in her throat. His skin radiated warmth, his hands curling instinctively against her.

And his presence—his very being—was like nothing she had ever felt.

A pulse of ancient energy seemed to hum within him, faint but undeniable. On his chest, a mark—faintly luminous, as if responding to her gaze. Not constant, not bright, but there. Almost.

Brand had arrived.

At dawn, the village gathered.

Golden light spilled across the sands as Oriana stepped into the open, Brand cradled in her arms. A hush fell over the crowd. Eyes turned to them, wide with reverence and curiosity, as if sensing the ripples this child had already sent through the Flow.

The elders stood in a semicircle, their robes whispering in the breeze. It was rare for the entire council to gather for any birth. The weight of this moment was evident.

Jekar stepped forward, his voice steady and clear.

"A child is born beneath the watch of the Flow," he said. "A child whose name will carry the weight of the past—and the promise of the future."

A soft murmur passed through the gathered villagers.

They had felt it too.

The presence.

The shift.

Brand was more than a child.

He was the beginning of something vast.

Oriana lifted her gaze, her voice steady despite the fatigue that clung to her bones.

"His name is Brand."

Silence stretched, long and weighty, as if the name itself rippled through the air—etched into the very fabric of history. Then, slowly, the elders nodded.

"A name of fire and renewal," murmured one.

"A name that will be remembered," said another.

Jekar inclined his head. "Then let the desert bear witness."

One by one, the villagers stepped forward, pressing their palms to the earth in an ancient gesture of acknowledgment. The desert wind stirred, carrying a whisper through the Flow. The moment felt sacred, as though the sands themselves had accepted the child into their endless embrace.

An elder woman, her face mapped with the lines of many seasons, approached. She traced a symbol in the air above Brand's forehead—a blessing once reserved for warriors and seekers alike.

"May the Flow guide you, and may your path be your own."

A shiver passed through Oriana as the words settled over them. She held Brand tighter, his heartbeat small but strong against her chest.

The Flow coiled gently around them, and in its hush, it spoke what she already knew—this was only the beginning.

And she believed it.

When the celebration faded and the villagers drifted back to their homes, Oriana returned to the solitude of her dwelling. The warmth of the gathering still clung to the walls, but so did something else—a heavy, consuming fatigue, like invisible chains around her limbs. Her vitality, once fierce and unrelenting, had been siphoned by the desert, by the temple, by the escape from the CABAL.

How long before they come again?

She sat beside the small woven basket where Brand now slept, his breath slow and even. The sight of him filled her with something vast—love, fierce and unyielding.

But also fear.

Not fear of what he might become.

Fear that she would not live long enough to see it.

Jekar entered the room without a sound, his presence as steady as ever. He studied her for a long moment before settling into the chair across from her. "You can feel it now, can't you?"

Oriana didn't bother pretending to misunderstand. She exhaled slowly, pressing a hand to her chest, where a dull ache had settled, deeper than flesh or bone. "Yes."

"The Flow does not give without taking." Jekar's voice was gentle but unyielding. "There must be balance. You may act according to its will, but to ask it to bend to yours—there must be balance. You have wielded power beyond mortal limits. The desert granted you strength, but it does not relinquish its gift without cost."

She glanced at her hands. They still trembled at times, not from fear, but from something far worse—weakness. The strength that had once surged through her veins, the energy that had allowed her to command the sands, was now fleeting.

Jekar reached forward, placing a weathered hand over hers. "Your time is not yet finished, but it is no longer what it once might have been."

She swallowed hard, her throat tight. "I thought I had more."

He nodded. "We all do."

Oriana's gaze drifted to Brand, his small form rising and falling in perfect rhythm. "He will need me."

Jekar followed her gaze, his expression unreadable. "Then make use of the time you have. Teach him, prepare him. Do not let regret weigh heavier than purpose."

She nodded, forcing past the lump in her throat. The Flow had already chosen its path, and no amount of defiance would alter it. But she still had time—not for herself, but for Brand.

And she would not waste a single moment.

In a town not far off, agents of the group known as the CABAL gathered for a progress report to the local leader.

The inn was silent, save for the low murmur of voices from the farthest table. Hooded figures sat in shadow, their words meant for no ears but their own.

"The search for the Artifact and Nodes continues." Then, after the briefest pause, "The child survived."

A longer pause followed. Then another voice, colder. "For now."

"He is still unformed. He does not know what he is."

"Then we will ensure he never learns."

A rustle of parchment. A symbol marked in ink. A name written in the margins.

Brand.

"Make preparations. Ashara is peaceful, but peace breeds weakness. If he remains here, he is nothing. But if he is shaped—"

A long silence. Then a final whisper.

"Then he must become ours."

A third voice, precise and calculated, interjected. "The objective remains unchanged. His potential must be either controlled or erased.

If we cannot mold him into an instrument of the CABAL, then he must be removed before he can be used against us."

Another pause, then the rustle of fabric as one figure stood. "We will not fail again."

The conversation ended, but in the shadows of Ashara, a future had already begun to take shape.

The days passed with an unrelenting certainty, each sunrise reminding Oriana of the urgency pressing against her soul. She had fought wars, tamed the desert's wrath, and wielded power that few could comprehend. But nothing had prepared her for the task before her now—passing on what she knew before time stole the chance away.

Brand was still an infant, his world no bigger than the warmth of her arms and the gentle rhythm of her heartbeat. But Oriana knew that the Flow did not wait for age—it moved through all things, whispering to those who could hear it. And Brand would hear it, of that she was certain.

One evening, as the desert sky bled orange and violet, she sat beneath the open sky with Brand nestled against her chest. The wind carried the scent of sand and sage, wrapping around them like a silent guardian.

"This world will not be kind to you," she whispered softly, her fingers tracing gentle, soothing patterns along his back. "But I will give you the tools to shape your own path."

Jekar stood a short distance away, watching the exchange with the quiet patience of a man who had lived long enough to understand the weight of legacy. He stepped forward, lowering himself beside her.

"He is too young to understand words," he murmured, though his tone held no reproach.

Oriana smiled faintly. "The Flow understands long before we do. And so will he."

She closed her eyes, exhaling slowly. She reached out—not physically, but with the awareness that lay beyond flesh and thought. The Flow stirred in response, soft and steady, wrapping around her, around Brand, binding them in something more profound than blood.

Jekar felt it too, though he did not move. "You would begin his training now?"

Oriana nodded. "Not in the way of warriors, not yet. But he must know the Flow before the world teaches him to ignore it."

She took Brand's tiny hand in hers, pressing his palm gently against the dry earth beneath them. The moment was small, almost imperceptible, but she felt the subtle shift—the acknowledgment of energy, of life beneath his touch.

"This is your first lesson," she murmured softly to him. "The world is alive. It speaks. One day, you will answer."

The infant stirred but did not cry. His small fingers twitched against the ground, his breath deep and steady.

Jekar exhaled. "The path you lay for him is unlike any before it."

Oriana met his gaze. "That is the only way he will survive."

They sat in silence for a long time after that, as the stars began to unfurl across the sky, bearing witness to the first whisper of a future not yet written.

Chapter 21:

The Fox Returns

The desert was a vast and living entity, stretching beyond the horizon in waves of golden dunes and jagged cliffs carved by time. To those who understood, it was never silent. The wind carried whispers, the sand shifted with unseen intention, and the stars blinked like watchful sentinels overhead.

At four years old, Brand was too young to grasp the full depth of these truths, but he could feel them. The desert called to him in ways he could not explain. It hummed beneath his feet, pulsed in the wind that tousled his unruly hair, and spoke to him in dreams that lingered even after he awoke.

One morning, as the first light of dawn painted the sky in soft hues of violet and orange, Brand wandered beyond the outskirts of the village. He moved with quiet curiosity, his small hands trailing through the cool sand, his senses alight with wonder.

Then, he saw it.

A fox—sleek and silver—standing atop a nearby dune. Its fur

shimmered, rippling like heat waves in the early morning light, and its eyes—deep, endless pools of blue—watched him with a knowing gaze.

Brand froze, his heart hammering in his chest. The fox did not move. It did not run, nor did it show fear. Instead, it tilted its head, as though measuring him.

The wind stirred around them, carrying a whisper that was neither voice nor thought, yet Brand understood it all the same.

You see me.

He took a hesitant step forward, his small fingers reaching out. The fox did not retreat. Instead, it blinked slowly, an invitation.

Brand crouched in the sand, mirroring its stillness, his young mind struggling to grasp what he was experiencing. He had seen animals before—jackals in the night, great desert hawks circling high above— but none like this.

A presence.

A guide.

He did not yet know the word for what this was, but he would come to learn it in time.

The Flow.

The fox twitched its ears, then, in the blink of an eye, was gone— vanishing as though it had never been there at all. The wind stirred once more, carrying the scent of distant rain and something else... something ancient.

Brand remained still for a long moment before rising. He didn't rush back to the village. He simply turned and walked, his small footprints tracing his path in the sand.

He didn't fully understand what had happened—not yet.

But he would.

Brand returned to the village in thoughtful silence, his small hands dusted with sand, his mind still caught in the lingering presence of the fox. The morning bustle had begun, with villagers tending to market stalls and preparing for the midday heat. But Brand barely noticed the familiar sights and sounds—his thoughts were fixed on what he had witnessed.

He found Oriana in the courtyard of their home, kneeling beside a basin of water, washing the morning's dust from her hands. Her movements were slow and measured, as always, but today he saw something else in them—a quiet weariness.

She looked up before he spoke, her sharp gaze scanning his face. "You wandered far today."

Brand hesitated, then, as though the words might vanish if he didn't speak them quickly, he blurted, "I saw a fox."

Oriana stilled. "A fox?"

He nodded, stepping closer. "Not a normal one. It... it looked at me. It spoke, but not with words."

She studied him, searching his face for something. "And what did it say?"

Brand frowned, struggling to recall the exact feeling of the moment.

"It said... You see me."

For the first time, Oriana's face betrayed a flicker of something—concern, curiosity, perhaps even recognition. She dried her hands and motioned for him to sit beside her. "There are many creatures in the desert," she said carefully. "Some are made of flesh, others are born of the Flow itself."

Brand tilted his head. "So it was real?"

She sighed, brushing a stray lock of hair from his face. "Real is a word that doesn't always mean what you think it does."

Unsatisfied with the answer, he pressed, "Have you ever seen one?"

Oriana hesitated before shaking her head. "Yes, before you were born. When I was a child, the elders spoke of spirits that walk alongside those meant for something greater." She placed a gentle hand on his shoulder. "The question is not whether the fox was real. The question is why it showed itself to you."

Brand opened his mouth to answer but paused. He didn't know. He had no idea what had drawn the fox to him, nor what it meant. But deep inside, he felt something—an anticipation, as though a door had opened that could never be closed again.

That night, they attended a festival near the local temple. The lights flickered in the night breeze, casting golden reflections across Oriana's face. She stood at the temple steps, watching the crowd, but her mind was elsewhere—tuned to something deeper, something just out of reach.

She had always sensed certain things before they happened: a shift in the wind before a storm, a heaviness in the air before bad news. But tonight, the feeling was different. It wasn't a premonition. It was more like a presence.

She turned her gaze to Brand. He was laughing, carefree, the way only the young could afford to be. But beneath the surface of his mirth, something pulsed—an unspoken restlessness she couldn't name.

Then, for the briefest moment, the festival disappeared. The noise, the fire, the people—all flickered like candlelight before her vision shifted.

In its place, she saw ruins. Ancient stones, whispering with the weight of time, and a shadow standing where Brand had been. The air was charged, vast, and unseen. And then—

A voice. Not spoken, but felt. "He carries the thread of what was lost."

Oriana blinked, and the vision vanished as quickly as it had come. The laughter of the festival returned, but her breath was short, her fingers trembling.

She looked at Brand again, but he was oblivious, caught in the joy of the moment.

She thought of the visions she had seen of his future and whispered to herself, barely audible, "What are you becoming?" She was reminded, yet again, that he would walk the path of danger and destiny.

The next day, as the sun began its descent, Brand sought out Jekar. The old elder sat outside his small hut, carving intricate patterns into a piece of bone. He didn't look up when Brand approached, but his voice, warm and familiar, filled the air. "You have questions."

Brand sat cross-legged before him. "I saw something in the desert."

Jekar's knife paused, then resumed its steady motion with a practiced hand. "Tell me."

Brand recounted the encounter, his words tumbling out in a rush, excitement and uncertainty intertwined. When he finished, Jekar remained quiet, his gaze sharp as he set his carving aside.

"There are things in this world that exist beyond sight, beyond sound," Jekar said, tapping his chest. "But not beyond knowing." He leaned forward slightly, eyes studying Brand intently. "The Flow touches all living things, but only some hear it. Even fewer are seen by it."

Brand frowned. "The fox was... the Flow?"

Jekar chuckled, shaking his head. "Not exactly. It was part of the Flow. A guide, perhaps. Or a test."

Brand shifted restlessly. "So what do I do now?"

Jekar smiled, his eyes crinkling at the edges. "You wait. And you listen." He tapped his chest again, a gesture laden with meaning. "And when the fox speaks again, you'll understand."

Brand wasn't sure he liked that answer, but something about Jekar's calm certainty soothed him. He stood, brushing the dust from his knees. As he turned to leave, the wind stirred around him, warm and familiar.

You see me.

Brand paused, glancing over his shoulder toward the distant dunes, where the last rays of sunlight kissed the horizon. He didn't see the fox again that day.

But he knew it was watching.

The night was still, save for the occasional gust of wind that swept the sand into gentle waves outside the village. Brand lay awake in his small sleeping area, staring at the ceiling, his thoughts swirling—of the fox, of Jekar's words, and of the unseen forces that seemed to be watching him.

He closed his eyes, breathing deeply, trying to feel what the elders spoke of—the Flow. The unseen current that ran beneath the world, touching all things, whispering to those who could hear it.

Nothing.

Brand huffed in frustration, sitting up. Maybe Jekar had been wrong. Maybe the fox had just been a trick of the light. But deep inside, he knew that wasn't true.

A gust of wind rattled the wooden shutters. Brand glanced toward them, and for the briefest moment, he thought he saw something move beyond them—a shimmer, like heat rising from the sand, but colder. Purposeful.

He swallowed hard, then slid out of bed. If the fox had chosen him, if the Flow was truly reaching out to him, then he would answer.

Brand stepped into the night, the cool desert air wrapping around him like a cloak. The village was silent now, the fires in the central courtyard reduced to little more than glowing embers. He walked slowly, his bare feet sinking into the sand, ears straining for anything beyond the whisper of the wind.

Then, he felt it.

It wasn't sound, nor sight, nor touch. It was something deeper, something that resonated within him like an unspoken word. A pulse in the air, faint but steady, waiting for him to notice.

The Spirit Fox stood at the edge of the village, just beyond the last hut, its silver form shimmering under the moonlight.

Brand took a hesitant step forward, and the fox flicked its tail, watching him closely. The wind picked up, swirling around him, and for a moment, the world felt... different. Lighter. As if gravity had lessened its hold.

He took another step, then another. The fox turned and began to walk, its paws leaving no imprint in the sand. Brand followed.

They moved through the dunes, the village shrinking behind them. Brand's heart raced, but not from fear. Instead, he felt something stirring within him—an awareness, a pull, growing stronger with every step. The fox led him to a rocky outcrop, where the desert stretched out before them. It stopped and turned to face him.

The wind stilled.

Brand stared at the fox, waiting. But it didn't speak. It simply watched him, its gaze expectant.

He licked his lips, suddenly feeling exposed. "I don't know what I'm supposed to do."

The fox blinked slowly.

Brand frowned, his frustration bubbling. "Jekar said I have to listen. But I don't hear anything."

The fox tilted its head, and then, without warning, it leapt toward him.

Brand gasped, stumbling backward. But the fox did not collide with him. Instead, it passed through him, leaving a sensation like cool fire washing over his skin. His vision blurred, and in that instant, he saw.

The desert stretched endlessly, but it was no longer empty. Threads of light wove through the sand—faint, yet undeniable, shifting with the breath of the world. Above, the stars pulsed in unison, each one connected by unseen strands of energy. The wind was no longer just air; it carried intent, movement, emotion.

Brand staggered, his knees buckling. The vision faded as quickly as it had come, and he found himself gasping for breath on the ground.

The fox stood nearby, watching.

Brand looked up at it, his mind whirling. "What was that?"

The fox's tail flicked once, and the wind carried a whisper.

The beginning.

Brand's fingers clenched into the sand. He understood now. The Flow wasn't just something to see or touch—it was something to feel. Alive. It was alive, just as he was. And for the first time, it had allowed him to glimpse its depths.

He exhaled slowly, nodding to himself. "I'll learn."

The fox's ears flicked, then, as it had before, it vanished into the night, leaving Brand standing alone beneath the vast, unbroken sky.

But he wasn't afraid.

For the first time, he thought he understood—the Flow wasn't just something to find. It was waiting for him to listen.

The next morning, Brand woke with fire in his chest. The vision from the night before still clung to him—glowing threads weaving through the desert, the stars pulsing with unseen energy, the power moving through the world. He had seen the Flow. Truly seen it. And now he wanted more.

He needed more.

Brand spent the morning shadowing Oriana as she prepared herbs and medicines, her careful movements betraying no sign of the fatigue that often weighed on her. But his thoughts were elsewhere, racing with questions and possibilities. Finally, unable to hold them back, he blurted, "I saw it."

Oriana paused, her hands steady over a bowl of crushed desert root. She didn't look up. "What did you see?"

"The Flow. The way it moves through everything." His voice buzzed with excitement. "I felt it—like the wind, but deeper. It was real."

Oriana finally looked at him, her expression unreadable. "And what did you do?"

Brand hesitated, then admitted, "Nothing. But I want to. I want to use it."

A long silence stretched between them. Oriana exhaled slowly, wiping her hands on a cloth. "Brand, the Flow is not a tool to be used. It is not a blade to wield or a storm to summon. It is life itself. There is also energy around us called the Flux." Her voice grew quieter, more cautious. "It may be used, but you must be careful not to become dependent on it."

She thought about the cost of misuse—the price she herself had paid—and felt a chill at the look in Brand's eyes. She was afraid of what he might become if he didn't understand the danger he faced.

Brand frowned, frustration tightening his chest. "Then why show it to me if I can't use it?"

Oriana studied him with a calm intensity, knowing she couldn't hide the truth much longer. But for now, she refused to give him more. Finally, she nodded toward the door. "Go. Find Jekar. Tell him what you've told me."

Without a word, Brand rushed through the village, brushing past vendors and neighbors as their calls faded behind him. He reached Jekar's small hut near the edge of the settlement, finding the elder outside, carving symbols into the surface of a staff.

"You are restless," Jekar observed without lifting his gaze.

Brand dropped to his knees in the sand, desperation in his voice. "I want to use the Flow."

Jekar set his carving aside and sighed, his tone measured. "Then show me."

Brand blinked. "What?"

"Show me." Jekar gestured toward a stone half-buried in the sand. "Move it."

Brand hesitated, then turned to the stone. He glanced back at Jekar, whose face remained unreadable—no sign of mockery, only quiet expectation.

Brand took a steadying breath. He had seen the Flow. Felt it. The way it moved through the desert, the wind, the stars. He knew it was there.

He reached out his hand, focusing on the space between his fingers and the stone. He imagined the glowing strands from his vision, weaving through the sand and bending to his will, surging forward at his command.

Nothing.

His brow furrowed, frustration bubbling up. He clenched his teeth and dug deeper, demanding the Flow to respond. Move.

Still, nothing.

His hands balled into fists. He had felt it. He had seen it! Why wasn't it working? Growling low under his breath, he threw himself into the motion, pushing with all his force—

The sand exploded in a violent burst. The stone tumbled a few feet away, but there was no grace to it, no flow. It was a chaotic, unrefined outburst of energy.

Brand stood there, panting, exhilaration racing through him. "I did it!"

Jekar's face remained stoic. Slowly, he shook his head. "No. You forced it."

Brand's chest tightened, his excitement dimming. "But I moved it."

Jekar met his gaze, the weight of his words heavy. "You moved it the way a storm moves the dunes—without thought, without balance. That's not the Flow."

"That was the Flux—not the Flow." Jekar's voice was low, but his words carried weight. He leaned forward, his weathered finger tapping Brand's chest. "You're not the CABAL, and even they can't do what they think they can. I pray they can't, for all our sakes. The Flow doesn't bend to force. You move with it."

Brand's jaw clenched. "I don't understand. How do I move with it if it won't even move? The Flux, at least, does what I want."

Jekar sighed and reached for a small cup of water, setting it gently before him. "Watch."

He dipped his fingers into the water, stirring slowly. The ripples spread, expanding in a deliberate dance. "The Flow moves like this. You can't grasp it." Without warning, he clenched his fist, splashing droplets everywhere. "When you try to control it, you lose it."

Jekar then placed his palm flat against the surface, letting the water settle peacefully around it. "But when you move with it—when you allow it to carry you—it will respond."

Brand stared at the water, his chest tightening. He didn't want to move with the Flow. He wanted to command it. The tension in his jaw and the tightness in his fists spoke volumes of his frustration.

Jekar studied him quietly for a long moment before speaking again, his voice soft but firm. "You are angry."

Brand's eyes shot up, and he snapped, "I'm not."

Jekar tilted his head slightly. "Not at me. Not at the Flow. But at what the world has taken from you."

Brand's throat tightened, and the words caught in his chest. He didn't want to admit it, but the truth gnawed at him. The world had stolen from him— he KNEW it. His mother's strength – though she tried to hide it; his father – gone from their lives for some mysterious reason, and the answers he needed for what made him special! Now, this force, this powerful, vast Flow, was slipping through his grasp too? NO! He would not ALLOW it!

Jekar sighed, standing slowly. "You'll learn, in time. But not today."

Brand clenched his fists, his mind still buzzing with frustration. He watched Jekar walk away, then glanced down at the stone he had moved, the sand still disturbed around it. He had felt something—a spark of power, even if it wasn't what Jekar had hoped.

For now, that was enough.

Chapter 22:

Lessons from the Trickster

The desert held more than shifting sands. Beneath its surface, in the silent spaces between time and motion, ancient forces stirred unseen. Brand had glimpsed these currents, brushed their edges—but they always slipped from his grasp. So, he turned to an unlikely teacher.

Belizar.

Unlike any other creature in the village, Belizar was an enigma. Larger than a typical desert lizard, its scales shimmered with a metallic sheen, and its luminous eyes gleamed with an unsettling intelligence. Some believed Belizar was once the creation of the CABAL—meant to be controlled, but long since escaped their grasp.

Now, it watched Brand with a look that seemed equal parts amusement and expectation.

Brand sat cross-legged in the sand, his eyes locked onto the creature. "Jekar says I need to listen to the Flow."

Belizar flicked his forked tongue. Jekar is wise. But listening is only the beginning.

No one could say for sure whether Belizar's voice was magic or mechanical, but it was unmistakable. At times, the lizard's form shimmered, seemingly growing larger and more human-like than just a reptile before settling back into his normal appearance. Belizar was a mystery, wrapped in scales.

Brand frowned. "Then what comes next?"

The lizard circled him slowly, its movements languid. Understanding takes time.

Brand's impatience flared. "I don't have time. I want to learn now."

Belizar's tail flicked against the sand. Impatience makes fools of the strongest. The desert does not rush to shift its dunes. The wind does not beg to move.

Frustration rippled through Brand. "I don't understand. When do I learn something important?"

You wish to learn? Then we begin.

Brand's breath quickened; his eagerness evident. "What do I do?"

Without warning, the lizard darted forward—so fast that Brand barely had time to react before it landed on his shoulder, its claws digging in just enough to hold steady.

Close your eyes, Belizar whispered.

Brand hesitated, then obeyed. The world around him dissolved into darkness.

Feel the sand beneath you. Not just with your skin—listen to it. Let it speak to you.

Brand furrowed his brow, focusing intently. At first, all he felt was the dry heat, the roughness of the grains. But then, something deeper—a faint vibration beneath the surface, like a pulse buried in the earth.

He inhaled sharply. "I feel it."

Good. Now, do not seek to move it. Let it move you.

Brand gritted his teeth, frustration simmering beneath the surface. He wanted to force it—to pull, to bend the Flow to his will. But he made himself wait.

Then, for a fleeting moment, he felt it.

The air around him chilled, the faintest breeze stirring where none had been. The sand beneath him shifted, as if responding to his presence. It was subtle, almost imperceptible—but real.

His heart raced. He hadn't forced it.

Belizar's voice came again, softer this time. Now you begin to understand.

Brand opened his eyes, but the desert was unchanged.

Yet, he knew something had shifted.

The days that followed tested Brand's patience in ways he hadn't imagined. Each morning, before the sun reached its full heat, he trained with Belizar in the dunes. The lessons were simple in theory, maddening in practice.

One morning, Belizar led him to ancient ruins. The crumbling structures stretched before him like the bones of a long-forgotten god.

Brand stood at the edge, fists clenched. Others had dared him to enter, but that wasn't why he was here.

He came because something deep inside him urged him to.

The air in the ruins felt different—not thick with dust, but with something older, more alive. It pressed against his skin, stirring in the spaces between his thoughts. It was the same feeling he had when he fought—when his body moved before his mind had decided.

A rock shifted behind him. Instinct took over, and he spun, faster than he should have. Too fast.

Belizar's voice sliced through the silence. You feel it, don't you?

Brand turned, breathing hard. The lizard stood perched on a broken pillar, its eyes gleaming with knowing.

"I don't feel anything," Brand said, his jaw tight.

Belizar clicked his tongue. Lies don't suit you. You move like someone listening to a song no one else can hear.

Brand frowned, unsure of how to respond. He didn't want an answer.

Belizar tilted his head. The ruins are not silent. They remember. But they won't wait forever.

Brand swallowed hard, his throat tight, and turned away from the ruins, stepping deeper into the shadows of the crumbling stones. Whatever this was—this gnawing itch beneath his skin, this quiet whisper of something far greater than he could understand—he wasn't ready to confront it.

Not yet.

The next morning, the ruins called to him again.

Standing before the stone walls, his fingers brushed the surface, tracing the intricate carvings. These weren't just ancient symbols; they were older than the village itself, older than any history he had been taught. They should have meant nothing to him.

But the moment his skin made contact, a surge of energy coursed through him. It wasn't warmth—it was raw, primal, untamed.

He jerked his hand back, but the sensation lingered, still vibrating in his fingertips.

The ruins are active, Belizar's voice, low and almost conspiratorial, broke the silence.

Brand's eyes snapped to him. "What does that mean?"

Belizar leapt gracefully onto a broken pillar, his tail flicking lazily. It means there's power here, but not one kind of power. There are two forces in this world, Brand—Flow and Flux.

Brand raised an eyebrow, crossing his arms. "Magic?"

Belizar's lips twitched in something between a sigh and a chuckle. Magic is a story, a fable told by those who don't understand. Flow and Flux are the truths behind all things. You've heard of them before— you know them. I'll remind you. Flow is purpose. It guides what is meant to be. Flux is potential—unbound, neither good nor evil. Just pure energy.

Brand frowned, a wave of confusion settling over him. "So what happens when you touch both?"

Belizar's expression grew sharp, his gaze fixed. Then you must be very careful which one you choose to listen to.

The following morning, they returned to the dunes for training.

Again, Belizar ordered, perched on a rock, watching Brand intently. Brand sat in the sand before him, muscles tight with the effort of concentration.

Feel the earth. Let it guide you.

Brand closed his eyes, exhaling deeply. He stretched his senses outward, trying to reach beyond the surface of things. He felt the warmth of the sun on his skin, the grains of sand shifting in the wind, the almost imperceptible hum of something deeper beneath it all. The Flow. It was there—but always just out of reach.

With all his focus, he tried to stop forcing, tried to let the Flow move through him, not command it. His fingers trembled, and the sand beneath him shifted, barely noticeable, like a breath of wind passing through.

Frustration mounted. It wasn't enough. It wasn't working.

Brand clenched his fists, feeling the weight of the desert air pressing down on him. "It's not working."

The words felt hollow in the vastness of the dunes.

Belizar flicked his tail, the movement sharp and dismissive. It does not bend to frustration. You continue trying to command what does not belong to you.

Brand's frustration flared, and he shot to his feet, brushing the sand from his clothes. "Then how do I make it mine?"

The lizard's golden eyes gleamed, narrowing. *It is never yours to claim. It is never anyone's. It simply is.*

Brand opened his mouth to argue, but before the words could form, the earth beneath them shuddered. A low, guttural growl echoed across the dunes, sending a chill down Brand's spine. Belizar stiffened, his scales raising in alarm. *Something comes.*

Brand spun, scanning the horizon. At first, the sand seemed endless—smooth, undisturbed. But then, shapes began to materialize from beyond the dunes, dark and unnerving. Jackals. But not the kind of creatures the desert had known. These were twisted, mechanical, their red-glowing eyes betraying their CABAL origins. Their lean bodies were enhanced with cybernetic modifications, and energy pulsed from them like a living storm.

Brand's pulse quickened. He had seen them before—always from a distance, always lurking, waiting. But never this close. Not to the village.

Belizar's tail flicked again, sharp. *Now, boy. You learn—or you die.*

Before Brand could respond, the first jackal lunged.

His body moved faster than his mind. He darted to the side, rolling to his feet, his hands scraping against the sand. The jackal's claws raked through empty air where he had been just moments before. Another beast followed, circling, seeking an opening.

Brand's instincts screamed at him—fight, run, survive. But then, something deeper tugged at him. The Flow. It throbbed beneath his feet, pulsing in rhythm with his heartbeat.

He had seconds to decide. He could force it, like he always had—command, control—or he could do what Belizar had taught him: yield, listen, move with it.

Taking a breath, Brand grounded himself, releasing the tension in his clenched fists. This time, instead of pushing forward, he leaned into the moment. He listened.

The wind shifted. The sand beneath him stirred, alive, responsive. His senses stretched, and his awareness expanded. When the next jackal leaped, he didn't dodge with conscious thought. He moved with the flow, with the rhythm of the earth beneath him.

The jackal missed him by inches, its movements thrown off, its balance disrupted by an unseen force. It crashed into the sand, skidding with a mechanical howl.

Brand froze, staring in disbelief. I did that.

But Belizar's voice rang clear in his mind: You did nothing. The Flow did.

Brand turned to face the remaining jackals, his heart pounding in his chest, his mind racing. He was far from mastering this power, far from understanding it fully, but something crucial had shifted.

He wasn't alone in the fight. The desert, the wind, the world itself—it was with him, and if he moved with it, it would move with him.

For the first time, Brand felt something that resembled control.

And the jackals sensed it, too.

The battle had been short, but its effects lingered in his muscles, the ache of exertion pulling at him. His mind was alive with the realization of what he had done—and what he had failed to do. He had moved with the Flow, felt its guidance, but it had been fleeting, instinctive. The power had slipped through his fingers before he could grasp it fully. He still didn't understand it.

Belizar watched from a distance, perched on a nearby rock as Brand knelt in the sand, trying to catch his breath. You're overthinking it.

Brand wiped the sweat from his forehead and looked up. "I almost died."

The lizard's golden eyes narrowed, unwavering. And yet, here you are. What does that tell you?

Brand clenched his jaw, his gaze drifting to the sand where the jackals had fallen. Their bodies were already dissolving, crumbling into the earth as the unnatural energy that kept them alive faded away. The village needed to know what had happened.

He rose slowly, brushing the sand from his clothes, and turned toward the distant glow of the village fires. "I have to go back."

Belizar didn't move. They will see you differently now.

Brand stopped, hesitation pulling at him. "What do you mean?"

The lizard's voice grew sharper. You fought something meant to kill you. And you won. He paused, his eyes gleaming with knowing. Not everyone will see that as a victory.

Brand's frown deepened, but he didn't argue. The truth in Belizar's words weighed on him. He could feel it already—the heavy burden of what he'd just done. The village had always been a sanctuary, a place of safety. But now, after what had happened, it felt smaller. His place here was no longer certain.

He entered the village just as the first light of dawn began to stretch across the sky. His body was still tense, his thoughts scattered, but he moved quickly, driven by a need to face what came next.

The square was eerily silent as he approached. The villagers were gathered, their faces a mix of curiosity, concern—and something darker.

Fear.

Jekar stood at the front, his arms crossed, his sharp eyes scanning Brand's face with an intensity that made the air feel heavy. "You fought them alone."

Brand nodded, his throat tight. "They were too close. I had no choice."

A murmur rippled through the crowd. One of the elders, an older woman named Tala, stepped forward. "No choice? Or did you seek them out?"

Brand stiffened. "I—"

"They've never come this close before," another man said. "Not until now." His gaze was heavy, accusing. "Not until you."

A cold sensation coiled in Brand's gut. "You think I called them?"

"We think," Tala said slowly, "that things are changing. And we do not know if that change is for better or worse."

Jekar raised a hand, silencing further debate. His gaze never left Brand. "How did you survive?"

Brand hesitated. He could feel the weight of their expectations, the silent demand for an explanation. Should he speak of the Flow? The way it had moved with him? Would they even believe him?

Finally, he settled on a half-truth. "I fought. And I was fast."

Jekar's lips pressed into a thin line, but he did not press further. Instead, he turned to the villagers. "We will discuss this later. For now, we must decide what to do next. If the CABAL's creatures are bold enough to come this close, we are no longer safe."

Brand exhaled, the tension easing from his shoulders. The moment passed, but he knew the questions would linger. They had seen something in him today—something they did not fully understand. And that made them wary.

As the villagers dispersed, Jekar motioned for Brand to follow him. They walked through the quiet pathways of the village until they reached the elder's small home. Jekar entered first, seating himself beside a dimly burning lantern. Brand remained standing.

"You didn't tell them everything."

Brand's throat tightened. "Would it have mattered?"

Jekar studied him for a long moment before sighing. "Perhaps not." He leaned forward, his hands resting on his knees. "You must understand, Brand. Power is not always seen as a gift. Some will fear it. Some will seek to use it." His gaze hardened. "And some will seek to end it before it becomes something they can't control."

Brand swallowed. He hadn't considered that. He had never thought of himself as something to be feared.

Jekar's voice softened. "Be careful, boy. The world is watching. You will need to prepare for what comes next. Train hard to fight—I will do what I can."

Brand nodded, but inside, he could not shake the feeling that everything had changed.

And whether he was ready or not, his path had already begun.

The sun had barely begun its ascent when the first riders appeared on the horizon. Their approach was swift and methodical, their silhouettes slicing through the golden morning light like phantoms against the dunes. The villagers knew them well—the Desert Rangers, nomadic warriors who patrolled the vast expanse of the wastelands, maintaining a fragile balance between law and chaos.

Brand had heard tales of them since childhood. Stories of their skill, their discipline, their ability to move unseen through the sands. And now, they were here—just as Jekar had predicted.

Captain Darrek, their leader, was the first to dismount. His mere presence commanded respect. Clad in light armor reinforced with ancient tech, his movements were precise, calculated. His sharp eyes scanned the gathered villagers before settling on Brand.

"You," he said, his voice thick with authority. "You fought the jackals."

Brand straightened, feeling the weight of the moment. "Yes."

Darrek's gaze remained locked onto him. "Tell me how."

Brand hesitated, glancing at Jekar. The elder gave a small nod. Brand took a breath, then spoke. "They came at me fast. I moved faster." He elaborated on the fight.

Darrek studied him for a long moment before turning to his squad. "He's telling the truth. I've seen it before." He looked back at Brand. "You're strong. But strength without training is reckless."

Brand frowned. "What do you mean?"

Another Ranger stepped forward, a woman with a long braid and a gaze just as sharp as Darrek's. "We've seen others like you. People who can move before the battle even starts. People who survive when they shouldn't." She paused. "Most of them don't last long."

Darrek nodded. "Because power alone isn't enough. It needs control. If you don't learn that, you'll die just as quickly as those jackals."

Brand felt a flicker of frustration. He had already struggled with control, with understanding the Flow. Now, these warriors were echoing the same words Jekar and Belizar had.

He clenched his fists. "Then teach me."

A slow smile spread across Darrek's face. "I thought you'd say that."

The Desert Rangers didn't believe in easy lessons. The very next morning, before the sun had fully risen, Brand found himself put to the test.

Darrek had him running across the dunes, his feet sinking into the shifting sands with every step. "Control your breathing," the captain commanded. "The desert doesn't care if you're tired. Slow down, and you die."

Brand gritted his teeth, pushing himself harder. Every muscle screamed, but he refused to fall behind.

Next came hand-to-hand combat. The Rangers didn't coddle him. They attacked with brutal precision, forcing him to react, to move, to adapt. Brand quickly realized that brute strength was useless if it wasn't used wisely.

One particularly fast Ranger—Revik—knocked him to the ground more times than Brand cared to admit.

"You're fast like your mother," Revik conceded, offering a hand to pull Brand up. "But you rely on it too much. Your enemy won't always give you time to dodge."

Brand accepted the offered hand, frustration simmering beneath the surface. He had always been strong. But strength was proving useless without discipline. He was also thrown by the mention of his mother. She never talked about having a history with the Desert Rangers. Well – if she could impress one of them – he knew he would be able to as well!

As the training continued, Darrek observed him closely. When the morning session ended, the captain pulled him aside. "You have potential," he said. "But you hesitate. Why?"

Brand exhaled, staring at the sand beneath his feet. "Because I don't know if I should be using what I can do."

Darrek tilted his head. "The Flow?"

Brand's eyes snapped up. "You know about it?"

Darrek's expression darkened. "I've seen men try to control it. I've seen what it does to them." He stepped closer. "Power without purpose is dangerous. But fear of power is just as deadly."

Brand swallowed hard. "So what do I do?"

Darrek smirked. "You train. You learn. Because if you don't, someone else will decide your fate for you."

Brand nodded, determination settling into his bones. He didn't have all the answers yet, but he had a path.

And for now, that was enough.

Chapter 23:

The Tinkerer's Touch

The training with the Desert Rangers had left Brand sore but exhilarated. His body ached from the grueling sessions, but there was a new energy flowing through him—a sense of purpose, of progress. Yet even as he immersed himself in the discipline of combat, something else tugged at him.

Tink.

She had always been there—his closest friend, his sharpest critic, the one person in the village who never treated him any differently. Where others saw mystery and potential danger, she simply saw Brand. And he found himself drawn to her more each day.

The village's small workshop was a place of organized chaos. Mechanical parts were strewn across wooden tables, half-assembled devices hummed with faint energy, and the scent of heated metal lingered in the air. Tink sat in the heart of it all, her hands stained with oil, her sharp eyes focused on the inner workings of a small machine she was piecing together.

Brand leaned against the doorway, watching her for a beat before speaking. "You spend more time talking to machines than people."

Without lifting her eyes, she smirked. "Machines listen. People just make noise."

Brand chuckled and stepped inside, weaving through the clutter until he reached her table. He picked up a small gear, turning it between his fingers. "And what's this one supposed to do?"

Tink sighed and finally looked up at him. "It was supposed to be a self-adjusting gear for one of the wind turbines, but it keeps slipping under pressure." She wiped her forehead with the back of her hand, leaving a streak of grease behind. "I'll figure it out."

Brand set the gear down. "You always do."

For the first time, she studied him. "You look different."

Brand shrugged. "Training."

She smirked. "Getting knocked around by those Rangers?"

He rolled his eyes. "Something like that."

She leaned forward, resting her elbows on the table. "And? Do you feel any different?"

Brand hesitated. He did feel different—stronger, more disciplined. But there was something else—a restlessness, an awareness that the life he had always known was shifting beneath him. He exhaled. "I feel like everything is changing."

Tink nodded slowly. "Yeah. I've felt it too."

They sat in silence for a beat, the hum of machines filling the air between them. Finally, Tink reached across the table, tapping his wrist. "Just don't get so caught up in training that you forget where you came from."

Brand met her gaze, something unspoken passing between them. "I won't."

Tink grinned. "Good. Because I'd hate to have to remind you."

After that, Brand found himself visiting the workshop more often. Some days, it was just to talk. Other times, he helped where he could—passing her tools, holding parts steady, learning the names of the intricate gears and wires that brought her creations to life. It was a world unlike the one shaped by the Rangers' training, a world where precision replaced brute force, where patience mattered just as much as power.

Tink never rushed him, never asked questions he wasn't ready to answer. She worked, and he observed, and in those quiet moments, he felt something settle inside him. A balance, perhaps, between the warrior he was becoming and the boy who had always been drawn to her presence.

One evening, as the sun dipped below the horizon, he lingered longer than usual. Tink had just finished a particularly difficult repair, and they sat on the roof of the workshop, watching the desert fade into the cool embrace of twilight.

"You know," Tink said, leaning back on her elbows, "you never used to be this serious."

Brand glanced at her. "Guess I never had to be."

She tilted her head. "Do you miss it? Before all of this?"

He considered the question. Before the Rangers. Before the Flow. Before the quiet war he was slowly realizing was creeping into his life. "Sometimes," he admitted. "But I can't go back."

Tink nodded, as if she understood more than he had said. "No, you can't." She smiled, though there was a hint of something else behind it. "But you don't have to leave everything behind, either."

Brand looked at her, really looked at her. The grease-streaked hands, the sharp intelligence in her eyes, the way she always seemed to know what he needed to hear before he knew it himself.

Something inside him shifted.

For years, she had been his best friend, the one constant in a world that seemed to be unraveling. But now, as the air between them thickened with unspoken words, he realized she was more than that.

Tink must have sensed it too. She turned fully to face him, her expression open yet unreadable. "Brand..."

He swallowed hard. "Yeah?"

She hesitated for just a moment before shaking her head with a small, soft laugh. "Never mind."

Brand opened his mouth, but no words came. Instead, he found his hand reaching for hers, his fingers brushing against hers before gently clasping them. Tink didn't pull away.

They sat like that, hand in hand, watching the stars slowly emerge one by one. The moment didn't need words.

For now, it was enough.

Brand's time was no longer his own.

As the weeks passed, his training with the Desert Rangers only grew more intense. Dawn after dawn, he pushed his body and mind to their limits, learning to fight, to move, to think like a warrior. His speed had always been his greatest weapon, but now he was refining it, sharpening his instincts into something lethal.

His mornings began long before the first rays of sunlight touched the dunes. The Rangers drilled him relentlessly—long-distance runs across shifting sands, controlled breathing under extreme conditions, and combat sparring that left his body bruised but his reflexes sharper.

Captain Darrek personally oversaw his hand-to-hand training, forcing him into scenarios where brute strength wouldn't save him. "You rely on speed," Darrek had said after knocking Brand flat for the third time that morning. "That's good. But if someone faster comes along, then what?"

Brand had no answer. He tried to think of what his mother or Belizar had taught him. He could only think of listening to the Flow or trying to move with the enemy rather than control them. But in his gut, he knew he'd always just rather be faster.

By midday, training shifted to tactical awareness and survival techniques. Tracking patterns in the sand, reading subtle shifts in the wind, understanding how the smallest movement could make the difference between life and death.

"The desert speaks," Revik, one of the Rangers, had told him. "Learn its language, and you'll never be caught off guard."

At night, there were drills in shadowed silence—learning to move unseen, to strike before being struck. The Rangers had no use for brute force alone. They were ghosts of the dunes, warriors who knew when to fight and when to disappear.

It was thrilling. It was exhausting. It consumed him.

And Tink noticed the change in him before he did.

"You barely come around anymore," she said one evening, adjusting a mechanical clamp. Her voice was light, but Brand sensed the edge beneath it—something unspoken that he wasn't sure how to address.

"I've been busy," he replied, wiping sweat from his brow. "Training takes time."

Tink scoffed, setting her tools down with a sharp clink. "Training takes all your time, apparently."

Brand sighed, a flicker of frustration passing through him. "It's important." He didn't want to acknowledge the growing anxiety in the village or his mother's certainty that the CABAL would come one day.

She turned to face him, arms crossed. "I know that. I just…" She hesitated, then shook her head. "Never mind."

A knot twisted in Brand's chest. He wanted to make her understand— what he was doing mattered, not just for himself but for the village, for her. But the words wouldn't come.

Tink picked up her tools again, her movements deliberate. "You should get back. Wouldn't want Darrek to think you're slacking."

Brand nodded slowly, but as he stepped out of the workshop, he felt an undeniable shift between them.

He was changing. And he wasn't sure if Tink would still be there when he finally understood what that meant.

The distance between them grew in the days that followed, widening like a crack neither of them knew how to mend. Brand tried to push it aside, focusing on his training, but every time he passed the workshop and glimpsed Tink bent over her work, something inside him twisted.

One evening, after an especially grueling session with the Rangers, he found himself standing outside the workshop, hesitating at the door. He wasn't sure if he was there to argue or to apologize.

Tink didn't look up when he entered. She was calibrating a small motor, the rhythmic turning of her wrench filling the silence.

Brand cleared his throat. "Need any help?"

She paused, wrench still in hand, but didn't meet his gaze. "Didn't think you had time for this kind of thing anymore."

He winced at the sharpness in her tone. "That's not fair."

Tink sighed, setting the wrench down with a deliberate clink. She leaned back against the table, crossing her arms. "Isn't it?"

Brand exhaled, rubbing his face. "I didn't mean to shut you out. Training—"

"Training is important, I know," she interrupted, her voice softer now, but still tinged with frustration. "And I get it, Brand. I do. You're doing something that matters, something bigger than this village. But you're not just changing—you're leaving."

Brand frowned, his chest tightening. "That's not true."

Tink studied him for a long moment, her eyes searching his face. Then she shook her head. "Maybe you don't see it yet. But I do."

He stepped closer, but the words he wanted to say stalled in his throat. She spoke first.

"I'm proud of you," she said, her voice quieter now. "I just don't want to wake up one day and find you gone."

Brand's chest constricted. He reached for her hand, his fingers brushing against hers, lingering, unwilling to break the connection. "I'm still here."

Tink met his gaze, and for the first time in weeks, something unspoken passed between them. A truth neither of them had dared to voice. She squeezed his hand, then let go, offering a small, sad smile.

"For now," she said.

Brand wanted to argue, to promise her that nothing would change. But the words stuck in his throat, because deep down, he knew the path he was walking was leading him further away from the life they'd shared.

And Tink wasn't wrong.

Chapter 24:

The Warrior's Path Begins

The desert stretched endless before Brand, the sun a relentless overseer, heat waves distorting the distant horizon. Sweat slicked his back as he sprinted, boots churning dust from the dry, cracked earth beneath him. The Rangers had given him no respite—"Push your body to its limit, then find out where the real limits are"—that was Darrek's philosophy.

Brand was still a teenager, but his frame was already taller and stronger than most his age, limbs wiry with muscle waiting to fully develop. Even so, the brutal pace of Ranger training pushed him well beyond what he had thought his limits were and into entirely new realms of exhaustion.

"Faster, boy!" Darrek's voice pierced the heavy air. "Think your enemies will wait for you to catch your breath?"

Brand gritted his teeth, lungs burning as he forced his legs to move faster, the weight of the wooden training sword strapped to his back thumping against him with every step, a harsh reminder of how much farther he had to go.

At the top of a ridge, Darrek raised a hand, signaling a stop. Brand dropped to his knees, gasping for air, sweat dripping into the sand beneath him.

"You fight with heart," Darrek observed, kneeling beside him, "but that alone won't keep you alive."

Brand wiped his brow with the back of his hand, nodding but too drained to speak. He understood. Strength wasn't enough.

Darrek scanned the horizon, his sharp eyes piercing the empty dunes. "You need to learn how to read your enemy. Anticipate their moves. And most of all, stop thinking of combat as brute force against brute force." He tapped his temple. "Outthink them."

Brand frowned, catching his breath. "How?"

Darrek's smirk tugged at the edge of his lips. "That's the part you have to figure out."

Later that evening, after the sun had long dipped behind the dunes, Brand sat outside his home, staring at the fading horizon. His muscles ached, the soreness settling into a familiar burn, a reminder of the day's grind.

His mother's voice interrupted his thoughts. "You're pushing yourself harder than usual."

Brand looked up, meeting her gaze. Oriana stood near the entrance, her silver-streaked hair flowing freely over her shoulders, her expression unreadable. She approached and sat beside him on the cool stone, her presence steady and quiet.

"I have to," Brand murmured, glancing at his scraped knuckles. "If I don't, I won't be strong enough."

Oriana sighed. "Strong enough for what?"

"To protect the village. To protect you."

She smiled, sad and proud all at once, brushing a hand through his unruly hair. "You're already strong, Brand. But strength isn't just in your fists or your feet. It's here." She pressed her palm gently to his chest.

Brand looked away. He wanted to believe her. But when he closed his eyes, all he saw were shadows slithering through the dunes—faces twisted by fear, pain, loss. Victims of the CABAL.

"I don't want to be weak," he whispered.

Oriana exhaled softly and reached out, lifting his chin until their eyes met. "Then listen, my son. The Flow isn't something you command. It's something you learn. A man who fights the current ends up drowning in it."

Brand frowned. "But the Rangers—"

"The Rangers will teach you how to fight," she said, voice like wind over still water. "But you must learn how to be. You're more than your sword. One day, you'll see that."

She leaned in and kissed his forehead, then stood and disappeared into the house.

Brand sat alone beneath the deepening sky, the wind stirring the dunes, whispering secrets he wasn't yet ready to understand.

Someday, maybe. But not tonight.

He stood in the center of the Rangers' makeshift sparring ring, a wide circle of hardened sand ringed by jagged rocks. Behind him, firelight danced, casting long, leaping shadows as night crept in.

Revik, a grizzled Ranger with a jagged scar carved down his left arm, stepped forward carrying two wooden training swords. He tossed one to Brand. "Let's see what all that training's worth."

Brand caught the sword. It felt familiar in his grip, but tonight it felt heavier—realer. He'd sparred before, but never with a full Ranger. A quiet ripple of interest moved through the gathered onlookers.

Darrek's voice rang out, steady and final. "Begin."

Revik stepped in, movements fluid but unhurried, blade angled casually.

Brand raised his own sword, ready to block—

Nothing came.

Revik circled. Watching. Waiting.

Testing him.

Brand shifted his stance, recalling Darrek's lesson—read your enemy.

He feinted left. Revik didn't flinch. Brand paused. Something felt wrong.

"You're thinking too much, boy," Revik said, and the smirk was the only warning.

Then he moved.

The wooden blade came down hard. Brand barely got his sword up in time to deflect it, the impact jarring through his arms. Before he could reset his stance, Revik pivoted sharply and struck him across the ribs.

Pain bloomed. Brand staggered back, breath catching in his throat as laughter rippled through the watching Rangers.

"Not bad," Revik said, circling him. "But you're still trying to control the fight." He spun his practice sword with effortless grace. "Move with your opponent's energy, not against it. Think of the space around you within the circle of your sword's reach as your ring and the sphere you get by rotating that ring as your domain. When you are alone – it is only your energy inside the sphere but when an enemy enters it – both of your spheres, your energies are available. The energy of movement, thought, focus, Flux and even ... well we will save that for another time. Just remember – you're not alone in this dance. Forgetting that makes you weak. Forgetting that could make you dead."

Brand clenched his jaw and reset his footing. He had to stop forcing the fight—stop thinking so hard. He exhaled, steadying his breath, letting the world narrow to the space between them. Trust the Flow.

Revik lunged again.

This time, Brand didn't try to anticipate. He let his instincts take over. He stepped just aside, feeling the air slice past his shoulder as the blow missed.

Then he struck.

Wood met wood with a loud crack, Brand's sword colliding against Revik's shoulder. The veteran staggered a half-step back, eyes widening. Then, slowly, a grin curved his face. "Better."

Brand's arms still shook, but a flicker of pride warmed his chest. He hadn't won—but for the first time, he'd felt it. The Flow wasn't something to chase. It moved with him.

Darrek crossed his arms, nodding once. "We'll make a Ranger of you yet."

Brand wiped the sweat from his brow. His muscles ached, but his smile came easy. Maybe he could do this.

The next morning, Darrek woke him before sunrise. "Today," he said, "you learn what real endurance is."

The trial was brutal.

Miles across shifting dunes. Stones hauled up jagged hills. Endless stances held beneath a blistering sun. No water. No breaks. Only pain and dust and grit.

Every time Brand faltered, Darrek pushed him harder. "Get up," he snapped. "This isn't about speed. It's about will."

Brand's legs buckled. His vision blurred. But something deeper— hot and stubborn—kept him going. A fire in his chest. A promise to himself.

By sunset, he stood at the top of a ridge, limbs trembling, soaked in sweat and dust. But still standing.

Darrek gave a rare nod. "You've got a warrior's heart, boy. But that's not enough. You'll need strength. Skill. Discipline. And you never stop building them."

Brand, barely upright, cracked a dry smile. "Then I'll keep going."

Darrek chuckled. "That's the spirit."

Brand had survived. But he knew this was only the beginning.

Before the first light of dawn, Darrek's voice cut through the silence. "Up. Now."

Brand jolted awake, his body already aching from the previous day. Every muscle protested as he sat up, legs stiff and heavy. The desert lay in shadow, its chill a brief reprieve before the heat returned.

Darrek tossed him a water flask. "You don't get another drink until you finish the trial."

Brand took a single sip, letting the cold water soothe his parched throat. Before he could take more, Darrek snatched it back.

"That's it," the Ranger said. "Move."

The moment their feet hit the sand, Brand knew this would be worse than anything before. The dunes shifted beneath him, swallowing each step. His boots sank, dragging him down with every stride. It felt like running through quicksand.

The sun rose fast, unrelenting, turning the air to fire. Sweat evaporated before it could fall. His lungs burned. His breath came in ragged bursts. His heart pounded like a war drum.

"Keep going," Darrek said, calm as ever, running beside him without missing a beat.

Brand clenched his teeth. He wouldn't fall behind. He couldn't.

His legs trembled, his vision blurred, but he kept moving. One step. Then another. And another.

At the base of a rocky hill, Darrek stopped and pointed to a pile of heavy stones. "Carry one to the top."

Brand dropped to a knee, choosing a stone nearly the size of his torso. He gripped it tight. Its jagged edges cut into his palms as he hoisted it to his chest. The weight crushed down on him like a living thing.

He staggered forward. The incline was steep, the path unforgiving. His arms screamed. His spine felt like it would snap. Breath tore from his lungs in gasps. The peak loomed above him like a cruel joke—so close and yet impossibly far.

But still, he climbed.

Halfway up, Brand's legs buckled. He dropped to one knee, the stone nearly slipping from his grasp. His arms screamed in protest. His vision blurred. Every part of him begged to quit.

No one would blame him if he stopped—if he let the stone fall and collapsed beside it.

But he wasn't just doing this for himself.

He thought of his mother. Of the village. Of Tink.

And he dug deeper.

With a grimace, he clenched his teeth and forced himself upright. His village needed him strong. His mother needed him alive.

With a final, guttural roar, he surged forward—step by agonizing step—dragging himself to the summit.

The instant he reached the top, he let the stone fall and collapsed beside it, gasping for breath, the world spinning around him.

Darrek arrived seconds later, his expression unreadable. Then he gave a single nod.

"Pain fades," he said. "Strength of Spirit doesn't."

Brand couldn't even answer. But something deep within him still burned.

He had survived.

And he would always survive.

Chapter 25:

Tink, the Heart of the Village

Brand wiped the sweat from his brow, leaning against the workbench as he watched Tink scowl at a rusted gear assembly. The small workshop reeked of hot metal and oil, the scent thick in the sweltering midday air. Tools clattered as she rummaged through a crate, muttering curses under her breath.

"Hand me the smaller wrench," she said, not looking up.

Brand reached for it, then hesitated, eyeing the clutter of bolts and half-assembled parts on the table. "Which one? You've got, like, five in here."

Tink shot him a glare and snatched the right one herself. "The one I always use, genius."

He smirked, arms folded across his chest. "You should label them."

"I don't label things. I just know." She jammed the wrench into place. "If you spent more time in here, you'd know too."

Despite the edge in her voice, he caught the ghost of a smile at her lips.

That was Tink—sharp tongue, sharper mind, and an uncanny knack for understanding machines better than most people understood each other. She'd been fixing and modifying village tools for years, bringing old things back to life with an ingenuity that never failed to impress him.

He watched her fingers move—quick, precise—as she tightened a bolt. A strand of dark hair fell into her face, and she huffed, blowing it away with an annoyed breath.

"You could tie that back," Brand offered, trying to sound casual and failing.

She paused, one eyebrow arched. "And take hair advice from you?" She gestured at his own wild, dust-caked mess. "No thanks."

He laughed. "Fair point." His eyes lingered, just for a moment, on the way the light caught her hair.

The tension eased. They slipped into their usual rhythm—Tink giving sharp commands, Brand double-checking every tool he passed her, steadying parts when needed. Despite all his combat training, there was something strangely calming about this—working with his hands, solving problems without violence. Here, there were no enemies, no drills. Just the quiet satisfaction of fixing something broken. The feeling of making something whole again or at least giving it new life. It felt good. He sometimes thought could understand why his mother chose life as a healer rather than as a fighter.

When they finally finished assembling the mechanism—a refurbished water pump meant to reroute water to the outer fields— Tink leaned back with a tired sigh, swiping her forearm across her brow. A streak of oil smeared across her cheek, but she didn't seem to notice.

Brand did.

He almost said something—almost reached out to brush the smear of oil from her cheek—but stopped himself. There was a weight in his chest, something strange and unfamiliar that pressed harder every time he looked at her lately.

Instead, he cleared his throat. "Think it'll work?"

Tink grinned, tapping the side of the device. "Course it will. I built it."

Brand chuckled, shaking his head. "No humility whatsoever."

She shrugged. "Why bother with humility when I'm always right?"

He rolled his eyes, but the warmth in his chest lingered. He wasn't sure when things had started to change—when their easy friendship had begun to feel like something more. All he knew was that lately, he was noticing things he'd never seen before.

And that scared him more than any battle ever could.

That evening, as the village settled into its usual nighttime hum, Brand found himself outside Tink's workshop again. The soft glow of lamplight flickered through the windows, casting shifting shadows across the worn walls. He hesitated, hands buried deep in his pockets, then stepped inside.

Tink was hunched over a delicate contraption, brass coils and tangled wires spread across the worktable. She didn't look up, but he knew she'd registered his presence—she always did.

"Didn't think you'd still be working," he said, trying for casual as he leaned against the wall.

"Didn't think you'd care," she replied, fitting a small gear into place.

He smirked, but her words settled heavier than he expected. He wasn't sure why.

She let out a quiet sigh and finally looked up at him. "Something on your mind?"

Brand hesitated, then shook his head. "Just... needed air."

Tink studied him for a beat longer before turning back to her project. "Well, you're taking up space. Either sit down or help."

He grabbed a stool and watched her hands move with familiar, effortless grace. He'd always admired her skill—but lately, he found himself drawn to other things too. The way she chewed her lip when deep in thought. The flick of her eyes toward him when she thought he wasn't looking.

Silence stretched between them—comfortable, but charged. The night carried faint echoes of laughter from the village square, but in here, it was just the two of them.

Finally, Tink spoke. Her voice was low, but certain.

"You've been different lately."

Brand tensed. "Different how?"

He wasn't sure what she meant—and her tone was different than their usual banter.

Tink set down her tools and turned to face him fully, arms crossing. "More distracted. More... tense." Her sharp gaze softened just a little. "More like you're carrying something you're not telling me about."

Brand swallowed. He wanted to tell her—about the weight of training, the pressure of expectations, the way his mother's voice still echoed in his mind.

But more than that, he wanted to tell her about how everything felt different when she was near. How she was the one thing that made him forget the rest.

Instead, he shrugged. "Just tired."

Tink studied him for a long moment, like she was deciding whether to push. Finally, she gave a small nod. "Well... try not to break under the weight of whatever it is."

She turned back to her work, but he didn't miss the way her fingers lingered on the edge of the table—like there was more she wanted to say but wouldn't.

Brand ran a hand through his hair and let out a slow breath.

Whatever was changing between them, it was happening—whether they acknowledged it or not.

And that scared him even more than facing a sword to his throat.

A week later, the tension hadn't gone away. It had deepened.

It was in the way their hands brushed when passing tools.

The way their gazes lingered just a moment too long.

The way Brand found excuses to be near her, even when there was no real work to do.

One evening, as they worked late in the dim light of the workshop, Tink reached for a wrench at the same time he did.

Their fingers collided.

Neither of them pulled away.

For a long heartbeat, neither moved.

Tink's breath hitched. Brand felt his heart pounding against his ribs. The warmth of her skin, the quiet of the night, the weight of everything unspoken pressed in around them.

He could step back. Laugh it off. Pretend nothing had changed.

Or he could stop pretending.

Slowly, Tink looked up at him, lips slightly parted, eyes searching his face—for something.

A challenge. A question.

An invitation.

Brand swallowed hard.

Was this real? Was this just another battle he wasn't ready for?

But before he could decide, she made the choice for him.

She leaned in.

It started as the softest brush of lips—hesitant, uncertain. But when Brand didn't pull away, she leaned in closer, her fingers curling into his shirt. Heat exploded in his chest, something deep and primal stirring awake. His hands found her waist, anchoring him as everything else faded away.

Whatever line had once existed between them had vanished.

Outside, the world was still dark, with the first hints of dawn creeping through the narrow slats of the workshop walls. The room smelled of oil and iron, but beneath that, there was something else—something new, something fragile.

Brand lay still, feeling the steady rhythm of Tink's breath against his chest, the warmth of her bare skin pressed against his. The weight of the night before settled in his mind, a mixture of wonder, satisfaction, and an undeniable awareness that nothing between them would ever be the same.

He exhaled slowly, careful not to wake her. His arm was draped around her waist, the curve of her back fitting perfectly against him as though they had always belonged there. He had fought battles, endured exhaustion beyond reason, trained until his body gave out— but this was something entirely different.

Tink stirred slightly, shifting against him, and Brand felt the memory of the night flood back with vivid clarity. The way she had pulled him toward her with an urgency that stole his breath, the softness of her lips against his, the tentative way they had explored each other—not with clumsy inexperience, but with the kind of deliberate reverence that came from knowing they were crossing a threshold that could never be uncrossed.

There had been whispers between them, names spoken in the dark. Hands that had traced familiar forms but in entirely new ways. Quiet, breathless laughter followed by a silence thick with meaning.

He had known Tink all his life, but last night, he had truly felt her—for the first time, in a way that made his chest ache with something deeper than desire.

A part of him had expected regret to settle in with the morning light, for doubt to creep in like an unwanted guest. But there was none.

What now?

Tink's fingers twitched against his arm, then curled slightly. A quiet sigh escaped her lips as she shifted onto her back, blinking up at the wooden ceiling. Her eyes, still heavy with sleep, found his almost immediately.

Neither of them spoke.

Brand swallowed, unsure of what to say. Should he reassure her? Tell her this hadn't been a mistake? That he'd wanted this for longer than he could admit even to himself?

But before he could form the words, she smirked—a small, sleepy thing, but undeniably, unmistakably Tink.

"Morning, warrior."

Relief washed over him like cool water, and he chuckled, letting his fingers brush against hers where their hands lay tangled between them. Still them.

"Morning, mechanic."

She stretched lazily, the blanket shifting with her, and Brand had to force himself not to get lost in the sight of her—the way her skin caught the early morning light, the familiar defiance in her eyes softening into something more open.

Her expression sobered just slightly. "So... what now?"

Brand hesitated. Not because he didn't know his answer, but because it terrified him just how much he meant it.

"We keep going," he said, his voice quiet but firm. "We figure it out."

Tink studied him for a long moment, then nodded. "Good answer."

She reached up, brushing a strand of hair from his face before leaning in, pressing a soft kiss to his jaw—a small, quiet promise.

Brand exhaled, a slow smile tugging at his lips. Whatever came next, they would face it together.

Chapter 26:

Discovery and Prosperity

The air was thick with heat as Brand and Tink made their way across the rocky outskirts of the village, the midday sun casting long shadows over the cracked earth. The weight of last night still clung to them—an unspoken change in the way they moved, the way their eyes lingered just a little longer, the way their hands brushed with newfound familiarity.

Brand adjusted the straps on his pack, glancing at Tink. She looked the same as ever—confident, steady—but he caught the flicker of something different in the small smirk that played at her lips when she noticed him watching.

"Don't look at me like that," she teased, nudging him with her elbow.

Brand smirked. "Like what?"

"Like you're still trying to figure out if last night really happened, and what it means."

He chuckled, shaking his head. "I know it was real." He hesitated before adding, quieter, "I just don't know what comes next."

Tink slowed, her gaze meeting his with a steadiness that made his stomach twist. "Then we figure it out."

She said it so simply, as if it were the easiest thing in the world. And maybe, for her, it was.

Before he could respond, she tilted her head toward the distant cliffs. "Come on, we've got work to do."

That morning, they set out to investigate a rumor whispered among the villagers—a place where the land guarded something forgotten, something valuable. The elders spoke of it in half-remembered stories, but no one had ever found it. Until recently.

A few days earlier, a minor earthquake had cracked open a portion of the canyon wall near the southern dunes. A few scouts had seen something glinting in the rock before turning back, spooked by the unfamiliar. The village needed resources—water, salvage, anything that could give them an edge against the drought and the ever-looming presence of the CABAL.

If there was something to be found, Brand and Tink intended to find it.

The path to the canyon was treacherous. Loose stones shifted beneath their feet, the heat baking the air around them. Brand led the way, his instincts sharp, each step measured. Tink followed close behind, occasionally stopping to examine unusual rock formations, her mind, as always, ticking away at possibilities.

When they finally reached the newly formed crack in the rock face, they stood in silence, taking in the sight before them. The fissure was wide enough for a person to slip through, leading into the darkness beyond.

Tink pulled a small lantern from her pack and ignited the wick. "Well? Are we going in, or are we just going to stare at it all day?"

Brand grinned. "Ladies first."

Tink snorted. "Nice try, warrior. Get in there."

Brand rolled his eyes but stepped forward, carefully slipping through the gap. The rock was cool against his skin, a sharp contrast to the sweltering heat outside. As he emerged on the other side, he inhaled deeply, the air inside tinged with the scent of something old—dust, rust, and something faintly metallic.

Tink followed a moment later, holding the lantern high. The glow revealed a vast chamber, the walls lined with what appeared to be ancient machinery, half-buried in sand and debris. Some of it had clearly been damaged by time, but others—others looked almost untouched.

Brand stepped forward, his boots kicking up dust. "What is this place?"

Tink knelt beside one of the machines, running her fingers along its surface. "It's not just ruins," she murmured. "This... this was a working facility."

Brand crouched beside her, inspecting the strange symbols etched into the metal. They were unlike anything he had seen before—not the markings of the village, nor the crude engravings left by scavengers.

Tink exhaled slowly, her excitement barely contained. "This could change everything."

Brand nodded. He felt it, too. Something about this place felt important—like they weren't just uncovering the past, but stepping into something much bigger than themselves.

For the first time in a long while, Brand wondered if their discovery was meant to be found... or if it had been left buried for a reason.

Tink's fingers brushed over the dusty surface of a console embedded in the wall. Unlike the rusted-out machines surrounding it, this one still hummed faintly with latent energy.

Brand watched as she knelt, prying open a side panel with practiced ease. "Be careful," he muttered.

Tink scoffed. "When am I not?"

Ignoring his smirk, she probed deeper, her lantern casting shadows across the hollowed-out facility. Inside the panel, wires twisted together in intricate, alien patterns—nothing like the crude circuitry they used in the village. Some still pulsed with a dim blue glow.

Brand stepped closer, his instincts on high alert. "That doesn't look dead."

Tink exhaled, her brow furrowing. "It's not."

The air between them grew thick, charged. The walls seemed to hum in response to their presence, as if aware of them. Dust shifted in unseen currents. A faint pulse of energy radiated from the console, so subtle that Brand thought he imagined it—until Tink's lantern flickered.

She froze. "Did you see that?"

Brand nodded, his muscles coiling. Something was still alive here.

A low vibration rolled beneath their feet. Not strong enough to be an earthquake, but enough to send grains of dust tumbling from the ceiling.

Tink exhaled slowly. "I think... I think this place is waking up."

Brand's pulse quickened. He reached out, gripping her wrist lightly. "Maybe we shouldn't—"

Before he could finish, a soft hiss of hydraulics echoed from deeper within the chamber. A panel slid open, revealing an inner corridor—dark and untouched by time. The air that rushed out was cool, metallic, and tinged with something distinctly unnatural.

Brand and Tink exchanged a glance, a silent understanding passing between them.

They had uncovered something far greater than they had expected.

And whatever it was—it had noticed them, too.

The soft glow of unseen lights flickered to life along the corridor's edges, a deep blue pulse illuminating the ancient walls. A rhythmic hum vibrated through the air, low and mechanical—like something stirring from a long, forgotten slumber.

Tink exhaled sharply. "I don't think we have a choice anymore."

Brand nodded, his grip tightening around the hilt of his knife. "Then we go forward."

Together, they stepped into the darkness, the weight of history pressing down around them.

The corridor stretched ahead, flanked by sleek, metallic walls that showed no rust or wear, as if untouched by time. The air inside was cooler, with a sterile, artificial scent. Unlike the outer chamber, where machinery lay dormant under layers of dust, this place felt preserved—waiting.

Tink reached out, trailing her fingers along the nearest surface. A faint blue glow followed her touch, as if the walls themselves responded to her presence. She turned to Brand, her eyes alight with curiosity and unease. "This isn't just an old ruin," she whispered. "It's something more."

A sudden click echoed from above, followed by a slow mechanical whirr. Both Brand and Tink froze, their eyes darting to the ceiling. Panels along the walls shifted slightly, as if unlocking.

Brand clenched his jaw. "We shouldn't be here."

Tink's lips pressed into a determined line. "And yet, here we are."

A faint hiss of escaping air sounded ahead of them. Then, a doorway slid open. The chamber beyond was vast—far larger than they had expected. Strange, vertical structures lined the walls, each encased in transparent material. And inside...

Tink inhaled sharply. "Are those... people?"

Brand stepped closer, his pulse hammering. No, not people. The figures within the glass-like enclosures were humanoid, their features elongated, their limbs slightly too slender. Their skin shimmered faintly, as though laced with something metallic. Some wore intricate plating over their chests and arms, their expressions frozen in eerie stillness.

Suspended. Sleeping. Waiting.

Tink took an uneasy step back. "This... isn't a facility," she murmured. "It's a Vault."

The word hung in the air, heavy with implication. This place wasn't forgotten. It had been sealed—on purpose.

The realization settled over them like a weight.

Brand swallowed hard, every instinct screaming at him to leave.

But before he could speak, a low hum rose from one of the pods.

A flicker of motion.

Then—

A pair of glowing blue eyes snapped open.

Chapter 27:

Secrets Beneath the Sand

Glowing blue eyes locked onto Brand and Tink, unblinking and eerily aware. The vault's silence thickened, as if time itself had paused.

Brand's grip on his knife tightened, his breath slow and steady, muscles coiled and ready for whatever came next. Beside him, Tink stood frozen, her fingers hovering near the inactive control panel, caught between hesitation and the urge to undo their actions.

Then, a sudden hiss filled the air as frost began to melt from the edges of the glass enclosure. The metallic casing released a series of sharp clicks, and the pod shuddered before splitting open with a pressurized burst. The figure inside didn't step out immediately. Instead, long, slender fingers flexed, joints stiff from disuse, before it slowly raised its head.

Tink took an involuntary step back. "That... doesn't look human."

Brand had already reached the same conclusion. The figure's skin gleamed in the dim light, a disturbing fusion of organic and metallic tones, as if crafted rather than born. Faint energy lines pulsed beneath its surface, glowing softly in patterns that mimicked the ones embedded in the walls around them.

Then, it moved.

A single, fluid step forward, its bare feet touching the ground with unexpected grace. It turned its head toward them, its expression neutral—neither hostile nor welcoming—just... observing.

A voice, mechanical yet layered with an unmistakable sentience, echoed from its lips.

"Designation: Unidentified. Origin: Unconfirmed. Status: Subjective Threat Assessment Pending."

Brand's fingers twitched on his weapon. "Did it just... scan us?"

Tink exhaled sharply. "I think it's... trying to figure out if we're enemies."

The figure's head tilted slightly. Then, for the first time, its lips moved of their own accord—not just repeating programmed speech, but forming something new.

"What era is this?"

The question sent a chill down Brand's spine.

Tink's eyes flicked to him. "That's not the question of someone who just woke up from a nap," she muttered. "That's the question of something... ancient."

The figure's gaze shifted between them, expectant.

Brand cleared his throat, forcing himself to speak. "We don't know what era you're talking about. We're from the village above, in the desert."

The figure blinked once. Then, a slow nod. Understanding. Recognition.

"Accessing CODEX terminal. Limited access available. I see. The surface endures... the Flow persists but is unstable."

Tink's brows furrowed. "The Flow?"

The being exhaled—not air, but something else, something intangible. A shift in the energy around them. It was the same kind of shift Brand had felt in his rare moments of connection to the Flow.

Before he could react, the vault trembled. A deep resonance passed through the walls, the pods, the very ground beneath them. A response.

More pods were waking.

Brand's pulse quickened. "I think we just set off something bigger than we realized."

The being—whatever it was—turned toward the other awakening chambers. Its expression darkened.

"Then we must leave. Now."

Brand hesitated. His instincts screamed at him to move, but his mind struggled to grasp the enormity of the moment. Who—or what—was this being? And why did it understand the Flow in a way he barely could?

Tink, always quicker to act, stepped forward cautiously. "Leave?

Why?"

The being's glowing eyes flicked toward the other pods, which pulsed with the same rhythmic hum as the one it had emerged from. More were waking.

"Containment was not meant to be breached. The cycle was not meant to resume. If you remain, you will not leave."

Brand's grip tightened on his knife. "And why should we trust you?"

The being turned its gaze back to him, its expression unreadable. "You activated the vault. Your presence stirred the dormant. If I meant you harm, you would already know."

Tink muttered under her breath, "Comforting."

The air in the chamber thickened. The temperature dropped. A faint mist curled at their feet, and the hum of the pods grew sharper, almost like whispers just beyond hearing.

The being turned sharply toward the nearest pod, its form suddenly more rigid, more alert. "They are not like me. Their purpose is different. Their purpose was war."

Brand exchanged a glance with Tink, his gut twisting. "And what was your purpose?"

A beat of silence.

Then, finally: "I was meant to stop them."

A crack splintered through the air as the second pod shuddered violently. A shadow stirred inside, its movements jerky and unnatural. The vault's ancient warning systems blared in a low, rhythmic pulse, and the air itself rippled with an unseen force.

The being's gaze snapped back to them. "You will not survive them. Move. Now."

Tink didn't wait for another warning. She grabbed Brand's arm, yanking him toward the corridor they had entered through. But as they turned, the heavy metal doorway slid shut with a deafening clang.

Brand spun, his pulse hammering. "That wasn't us."

The being inhaled deeply, its glow intensifying beneath its skin. "No. The vault has sealed. The cycle will resume."

Tink's voice was tight with urgency. "That doesn't sound good."

Brand swallowed hard, his mind racing. They'd just stumbled into something far bigger than themselves.

And now they were trapped inside with it.

The vault trembled as another pod released a sharp, metallic hiss, its frost-coated glass cracking from within. A dark figure pressed against the transparent surface, jerking unnaturally, its movements grotesque.

Brand's muscles coiled. He could feel it—a presence twisted with disharmony, a ripple in the Flow that made his skin crawl.

Tink cursed under her breath, her grip tightening on Brand's arm. "Tell me we're not about to fight something we don't understand."

The being—their supposed ally—stepped forward, its glowing eyes fixed on the trembling pod. "They are incomplete. Corrupted. They should not wake."

Brand's heart skipped a beat. "What does that mean?"

"They are echoes of what once was. Shadows without purpose. But they will see you... as prey."

Before they could react, the first pod exploded outward, shards of reinforced glass scattering across the floor. A humanoid form staggered forward—its body twisted, limbs unnaturally long, and its face a hollow mask of metallic ridges where eyes should have been.

Then it twitched toward them.

Brand barely had time to react. The thing lunged, a blur of sinew and metal. Instinct screamed through him as he shoved Tink aside and brought his knife up to block—

But the moment his blade made contact, a surge of red energy crackled through the creature's limbs, forcing him back. The impact sent him skidding across the floor, his muscles straining against the unnatural resistance.

Tink scrambled to her feet, reaching for her toolkit. "That's not normal."

The awakened being lifted a hand, and a pulse of blue energy erupted outward, slamming into the creature with a force that made the vault's walls groan. The malformed thing shrieked, spasming violently—then, it crumbled into itself, dissolving into a mist of flickering red light before vanishing entirely.

Brand panted, his grip tightening on the knife. "What the hell was that?"

"A failure. A remnant." The being's glowing blue eyes flicked to the remaining pods, where shadows twisted violently inside. More were waking.

Tink didn't wait for a response. She rushed to the nearest control panel, flipping open a rusted casing. "I can try to override the system. Shut the pods down before more of those things crawl out."

Brand turned to the entity. "Can she do it?"

The being hesitated, its gaze lingering on the pods. "Not without consequence. The vault was built on balance. Force it shut, and it may not open again."

Brand's jaw tightened. They were running out of time.

Tink cursed as another pod hissed open, shards of glass splintering. "Brand, make a choice—fight or flee?"

Brand's pulse raced. His life had always been about fighting—his strength, instincts, speed, honed for moments like these. But the Flow... the Flow wasn't about force. It didn't bend things to its will. It guided.

For the first time, Brand listened.

A sensation rippled through him—not fear or panic, but something else, something deeper—a path.

He turned to Tink. "Shut it down."

She didn't argue. Her fingers flew over the interface, sparks flying as she worked. The vault groaned, the walls trembling, resisting.

The awakened being stiffened. "They will fight back."

The pods began to crack, their occupants stirring violently. But Brand stepped forward, grounding himself. He didn't fight the Flow; he let it guide him.

When the creatures lunged, he was already in motion.

The Vault roared to life as Tink's fingers moved with frantic precision, sparks flying from the console. The air thickened with a deep, pulsing energy—a resistance that fought back against their attempt to shut it down.

Brand moved with fluid precision, dodging the remnants as they lunged toward him. He didn't force; he flowed.

When one of the twisted figures charged, Brand pivoted effortlessly, letting its own momentum betray it. With a flick of his wrist, his blade cut through the corrupted mass, but instead of crumbling, the creature reformed—its severed limbs knitting together with red-hued energy.

"They're not stopping," Brand growled.

"They won't," the awakened being said, lifting its arm. A pulse of blue energy radiated outward, slamming into the nearest creatures, forcing them back. But they only snarled in response, their hunger growing.

Tink let out a frustrated shout. "I'm locked out! Something's overriding the shutdown!"

Brand's gut twisted. "Then we need another way!"

The awakened being's head tilted, its glowing eyes flicking to the far end of the chamber. "There is one way."

Tink wiped sweat from her brow, glancing up. "Yeah? Now would be a good time to share."

The entity turned toward Brand, its expression unreadable. "You must sever their connection to the Flow. Without it, they will collapse."

Brand's mind raced, his chest tight with the urgency of the task. He barely understood his own connection to the Flow—how was he supposed to sever theirs? But there was no time to hesitate.

Closing his eyes, he steadied his breath. Feel, don't force. Let it guide you.

The creatures moved faster now, their movements sharp and predatory. Red energy coiled around them like a storm gathering strength. They sensed a shift. They sensed danger.

Brand reached out—not with his hands, but with his mind. He sought the wrongness, the disharmony in the air, and there it was: a tether, thin but strong, connecting the creatures to something far darker.

Brand inhaled sharply. This is what the CABAL does. This is what I must not become. But there was no time for doubt. Instead of trying to bend it to his will, he let himself become a conduit, a bridge for the Flow's power.

When he exhaled, an unseen ripple of force radiated outward from him, a wave across the surface of a lake. The moment it touched the tether, it snapped—severed and recoiled, pulled back into the walls like a broken string.

The vault shuddered. The creatures froze. Their forms flickered, uncertain, like they were questioning their very existence. The red energy around them fractured, pulled away, dissipating into the void.

One by one, they crumbled to dust.

The silence that followed was heavy, unnatural, oppressive. The hum of the vault shifted, now infused with something different—a purer, untainted energy.

Tink exhaled a long, shaky breath. "Tell me that was supposed to happen."

The awakened being studied Brand with a measured gaze. "Not all who touch the Flow can unmake. You are... more than I expected."

Brand staggered slightly, exhaustion sweeping over him like a cold wave, but he steadied himself. "We're still locked in, aren't we?"

Tink's lips quirked in a dry laugh. "Yeah. But I think I can fix that." She turned back to the console, her fingers flying over the interface now that the interference was gone.

The awakened being stepped closer, its voice lowering. "You severed their link. But their master will know."

Brand met its gaze, the weight of its words pressing down on him. "Then tell me what we just fought."

A pause, heavy with implication. The entity's glowing eyes didn't blink. "Not what. Who. The CABAL were not the first to seek control of the Flow. You have awakened an ancient war."

The words settled into Brand's chest like a stone, sinking deep, their meaning a cold truth that gnawed at him. Before he could respond,

Tink let out a triumphant shout.

With a deafening groan, the vault doors slid open, a crack of escape.

"Time to go," she said, urgency sharp in her voice. "Before something else wakes up."

Brand nodded, his eyes still locked on the entity for a moment, something unspoken passing between them. A warning. A promise.

Whatever war had begun long ago, it was clear now: it wasn't over. And they had just stepped into its path.

Chapter 28:

The Time of Awakening

The desert wind hit them the moment they emerged from the vault—hot and dry, carrying the sharp scent of sunbaked sand and the distant promise of vegetation. Brand inhaled deeply, grounding himself. After the heavy, electric stillness of the underground facility, the open sky felt almost unreal, like a dream on the edge of fading.

Tink wiped the sweat from her brow, squinting toward the silhouette of the village in the distance. "I don't know about you," she muttered, "but I'm ready to pretend none of that ever happened."

Brand exhaled slowly, the implications of their discovery still pressing on him. "We don't have that luxury."

The awakened being followed them silently, its movements unnervingly smooth, as if it were adapting to the world beyond the vault. Its glowing blue eyes flickered, scanning the horizon with an expression that was both eerily familiar and entirely alien.

"You said we woke something up," Brand said, breaking the silence. "What happens now?"

The entity's gaze turned toward him, its face unreadable. "The balance has shifted. Those who seek to control the Flow will know. The CABAL will move."

Brand's stomach twisted at the confirmation. He'd feared this answer, but hearing it solidified the reality of their situation. They hadn't just fought remnants—shadows of a long-forgotten war. The true enemy was still out there. Watching. Waiting.

Tink crossed her arms, her posture tight with resolve. "Then we need to warn the village."

Brand nodded, his mind racing. "And we need to figure out what to do next."

The walk back to the village felt longer than before, the weight of their discovery pressing down on them like an invisible force, the desert air thick with unspoken tension. As the village came into view, small figures moved between sun-bleached structures, and the scent of cooking fires carried on the breeze. Life went on, unaware of the catastrophe that had just been unearthed beneath the sands.

Brand could feel the weight of responsibility settle heavily in his chest.

When they stepped across the village perimeter, familiar faces turned toward them. Belizar, lounging lazily on a shaded ledge, flicked his tail in amusement at their dust-caked forms. "You two look like you've been dancing with ghosts."

Tink shot him a glare. "Something like that."

Before Brand could speak, a voice rang out. "You're back."

He turned to see Tink's father, Jorek, approaching. His face was impassive, but the tension in his posture was undeniable. "There's been talk of a disturbance in the dunes."

Brand exchanged a glance with Tink, then replied, his voice low and steady. "We found something. Something buried."

Jorek's eyes flicked past him, landing on the awakened being standing silently at Brand's side. The air between them seemed to freeze, thick with an unspoken recognition, an unsettling silence that hung heavy.

Tink swallowed, her voice barely a whisper. "It's... complicated."

Jorek's jaw tightened, his patience clearly wearing thin. "Then start explaining."

Brand took a steadying breath. He had known this moment was coming, but the weight of it still pressed down on him. This was only the beginning.

Word spread quickly through the village—their return was no ordinary one. The villagers gathered in clusters, eyes drawn to the strange figure at their side. The air was thick with suspicion. A few exchanged murmurs, others eyed the newcomer with open wariness. They had seen outsiders before. The last one had been a CABAL agent.

Jorek's gaze was sharp, cutting through the crowd, and his voice demanded answers. "You brought something back with you?"

Brand stood firm. "It's not something. It's someone. It helped us escape the vault."

A low murmur rippled through the crowd, some of it disbelief, some of it fear. Elders huddled together, whispering in urgent tones. The younger villagers eyed the being, their hands twitching near weapons.

Erdan, one of the oldest of the elders, stepped forward. His staff thudded against the ground, the sound like a declaration of authority. "What is it?"

The awakened being—Vaelin—shifted its gaze to the elder, its blue eyes unreadable, almost too calm in contrast to the tension rising in the crowd. "I am a protector of balance. My name is no longer relevant, but I was once called Vaelin."

Tink let out a sharp breath, the first sign of frustration breaking through her composure. "So, you do have a name."

Vaelin's head inclined, a gesture that seemed almost... reluctant. "A designation. Nothing more."

Jorek's frown deepened, his voice now laced with suspicion. "And why should we trust you?"

Brand met his gaze evenly, not flinching. "Because without it, we wouldn't have made it out alive."

Silence hung between them like a storm on the horizon. The crowd was waiting, breath held, as the weight of Brand's words settled over them. It was Belizar's voice that shattered the stillness, but it was far from his usual joking tone. His words cut through the tension with unsettling seriousness. "Then perhaps the better question is—what exactly have you brought back with you?"

Brand hesitated. The enormity of the truth was clawing at him, but the village had a right to know. He looked to Tink, who gave him a small nod. They couldn't keep secrets now.

Taking a deep breath, Brand faced the villagers. His voice carried the gravity of their discovery, every word wrapped in the urgency of what lay ahead. "We found something buried deep beneath the sands. An old war, locked away. And now... it's waking up."

Gasps followed, as if the air had been sucked out of the village. Murmurs spread like wildfire through the gathered crowd. A mother instinctively pulled her child closer to her, while one of the young hunters visibly tensed, his hand moving to the hilt of his blade.

Erdan's eyes narrowed as he assessed Brand, as if weighing every word for its true meaning. "Then you've endangered us all."

Brand's fists clenched, his frustration bubbling to the surface. "No. We have a chance to prepare. The CABAL will come for this knowledge. But now we know they're not the only ones who seek the Flow's power. We have the strength to stand against them."

Jorek ran a hand through his graying hair, his eyes searching the horizon as if he could already see the storm brewing. He exhaled sharply, the weight of their predicament settling in. "This is bigger than just us." He turned toward the elders, his voice now full of authority. "We need a council meeting. Now."

The villagers slowly dispersed, their voices low and wary as they exchanged uncertain glances. Some cast lingering looks at Vaelin, who stood unmoving, watching them all with an eerie calm.

Tink nudged Brand, her voice laced with dry humor. "Well. That went about as well as expected."

Brand sighed, rubbing a hand across his face. "Better, actually."

She smirked, her eyes glinting with the sharp edge of sarcasm. "Then I'd hate to see worse."

Vaelin's voice cut through the quiet like a whisper on the wind. "They are afraid. This is natural. But fear will not stop what is coming."

Brand turned to meet its gaze, his jaw tightening. "Then we need to make them ready."

The last light of the setting sun stretched long shadows over the village, casting an ominous glow over the sand. In the distance, the dunes seemed to shift as if something unseen stirred beneath the surface.

The council hall was a simple structure, built from sun-baked stone and reinforced wood, yet tonight, it felt as though the weight of the world rested within its walls. The air inside was thick with tension, heavy with the unspoken fears of the gathered elders. Torches flickered along the walls, casting erratic shadows that seemed to dance over the faces of those present, their expressions unreadable.

Brand stood at the center of the circle, flanked by Tink and Vaelin. All eyes were upon them, heavy with scrutiny. The elders' stares were sharp, skeptical, probing.

Jorek, standing at the head of the gathering, his posture stiff with authority, spoke with firm resolve. "We have all heard what Brand and Tink claim. They uncovered something buried beneath the sands— something that should have stayed buried."

Erdan's voice was a low grunt, his weight shifting as he leaned on his staff. "And they brought it back here." His eyes narrowed as he studied Vaelin. "They brought back an unknown."

Tink scoffed, rolling her eyes as she crossed her arms. "Would you rather we let the CABAL find it first?"

Erdan's glare was sharp enough to cut, but before the argument could escalate further, Maris, one of the younger elders, spoke up. Her voice was steady, commanding attention despite her age. "The boy is right about one thing. If the CABAL learns of what they uncovered, they will come. They have always craved control of Flow....artifacts." This last was said with a glance back at Vaelin.

Kett, a more reserved elder, frowned deeply, his gaze fixed on the ground as if he were weighing the consequences of their words. "Then we should do everything in our power to ensure they do not learn of it."

Brand's hands clenched at his sides, his knuckles white with tension. "It's too late for that. They will know. If I could feel the disturbance, they will, too."

Jorek's sharp gaze fixed on him, his voice hard with the weight of responsibility. "Are you certain?"

Vaelin's presence seemed to grow colder as he spoke, his voice carrying an unnatural stillness that made the room feel even heavier. "The CABAL's reach is vast. The remnants we faced in the vault were but echoes of a war they seek to rekindle. They do not need to find this place. They already know it exists."

A murmur rippled through the council. For some, this was the first time they had heard of the CABAL's true nature. For others, it confirmed an old, lingering fear.

Erdan's grip on his staff tightened. "Then we must abandon the village. Leave before they come."

Brand stepped forward, shaking his head. "No. We stand."

Jorek's expression hardened. "And fight? Against a force that has existed longer than any of us?"

Brand met his gaze, unwavering. "Yes."

A long silence followed. A choice stood before them—stay and prepare, or flee into the unknown.

Maris was the first to break the stillness. "We do not have the luxury of running. The desert is not kind to those without a home."

Belizar, silent until now, flicked his tail and spoke from his place near the edge of the room. "And where would you go, old man?" He tilted his head toward Erdan. "Everywhere else is worse than here."

The elder scowled but held his tongue.

Jorek ran a hand down his face. "Then we must prepare." He turned to Vaelin. "You claim to be a protector of balance. If that's true, help us defend it."

Vaelin inclined his head slightly. "I will teach you what I can. But if you fight the CABAL, understand this—this war is older than your village. Older than your ancestors."

Brand exhaled, feeling the weight of what was to come settle in his chest. "Then we'd better learn fast."

Jorek gave a sharp nod. "At first light, we begin preparations. Every able-bodied fighter will train. Every scout will learn to move unseen." He turned back to Vaelin. "And you will show us how to use what we have against them."

Vaelin met his gaze. "Weapons alone will not win this fight. To stand against the CABAL, you must understand the Flow. Not everyone can access it directly, but if the group unites in purpose, it will aid those who can."

The council murmured again, but this time, it was not fear that stirred them. It was resolve.

The village had chosen its path.

The battle for survival had begun.

The first light of dawn stretched long across the desert, casting golden hues over the village as its people gathered. Today was different. There was no morning chatter, no slow start to the day. Only tension—a sharpened awareness of what lay ahead.

Brand stood near the center of the training ground, watching as the villagers assembled. They were farmers, merchants, scavengers—but today, they would begin learning how to fight.

Vaelin moved among them, his presence unnerving yet strangely magnetic. He didn't look like them, but there was something in the way he carried himself that commanded respect.

Jorek crossed his arms, standing beside Brand. "I hope you're right about this."

Brand kept his eyes on the villagers. "We don't have a choice."

Vaelin turned toward the gathering, his voice cutting effortlessly through the murmuring crowd. "You wish to fight the CABAL. But you do not understand what you face. Strength alone will not save you. Fear will be your downfall."

The crowd stilled.

Tink, standing nearby, muttered, "Great motivational speech."

Vaelin ignored her. "Your weapons are crude, your skills untested. But there is something more important than blades or speed. The Flow exists within all things. Learn to listen to it, and you will survive. Ignore it, and you will die."

Jorek stepped forward. "Then start teaching."

Vaelin surveyed the faces before him, then motioned toward Brand. "He will be your first lesson."

Brand blinked. "What?"

Vaelin extended his hand. "Attack me."

A murmur swept through the crowd. Brand hesitated. He had fought before—trained with the Rangers, survived battles against beasts and men. But this was different.

Jorek leaned in. "Better not embarrass yourself, boy."

Brand exhaled sharply, then with a measured step, lunged.

He aimed for precision, speed—his blade flashing toward Vaelin's side. But before it could land, the air itself seemed to shift.

Vaelin did not move. And yet, Brand felt something push back against him, subtly redirecting his momentum. His strike missed.

He narrowed his eyes, adjusting his stance. He struck again—faster, stronger. But each time, the air shifted, as if unseen hands guided him away.

The villagers watched in stunned silence.

Finally, Vaelin stepped forward. With a single motion—smooth, effortless—Brand was on his back, the wind knocked from his lungs.

A collective inhale swept through the crowd.

Vaelin offered him a hand. "You fight against the current when you should move with it. Learn the Flow, or fall like the rest."

Brand took his hand, pulling himself to his feet. This was going to be harder than he thought.

Chapter 29:

A Warrior's Path

The days following the first lesson passed in a grueling haze. The village had committed to training, but commitment didn't equal readiness. Farmers, merchants, and scavengers alike struggled to hold their weapons properly, their stances unsteady, their swings wild. It was clear—they had courage, but courage alone would not be enough.

Brand spent every waking moment under Vaelin's watchful eye. He was stronger than the others, faster—but he still could not grasp the Flow. Every time he tried to fight with instinct, Vaelin countered effortlessly, knocking him aside as though he were a child.

"You think too much," Vaelin said after their latest sparring match, standing over Brand's sprawled form. "The Flow is not logic. It is not strength. It simply is."

Brand groaned, rubbing his sore ribs. "That's real helpful."

Tink smirked from the sidelines. "I think what he's saying is, stop trying to punch a river."

Vaelin nodded approvingly. "She understands."

Brand muttered under his breath but remained silent. He knew he had to learn, but his instincts rebelled against surrender.

That evening, as he sat by the fire, turning over the lessons of the day, Jorek approached. The older warrior sat beside him, his gaze on the horizon.

"You're frustrated."

Brand exhaled. "I don't understand how to fight without fighting."

Jorek smirked. "That's because you've always fought one way. Strength. Strategy. You think control is the key."

Brand frowned. "It isn't?"

Jorek shook his head. "Control is an illusion. The best warriors don't control. They respond." He paused. "There's a difference."

Brand mulled over the words, staring into the flames. Maybe Vaelin wasn't trying to teach him how to fight. Maybe he was trying to teach him how to let go.

He clenched his fists. Could he?

As he stared into the fire, the wind shifted around him. It whispered through the dunes, carrying something unseen—a feeling, a pulse—

And for the first time, Brand didn't resist it.

The Flow moved, and he moved with it.

Morning came too soon. The cool air of dawn had barely settled when Vaelin called Brand to the training grounds, the rest of the village watching in silent anticipation. Today's lesson would be different.

Brand stepped into the circle, expecting another sparring match, another moment of frustration. But Vaelin stood still, arms folded, watching him.

"Close your eyes," Vaelin instructed.

Brand hesitated. "Why?"

Vaelin's voice was calm but firm. "Because if you must see, you are already too late."

A murmur spread through the crowd. Brand clenched his jaw but obeyed, closing his eyes, shutting out the rising sun and the faces of those watching him.

"Now," Vaelin continued, "defend yourself."

Brand's muscles tensed. He heard nothing. Felt nothing.

Then, the attack came.

It wasn't the slow, measured strike of a sparring match. It was fast, unpredictable—a blur of motion that should have sent him sprawling—

But this time, he didn't think. He didn't force. He simply moved.

His body twisted, avoiding the strike by the smallest fraction. His pulse thundered, not from panic, but from awareness. The air shifted before the attack came, ripples spreading through the world around him.

The Flow had warned him.

A second strike followed. This time, he reacted before it landed. His arm moved to block, and instead of meeting resistance, he allowed the momentum to guide him, redirecting the force away.

Gasps rippled through the crowd.

Brand opened his eyes. Vaelin stood before him, his expression knowing.

"You are beginning to listen," Vaelin said. "But it is only the beginning."

Brand exhaled slowly, his chest rising and falling. For the first time, he wasn't fighting the Flow. He was in it.

And he knew there was no turning back.

Training continued over the next several days, and Brand could feel the difference. He shared his lessons with Tink in the evenings when they could be alone together. Somehow, spending time with her helped him stay connected to the inner sensations he was developing to better connect with the Flow. During the days, his body moved in ways it never had before—not just with power, but with intent. He no longer lunged at an opponent blindly but let their movements dictate his responses—adjusting, flowing. It was no longer a fight against resistance. It was a dance.

But Vaelin was not satisfied.

"You learn quickly," the being said, watching Brand outmaneuver a sparring partner with ease. "But you have not been tested."

Brand wiped sweat from his brow. "You mean more sparring?"

Vaelin shook his head. "No. A real test."

Brand frowned. "What does that mean?"

Vaelin gestured toward the dunes beyond the village. "There's something waiting for you out there. A force that will not hold back. If you wish to understand the Flow, you must face it."

A murmur rippled through the villagers. Jorek stepped forward, arms crossed. "You're sending the boy into the wilds?"

Vaelin met his gaze evenly. "Not alone." He turned to Tink. "You will go with him."

Tink blinked. "Uh, what?"

Brand straightened. "Why?"

"Because the Flow is not just about battle," Vaelin said. "It's about connection. You must trust yourself, but also another. You must feel not just your own instincts, but hers."

Tink scoffed. "And what exactly are we supposed to be facing?"

Vaelin's expression darkened. "You'll know when you find it."

Brand exchanged a glance with Tink. He had learned to listen to the Flow, but now, he had to trust it completely.

Out there, amid the shifting dunes, something waited.

The desert stretched endlessly before them, dunes rolling like frozen waves beneath the blistering midday sun. Brand and Tink moved in silence, the only sounds their steady footsteps and the distant whisper of the wind.

Brand felt it in his bones—something was definitely out here.

Waiting.

Tink adjusted the strap on her pack. "Any idea what we're looking for?"

Brand shook his head. "Vaelin said we'd know."

Tink snorted. "Great. Love cryptic instructions."

As they pressed deeper into the dunes, the air began to change. The heat remained the same, but something in the space around them felt denser—heavier. The Flow was shifting.

Then, Brand felt it—a presence.

He turned just as the sand erupted beside them.

Something was rising from beneath the dunes.

And he had been right—it had been waiting for them.

Chapter 30:

The Trial of the Dunes

S and surged upward in a spiraling column, a living tempest of dust and shadow. Tink stumbled back, shielding her face as Brand steadied himself, feeling the weight of the Flow coil in the air around them.

The force rising from beneath the dunes was no mere creature. It was ancient, aware, and watching.

A shape formed within the storm—a figure with shifting, liquid contours, humanoid yet unbound by a fixed form. Its eyes burned with pale blue fire, flickering like dying stars. When it spoke, its voice did not carry on the wind. It echoed within their minds.

"You have come seeking understanding. You will find only what you bring with you."

Brand swallowed hard, his heart pounding as he gripped the hilt of his blade. He could feel the energy pulsing from the entity, not malevolent, but immense. A being entwined with the very desert itself.

Tink nudged him, her voice tight. "What... is that?"

Brand shook his head. "A challenge."

The entity extended a hand, and the Flow around them shifted violently. The dunes trembled, and a wave of force slammed into them.

Brand barely had time to react. He let his body move—not resisting, not forcing. He flowed with the energy, twisting his stance, rolling as the impact carried him.

Tink wasn't so lucky. The shockwave lifted her off her feet, sending her tumbling across the sand. She landed hard, coughing as dust filled her lungs.

Brand pushed himself up, heart pounding. "Tink!"

She groaned, waving a hand. "I'm fine. Just got tossed like a rag doll."

The figure watched them with silent intensity. "You are not ready. You rely on instinct, but not wisdom. The Flow is not merely to be wielded—it must be understood."

Brand clenched his jaw. "Then teach us."

The entity's burning eyes flickered. It raised both hands, and the sand beneath them began to sink.

The ground swallowed their feet, dragging them into the depths of the dunes.

The challenge had begun.

Darkness consumed them as they fell. Brand felt the cold embrace of the earth closing around him, the shifting dunes swallowing him and Tink whole. The weightless descent felt endless, the air thick with something unseen.

Then, suddenly, they stopped.

Brand landed on solid ground, the impact jarring but not violent. His body tensed as he inhaled sharply, his fingers digging into the compact sand beneath him. A faint luminescence surrounded them— pale blue strands of energy twisting through the air like wisps of firelight.

Tink landed beside him, groaning as she pushed herself up. "I hate magic sand," she muttered, shaking dust from her hair.

Brand scanned their surroundings. They were no longer in the desert. At least, not as they had known it. Instead, they stood within a vast underground cavern, its walls carved from smooth, glass-like stone. Strange symbols glowed faintly along the curved surfaces, shifting as though alive.

Tink touched one of the walls, her fingers trailing over the glowing inscriptions. "This place... it's ancient."

Brand nodded, sensing something much older than them, woven into the Flow itself.

A voice echoed through the chamber, though the entity that had cast them down was nowhere to be seen.

"The Flow is balance. You seek strength, but strength alone leads to ruin. Prove that you understand. Prove that you are worthy."

The ground trembled beneath their feet. Figures began emerging from the shifting walls—shadows solidifying into form.

Tink inhaled sharply. "That's... not good."

Brand's muscles coiled. The trial had begun.

The figures took shape, their forms flickering like mirages, shifting between solidity and shadow. They were not just enemies—they were echoes. Reflections of warriors long past, beings who had walked the path of the Flow before.

Brand steadied his breath, tightening his grip on his blade. Tink stepped beside him, her fists clenched. "I hate ghosts," she muttered.

The first figure lunged.

Brand moved on instinct, sidestepping the strike. But as his blade met the creature's form, it passed through like water.

His heart pounded. "They're not real."

The entity's voice resonated through the chamber. "Real enough. Strike without understanding, and you will never land a blow."

Tink rolled away as another figure attacked, barely dodging a slash that seemed to distort the air itself. "Okay, great. So, what do we do?"

Brand exhaled. He had to think. No—he had to feel.

He closed his eyes, opening himself to the Flow. The air around him shimmered, and for a moment, he could see without sight. The creatures were not fully formed; they existed within the Flow, their movements dictated by energy, not matter.

He adjusted his stance, releasing the need to control. When the next creature lunged, he didn't strike—it was not about resistance, but redirection.

The moment he guided its force, the figure shattered, dissolving into the air like mist.

Tink gasped. "That worked?"

Brand nodded. "Don't fight them. Flow with them."

The remaining figures advanced. This time, Brand met them with harmony rather than brute force. He moved between them, each touch redirecting their energy, unraveling their forms. Tink followed his lead, adjusting her movements, using feints and misdirection instead of resistance.

One by one, the shadows faded.

And then, silence.

The luminescent strands of energy in the chamber pulsed brighter. The entity's voice returned, softer now. "You have begun to understand. But the Flow is not just movement—it is choice."

A path illuminated ahead, carved into the stone. Two doors.

Brand swallowed hard. The trial wasn't over.

Tink glanced at him. "I take it we don't get to go home yet?"

Brand shook his head. "Not yet."

He stepped forward.

And the next phase of the test began.

Brand and Tink stood before two doors, their surfaces shimmering with flowing inscriptions, each pulsing with energy. One door glowed faint blue, the other deep crimson. Both radiated power—but their meanings were unknown.

The entity's voice resonated through the chamber. "Every warrior reaches a crossroads. Strength or wisdom. Power or balance. Control or surrender. Choose."

Tink shifted uneasily. "I don't like this."

Brand studied the doors. One path led forward, the other... somewhere else entirely.

His instincts pulled him toward the blue door—a familiar presence, an energy that resonated with the Flow. But a part of him, the part that had always fought, felt the allure of the red. The CABAL's energy had always been red. Was this a test of temptation?

Tink exhaled, stepping closer. "So, what's it going to be?"

Brand closed his eyes, inhaling deeply. Feel, don't force. The Flow is not about control—it is about movement.

When he opened them, his fingers reached for the blue door.

The instant they brushed the surface, the chamber trembled. The red door flared with violent energy—was it a warning, or punishment for his rejection?

The blue door slid open, revealing a long corridor bathed in cascading light, like water flowing through the air.

Brand turned to Tink. "This is the path."

She exhaled in relief. "Good. I was really hoping we weren't taking the creepy red one."

The entity's voice returned, softer now. "You have chosen the path of harmony. You understand that power alone is not mastery. The Flow accepts you."

As they stepped forward, the chamber behind them dissolved into darkness.

The trial was over.

But their journey had only just begun.

Chapter 31:

The Return to the Surface

The corridor of cascading light surrounded them, its glow not blinding nor dim, but somewhere in between—a presence more than an illumination. Brand and Tink moved forward cautiously, their reflections rippling through the air as though they were passing through liquid time.

"Okay," Tink muttered, glancing around. "Officially weirded out."

Brand nodded, but fear didn't touch him. The Flow was there, guiding them.

With each step, the weight of the desert's trial lifted, the pressure of the challenge fading behind them. The walls of light pulsed with rhythm, as if they were responding to their every movement. Ahead, the corridor began to narrow, spiraling upward.

"The way out," Brand said. "We're being led back."

Tink exhaled sharply. "Let's hope it's as simple as it seems."

They ascended, the walls shifting with them, the air thickening, wrapping around them like unseen hands, lifting them with a soft, invisible force. The Flow carried them now, instead of gravity.

Then—light erupted outward.

They were thrown into the open air, sand scattering beneath them as they landed on solid ground. The desert stretched around them again, the sky a deep amber, the sun setting in the distance.

Tink groaned. "I think I'm going to be dizzy for a week."

Brand scanned the dunes. The entrance to the underground chamber had vanished—gone, as if it had never existed.

But something had shifted. The desert was silent. No wind. No shifting dunes. Only stillness.

Vaelin stood a few paces away, watching them, waiting.

Brand exhaled, brushing the sand from his clothes. He met Vaelin's gaze. "You knew this would happen."

Vaelin's expression remained unreadable. "It was necessary."

Tink pushed herself up, still recovering from the experience. "So... do we get a reward, or what? Because I feel like I earned a medal or something."

Vaelin ignored her and stepped forward. "What did you learn?"

Brand hesitated. The trial had been more than just a test of skill— it had tested his self-awareness. He had learned that power without wisdom led to destruction. That the Flow wasn't something to control—it was something to harmonize with.

"That control is an illusion," he said finally. "The Flow moves through everything. We don't take from it. We move with it."

Vaelin gave a slight nod. "Then you are ready."

Tink scoffed. "Ready for what?"

Vaelin's gaze didn't flicker. "For what comes next."

A shift in the air—a ripple in the energy of the dunes. Brand felt it before he heard it.

Then—a warning pulse surged through the Flow.

Brand's stomach clenched. Something was approaching.

The pulse of energy washed over them, a tremor in the unseen fabric of the world. Brand instinctively moved forward, positioning himself between Tink and the open expanse of the dunes. Whatever was coming, it was close.

Vaelin remained still, his gaze fixed on the horizon. "Do you feel it?"

Brand nodded. "It's... strong."

Tink frowned, placing a hand over her chest. "It's more than that. It feels... wrong."

The sky darkened, even as the sun lingered low on the horizon. The air thickened, charged with something unnatural.

Then the dunes began to stir.

At first, it was subtle—a ripple, a faint disturbance. Then, the sand erupted, twisting into spiraling tendrils that seemed to bend against nature, as if some unseen force was pulling the desert into motion. A shape began to form within the storm—dark, shifting, a presence that radiated malice.

Brand's grip tightened on his blade. "Is it CABAL?"

Vaelin's voice was low and grim. "No. This is older."

The swirling mass lunged forward, the sand coiling around it like armor. The figure within began to take shape—tall, lean, pulsing with red-hued energy. Its eyes burned with an unnatural light, filled with hunger.

Tink took a cautious step back. "That's bad, right? I mean, I really feel like that's bad."

Vaelin's expression remained impassive. "It's a wraith. A remnant of the past, tied to the Flow but corrupted by those who sought to bend it."

Brand's breath hitched. A remnant... of the same force they had faced beneath the sands.

The wraith lifted a clawed hand, and the wind howled. The energy around them turned volatile. It had sensed them.

Then it struck.

The storm surged forward, tendrils of energy cracking through the air like whips. Brand barely managed to dodge, rolling to the side as the sand where he had stood exploded in a violent shockwave.

Tink yelped, scrambling backward. "Okay, definitely bad!"

Vaelin moved with fluid precision, stepping between them and raising his hand. The Flow around him rippled outward, creating a counterforce against the wraith's attack, slowing its advance. "This battle is not yours alone, Brand. Feel, and move with it."

Brand gritted his teeth, feeling the Flow shift around him. The wraith was tethered to it, but in a fractured, unnatural way—raw and chaotic, unlike anything he'd ever faced.

The wraith lunged again, and this time, Brand didn't strike. He listened.

The Flow whispered its rhythm, offering a path through the storm.

He exhaled, then stepped into it.

And for the first time, he didn't resist.

He moved with the wind, his blade following a trajectory he didn't fully control—but didn't need to. The strike landed, not with force, but with precision. The wraith recoiled, its form shuddering.

Vaelin watched silently, his expression unreadable. "Now you understand."

The wraith shrieked, an unearthly sound as its body fractured at the edges. But the battle was far from over.

Its form contorted, the red-hued energy within it pulsing erratically. It was wounded, but not defeated. The wind howled louder, sand swirling in chaotic waves, obscuring their sight and warping the sounds around them.

Vaelin moved forward, his voice steady amidst the chaos. "The Flow is harmony, Brand. But the corrupted do not listen. They only consume."

Brand could barely hear him over the wraith's piercing cries. It lashed out again, tendrils of its form elongating and seeking purchase in the physical world. It was trying to anchor itself.

Tink's voice rang out. "So how do we kill something that won't die?"

Vaelin's reply was calm, resolute. "We do not kill. We release."

Brand's breath caught. He had spent years learning to fight, to survive, to overpower his enemies. But this? This was something else entirely.

The Flow pulsed around him, a rhythm that transcended thought, beyond action. It was a current—he had to move with it.

The wraith lunged once more, but Brand didn't meet it with force. Instead, he let go.

His feet shifted with the wind, his blade tracing an arc through the air—not to strike, but to part the energy. The wraith howled as its attack was redirected, its essence unraveling.

The red hue dimmed, the corruption unraveling. It fought to remain whole.

Vaelin raised his hand. A ripple surged through the Flow, engulfing the wraith in a wave of energy.

Brand stepped forward, exhaling. One final movement. His blade cut through the air, severing the last tether that held the wraith together.

The creature released a final, shuddering cry—then it vanished.

Silence descended over the desert. The wind, once fierce, softened to a whisper.

Tink exhaled a breath she'd been holding. "Okay. That was terrifying."

Brand lowered his blade, his eyes locked on the empty space where the wraith had been. He hadn't destroyed it. He had unmade it.

Vaelin's gaze met his. "Now you understand."

Brand exhaled. He did.

This was the cost of moving with the Flow.

Chapter 32:
The Path Ahead

The desert lay still in the wake of the battle. The wraith was gone, yet its presence lingered in the air like a fading echo. The wind, once howling with unnatural fury, had eased into a hushed stillness, as though the very dunes held their breath. The vast expanse of sand stretched endlessly, the shifting patterns on its surface undisturbed, as if nature itself refused to acknowledge the violence that had unfolded.

Brand still felt the energy of the Flow coursing through him—raw, electric, but now refined, as though he no longer had to struggle against it. His pulse slowed, and beneath the storm, he sensed a newfound calm. Every nerve in his body felt heightened, as if he could sense the faintest ripple in the air, the heartbeat of the world itself. The sky above was streaked with deep purples and reds, the last remnants of daylight casting long, dramatic shadows across the landscape.

Vaelin stepped forward, his gaze studying Brand with quiet intensity. His presence, always enigmatic, now carried a subtle air of approval. "You've crossed the threshold."

Brand exhaled, his grip on the blade loosening. "It didn't feel like a fight. It felt... different."

Vaelin nodded. "Because it was." He gestured toward the dunes. "You're beginning to understand that the Flow isn't a weapon. It's not a force to be commanded. It's a path."

Tink dusted herself off, her legs still unsteady from the intensity of their ordeal. Her fingers trembled as she wiped the sweat from her brow. "That's great and all, but what happens now? Do we get a break, or is another magical nightmare about to attack us?"

Vaelin's lips curled into the faintest ghost of a smile. "There are no breaks. Not for those who have chosen this road."

Brand glanced at the horizon, the sun dipping lower, casting golden hues that made the desert glow like molten glass. He felt different, lighter—but also burdened. Understanding the Flow hadn't just changed the way he fought—it had changed him.

Returning to the village, the sands whispered beneath their feet, shifting in gentle waves, as though nature itself acknowledged their passage. The night air was crisp, carrying the scent of distant fires and dry earth. Overhead, the first stars flickered into existence, scattered across the sky like fragments of an ancient puzzle.

Brand's mind churned. He could still feel the remnants of the wraith's presence, the way it had twisted the Flow, the way it had fought against release. The sensation left an imprint on him—like a shadow lingering at the edges of his perception. How many more of these things were out there?

He turned to Vaelin. "What was that thing, really?"

Vaelin didn't answer immediately. His eyes followed the shifting dunes, lost in thought. Finally, he said, "A fragment."

Tink frowned, adjusting the strap on her gear. "Of what?"

Vaelin's expression darkened, his usual stoicism weighed down by something heavier. "Of a past that refuses to stay buried. The CABAL isn't the only force that seeks to bend the Flow to its will. Others have tried. Some succeeded—for a time."

Brand felt a cold weight settle in his chest. "And they left behind... things like that?"

Vaelin nodded. "Yes. Some remnants still roam the world, echoes of those who sought to take what was never meant to be held."

Tink shuddered, wrapping her arms around herself despite the desert's lingering heat. "Fantastic. Ghosts of power-hungry lunatics. Just what we needed."

Brand looked ahead, the village lights flickering in the distance. Even from here, he could make out the familiar shapes of buildings, the faint hum of life returning to normal. It looked so small from here— as though the world they'd just stepped into belonged to another time.

"Then we must prepare—for whatever comes next," he said, his voice steadier now, tempered by resolve.

Vaelin placed a hand on his shoulder, his grip firm but not oppressive. "Understanding the Flow is just the first step. There will be more challenges ahead."

Brand met his gaze. "I know."

And for the first time, he felt ready.

By the time Brand, Tink, and Vaelin arrived at the outskirts of the village, it was alive with murmurs. The flickering lanterns lining the dirt pathways cast long, wavering shadows against the clay walls of the simple homes. Smoke curled from cookfires, the rich scent of roasted grains and spiced meats filling the air, but the usual warmth of the village felt subdued—as though the people sensed the change before they even saw them.

Brand could feel their eyes on him, watching from doorways and behind tattered cloth drapes. They knew something had happened. The Flow in this place had shifted, and while most couldn't feel it as he did, they sensed it in their own way.

A small group had gathered near the center of the village, their whispers barely veiled. Among them, the village elder, Eoran, a wiry man with deeply lined skin and sharp, perceptive eyes, stepped forward. His gaze flickered between Brand and Vaelin, lingering for a moment before he spoke.

"You went beyond the dunes," Eoran said, his voice even but heavy. "And returned changed."

The villagers behind him murmured, shifting uneasily. The desert was sacred—a place of secrets. Those who returned from its depths were never the same.

Brand met his gaze, standing taller. "We fought something... something old." He hesitated, then added, "Something wrong."

Eoran's expression didn't change. "And did you destroy it?"

Brand hesitated. "No."

A flicker of something unreadable passed through the elder's eyes. "Then you learned something."

Tink, standing beside Brand, exhaled. "Understatement of the year."

Eoran nodded slowly. "The Flow doesn't exist only in the bodies of warriors. It lives in the land, the sky, the hands that build, and the voices that call for change. You've returned, but you are not the same as when you left." He looked directly at Brand. "What do you see now that you did not before?"

Brand glanced around. Everything looked the same—the same homes, the same pathways, the same faces. But the world no longer felt small. He could feel the current beneath it all, a quiet song running through the village, connecting every voice, every breath.

"I see the Flow in everything," he said finally.

Eoran's expression softened, his head inclining slightly in approval. "Then you've taken your first step toward wisdom."

A silence settled between them, broken only by the shifting wind. The villagers still watched, uncertain, but Eoran turned to them. "Tonight, we eat. Tomorrow, we listen."

There was no argument. The tension eased, replaced by quiet understanding. They didn't yet know the full extent of what had happened beyond the dunes, but they would hear it in time. For now, there was food, warmth, and fire.

Tink let out a breath. "Finally, something I can get behind."

Brand, however, paid only half attention. His mind lingered on the horizon. This was just the beginning.

The celebration slowed as the fires burned low, the sounds of laughter and conversation fading into the stillness of the night. The scent of roasted meat and spiced ale hung in the air, but Brand barely noticed. His thoughts spiraled like the embers drifting into the dark sky.

He and Tink walked in silence through the narrow paths between the mudbrick homes, their steps unhurried, each one slow and deliberate. The village was settling, lanterns casting soft glows through open windows, their light stretching long, sleepy shadows across the sand. It felt different now—everything did.

Tink broke the silence. "You looked lost back there."

Brand smirked. "Maybe I am."

She nudged him lightly. "You? The guy who fought off a nightmare made of sand and shadow? Please."

He exhaled, glancing at her. "It's not that simple. I thought I knew what it meant to fight, to be strong. But now..." He trailed off, his mind searching for the right words. "It's like I was seeing with my eyes when I should have been listening. Like the world was speaking, but I never knew how to hear it."

Tink studied him for a moment, then nodded. "You're different."

He met her gaze. "Do you think that's a bad thing?"

She shook her head, her expression softer than usual. "No. Just means I've got to keep up."

They reached the small hut where Tink stayed, a modest space tucked away at the village's edge, far from the busiest paths. The wind had picked up, cool against their skin, carrying the scent of sand and desert blooms.

Brand hesitated at the doorway. "I don't know where this path leads."

Tink arched an eyebrow. "Since when do you need to know?"

He chuckled. "Fair point."

She stepped inside, leaving the door open for him. "You planning to stand out there all night?"

Brand hesitated for only a moment longer before following her in. The space was small but comfortable, warmed by the dying embers of a fire. The flickering light danced across her face as she turned to him, something unspoken passing between them.

She reached up, fingers tracing his jawline softly. "Stay."

He didn't answer with words. Instead, he pulled her close, feeling the steady rhythm of her heartbeat against his chest. Despite the chaos, the uncertainty—it felt real. It felt grounding.

The night stretched on outside, the desert vast and endless. But in this moment, there was only them.

Chapter 33:

A New Purpose

The first light of dawn crept over the horizon, bathing the desert in hues of gold and rose. A gentle breeze whispered through the village, stirring the dust along the narrow paths. The world felt quiet, expectant—as if it, too, was waiting for something.

Brand stirred awake, the warmth of Tink's body still pressed against his. Her steady breathing filled the small space, grounding him. For a moment, he let himself savor it—the rare peace of it all.

But the weight of the previous day settled quickly. The trial. The battle. The understanding that had taken root within him.

He carefully untangled himself and sat up, running a hand through his hair. As soon as he moved, Tink groaned softly and blinked at him. "If you're about to sneak out, don't."

He smirked, trying to lighten the mood. "You say that like I'm running."

She propped herself on one elbow, her gaze sharp even through the haze of sleep. "Aren't you?"

Brand exhaled, accepting the seriousness of the moment as he shook his head. "No. But... I need to talk to Vaelin."

Tink studied him for a moment, then nodded. "Figures. Go be all mystical and broody. I'll catch up later."

He leaned down and kissed her forehead before slipping out into the cool morning air.

Vaelin was waiting for him.

The old warrior stood on the outskirts of the village, his back to the rising sun, his presence as unmoving as the dunes. He didn't turn as Brand approached, only speaking once the younger man was close enough to hear.

"You have questions."

Brand nodded. "I don't know what comes next."

Vaelin finally faced him, his sharp eyes studying him as if weighing his very soul. "You know more than you think."

Brand crossed his arms. "I know I can't stay here. I know there's something bigger waiting out there. But I don't know where to begin."

Vaelin nodded slowly. "The Flow has opened itself to you. But you must decide how to walk with it. That is the burden of knowledge." He gestured toward the open desert. "You will not find your answers by standing still."

Brand followed his gaze, the endless horizon stretching before him. He had always known he would leave one day. That the village was never meant to be his final home.

But now, he understood why.

The village stirred with the quiet urgency of morning. Merchants unfurled their fabrics, laying out their wares, the scent of fresh bread and roasted grains drifting through the air. The world moved forward as it always did, but to Brand, everything felt different.

He walked with purpose through the winding paths, his steps deliberate, his senses attuned to the energy flowing through the village. The Flow was here too, in the smallest details—the laughter of a child, the rhythmic hammering of a blacksmith, the chants of an elder preparing morning prayers. He had walked these paths countless times, but today, he saw them with new eyes.

As he approached the central gathering space, familiar faces emerged from the crowd. Jorek, the ranger who had trained him, stood with arms crossed, his usual smirk tinged with something unreadable. Eoran, the village elder, stood near the temple steps, his sharp gaze locking onto Brand with knowing certainty. And beyond them, Tink.

She stood at the edge of the market, hands on her hips, waiting.

Brand slowed as he reached her, and for the first time, he hesitated. Leaving was one thing. Saying goodbye, another.

Tink sighed, shaking her head. "I knew this was coming."

Brand offered her a half-smile. "You always know things before I do."

She stepped closer, lowering her voice so only he could hear. "So, this is it? You walk off into the dunes, chasing fate?"

He exhaled. "It's not fate. It's choice."

Tink studied him, searching his face for something unspoken. After a long pause, she let out a quiet chuckle. "You're terrible at goodbyes."

Brand smirked. "Never had to make one like this before."

She reached up, fingers grazing the edge of his jaw, her touch lingering. "Then let's not make it a goodbye."

For a moment, he let himself absorb everything—the warmth in her eyes, the way the wind tugged at her hair, the steadiness of her voice. He would come back. He had to.

Behind them, Jorek stepped forward, breaking the moment. "Don't forget what I taught you, boy. If you die out there, I'll find a way to resurrect you just to kick your ass."

Brand chuckled. "Noted."

Eoran raised a hand, signaling the village's acknowledgment of his departure. There were no grand speeches, no drawn-out ceremonies. Only understanding.

Brand turned once more to Tink. She gave him the slightest smirk and nodded. "See you around, Striker."

The name felt different now. It was no longer just something he had made up in his youth. It was becoming who he was.

Without another word, he turned toward the dunes.

The desert awaited.

Brand's boots sank slightly into the shifting sand as he walked further from the village, each step heavier than the last. Before him stretched the vast expanse of golden dunes, bathed in the soft glow of the morning light. The sky was a clear, brilliant blue, unmarred by clouds. It was beautiful, yet it carried the weight of solitude.

The sounds of the village had faded behind him, swallowed by the vastness of the open desert. He could still feel their presence—the warmth of the people who had raised him—but it was already fading into memory, a place left behind. This was the path he had chosen, and though it did not make the distance easier to bear, it was his choice to make.

He turned once more, catching sight of the village one last time. It looked smaller, almost fragile, against the rolling dunes. He let the image linger, etching it into his memory. It wasn't just home—it was the foundation upon which everything else would be built.

A familiar presence brushed against his awareness. He didn't need to turn to know that Tink still watched from the edge of the village, standing where they had last spoken. She hadn't called out, hadn't run to stop him. But he knew she was there.

His fingers tightened around the hilt of his blade. He would return— one day.

The wind picked up, carrying the scent of dry earth and distant stone. It whispered through the dunes, a voice older than any language, guiding him forward. The Flow wasn't pulling him—it was walking beside him.

With a final breath, he set his sights ahead and took the next step.

The desert did not welcome. It tested.

And so, he walked into the unknown.

Chapter 34:

The First Trial of the Journey

The sun climbed higher, its relentless heat pressing down on Brand's shoulders as he trudged forward. The dunes stretched endlessly, rolling hills of golden sand that offered no shade or reprieve. The desert was not kind to travelers—it only demanded endurance.

The first few hours had been manageable. Now, every step felt heavier. His muscles burned, his breath slowed, and the weight of his supplies pressed relentlessly against his back. The village was long behind him, its warmth already fading into distant memory. Ahead, only the unknown remained.

He adjusted his pack, scanning the horizon. No map, no clear path— just instinct and the Flow.

A faint shimmer wavered on the horizon, just beyond the heat distortion. Something was there. A rock formation? A ruin? Or something less welcoming? The wind stirred behind him, whispering as it curled through the dunes.

Then, movement.

A low growl cut through the stillness, and Brand's body tensed. He turned his head slightly, listening. The sound was deep, guttural, unnatural.

His fingers tightened around the hilt of his blade.

From behind a cresting dune, a massive creature emerged, half-hidden by the shimmering heat. It stood on four legs, its body covered in thick, sand-colored fur that blended seamlessly with its surroundings. Its eyes glowed with an eerie amber light.

A sand prowler.

Brand had heard of them from the Rangers—pack hunters, stealthy, relentless. But this one was alone. Why?

The creature sniffed the air, locking onto him. A test. A warning. Or a hunt?

Brand lowered into a stance, letting his breath slow. The Flow stirred around him. He would not strike first.

The beast took a step forward, its muscles coiling.

Then, the air shifted.

A distant bell rang, soft but clear. The creature hesitated, its ears twitching. Brand turned his head in the direction of the sound. A caravan.

Emerging from behind the dunes, a line of riders and pack animals appeared, their forms draped in long, protective cloaks. They moved at a steady pace, their banners rippling in the dry wind. Merchants? Nomads? Or something more?

The prowler let out a final, warning growl before slinking away, disappearing into the dunes as if it had never been there.

Brand straightened, exhaling slowly.

This journey was not going to be as simple as he'd thought.

With one last glance at the fading silhouette of the creature, he turned toward the caravan.

Perhaps fate had set this path before him.

Brand approached the caravan cautiously, his hand hovering near the hilt of his blade. The desert had taught him well—not all travelers were friendly, and though these figures showed no signs of hostility, appearances could deceive.

As he drew closer, the lead rider pulled back his hood, revealing a weathered face marked by sun and time. His eyes were sharp, assessing. The cloak he wore bore intricate markings along the hem—symbols of trade, not war.

"You walk alone, boy," the man said, his voice rough, like sand grinding against stone.

Brand inclined his head. "For now."

The man studied him a moment longer, then gestured toward the pack animals. "Lone travelers don't last long out here. You carry yourself like one who's seen battle, but you tread with care. Where are you headed?"

Brand hesitated. Did he even know?

"The old paths," he said at last, letting the Flow speak through him.

The merchant's brow creased, but he asked no more. Instead, he turned to the others and motioned for the caravan to keep moving. "Walk with us a while," he said. "The road is less cruel with company."

Brand nodded and fell into step beside them. Their pace was steady, slow enough to preserve strength beneath the sweltering sun. The only sound was the soft crunch of sand beneath boots and hooves. The merchants spoke in low tones, their dialect slightly different from the village tongue, but familiar enough for Brand to follow fragments.

He caught murmurs of a place ahead—a ruin lost to time, where spirits wandered and the wind carried whispers.

A test of the Flow... or something darker?

A younger rider, perhaps his age, rode closer and gave him a curious glance. "You really mean to go to the ruins?" he asked, half-incredulous.

Brand met his gaze. "I go where I'm needed."

The young man snorted. "Then you're either a fool or a man with death chasing his heels."

Brand smirked. "Maybe both."

The caravan moved on, each step drawing them closer to the edge of the known world. And with it, the mystery of the road ahead deepened.

The caravan pressed forward, the rhythmic clinking of harnesses and low murmurs of the men blending with the desert wind that whispered through the dunes. The sun blazed overhead, casting elongated shadows that danced across the rippling sands. Ahead, a jagged outcrop of black stone jutted from the earth like the ribs of a buried beast, marking the entrance to the ruins.

Brand felt it before he saw it—the subtle shift in the air, the weight of something unseen pressing against his senses. The Flow trembled here, uneasy, as if the land itself was holding its breath.

One of the older merchants muttered a prayer under his breath, his fingers grazing a carved pendant hanging around his neck. The young rider from earlier, walking his camel alongside Brand, leaned in, his voice barely above a whisper. "You feel it too, don't you?"

Brand didn't answer immediately. He let the sensation wash over him—a presence woven into the wind, something ancient and watchful.

"I do," he said finally.

The merchant leader, his sun-browned face hardened by years of desert travel, raised a hand, signaling the caravan to slow. "We make camp here," he announced, his voice grave. "No one goes beyond the stones."

Brand studied the ruins ahead. What remained of the ancient structures was slowly being consumed by the desert, their edges worn smooth by centuries of wind. Something had stood here once— something powerful.

The merchants wasted no time setting up camp, driving stakes into the sand and draping fabric over their beasts of burden. Fires were kindled, the rich scent of spices and dried meat quickly filling the air. But beneath their mundane movements, an unspoken tension lingered, thick as the desert air.

Brand turned his attention back to the ruins, his gaze drawn toward the dark passageways that led deeper into the remnants of another age.

The wind howled through the broken stone, carrying whispers too faint to be understood.

He had the distinct feeling that something was waiting.

Night fell, settling over the desert in a thick shroud of silence. The fires from the caravan flickered weakly, their light barely cutting through the creeping darkness. Above, the sky stretched into infinity, a sea of glittering stars too distant, too indifferent to the world below.

Brand sat near the edge of the camp, his eyes fixed on the ruins. They were waiting. Not just the stones, not just the wind curling through the shattered walls—but something unseen, something ancient.

The merchants had retreated into their tents, their voices low, their laughter and stories softer than they'd been earlier in the night. Even the firelight seemed subdued, casting long, flickering shadows that danced along the sand.

The young rider who had spoken to Brand earlier sat nearby, sharpening a curved blade with slow, absent strokes. "You're thinking about going in, aren't you?" he asked, not looking up.

Brand exhaled, slow and steady. "I need to know what's inside."

The young man gave a dry, humorless chuckle. "People who go in don't usually come out."

Brand glanced at him. "And how do you know that?"

The rider's hand stilled on the whetstone. "Because my father was one of them."

Silence stretched between them, broken only by the soft hiss and pop of the fire. Brand studied the young man's face—there was a shadow there, something hollow in his gaze.

Before Brand could speak again, the wind shifted.

The campfires dimmed, their flames curling inward as though gripped by unseen hands. The air grew dense and heavy, pressing down like the first breath before a storm.

Then came the whispers.

Not from the men. Not from the wind.

From the ruins.

A chorus of voices—layered, echoing, distant. They spoke in a language Brand didn't know, yet somehow understood. The sound stirred something ancient within him, something the Flow recognized even if he did not.

His pulse quickened. The Flow beneath his skin shivered, vibrating with the same unsettling rhythm as the voices.

Beside him, the young rider had gone pale. "It's starting again," he murmured.

Brand rose, eyes fixed on the crumbling archways beyond the camp.

Something had awakened in the ruins.

And it was calling to him.

Chapter 35:

Into the Forgotten Depths

The wind howled through the ancient ruins, its whispers twisting through the broken corridors like unseen fingers reaching for something lost. The firelight of the caravan had faded to embers, but the murmurs of unease among the travelers persisted. The ruins were awake. And they were watching.

Brand stood at the edge of the camp, his fingers resting lightly on the hilt of his blade. Every instinct told him that stepping inside would change him. That nothing beyond the crumbling archways would be as it was before.

And yet, the pull was undeniable.

The young rider from earlier, still seated by the fire, watched him with quiet intensity. "If you go in, you go alone," he said. "No one will follow."

Brand nodded, unsurprised. The caravan feared the ruins, their stories speaking of men who entered, only to vanish without a trace. To them, it was cursed ground.

He drew a deep breath and stepped forward.

The first thing that struck him was the silence. The moment he crossed the threshold of the ruins, the wind outside ceased. The air hung heavy, unmoving, as though sound itself had been swallowed whole. His own footsteps barely echoed, muffled by the weight of time pressing in around him.

Stone columns rose from the sand like skeletal remains of a forgotten civilization, their surfaces etched with symbols that pulsed faintly in the dim light. Not dead. Not alive. Something in between. The columns stretched high above him, their tips broken and jagged, their very presence a testament to a time long past. The air carried the scent of old stone and the dry musk of sand trapped in forgotten places.

As he ventured deeper, the shadows seemed to shift, stretching unnaturally, as if they were watching him. Every few steps, his foot brushed against something buried in the sand—shattered pottery, rusted metal, remnants of lives erased by time.

Brand traced his fingers over the carvings. The moment his skin touched the stone, the whispers shifted.

No longer distant. Now, they were inside him.

His breath caught as his vision blurred, the world tilting around him. The symbols glowed brighter, their pulsing light spilling over his hands, crawling up his arms like veins of energy.

The stone beneath his feet softened—no, not softened. Shifted.

The ruins dissolved, and suddenly, he was not standing in a ruin—

He was somewhere else.

Somewhere ancient.

Somewhere, waiting for him to remember.

The world around him coalesced into something solid, something real. A vast city stretched before him, its towering spires glistening under the light of twin suns. The sky was an endless gold, and the streets thrummed with life, figures robed in flowing garments, their voices merging into a rhythmic hum—chanting, or perhaps a song carried on the wind.

Brand gasped, staggering back. But the vision did not break.

He was there. A city that should not exist, yet felt more real than anything he had ever known.

And deep in its heart, something was calling him forward.

Brand's breath came in shallow draws as he steadied himself. The city before him pulsed with life, untouched by time's decay. The golden glow of the twin suns painted long shadows across the stone pathways, their light refracting off the polished white towers that stretched toward the sky. But there was no heat. No wind. Only the overwhelming sensation that this place had been waiting for him.

He turned, expecting to see the ruins—the broken remnants of whatever civilization had once stood here. But they were gone.

Instead, the city lived.

Figures moved through the streets, their robes flowing like rippling silk. Some carried bundles wrapped in fine cloth; others walked in tight groups, their voices merging into an unceasing murmur that ebbed and flowed like the tide. They did not see him. Or if they did, they did not acknowledge his presence.

He took a hesitant step forward. The ground felt solid, real. The stone beneath his feet hummed with energy, warm, as if something vast and unseen coursed through it.

A distant chime rang out, deep and resonating, sending a pulse through the air. The figures all turned at once, their heads tilting toward the sound, their movements synchronized, as if guided by an unseen force.

Brand's skin prickled. This was not just a vision. This was a memory.

A rush of voices filled his mind—

"...the Flow is balance..."

"...the One watches all..."

"...harmony must be preserved..."

The words were not spoken aloud, yet he heard them. Felt them.

Then, as suddenly as it had begun, the world around him shuddered. The edges of his vision wavered, the golden sky darkening, the humming voices distorting into something less human.

The figures in the city ceased their movements.

One by one, they turned to face him.

Their faces—once serene—began to shift, their features melting away like wax, replaced by dark voids where eyes should have been. Their robes withered, their forms flickering between what was and what had been.

A voice, clear and resonant, sliced through the distortion.

"You should not be here."

Brand's pulse hammered in his ears. He turned toward the source—

And found himself staring into the eyes of something ancient.

Then the vision convulsed—the city fractured before his eyes, and slowly, the ruins rushed back.

Brand staggered back, gasping, the desert heat once again pressing against his skin. The carvings beneath his fingers had gone cold. The whispers had fallen silent.

But he could still feel it.

Whatever he had just witnessed—it had witnessed him too.

Brand stood frozen, his breath ragged, his heart pounding like a drum against his ribs. The presence before him was unlike anything he had ever encountered. It was neither flesh nor shadow, neither fully seen nor unseen. It stood just beyond the veil of reality, shifting in and out of form like a mirage in the desert heat.

The entity's eyes—or what he assumed were eyes—were pinpricks of white fire set into a figure composed of flickering gold and obsidian light. Its shape was humanoid, but only just. The lines of its body blurred, the energy within it barely contained, as though it existed in a state of perpetual unraveling.

Brand instinctively took a step back, but the entity remained unmoving, watching. The weight of its presence pressed down on him, a force beyond comprehension.

"Who are you?" Brand asked, his voice hoarse.

The figure did not respond immediately. Instead, a pulse of energy rippled outward, causing the ruins around him to distort momentarily—as though reality itself had been folded and reshaped.

Then it spoke, and the voice was not one but many, layered upon itself like echoes from different times.

"You do not belong here."

Brand clenched his jaw. "I didn't exactly ask to be here."

The figure tilted its head, studying him. "Yet you have come. Drawn by the remnants of what was. By echoes not meant for mortal minds."

Brand swallowed hard, his fingers twitching near the hilt of his blade, though he knew instinctively that no weapon could harm whatever this was. "The city—what was it? A memory?"

The light within the entity flared, casting long, jagged shadows across the crumbling ruins. "A warning."

Brand narrowed his eyes. "A warning of what?"

The air around him crackled, as if the ruins themselves resisted the answer. "Of what happens when the Flow is twisted. When balance is shattered." The figure's voice was calm, but beneath it was something vast—too ancient to be contained by words.

Brand exhaled slowly, his mind racing. The city—the people—it had all seemed so real. But if it had been a warning, then something had happened. Something catastrophic.

"You were part of it," Brand realized aloud. "Weren't you?"

For the first time, the entity moved, its form shifting closer, mere inches from him now. The temperature dropped, and the space between them hummed with energy that made Brand's skin prickle.

"I was the Guardian." The voice softened, almost mournful. "I protected what should never have been lost. But I was not enough."

Brand felt the weight of those words settle over him. A Guardian. A protector of something vast and powerful. And yet, they had failed.

A gust of wind rushed through the ruins, stirring the dust. The entity raised a hand—not quite solid, not quite light. The moment it did, the whispers returned, no longer warnings but pleading.

Brand gritted his teeth. "If this is a warning, then tell me—what am I supposed to do?"

The Guardian's form flickered, its edges unraveling like embers caught in the wind. "You must not follow the path of those before you. You must not seek control of the Flow."

The words sent a chill down Brand's spine. Control. It was the one thing he had always struggled with. The thing the CABAL wanted above all else.

The Guardian's voice grew fainter, the ruins around them seeming to collapse inward, shifting back to the real world. "You must..."

Brand took a step forward. "I must what?"

But the Guardian was already gone.

The ruins snapped back into focus, the weight of the moment vanishing like breath in the wind.

Brand stood alone.

But the warning remained.

Brand stood in the silence of the ruins, the Guardian's final words echoing in his mind, unshaken, like the reverberations of a forgotten bell. The air around him felt heavier now, as though the weight of ages lost pressed against his shoulders. You must not seek control of the Flow.

He exhaled sharply, scanning the broken temple around him. The carvings along the walls no longer pulsed with light; they had gone cold, dormant once more. Whatever connection had been awakened was slipping away, like water through his fingers.

But something remained. A presence. A knowledge buried deep within the ruin.

Brand took slow, measured steps, his boots crunching against the shattered stone. The Flow in this place was ancient, tangled with the remnants of what once was. He could feel it just beneath the surface, like the last flickers of a dying ember.

A glint caught his eye—a sliver of polished metal jutting from beneath a collapsed archway. He crouched, brushing away the dust and debris until his fingers closed around something smooth and cold.

With a sharp tug, he unearthed it.

A dagger.

But not just any dagger. Its blade was curved, its edge lined with strange markings that seemed to drink the light rather than reflect it. The hilt was wrapped in darkened leather, worn but intact. The weight was perfect in his hand, as if it had been forged for him.

As he turned it over, a sensation hummed through his body—not power, but recognition.

This weapon had been here for a reason. It had been waiting.

His fingers traced the inscriptions. He couldn't read them, but the meaning pressed into his mind nonetheless. A tool of balance. A blade not for conquest, but for... restoration?

Brand swallowed hard. He had never believed in destiny, but this... this felt different. The Flow had brought him here. The ruins had called to him.

A gust of wind rushed through the temple, sending a fresh wave of dust swirling around him. The whispers had faded, the Guardian gone, but the message was clear:

This was only the beginning.

Brand sheathed the dagger at his side and turned toward the exit of the ruins. The night stretched before him, vast and uncertain.

But he was no longer walking blindly.

He had a purpose now.

And he would see it through.

Chapter 36:

The Road Ahead

The ruins loomed behind Brand as he stepped back into the vast desert night. The air was sharp and cold, a stark contrast to the suffocating heat of the day. Above him, the stars burned brightly, scattered like shards of glass across an obsidian sky.

He adjusted his pack, feeling the weight of the dagger at his hip. A tool of balance, not conquest. The words echoed in his mind, reinforcing the Guardian's warning. Yet, he still had more questions than answers.

The campfires of the caravan flickered in the distance, their glow faint against the endless sea of sand. He had not expected them to wait for him.

As he approached, the young rider who had spoken to him earlier stood up from where he had been tending the fire. His expression was unreadable, but something in his stance—perhaps readiness, perhaps silent understanding—made Brand pause.

"You're still among the living," the rider said, his tone a mix of disbelief and reluctant respect.

Brand smirked. "Neither did I."

The merchant leader, the older man with the sun-worn face, rose from his seat. His eyes flicked to the dagger at Brand's side, but he said nothing. Instead, he motioned to the caravan.

"We leave at first light," he said. "If you're coming, be ready."

Brand nodded. He didn't know where this road would take him, but one thing was certain—

He was no longer just a boy from the desert. He was walking his path now.

And whatever lay ahead, he would face it.

The desert night stretched endlessly, the shifting sands illuminated only by the dim glow of campfires. Brand took a slow breath, feeling the cool air fill his lungs as he settled near the caravan's center, where the scent of charred meat and spiced grains mingled with the lingering smoke. The firelight cast flickering shadows over the gathered travelers, their faces worn by years of wandering beneath the relentless sun.

Soran, the merchant leader, sat on a thickly woven rug, a small metal cup in hand. His gaze flickered from the flames to Brand, as though measuring his worth, weighing something unspoken. The deep lines of his face, carved by the desert's cruelty, made him appear older than he likely was.

"You are not like the rest of us," Soran said at last, taking a slow sip from his metal cup. His voice carried the low, steady cadence of a man accustomed to command. "A man who steps into cursed ruins and walks out alive is either a fool or something else entirely."

Brand met his gaze, feeling the weight of unasked questions hovering in the space between them. "And which do you think I am?"

Soran's lips curled slightly. "Yet to be decided."

Across the fire, the young rider—Kaelen—huffed in amusement, tearing a piece of flatbread in half. "I say fool. Probably half-dead in there and too stubborn to realize it."

Brand smirked. "Maybe. Or maybe I just don't die easy."

Kaelen's grin widened. "That makes two of us."

A ripple of chuckles passed through the caravan members, their earlier unease fading. These men and women were survivors, traders, desert-born navigators who understood the weight of unspoken fears. But trust—trust was earned in the sands, where a man's word mattered more than any currency.

Soran tapped a ringed finger against his metal cup. "You plan to travel with us, then?"

"For a time," Brand replied. "I have no destination—just forward."

Soran nodded, as though expecting this answer. "Then you ride as one of us and abide by our laws."

Brand nodded in return. "Fair enough."

Soran's sharp eyes studied him for a moment before he gestured toward a leather pouch near the fire. "Then eat. A man walking his path still needs food."

Brand took a strip of dried meat and a handful of dates, the simple fare feeling more welcome than any feast. As he ate, the murmurs of the caravan surrounded him—discussions of trade routes, whispers of rising warlords in the north, and the ever-present dangers of the desert. He was among them now, but his path remained his own.

Still, for the first time since leaving the village, Brand felt the weight of the journey lighten—if only for a moment.

The night deepened, the once distant stars now sharp against the obsidian sky. The caravan's fires burned low, crackling softly as the travelers settled in—some wrapping themselves in thick cloaks, others dozing with weapons within arm's reach. The desert was quiet, but silence in the sands was rarely a comfort.

Brand remained awake, his back against a supply crate near the fire's edge. His fingers traced the hilt of his new dagger, its weight a constant reminder of the unseen forces now guiding his path. Across from him, Kaelen sat cross-legged, sharpening his curved blade with deliberate, rhythmic strokes.

"You should rest," Kaelen muttered without looking up. "You'll need your strength for the road ahead."

Brand exhaled, but he made no move to close his eyes. "I will."

Kaelen smirked. "You don't trust the dark, do you?"

Brand's fingers tightened around the dagger's hilt. "It's not the dark I don't trust. It's what moves in it."

A low breeze swept through the dunes, carrying with it a faint, unfamiliar scent—not the dry musk of sand and rock, but something else. Something unnatural.

Kaelen's expression darkened as he inhaled sharply. He moved fluidly to his feet, his blade now resting in his grip. Brand followed suit, his own senses sharpening. The Flow stirred—uneasy.

Soran, still awake and leaning against a saddle, lifted his head at their sudden movement. He studied them for only a second before speaking in a low, steady voice. "What is it?"

Kaelen's grip tightened on his weapon. "Something's watching us."

The wind shifted again, followed by a low, guttural sound.

It was distant, barely audible above the whisper of the dunes, but it sent a chill down Brand's spine. A growl. Not from a jackal, nor any desert beast he knew. This was different. Lower. Hungrier.

Soran cursed under his breath, rising slowly. His blade appeared from beneath his cloak. The caravan had faced dangers before—but this was something else.

Then, the growl came again. Closer.

The night, once still, came alive with unseen movement.

The air grew colder, thick with the scent of something wrong—a predator's scent. The low growls turned into a chorus, distant but circling, as if the creatures knew their prey had already sensed them.

Brand adjusted his stance, his grip tightening on the dagger. The weapon felt almost alive in his hand, its unfamiliar markings pulsing faintly under the moonlight. The Flow churned. It was no longer whispering—it was warning.

Kaelen moved beside him, shoulders squared, his curved blade held loosely but ready. "Jackals don't move like this," he muttered. "This is organized."

Soran stepped forward, his sword half-drawn. "Because they're not normal jackals," he said, his voice grim. "They're trained."

The realization struck Brand like a thunderclap. The CABAL. They had used these beasts before—twisted, engineered versions of desert predators, bred to track and kill.

Then, silence. Complete silence.

And then—A blur of movement.

The first beast lunged from the darkness, a massive form covered in black, matted fur. Its eyes glowed an unnatural, blood-red, locking onto Brand's throat. He had no time to think—

His body moved before his mind could. The Flow took hold.

Brand sidestepped, twisting just enough to avoid the snapping jaws. His dagger flashed in the firelight as he drove it downward, sinking deep into the creature's side. A shriek split the air, high and keening.

But there was no time to breathe.

More of them erupted from the dunes. Five. No, six.

The camp exploded into chaos. Swords drawn, shouts echoing in the night, the clash of metal against unnatural flesh. A merchant screamed as a beast dragged him down, its claws raking across his chest.

Kaelen moved with practiced grace, his blade cutting the air. A second beast lunged at him, but he pivoted, slicing through its throat in a single, fluid motion. Fast. Efficient. Deadly.

Soran, less graceful but equally effective, met his opponent head-on, catching its snapping jaws with the edge of his sword before kicking it back, sending it tumbling into the fire.

Brand turned just in time to meet another set of glowing eyes. This one was larger, its movements deliberate. A leader.

It circled him, testing, waiting. Intelligent.

Brand exhaled slowly, the Flow swirling around him, his body feeling lighter, faster. The dagger hummed in his hand, eager.

The creature lunged.

This time, Brand didn't move away. He moved forward.

With a twist of his wrist, he slashed across its snout, forcing it to recoil. He followed through, driving the dagger deep into its neck before ripping it free in a burst of dark, unnatural blood. The beast staggered, gurgling, and collapsed into the sand.

Around him, the battle was ending. The last of the creatures—those that had survived—fled into the darkness, their howls fading into the vast emptiness of the dunes.

A heavy silence followed.

Kaelen wiped his blade clean on a strip of cloth. "That was no random attack."

Soran sheathed his weapon, his expression dark. "No. It wasn't."

Brand exhaled, his heart still pounding in his chest. The Flow had saved him—had guided him. But the CABAL had found him.

And they would come again.

Chapter 37:

Signs of the Hunt

The first light of dawn painted the desert in hues of deep crimson and gold, but the beauty of the sunrise was lost on the weary caravan. The battle had left its mark—scorched sand, bloodied earth, and bodies, both human and beast, lying still beneath the morning sun.

Brand crouched beside one of the fallen creatures, his dagger still slick with its dark, unnatural blood. Up close, the beast was even more disturbing—its muscles unnaturally thick, its eyes still glowing faintly with the remnants of whatever dark energy had twisted it into existence. The CABAL's work.

"They won't stop." Kaelen muttered from behind him, his arms crossed over his chest. His usual smirk had vanished, replaced by something colder. "They've marked us now."

Soran, kneeling beside another corpse, wiped a hand over his face. "They were testing us."

Brand looked up, brow furrowing. "Testing?"

Soran nodded grimly. "These things hunt by design. They weren't here to kill us outright. They were here to see what we'd do." He gestured toward the largest of the beasts—the one Brand had slain. "And now they know."

Brand swallowed hard, his fingers tightening on the hilt of his weapon. The CABAL knew where he was now.

He straightened and turned toward the caravan, where the remaining merchants worked in grim silence to pack their belongings. The attack had cost them—two men lost, three injured, and one of the wagons ruined. Yet no one spoke of turning back. The desert was unforgiving, but retreat was never an option.

Kaelen let out a breath. "If we move fast, we might outrun them."

Soran shook his head. "We won't."

Brand met his gaze. "Then what do we do?"

Soran's eyes were dark with understanding. "We prepare. Because next time, they won't just be watching."

The desert stretched out before them, vast and indifferent, the endless dunes hiding whatever unseen forces now stalked them. The rising sun did little to ease the unease that clung to the caravan. The scent of burned flesh and blood still tainted the morning air, a reminder that the battle had been more than just a test—it had been a warning.

Soran moved among the survivors, speaking in hushed tones with the caravan's remaining fighters. They carried fresh wounds, their bodies bruised and battered, but their hands remained steady on their weapons. There was no fear left—only the hardened determination of men and women who had spent their lives surviving the desert.

Brand stood near the remnants of the broken wagon, watching as Kaelen finished wrapping a fresh bandage around his arm. A shallow cut ran just below his elbow—a lucky escape.

"Think they'll hit us again tonight?" Kaelen asked, his tone casual, but the tightness in his voice betrayed him.

Brand exhaled sharply. "They won't wait that long. They tested us once. Next time, they won't play games."

Kaelen scoffed. "Good. I was getting bored." But his fingers flexed over his blade's hilt, betraying his own readiness for the inevitable.

Soran approached, his expression grim. "We push forward. The nearest trade outpost is three days from here. If we move quickly, we can reach it before they strike again."

Brand glanced toward the horizon. The thought of running didn't sit well with him. "And what if we don't make it before they come?"

Soran's jaw tightened. "Then we make sure they regret it."

The others gathered as Soran laid out the plan. They would travel in tighter formation, keeping the remaining wagons within close range of the fighters. Scouts would ride ahead and behind, scanning for signs of another ambush. Every man and woman capable of wielding a weapon would carry one. They were no longer traders—they were survivors in a war they had never asked to fight.

Brand ran a hand over the hilt of his dagger, the cool metal grounding him. He had entered this caravan as a traveler. Now, he was something else.

His gaze drifted toward the distant dunes. The Flow stirred in him again, whispering something he couldn't yet understand. This fight was coming for him, whether he was ready or not.

And this time, he wouldn't just be defending himself.

He would be hunting them.

The caravan moved with quiet urgency, the rhythmic creak of wagon wheels blending with the soft crunch of hooves pressing into the sand. The desert sun hung high, an unforgiving eye that bore down on them with unrelenting heat. Despite the warmth, a chill ran through the travelers. They were being watched.

Brand rode near the front, his gaze fixed on the dunes ahead. The feeling had started just before midday—a prickling at the back of his neck, a shift in the air that set his nerves on edge. The Flow stirred again, not in warning, but in awareness. Something unseen was moving beyond the horizon.

Soran rode up beside him, his eyes sharp with the weight of experience. "They're out there." It wasn't a question. It was a fact.

Brand's fingers tightened on the hilt of his dagger. "They've been following us for hours... waiting," he thought, his heart pounding with both fear and resolve.

Kaelen, riding just behind them, let out a breath. "I hate waiting." His fingers drummed idly against the hilt of his blade, his body tense with anticipation. "Feels like they're toying with us."

Soran's expression darkened. "They are. That's what makes them dangerous."

Brand exhaled slowly, scanning the endless stretch of dunes. "We need to see them first."

Soran glanced at him, considering, then nodded. "We send scouts. Two riders ahead, two behind."

Kaelen grinned, already nudging his horse forward. "I'll go."

Brand turned to him. "I'm coming with you."

Soran didn't argue. "Take a wide path. Don't engage. Just get eyes on them."

Brand tightened his grip on the reins. "Understood."

The two of them peeled away from the main caravan, guiding their horses into the dunes. The terrain shifted beneath them, the golden sands stretching endlessly in all directions. Every crest they crossed felt like stepping deeper into unknown territory. They were hunters now, tracking shadows that refused to reveal themselves.

For a while, there was nothing but the rhythmic pounding of hooves and the unrelenting silence of the desert.

Then, Brand saw it.

A glint of movement—a ripple where there should be none. He yanked on the reins, bringing his horse to a sharp stop. Kaelen followed, his gaze darting to where Brand was looking.

The sand had shifted, but not from the wind.

Brand dismounted, his boots sinking slightly into the heated dunes as he crouched, running his fingers through the disturbed earth. Tracks. Not from animals. Too orderly. Too precise.

Kaelen let out a low curse. "That's not good."

Brand's jaw clenched. "No. It's not."

These weren't the tracks of beasts. These were the boots of men.

And they were closing in.

A gust of wind swept over the dunes, scattering fine grains of sand into the air. Brand remained crouched, his fingers pressed against the fresh tracks, his heart pounding in a slow, measured rhythm. The CABAL was here. Close.

Kaelen scanned the horizon, his fingers tightening around his blade. "We should get back."

Brand rose to his feet, his gaze locked on the undisturbed dunes ahead. He exhaled slowly, letting the tension settle deep into his muscles. No. If they were close enough to leave tracks, retreating wasn't an option.

"We're not alone," Brand murmured, his voice low.

Kaelen shifted slightly, his stance subtly adjusting. "How close?"

Brand's hand hovered near the hilt of his dagger. "Too close."

A silence settled between them, stretching long enough to feel unnatural. Even the wind had died, leaving only the vast emptiness of the desert around them.

Then—A flash of movement.

Brand's instincts screamed, and he twisted just as a bolt of searing energy ripped through the air where he had been standing. The heat of it singed past him, striking the sand and sending a plume of molten glass scattering into the wind.

Kaelen cursed, drawing his blade in an instant, his body shifting into a defensive stance. "Shit—snipers!"

Brand barely had time to register the warning before another blast erupted from the dunes. This time, he didn't dodge. He moved with the Flow.

His body twisted, his feet shifting in perfect rhythm with the pull of energy around him. The blast grazed his shoulder, but he was already moving, already pushing off the sand with a force that sent him barreling toward cover—a jagged rise of rock that barely offered enough protection.

Kaelen dropped down beside him, breathless, his blade ready. "I counted three. Maybe more."

Brand nodded, his pulse steady despite the rush of adrenaline. "They're flushing us out. They want us to run."

Kaelen's smirk was sharp despite the tension. "Well, they don't know me very well, then."

Brand exhaled, pressing his back against the rock, his mind racing. Three, maybe more. Snipers. That meant trained soldiers, not just CABAL hounds.

A voice cut through the silence, amplified by something unseen.

"We know who you are, boy. You can run, but we will always find you."

The voice was calm. Controlled. A hunter speaking to prey.

Brand's fingers curled around his dagger. They thought they were hunting him.

They were wrong.

He looked to Kaelen, his expression set. "We're not running."

Kaelen grinned. "Didn't think so."

Another blast tore through the air, but this time, Brand wasn't dodging. He was advancing.

Chapter 38:

Hunters and Prey

The scent of scorched sand filled the air as another energy blast struck the ground mere feet from Brand's cover. The heat pulsed against his skin, but his focus remained steady. This wasn't just an ambush—this was a calculated hunt.

Kaelen crouched beside him, eyes sharp, blade poised. "Three snipers, you said?"

Brand gave a curt nod, his senses attuned to the Flow, mapping the unseen currents of energy in the battlefield around them. The CABAL hunters were positioned well, high on the dunes, forcing them into predictable movements.

But the CABAL didn't understand him.

Not yet.

Brand closed his eyes for half a second, letting the Flow settle. His heartbeat slowed, the pull of energy shifting around him. The Flow didn't want to be commanded, only guided.

He exhaled, opening his eyes just as another shot streaked through the air. This time, he didn't dodge. He moved.

Launching himself forward, he rode the energy as though the desert itself propelled him. Sand kicked up in his wake as he sprinted up the nearest dune, his dagger gleaming in the rising light. The sniper atop the ridge barely had time to react.

Brand reached him in a blur, twisting past the barrel of the energy rifle before driving his dagger deep into the soldier's side. The CABAL agent gasped, his red-glowing eyes widening in shock as he fell. The hunt had just changed.

Kaelen wasn't far behind. The second sniper barely managed a shot before Kaelen's blade swept through the air, severing the man's throat. The body hit the sand with a dull thud, lifeless.

Brand turned, scanning for the third. The final hunter was already fleeing.

"Not this time," Brand muttered, giving chase.

The dunes stretched endlessly before him, but he was faster now. The Flow guided his steps, each push of his legs sending him forward. His heartbeat synced with the energy around him. The CABAL soldier turned, attempting to fire, but Brand was already on him—already striking.

His dagger struck true, slipping between the armor plates in the hunter's back. The soldier gurgled once before collapsing into the sand.

Silence fell over the desert.

Brand straightened, wiping the blood from his blade as he turned back toward Kaelen, who was still catching his breath beside the bodies.

Kaelen grinned. "Remind me never to hunt you."

Brand sheathed his dagger, his expression hard. "They weren't hunting me." His gaze drifted toward the horizon, where more of them waited. "They were just the first wave."

The wind carried the scent of blood and scorched sand, mixing with the faint, acrid tang of energy burned into the air. Brand stood over the fallen CABAL soldiers, his dagger still warm in his grip. The battle was over, but the war had just begun.

Kaelen wiped the sweat from his brow, surveying the dunes. "We need to get back to the caravan before more show up."

Brand nodded, scanning the horizon. The Flow still trembled, a warning that something was out there, just beyond sight. More were coming—it was only a matter of when.

They moved swiftly, their boots kicking up sand as they descended back toward the caravan's path. The sun burned hotter now, casting long shadows over the dunes, but the heat did nothing to thaw the cold tension in Brand's chest.

As they approached, Soran was already waiting, his sharp gaze locked onto them. "What did you find?"

Brand didn't hesitate. "Three CABAL hunters. Trained. They were positioned to box us in."

Soran's jaw tightened. "Casualties?"

"Not ours," Kaelen said with a smirk, rolling his shoulders. "But they'll be back."

Soran exhaled, glancing toward the others. The caravan members had gathered, sensing the shift in the air. They were no longer just merchants. They were survivors in a fight they hadn't chosen.

Brand took a step forward, voice steady. "We can't keep running. If we do, they'll pick us off one by one."

Soran eyed him carefully. "You have a plan?"

Brand met his gaze, the weight of the moment pressing down on him. "We turn the hunt on them."

A murmur rippled through the group. Some looked uneasy, others thoughtful.

Kaelen crossed his arms. "You want to set a trap?"

Brand nodded, his grip tightening on the hilt of his dagger. "They think we're prey. It's time we prove otherwise."

Soran considered this for a long moment before nodding. "Tell me what you're thinking."

Brand's fingers brushed the hilt of his dagger. He had spent his whole life learning to survive. Now, he would teach the CABAL what it meant to be hunted.

The midday sun blazed overhead as the caravan gathered in a loose circle, the weight of what was to come pressing heavily on their shoulders. The merchants, once wary travelers simply hoping to avoid trouble, now stood as something else—people preparing to fight for their survival.

Brand crouched, dragging his dagger through the sand to sketch a rough map of their position. "We use the terrain against them. The dunes are shifting, but the rock formations ahead provide cover. We force them into a narrow approach."

Soran nodded, studying the plan. "And when they come?"

Brand's gaze hardened, his voice low. "We hit them first."

Kaelen smirked, his hands already flexing around his blade. "I like this plan already."

Soran crossed his arms, his expression grim. "We don't have their numbers, or their technology."

Brand looked up, meeting Soran's gaze. "We don't need either. They think they're the hunters, but they don't know what it's like to be hunted. We lure them in, separate them, and take them down before they can regroup."

A murmur ran through the gathered fighters. Some nodded, others clenched their weapons tighter. The fear was still there, but it was beginning to shift—becoming something else.

Soran studied Brand for a long moment before exhaling slowly. "Alright. We do this on our terms."

The next hour passed in hurried preparation. Traps were laid— pits carefully disguised beneath layers of sand, jagged rocks placed strategically to break the enemy's advance. Those who could wield weapons were stationed at key vantage points, while the remaining caravan members were sent to the safest position they could find—if such a thing even existed.

Brand stood at the highest dune, watching as the last preparations were made. The Flow pulsed around him, swirling in a delicate dance of whispers through his senses. Something was coming.

Kaelen stepped up beside him, arms folded. "You sure about this?"

Brand exhaled slowly, his gaze still fixed on the horizon. "No. But running isn't an option."

Kaelen's grin returned, his eyes glinting with excitement. "Good. Would've hated to think you were losing your nerve."

A silence stretched between them as they stared out at the endless horizon. Then—a flicker of movement.

Dust rising in the distance. Shadows shifting, faint but unmistakable. The CABAL were coming.

Brand's grip tightened on his dagger, its hilt cool beneath his fingers. The trap was set. Now, all that remained was the fight.

The desert held its breath.

The caravan warriors crouched low, hidden behind ridges of sand and jagged stone. The heat pressed against them, beads of sweat trickling down their necks, but none dared move. Their moment was coming.

Brand knelt behind a formation of rock, his dagger gripped tight, his body coiled like a spring. The Flow pulsed at his fingertips, a soft hum of energy running through him. The CABAL had arrived.

Across the dunes, dark figures moved with calculated precision.

Their armor gleamed in the harsh light, sleek and deadly, their movements honed by ruthless training. These were not scavengers or wandering mercenaries. These were killers.

Soran signaled to the others, his fingers flashing a series of commands. Hold. Let them come closer.

Kaelen was tense beside Brand, his breath shallow. "They're too confident."

Brand nodded, his eyes locked on the approaching enemy. "They think this is another ambush."

"They're right," Kaelen smirked, his voice low. "Just not the one they planned."

The CABAL soldiers spread out, their eyes scanning the landscape, searching for the remnants of the caravan. They passed over the carefully concealed pits, oblivious to the dangers beneath the sand. The moment was now.

Brand moved first.

With a flick of his wrist, his dagger sliced through the air. The blade found its mark, embedding deep into the throat of the nearest soldier before he could even raise a cry. The man crumpled to the sand, lifeless.

And then—chaos erupted.

From the dunes, arrows rained down in a deadly storm. Hidden fighters exploded from the sand like wraiths, steel flashing in the sunlight. The trap had been set, and now it snapped shut around them.

The CABAL reacted quickly, their discipline keeping them from breaking rank. But it didn't matter. The shifting terrain, the unpredictable strikes of the caravan warriors, and the sheer savagery of their counterattack tore through their formation.

Kaelen moved like a shadow, his blade a blur as it carved through the enemy lines. Soran fought with brutal efficiency, his heavy weapon smashing through armor and bone alike.

Brand fought without thought, the Flow guiding his every movement. His blade struck with deadly precision, a blur of motion that was both fluid and brutal. He wasn't the hunted anymore. He was the storm.

The battlefield became a vortex of blood and steel. One by one, the CABAL soldiers fell. The few who managed to retreat fled into the desert, their formation shattered, their mission a failure.

Silence returned to the battlefield.

Brand exhaled, his pulse steadying. The Flow settled around him, its whispers fading as the chaos ebbed.

Soran wiped his blade clean, the blood smeared across the edge. "That was the easy part."

Kaelen grinned, rubbing his shoulder. "Easy? I think I pulled something."

Brand turned his gaze to the horizon. They had won this battle—but the war was far from over. The CABAL would not let this defeat go unpunished. His heart still beat with the anticipation of what would come next.

Chapter 39:
The Aftermath of Victory

The battlefield was silent now, yet the scent of blood still lingered in the air. The dunes were littered with the bodies of the fallen—CABAL soldiers sprawled where they had dropped, their once-imposing forms reduced to lifeless husks beneath the unyielding sun. The golden sand, once pristine, was marred by dark crimson stains.

Brand wiped his blade clean on a fallen soldier's cloak, his breathing steady but deep. They had won. But at what cost?

Around him, the caravan warriors moved through the wreckage, retrieving arrows, tending to the wounded, and ensuring no enemy had been left alive. Some of the merchants stood apart, their faces pale as they absorbed the carnage. They had expected danger, but not war.

Soran paced through the remnants of the fight, his gaze hard. "We struck first, we struck hard," he muttered. "But this won't be the end of it."

Kaelen sat on an overturned crate, pressing a strip of cloth to a wound on his arm. He smirked despite the pain. "I'd say we did pretty damn well, all things considered."

Brand crouched beside one of the fallen CABAL soldiers, turning the corpse over. The soldier's armor was branded with unfamiliar markings—a higher rank than the others they had faced. That was troubling. This wasn't just a scouting party. It was a sanctioned hunt.

He exhaled sharply. "They'll send more."

Soran nodded grimly. "And they'll be better prepared next time."

One of the younger caravan members, a boy barely old enough to hold a blade, approached with hesitant steps. "What do we do now?"

Brand looked past him, past the dunes, to the vast horizon beyond. Running wasn't an option anymore. They had bloodied the CABAL, and the CABAL never forgot.

"We move," he said, finally. "And we prepare for what's coming."

Soran clapped a hand on his shoulder, his grip firm. "Then we ride at first light."

Brand nodded, but deep in his heart, he knew—this fight was far from over.

The sun hung low in the sky, casting long shadows over the battlefield. The dead had been counted. The wounded had been treated. But the scars of the battle ran deeper than torn flesh or broken bones.

Brand sat at the edge of the camp, sharpening his dagger with slow, deliberate strokes. His mind still lingered in the rhythm of the fight— the way the Flow had guided him, the ease with which he had taken lives. It had felt natural. Too natural.

Soran approached, his presence heavy. "You fought well."

Brand didn't look up. "We all did."

Soran sighed, settling onto a crate beside him. His armor was scuffed, dried blood staining the edges. "You know what this means, don't you?"

Brand nodded. "They won't stop."

"They never do." Soran's voice was grim. "But we're not the same as we were before. The caravan's hardened. They've seen battle. They know what's at stake."

Brand glanced toward the others. The survivors sat in clusters, some speaking in hushed tones, others staring into the fire, lost in thought. The air was thick with exhaustion, but beneath it, something else lingered—a quiet, growing resolve.

Kaelen limped over, his usual grin subdued but still present. "If this is what every damn trip across the desert is like, I might start charging extra."

Soran chuckled, though the humor didn't reach his eyes. "If you live long enough to collect."

Kaelen smirked. "Oh, I plan to."

Brand exhaled, letting the tension in his shoulders ease just slightly. He had no illusions—this was only the beginning. The CABAL wouldn't let this insult stand. Their retribution would come, and it would be swift.

But for now, they had survived. And survival was a kind of victory in itself.

Soran stood, rolling his shoulders. "Get some rest, Brand. We move at first light."

Brand nodded, though he knew sleep would come hard. Not with the ghosts of battle still whispering in his mind.

As the fire crackled beside him, he tightened his grip on the dagger at his side. He wasn't just fighting for himself anymore.

The first hints of dawn painted the horizon in muted shades of violet and gold, but the caravan was already moving. There was no time to linger. The battle had bought them a sliver of freedom, but that freedom was fragile—the CABAL would return, and they wouldn't be so easily fooled again.

Brand rode near the front, his eyes scanning the terrain ahead. The dunes stretched endlessly, rolling waves of golden dust shifting under the wind's touch. But his thoughts weren't on the landscape. They were on what lay ahead—and what they had left behind.

Soran rode beside him, silent for a long while before speaking. "We're heading into rough territory."

Brand nodded. "The kind the CABAL doesn't control?"

Soran gave a small, humorless smile. "No such place exists. But they don't have as much sway here. The outposts ahead—some are neutral, some dangerous—but all are better than dying in the sand."

Kaelen, a few paces behind, groaned. "That's some real inspiring rhetoric, Soran."

The older warrior smirked. "You want inspiration, find a poet."

Brand allowed a small chuckle, but his focus remained ahead. The Flow was restless, whispering warnings he couldn't fully decipher, hints of danger beyond what they could see. The path ahead was uncertain, but one thing was clear—he was moving toward something. A crossroads. A turning point.

A gust of wind stirred the sand beneath them, and Brand caught sight of jagged rock formations in the distance, rising like the bones of a long-dead beast. The path ahead narrowed, forcing the caravan into a tight line as they navigated between the stone walls. It was the perfect place for an ambush.

Soran seemed to share the same thought. He muttered something under his breath before turning to Kaelen. "Double the scouts. I don't want surprises."

Kaelen nodded and fell back to relay the order. As he did, Brand spoke. "What kind of outpost are we heading for?"

Soran exhaled through his nose. "A trade hub of sorts. Small, but important. It sits at the edge of multiple territories, so it sees all kinds. Thieves, smugglers, mercenaries. The CABAL doesn't officially control it, but that doesn't mean they don't have spies there."

Brand frowned. "So we're walking into a nest of snakes."

Soran's mouth twitched in dry amusement. "That's one way to put it. But it's the best option we've got."

Brand's gaze drifted toward the horizon again. Something about this felt inevitable.

The caravan's pace increased, the weight of survival pressing them onward. They would reach the outpost by nightfall, a place where news traveled fast and eyes watched every stranger who entered. A place where the next step in Brand's journey would begin.

And he had the distinct feeling that whatever came next would change everything.

The outpost emerged from the desert like a scar upon the landscape—a sprawl of sand-blasted stone buildings, makeshift tents, and weathered metal structures battered by time and heat. It was no city, but it pulsed with life. Merchants bartered, voices rising over the distant clang of metal on metal as blacksmiths worked. The air smelled of spice, sweat, and the sharp bite of burning fuel.

Brand took in the sight from atop his horse, his fingers tightening around the reins. The place was alive, but something felt wrong. The Flow rippled around him, carrying whispers of tension—unseen currents of conflict woven deep into the fabric of this settlement.

Soran guided his horse alongside him. "Welcome to Ashara Outpost," he muttered. "Not as bad as it looks. But not much better, either."

Kaelen let out a low whistle. "Smells like a marketplace and a graveyard had a child."

Soran smirked. "That's not far from the truth."

They entered the main thoroughfare, weaving through the crowd. Eyes followed them—some curious, some wary, others calculating.

A group of men in patchwork armor stood near a supply station, their weapons visible but at rest. Hired muscle. They watched the newcomers with practiced indifference—the kind that masked a readiness for violence.

Soran leaned toward Brand. "Keep your weapons in sight, but don't reach for them unless you have to. The outpost has its own rules, and you don't want to learn the hard way what happens if you break them."

Brand nodded, but his senses remained sharp. Something about this place made him uneasy.

They rode toward a low, circular building near the center of the outpost. A large sigil was carved above the entrance—an ancient symbol, weathered but still recognizable. It marked this place as neutral ground, a hub where alliances could be formed—or betrayed.

Soran dismounted first. "We'll find a place to rest here. But keep your guard up."

Brand followed suit, his boots hitting the ground with a muted thud. The outpost buzzed with movement, but beneath the noise, something deeper stirred.

He didn't know what it was yet, but he would soon find out.

Chapter 40:

Whispers in the Dark

The air inside the circular building was thick with the scent of burning incense and aged wood. Dim lanterns cast flickering shadows against the stone walls, their soft glow barely cutting through the gloom. The low murmur of voices echoed through the space—a mixture of traders, mercenaries, and travelers gathered beneath the same roof, all seeking shelter, information, or simply a place to disappear.

Brand stepped forward cautiously, his senses alert. The Flow here was dense, tangled with energies from too many people bearing too many secrets.

Soran led the way, weaving through the crowded room toward a raised platform at the back, where a woman in long, embroidered robes sat. She was older, her face lined with experience, but her eyes remained sharp—taking in every new arrival with the ease of someone who had survived far too long in a place like this.

Soran gestured toward her. "That's Rasha. She runs this place. If there's news worth knowing, she's already heard it."

Kaelen leaned in slightly, smirking. "She doesn't look dangerous."

Soran's lips twitched. "That's what makes her dangerous."

Brand felt it now—the weight of Rasha's presence. Not physically, but something deeper. She commanded influence here, power forged not by force but by knowledge.

As they approached, Rasha's gaze fixed on them. "You bring trouble with you, Soran."

Soran sighed. "We usually do."

Her eyes flickered toward Brand, studying him with unsettling intensity. "And this one? He's different."

Brand met her gaze, saying nothing. He'd learned long ago that silence could carry more weight than words.

Rasha leaned back, a slow smile curving her lips. "I've heard whispers. The CABAL is moving. They're looking for something—or someone."

Soran's expression darkened. "We know. We ran into some of their scouts."

She nodded, unfazed. "Then you understand why you need to be careful here."

Kaelen crossed his arms. "We're always careful."

Rasha chuckled softly. "No, you're not."

Brand exhaled, his fingers brushing the hilt of his dagger. The Flow stirred again, the weight of unseen eyes pressing against him.

Someone was watching them.

And whoever it was—they were already moving.

Rasha's gaze lingered on Brand a beat too long, her fingers tapping lightly against the worn wood of the table. She was calculating. Weighing something. Finally, she gestured to the empty chairs across from her. "Sit."

Soran didn't hesitate, sinking into a seat with the ease of someone well-accustomed to dealings like this. Kaelen leaned against the back of a chair but didn't sit, his usual smirk still firmly in place. Brand, however, remained standing.

Rasha's eyes gleamed with quiet amusement as she studied him. "Distrustful. Smart."

Brand crossed his arms. "You said the CABAL is looking for someone. How much do you know?"

Rasha exhaled slowly, weighing her response. "More than most. Less than I'd like." She flicked a glance toward the room behind them. "Word travels fast in places like this. When the CABAL starts moving in ways that break from their usual patterns, people notice."

Soran nodded, eyes narrowing. "And?"

She leaned forward, her voice dropping to a near-whisper. "They're looking for a boy. One who shouldn't exist. One who—" She paused, her gaze flicking over Brand again, this time more calculating. "One who carries something inside him that they fear."

Brand's jaw tightened. The Flow surged violently, almost as if it were trying to escape him.

Kaelen's expression sharpened. "You're saying they're scared of him?"

Rasha's lips twitched into a half-smile. "Not yet. But they will be."

A heavy silence followed.

Finally, Brand sat, his muscles coiled like a drawn bowstring. "What do you want from us?"

Rasha chuckled softly, shaking her head. "Straight to the point. I like that." She lifted a hand, palm up. "I deal in knowledge. And knowledge, my dear boy, is far more valuable than gold."

Soran leaned forward, eyes hardening. "And what would it cost to buy yours?"

Rasha's smile deepened. "A favor. A small one."

Kaelen groaned. "It's never small."

Rasha ignored him. "There's a man here. Dangerous, even by this outpost's standards. He deals in things that shouldn't be sold. And I want him gone."

Brand exhaled slowly. "You want us to kill him."

Rasha's face remained unreadable. "I want him removed. How you do it is your choice."

Soran rubbed his temple, his frustration evident. "And in return?"

Rasha's eyes gleamed with something dangerous. "I'll tell you exactly what the CABAL is after—and where they plan to strike next."

Brand exchanged a brief glance with Soran, then Kaelen. The decision was easy.

He leaned forward, his voice a low rasp. "Where do we find him?"

Rasha's slow smile was all the confirmation he needed.

The air in the outpost had shifted.

Rasha's words still echoed in Brand's mind as he, Soran, and Kaelen moved through the twisting alleyways between the stone structures of Ashara Outpost. The familiar scent of spice, sweat, and smoke clung to the narrow corridors, but beneath it all, something darker stirred—something that set the hairs on the back of Brand's neck on edge.

Brand adjusted the dagger at his side, his gaze fixed ahead. "Who is he?"

Soran's stride remained unbroken. "Garron Vale. A trader, by title. But what he deals in isn't just goods—it's people, secrets, weapons. The kind that make men disappear."

Kaelen scoffed. "Charming."

Brand's expression hardened. "Why does Rasha want him gone?"

Soran's eyes flicked briefly to the side. "She didn't say. But men like him don't last long in places like this unless they've got powerful friends. And Rasha doesn't make moves unless she's sure the odds are in her favor."

Kaelen grinned. "Meaning we're the odds."

As they moved deeper into the outpost, the atmosphere shifted. The northern quarter was quieter—its buildings old, worn by time and desert winds. The kind of place where the law had long been forgotten.

They arrived at a squat, multi-leveled structure of reinforced stone and metal. The entrance was guarded by two men in dark clothing, weapons holstered but ready. They weren't watching for trouble. They were expecting it.

Brand slowed, his instincts flaring. "We're walking into a trap."

Soran exhaled sharply, a dry laugh in his voice. "We always are."

Kaelen cracked his knuckles. "So, what's the plan? Knock on the door and see if he's home?"

Brand's hand flexed around the hilt of his dagger. There was no avoiding this fight. But they could control how it started.

His eyes scanned the structure. There were other ways in. Other paths.

He smirked. "No. We go in from above."

Kaelen blinked. "Above?"

Soran followed Brand's gaze, then nodded slowly. "That could work."

Brand's movements were already decisive, his mind mapping their route. "Then let's move before we lose the advantage."

As they slipped into the shadows, the weight of what was coming settled on them like a storm cloud.

Garron Vale's time had run out.

The rooftop beneath Brand's palms was rough and warm from the day's heat. He crouched low, breathing steady, eyes fixed on the dim balcony ahead. This was their entry point.

Kaelen shifted beside him, voice barely a whisper. "I'm still voting for kicking in the front door."

Soran shot him a sharp look. "And walking straight into an ambush? No."

Brand's smirk stayed in place, but his focus remained razor-sharp. "This way, we control the fight."

Below them, the guards at the entrance stood unmoving, their postures relaxed but alert. Mercenaries, most likely. Men who could kill without a second thought—men who worked for Garron Vale.

Brand exhaled quietly. "Fast. Quiet. Take out anyone between us and Vale."

Soran gave a curt nod. "No wasted movement."

Kaelen sighed, stretching his neck. "Fine. Your way. For now."

Without waiting, Brand launched himself across the gap between the buildings. His landing was soft, controlled. He rolled forward, the impact absorbed, and pressed his back against the stone railing. The shadows swallowed him whole.

Soran and Kaelen followed, their movements swift and practiced. Seconds later, they were inside.

The corridor ahead was dim, the scent of old leather mingling with the acrid tang of burning oil. Brand held up a hand, signaling them to stop. Faint voices echoed from further ahead.

Soran drew his blade with a smooth, deliberate motion. Kaelen followed suit, his grin predatory. They had done this many times before.

Footsteps echoed down the hall from their right. A guard. Alone.

Brand didn't hesitate. He moved like a shadow, a quick wrap around the guard's throat, pulling him into the darkness. The man struggled, but it was over before he could make a sound.

Kaelen whistled low. "Efficient."

Brand's eyes never left the hallway. They were close now.

Ahead, a heavy door was slightly ajar, flickering light spilling from inside. Voices drifted toward them.

"—the shipment's on schedule. If she doesn't pay, we sell the lot elsewhere."

A second voice, deep and controlled. "She'll pay. She always does."

Soran's face darkened. "That's Vale."

Brand's grip on his dagger tightened. This was it. Time to finish it.

He pushed the door open, moving without a moment's hesitation.

Garron Vale sat behind a desk, his sharp features lit by the flickering lantern. His eyes widened in shock, just a moment too late, before Brand was on him.

Chapter 41:

Disappearing Act

The flickering lantern cast jagged shadows across the walls as Brand lunged. Garron Vale's reaction was swift—too swift for a mere merchant. His chair flew back as he reached beneath the desk with practiced ease.

Brand spotted the flash of steel before Vale even cleared the wood.

He was ready.

Brand twisted mid-strike, narrowly dodging the upward slash. His dagger flashed, slicing across Vale's forearm. A sharp curse escaped Vale's lips as the weapon dropped from his grip, blood spraying dark against the firelight.

Soran moved in immediately, his blade striking the edge of the desk, splintering wood as he pushed forward. But Vale was no ordinary trader.

With a fluid roll, Vale sprang to his feet, cradling his injured arm against his chest. His breath was ragged, but his eyes were calculating. No panic. Just strategy.

"Who sent you?" Vale rasped, voice rough yet steady.

Brand didn't answer. His focus remained razor-sharp.

Kaelen emerged from the shadows, cutting off Vale's only escape route. "No one important." He grinned, his voice dripping with sarcasm. "You, on the other hand... not so lucky."

Vale's lips twitched, his fingers twitching at his side. Something was wrong.

Brand felt it in the Flow—an unsettling surge, an unseen force gathering like a storm inside him. His pulse quickened.

Then he saw it.

Vale's good hand, still resting at his side, his fingers slowly curling. Not from pain—but from preparation.

Brand's heart skipped. He barely had time to react before it hit.

An explosion detonated beneath the desk with a deafening roar, hurling Brand and Soran backward. The lantern shattered, plunging the room into near-total darkness. Smoke, dust, and the acrid scent of scorched wood filled the air.

Coughing, Brand shoved himself to his feet, his ears ringing. His eyes locked on Vale—bloodied, but still moving. Still alive.

And escaping.

Soran was already recovering, shaking off the blast. "We can't let him slip away."

Brand didn't need the reminder.

He surged forward, his boots pounding against the wooden floor as he bolted toward the shattered door. The night air hit him like a punch, thick with smoke and the iron tang of blood.

Ahead, Vale was already moving, fast despite his injury. He weaved through the labyrinth of narrow alleyways, his cloak trailing like a shadow, vanishing into the chaos of Ashara Outpost.

Soran was only a step behind, blade drawn and steady. "Split up—cut him off!"

Without hesitation, Brand veered left, springing onto a stack of crates before pulling himself onto the rooftops. From his vantage point, he saw the chaotic paths of the outpost below—Vale's desperate figure knocking over barrels and shoving past startled merchants.

Kaelen stayed grounded, tearing through the narrow streets, his breath ragged but focus sharp. "Keep him heading toward the docks!"

Vale's speed was unnatural. His movements were too precise, and the deep gash on his arm seemed to have no effect on his stamina. Brand's thoughts raced. The Flow had been warning him—Garron Vale wasn't just a merchant. He was something more.

Vale darted into a side street, vanishing from view. Brand leapt from the rooftop, landing heavily and rolling to his feet. He expected an ambush—but the alley was empty.

Too empty.

He slowed his steps, dagger drawn, the Flow whispering warnings in the back of his mind. Something wasn't right.

Then—movement.

Vale wasn't fleeing. He wasn't panicking. He was waiting.

Brand barely had time to react before Vale struck. His movements were impossibly fast—far beyond what any normal man could achieve.

A knife flashed—Brand twisted, but the blade grazed his shoulder, a searing sting through his cloak. He countered immediately, slashing with deadly precision, but Vale was already gone, a shadow vanishing into the dark.

Soran rounded the corner just in time to see the flicker of Vale's retreat. "What the hell—?"

Kaelen skidded in behind him, his eyes narrowing. "What is he?"

Brand's breath steadied, his grip tightening on his dagger. He wasn't sure what Vale was, but one thing was clear:

Garron Vale wasn't just a man.

And he wasn't planning on dying tonight.

Brand's heartbeat pounded in his ears as the night air grew thick with tension. There was no fleeing now—Vale stood in the alley, poised and deliberate. He was no man running for his life; he was a predator, choosing his moment.

Soran and Kaelen flanked Brand, weapons raised. The shadow beneath Vale stretched long in the dim torchlight, but it wasn't right—it moved unnaturally, as if it didn't belong to him.

"Stay sharp," Soran muttered. "He's not human."

Vale exhaled a slow breath, his wounds should have been slowing him down. Instead, he looked stronger, more alive than before.

"You're persistent," Vale said, his voice unnervingly calm. "But you don't understand what you're chasing."

Kaelen snorted. "We're chasing a dead man."

Vale's lips curled into a smirk. "Are you?"

Then he moved.

Not with the frantic pace of a man fleeing death, but with the seamless grace of something far beyond human. His movements were fluid, disjointed in a way that made the world itself seem to bend around him.

Brand felt it instantly. The Flow. But it wasn't the natural current he knew. This was something controlled—twisted.

"Move!" he barked, urgency bleeding into his voice.

Vale struck first, a blur of motion, his blade flashing. Brand ducked just in time, the cold bite of steel grazing the air where his throat had been. Soran lunged, his sword cutting a wide arc, but Vale dodged, too fast—twisting in mid-air, like he'd seen the strike coming before it happened.

Kaelen charged from the side, but Vale's reflexes were inhuman. He caught Kaelen's wrist mid-strike, twisting with such force that the crack of bone echoed through the alley. A sharp cry. Kaelen crumpled, clutching his arm.

Brand didn't hesitate. He drove forward, dagger raised, aiming for Vale's ribs.

The blade struck, but instead of sinking into flesh, it met resistance—

something invisible, a barrier not of matter, but of energy. A distortion.

Vale's grin widened, cold and knowing. "You're learning."

Then, without warning, he vanished.

Not fled. Not running. Simply gone.

Brand's heart hammered in his chest. The alley was deathly silent. No movement. No sound. Only the dry whisper of the desert wind.

Kaelen groaned, pushing himself up with one hand. "What the hell was that?"

Soran's face was grim, his eyes shadowed with realization. "He's not a man."

Brand sheathed his dagger, his fingers still trembling from the encounter. CABAL agents bent the Flow to their will—mimicking the power of the gods themselves. But Vale wasn't just one of them.

Vale was something worse.

The silence stretched, unnatural, suffocating. The wind carried no sound, no trace of Vale's presence—just the cold chill of something unnatural lingering in the air.

Brand turned slowly, scanning the shadows. His mind churned, piecing together what they had just witnessed. Vale had bent the Flow—but not like Brand. This wasn't a man attuned to the Flow. This was something entirely different.

Soran exhaled sharply, wiping sweat from his brow, his gaze still fixed on the empty alley. "That wasn't an assassin. That was something... worse."

Kaelen flexed his injured arm with a grimace. "So, what's our plan? Ghost? Demon? Because whatever the hell that was, it's way beyond what we signed up for."

Brand didn't respond immediately. Instead, he moved toward the spot where Vale had vanished, his eyes scanning the air. The disturbance was still there—a subtle tension, as if the fabric of reality itself had been warped.

"We weren't meant to kill him," Brand muttered under his breath. "We were meant to see him."

Soran's gaze sharpened. "What do you mean?"

Brand's jaw tightened. "Rasha knew exactly what he was. She sent us after him, knowing full well we'd be walking into something we couldn't fight."

Kaelen's breath was sharp, disbelief mixing with anger. "So we were bait?"

Brand nodded grimly. "She wanted to see if we could survive it."

Soran's eyes narrowed, the realization settling over him. "Then we need answers. Now."

They retraced their steps through the winding alleys of Ashara Outpost. The usual murmur of trade and commerce seemed distant, swallowed by the weight of the truth they had just uncovered. What had started as a simple bounty was now something far darker, more complex.

When they reached Rasha's quarters, Brand could feel her presence even before they stepped through the door. She was waiting for them.

The door stood ajar.

They entered.

Rasha was seated at her usual place, hands folded, eyes unreadable. She didn't react to their arrival.

Brand didn't waste a moment. "What is he?"

Rasha's head tilted slightly, a curious glint in her eyes. "You tell me."

Soran took a step forward, his patience snapping. "He disappeared. He should be dead. And yet he's out there, waiting for us."

Rasha's lips curled into a smile, but it was devoid of warmth. "So you understand now. The CABAL's influence reaches far beyond just warriors. They've created... projects. Things twisted by the Flow, but no longer bound by it."

Brand's hand clenched around the hilt of his dagger. "You knew what he was. And you sent us anyway."

Rasha leaned forward slightly, her voice low. "I needed to see if you were ready."

The room went still. The air thickened with the weight of her words.

Kaelen scoffed, shaking his head. "Ready for what?"

Rasha's eyes locked onto Brand's, unblinking. "For war."

Chapter 42:

The War in the Shadows

The air inside Rasha's chambers was thick with unspoken tension, each word hanging like a weight they couldn't escape.

Brand's fingers flexed at his sides, the memory of Vale's impossible movements still reverberating in his mind. "You knew this would happen," he said, his voice low and edged with accusation.

Rasha's head tilted slightly, her expression unreadable as always. "I knew it was possible. I needed to see how you'd handle it."

Kaelen scoffed, his patience finally snapping. "Oh, we handled it alright. And in return, he nearly took my damn arm off." He flexed his fingers, wincing as pain shot through the joint.

Soran stepped forward, his voice steady but sharp. "You said the CABAL has projects. What does that mean?"

Rasha leaned back, fingers tapping a slow rhythm on the armrest, her eyes never leaving them. "It means they've long since stopped relying on soldiers. They've begun experimenting—on men, on the Flow itself. They want to shape it, control it, and, in doing so, create something beyond human."

Brand's jaw clenched, a knot of dread tightening in his gut. This was worse than he'd feared.

Kaelen's smirk faltered. "So we're not just fighting tyrants, but their freakish science experiments too?"

Rasha's nod was slow, deliberate. "Exactly."

Soran's arms crossed, his voice turning colder. "And Vale?"

Rasha's gaze darkened, her lips tightening into a thin line. "He was one of their successes."

Brand exhaled sharply, running a hand through his hair. "Then why let him live?"

Rasha's smile was ice. "Because the CABAL doesn't tolerate failure. Vale was meant to be untouchable, unseen. You forced him into the light."

Soran's brow furrowed. "So you're saying they'll come for him?"

Rasha's eyes flickered, a brief flash of something unreadable. "No. I'm saying they'll come for you."

The weight of her words slammed into them like a wave. There was no time to process it, no room for hesitation. The CABAL was coming—and they weren't prepared.

Brand forced his thoughts to the present, pushing aside the dread gnawing at the back of his mind. "How long do we have?"

Rasha's eyes were unreadable as she answered. "Not long. A day, maybe less. They'll want to eliminate you before you can vanish."

Soran's sharp exhale cut through the silence. "Then we prepare now."

Kaelen winced as he rolled his injured shoulder. "As much as I love a good fight, we're not exactly an army. We barely survived Vale, and we still don't even know what the hell he is."

Brand's fingers twitched at his side, still feeling the strange distortion Vale had left in the Flow. Fighting him had been like striking at a mirage—something that didn't quite exist.

Rasha stood and moved toward a set of shelves along the back wall, her fingers brushing across the spines of ancient tomes. She selected one, opening it to reveal pages filled with symbols Brand couldn't make sense of.

"These experiments the CABAL is running," she said, flipping through the book, "they're not new. The knowledge they've rediscovered is ancient—twisted, weaponized."

Brand stepped forward, eyes scanning the symbols. "And you have this knowledge?"

Rasha smiled faintly. "Enough to understand what we're facing. Not enough to stop it. Not yet."

Soran's arms crossed tightly, his voice sharp. "So what do we do?"

Rasha closed the book with a decisive snap. "Leave Ashara Outpost. The CABAL will burn it to the ground if they think they're harboring you."

Brand's gaze sharpened. "You're sending us away?"

She shook her head, her eyes steely. "I'm giving you a chance to choose the battlefield."

Kaelen raised an eyebrow, his lips curling into a smirk. "Now that, I like."

Brand let out a slow breath. This was no longer just survival—it was about gaining the upper hand.

His gaze met Rasha's, steady and unwavering. "Where do we go?"

Rasha hesitated for only a moment. "To the ruins west of here. There's something buried there. Something the CABAL desperately wants."

Soran frowned. "And you think we'll get to it before they do?"

Rasha's expression darkened. "You don't have a choice."

Brand felt the weight of her words settle over him, heavy and undeniable. The war had already arrived. The only question was who would strike first.

The outpost felt unnaturally quiet now. Not peaceful, but the kind of silence that only came before a storm—thick with the promise of bloodshed.

Brand moved quickly through the alleys, his steps light but purposeful. They needed to be gone before the CABAL arrived.

At the stables, Kaelen was already securing their supplies. "So, I guess no goodbye speeches, huh?" he said, tightening the final strap on his pack.

Soran stood beside him, checking his weapons. "No goodbyes. Just distance."

Brand glanced back at Ashara Outpost, the place that had briefly been a refuge—and now was a target. "They'll come for Rasha."

Soran's nod was grim. "She knows."

Rasha had insisted they leave, but something didn't sit right with Brand. She had known about Vale, sent them after him, used them as pawns. But for what? What was she waiting for?

A shadow flitted along the rooftops, barely a flicker against the rising dawn. They weren't alone.

Brand's head snapped to the side, scanning the ridge of buildings. Nothing. Only the oppressive silence, as though the world itself was holding its breath.

"Let's move."

They mounted their horses, the western path stretching ahead. The ruins. The answers. And the CABAL, lurking in the wings.

As the outpost receded into the distance, Brand knew—this wasn't just an escape. It was the beginning of something far bigger.

The desert lay before them, endless and unforgiving. A sea of shifting dunes, their crests bathed in the first light of the sun, beckoned them forward.

The air was still cool, but the promise of heat was already pressing against their backs. Brand kept his focus straight ahead, his senses on high alert. The CABAL wouldn't be far behind.

Soran rode alongside him, scanning the horizon. "We've got a lead, but not much to go on."

Kaelen, further behind, chuckled darkly. "Still better than waiting around to be skewered."

Brand didn't respond, his mind fixed on the ruins ahead. Why had Rasha sent them? What lay buried there that the CABAL craved? And why them?

The wind shifted, carrying a strange chill—a whisper of something unseen.

Brand's grip on the reins tightened. He turned his head just enough to catch a shimmer on the horizon. Like heat rising from the sand— but wrong. Too deliberate.

Soran saw it too. "We're being followed."

Kaelen muttered a curse under his breath. "Didn't take long, did it?"

Brand's thoughts raced. They were too exposed. The CABAL could cut them down before they even reached the ruins.

But this wasn't an attack. Not yet.

"They're watching us," Brand murmured. "Studying."

Soran's frown deepened. "Then let's make it hard for them."

Brand nodded, eyes narrowing. "Ride hard. If they want to follow, let's see how far they'll go."

The three of them spurred their horses into action, dust trailing in their wake as they galloped toward the ruins. If the CABAL wanted them, they'd have to earn it.

And Brand was ready to test just how far they were willing to go.

Chapter 43:

Hidden Under the Sand

The ride was grueling, the desert stretching endlessly beneath a relentless sun. Each mile put more distance between them and Ashara Outpost—but not between them and their pursuers. The CABAL's presence lingered, a shadow brushing the edges of their awareness, always just out of sight.

Brand's grip tightened around the reins, his gaze fixed on the ruins ahead. Half-buried in the sand, the jagged spires rose like the bones of a forgotten creature, ancient and warped by time. This wasn't just an abandoned site. The air here was different—thicker, heavier, as if the very ground whispered secrets from a time long lost.

Soran slowed his horse, his eyes scanning the horizon. "Rasha didn't exactly tell us what we're walking into." His voice was even, but the tension was clear—a thread of unease threaded through his words.

Kaelen snorted, wiping sweat from his brow. "Yeah, that's reassuring. Last time we followed her advice, we nearly died."

Brand dismounted with a soft crunch as his boots sank into the sand. The Flow trembled beneath him, not in its usual ebb and pull but with something deeper—an ancient hum, an energy that felt both foreign and familiar. He pressed his fingers to the hilt of his dagger, the faint pulse of power radiating from the ruins. Whatever the CABAL sought, it wasn't just buried—it was alive in some way.

"We make this quick," Brand muttered, his voice low and tight. His eyes scanned the dunes, searching for any sign of movement. The desert was deceptive—what appeared lifeless could hide dangers beyond imagining.

Soran moved first, heading for the crumbled stone entrance—a massive doorway, half-collapsed, leading into the darkness. The stone was covered in symbols, worn by time but still visible beneath the sand's shifting surface. Brand had seen these symbols before. Too many times.

Kaelen's footsteps slowed as he took in the sight. "Anyone else feel like we're walking into something we can't walk out of?"

Brand exhaled slowly, brushing his fingers across the ancient carvings. "If we turn back now, we'll never know what the CABAL wants."

Soran ran his gloved fingers over the markings, his frown deepening. "And if we go in, we might not come back at all."

Kaelen's sigh was heavy, a dry laugh slipping from his lips as he rubbed the back of his neck. "Well, when you put it like that, I guess we'd better make it worth the trouble."

Brand glanced once more at the horizon. The CABAL was coming. That much was certain. But whatever lay buried in these ruins might be the key to stopping them.

He stepped forward, past the fallen stone and into the deep shadows.

The ruins swallowed them whole.

As soon as Brand crossed the threshold, the air thickened. The heat of the desert was replaced by a heavy stillness, stifling and ancient, filled with the scent of long-forgotten dust—and something older, deeper.

Soran followed closely, his hand resting lightly on his sword hilt. "Stay sharp. Places like this don't stay untouched by accident."

Kaelen exhaled, shaking the last of the sand from his cloak. "Yeah, and I'm dying to know what made this place so special. Before we find out the hard way."

The passage descended, walls narrowing as they pressed deeper. The stone underfoot was uneven, worn smooth by time, but the precision of the carvings—too intricate for mere desert dwellers—spoke of craftsmanship that belonged to another age.

Brand traced his fingers lightly over the symbols carved into the walls. The same ones from the entrance. They pulsed faintly under his touch, as if alive, echoing a forgotten power.

"The Flow is stronger here," he muttered. It wasn't passive—it was active, alive in its presence, almost sentient.

Soran nodded. "Which means whatever's buried here isn't just relics. It's something... more."

Kaelen exhaled sharply, his voice laced with dark humor. "Great. So it's cursed. Just what I needed today."

The narrow tunnel opened into a vast chamber, the ceiling lost in shadow. Massive stone pillars lined the space, some shattered, others standing proud, etched with the same strange glyphs. At the far end, a broken altar stood—imposing, even in its decay.

Soran moved first, eyes sweeping the room warily. "This place... it was important. Too important to be left alone."

Brand stepped toward the altar, his boots stirring up clouds of dust. The Flow around him shifted, not resisting—but welcoming him, recognizing him.

As if in response to his presence, the glyphs on the walls and pillars began to glow.

Kaelen stepped back, a look of stark disbelief crossing his face. "Nope. No, thank you."

Soran's hand tightened on his weapon. "Brand—"

Brand's pulse thundered in his ears, the Flow thrumming around him, pulling him toward the altar. His hand touched the stone, and in that instant—

The ruins stirred to life.

The air shimmered, a deep hum vibrating through the ground. The glow of the symbols flared, ancient markings igniting as if something long dormant had finally awakened.

Far beyond the chamber's walls, something stirred.

Kaelen's breath was slow, deliberate. "So, ancient ruins waking up after a few centuries... totally normal, right?"

Brand didn't answer. His eyes were locked on the swirling symbols, their light shifting and folding in patterns that felt... familiar. Almost as if they were trying to communicate.

Then, a voice.

It wasn't spoken aloud. It reverberated in his mind, vibrating through his bones.

"You have come at last."

Brand stumbled back, breath caught in his throat. He spun, searching for the source, but found nothing. Only the hum of the ruins, the lingering echoes of something buried deep.

Soran's gaze was intense, narrowed. "You heard that?"

Brand nodded, still shaken. "A voice."

Kaelen's grip tightened on his weapon, his voice dry. "Of course you did. Because this place wasn't eerie enough."

The symbols pulsed again, the air around them shifting.

The walls grew translucent, revealing flashes of another time.

Figures in flowing robes stood where they did now, hands raised toward the altar, energy swirling around them. The Flow—harnessed with skill Brand had never seen—buzzed in the air, the symbols etched in the stone burning brightly.

Then, the vision faltered. The air thickened with shadows, the figures twisted, contorted. Their eyes glowed unnaturally, their forms no longer human. The Flow cracked, unraveling, twisting into chaos.

Screams—horrible, wrenching—echoed through the chamber.

And then... silence.

The ruins fell still again, the glow fading, the images vanishing like whispers in the wind.

Brand's breath was shallow, pulse racing. "This place... it was a sanctuary. Until it turned."

Soran's face was unreadable. "What happened to them?"

Brand's fingers traced the ancient carvings, his thoughts a tangled mess. He wasn't sure. But the sinking dread in his chest told him that whatever had destroyed them... was still waiting.

And the CABAL was hunting for it.

The glow from the symbols pulsed steadily, a rhythmic heartbeat that reverberated through the silence. Ancient energy crackled in the air, thick with something unresolved—a presence that refused to fade with time.

Brand took a step forward, his fingers brushing the altar. The stone was cold, yet it throbbed with life beneath his touch. He exhaled slowly, trying to steady the storm inside him.

Kaelen shifted nervously. "Tell me this doesn't involve a blood sacrifice."

Soran shot him a sharp look, but Brand didn't respond. His focus was elsewhere—pulled deeper into the Flow, lost in the echoes of the past.

Then, the chamber trembled.

The walls groaned, stone scraping against stone. A long-dormant mechanism, awakened by Brand's presence, clicked into motion. Dust cascaded from the ceiling as a hidden doorway—previously unseen—crept open at the far end of the chamber.

Kaelen took a careful step back. "No. That's sealed for a reason."

Soran ignored him, eyes fixed on the dark passage now stretching before them. "It's opening for you."

Brand's heartbeat quickened, matching the pulsing energy around him. He wasn't just feeling the Flow anymore—he was entwined with it. The power wrapped around him, coaxing him forward.

From the shadows beyond the threshold, a whisper coiled through the chamber.

"You were never meant to leave," the voice intoned, sorrowful and ominous.

The temperature dropped sharply. The torches flickered, their flames shrinking as if smothered by the unseen force. A deep hum filled the air, a presence stirring from the depths of time itself.

Soran's fingers tightened on his blade. "We need to move."

Kaelen's voice trembled. "We need to run."

But Brand did neither. The Flow had brought him here. And whatever waited beyond that door... he had to face it.

Taking a steadying breath, Brand stepped into the darkness.

The doorway slammed shut behind him.

Chapter 44:

The Depths Below

As the doorway sealed behind him, the air thickened, heavy with silence that swallowed even the sound of his breath. No turning back now.

Brand adjusted his stance, eyes scanning the corridor ahead. Darkness stretched before him, broken only by faint blue glimmers pulsing through the stone, like veins in a long-dead giant. The Flow still thrived here—trapped beneath the sands, waiting.

He stepped forward, and the energy stirred. The walls shivered, as if the stone itself whispered beneath his touch. Whatever was buried here was awakening.

A shadow flickered in his peripheral vision, just beyond the dim light. Brand froze, every muscle coiled tight.

Then, a voice.

Not a whisper, but a chorus—ancient and layered—speaking in a language that bent meaning like a knot in time.

"He walks the path. But does he seek the truth?"

Brand's pulse quickened. He spun, searching the void, but saw nothing. Just the stone—quiet, shifting with the weight of time.

Another step forward.

The ground beneath him crumbled.

Before he could react, the stone gave way, sending him plunging into the depths below.

The fall stretched on, too long, as though space itself had twisted. Then, impact. Hard stone slammed into his back, knocking the breath from his lungs.

Pain flared, and he rolled, gasping, his vision swimming. Above him, the hole had vanished—as if it had never existed.

The darkness pressed in.

But it was not empty.

Something stirred in the black.

Brand forced himself upright, wincing as the ache in his back sharpened. The air here was thick—suffocating, like unseen hands closing in.

He steadied his breath, reaching out through the Flow. It was everywhere—alive, rippling through stone, air, and his very skin. Watching. Waiting.

A whisper brushed his mind—no sound, just a presence, a fleeting touch against the edges of his thoughts.

"You have come far, but not far enough."

Brand stiffened, his hand instinctively sliding to the dagger at his side. "Who's there?"

The silence stretched, then shifted—as if the ruins themselves were listening.

And then the whispers returned—layered, overlapping, voices that slipped through his thoughts like threads in a forgotten tapestry.

"He seeks. He questions. But does he understand?"

A gust of unseen wind stirred the dust at his feet. The walls pulsed with rhythmic light, deliberate, not random—each beat a silent question.

Footsteps echoed softly, measured, deliberate.

Brand whirled, dagger drawn, his senses alight. From the shadows, a figure emerged—half-formed, flickering like a flame caught between existence and memory. Cloaked in deep robes, its face hidden behind an obsidian mask, it radiated an eerie power.

"Who are you?" Brand demanded, his fingers tightening around the hilt of his blade.

The figure tilted its head, a motion almost human, but not quite. "We are the Echoes. The memory of what was. The guardians of what must not be forgotten."

The words settled heavily on Brand's chest. His pulse hammered in his ears. "Why am I here?"

The Echo's voice softened, but its resonance was ancient, distant, yet somehow familiar. "To remember. And to choose."

The ground trembled beneath him. Without warning, the walls began to shift. Not crumble, not collapse—but change. The stone smoothed, symbols igniting with fresh light, revealing fleeting glimpses of a time long lost to the sand.

A time before the CABAL. Before corruption. Before the Flow twisted to serve ambition.

Brand staggered as a surge of energy hit him—not an attack, but an awakening. Images flashed in his mind—battles in lands he had never known, faces both foreign and familiar, power wielded with a mastery he couldn't begin to understand.

The Echo's voice grew stronger, no longer a whisper, but a command.

"Remember. Or be forgotten."

Brand's vision swirled, and the world twisted again.

In an instant, reality fractured. The ruins dissolved into a cascade of light and memory, then... snapped back, leaving him breathless and alone. The Flow rushed around him, pulling him deeper, into something older, ancient.

He was no longer in the chamber.

Instead, he stood on a vast plateau, the sky split between day and night—an impossible space, outside of time. Below him sprawled a great city, its streets alive with figures in flowing garments, their hands tracing symbols through the air—shaping the Flow with a mastery beyond Brand's comprehension.

Yet beneath the grandeur, something darker pulsed—an undercurrent of power that set his teeth on edge.

"The Age of Balance," the Echo's voice resonated again, though Brand could no longer see them. "Before the Sundering."

Brand spun, his breath shallow. "The Sundering?"

The scene twisted violently—the city plunged into darkness, its light snuffed out as if it had never existed. Shadows rose from the earth, curling through the streets, consuming everything in their path.

The same figures who had once shaped the Flow now battled against it, their power turned back upon them.

Screams echoed through the vision. The Flow cracked.

"The first betrayal," the Echo's voice whispered, carrying the weight of centuries. "The first war for control."

Brand watched, transfixed, as warriors—monks, protectors of the old ways—stood firm against the encroaching darkness. Their energy burned blue, striking against the red fire of their enemies. The same color as the power inside him.

His hands clenched into fists. "The CABAL."

The vision flickered violently, speeding through devastation— through a last, desperate stand at a temple. A final sacrifice.

"Their knowledge was sealed away, hidden beneath the sands, waiting for one who could hear the call."

Brand felt the truth settle over him like a shroud. "Me."

The vision shattered, and in an instant, the chamber's walls rushed back into place. His head spun, pulse pounding in his ears. The Echo remained, its masked face unreadable.

"You must understand," it intoned, its voice echoing in the chamber's depths. "Power is never lost—only buried."

Brand's throat tightened. The truth sank in. This was what the CABAL sought—this was the power they feared and craved.

And here, in this place, he stood at its very heart.

The Echo's words reverberated through his mind. Power is never lost—only buried.

The air around him pulsed with residual energy, charged and waiting, as if it, too, awaited his next move. He drew in a sharp breath, trying to steady the storm in his chest. The first war. The Sundering. The Flow splintered. And now, centuries later, the CABAL was here to finish what had been started.

"Brand."

Soran's voice sliced through the stillness.

Brand blinked, disoriented. He was back. The chamber was the same—its walls now dim, the glow receding like a fading memory. Soran and Kaelen stood a few feet away, watching him with a mix of concern and wariness.

Kaelen crossed his arms, his gaze sharp. "You went stiff as a corpse. What the hell did you see?"

Brand exhaled, his voice rough. "The beginning of everything."

Soran's frown deepened. "Explain."

Brand ran his hand over the cold stone of the altar. "This isn't just a ruin. It's a vault—locking away something the CABAL desperately wants. The Flow was once whole, balanced. Until someone tried to twist it, to control it." He glanced at them, his eyes sharp with realization. "The first war was fought over that power."

Kaelen's brow furrowed, a wry smile tugging at the corner of his lips. "Let me guess—those who wanted control wore a lot of red?"

Brand nodded grimly. "And those who fought against them? Blue."

Soran's jaw clenched, his gaze hardening. "History repeats itself."

A deep hum reverberated through the chamber again, vibrating through the stone. Brand felt the weight of the Echo's presence—its warning still lingering in the air like a storm on the horizon. This was why they had come here. Not just to flee the CABAL, but to understand the true cost of what they were fighting for.

Brand turned toward the exit, his steps quickening. "We can't stay. The CABAL knows about this place. They're on their way."

Kaelen let out a breath, half exasperated, half amused. "Oh good. Because things were getting a little too peaceful."

Soran sheathed his weapon, his expression grim. "Then let's move."

Brand hesitated for a moment, casting one last glance at the altar. The power here was undeniable, but it was just a fragment of something far bigger. If the CABAL was after the Flow, they would need more than this forgotten ruin.

And so would he.

As they moved toward the exit, the whispers of the Echoes faded into the darkness behind them.

But their warning—still fresh, still urgent—remained.

Chapter 45:

The Pursuit

The desert wind howled, fierce and unrelenting, as Brand, Soran, and Kaelen emerged from the ruins. The midday sun blazed overhead, its heat pressing down on them like an invisible hand, suffocating in its intensity. They had no time to waste.

Brand cast one final glance over his shoulder at the ruins. The echoes of the past still hummed in his mind—visions of power, of the Sundering, of a civilization lost to time. What they had uncovered could change everything. But reflection would have to wait. The CABAL was coming.

Soran was already scanning the horizon, his posture stiff with tension. His eyes flicked westward, where faint trails of dust curled into the sky. Riders? Scouts? Or worse—agents of the CABAL. "We need to move. Fast."

Kaelen wiped sweat from his brow and adjusted his grip on the reins. "Oh, great. Nothing quite like being hunted by a bunch of power-hungry lunatics." His voice was light, but there was an edge beneath it—an unease that Brand could feel in his gut.

Brand ignored the remark and swung himself into the saddle. The horse snorted, sensing the urgency in his movements. "We head east—through the rock canyons. It'll give us cover and slow them down if they follow."

Soran nodded, pulling himself up into the saddle with practiced ease. "If we're being tracked, we'll know soon enough."

Kaelen climbed onto his horse with a dramatic sigh. "Well, let's just hope that happens later rather than sooner."

They spurred their horses into motion, riding hard through the desert. The wind whipped around them, the shifting dunes casting ever-changing shadows. Each mile felt heavier than the last—not from fatigue, but from the weight of what they were carrying. They weren't just running anymore. They were carrying something the CABAL would stop at nothing to possess.

Brand's grip on the reins tightened, his senses stretched thin. He felt it—something pulling at the edges of his awareness. Not just the Flow, but something else. A presence. A cold, watchful gaze. An unnatural stillness in the air.

Soran slowed his pace slightly, his voice low but urgent. "You feel that?"

Brand's jaw tightened as he gave a curt nod. "We're not alone."

Kaelen, about to take a swig from his water skin, froze. His hand paused mid-air, and he capped the skin with a click. "Perfect. Just what I was hoping for—more company."

The wind kicked up, swirling the sands around them in a chaotic dance. The ridges of the dunes began to shift, no longer looking quite the same—as though something beneath them had stirred.

Soran's voice cut through the tense silence. "Keep moving. But stay sharp."

Brand's fingers brushed the dagger at his side, his pulse steady despite the unease gnawing at him. The CABAL was close—he could feel it—but something else stirred in the air. Something more elusive, more dangerous.

Whatever it was, it was waiting. Watching.

The wind whispered through the dunes, the landscape shifting as though the desert itself conspired against them. The deeper they rode into the canyons, the heavier the air became—thick with tension, like the world itself was holding its breath.

Brand kept his senses stretched tight, searching for the source of the crawling unease that prickled his skin. It wasn't just the CABAL. There was something else moving in the sands.

Soran rode slightly ahead, scanning the ridges above them with narrowed eyes. His jaw was clenched tight, and his fingers flexed, restlessly gripping the reins. "I don't like this. They should've caught up by now."

Kaelen exhaled sharply, his voice laced with suspicion. "That's what's bothering me. If they're tracking us, they're taking their sweet time." He glanced around, his gaze flicking over the canyon walls. "Feels like we're walking into a trap."

Brand nodded grimly, his grip tightening on the reins. The CABAL wasn't reckless. They didn't rush. They stalked. They waited for their prey to move exactly where they wanted.

A faint sound broke through the wind—a whistle, high and sharp.

Soran halted his horse, pulling it to a tense stop. "Did you hear that?"

Kaelen's brow furrowed, and he looked around, uneasy. "Yeah. That didn't sound natural."

Brand inhaled deeply, sensing the Flow ripple around them. Something was moving fast, just out of sight. The shifting sand along the ridges betrayed its presence—figures, barely visible, shifting with the dunes.

And then the silence shattered.

A blur of motion, and suddenly arrows rained down from above, striking the ground with deadly precision.

"Move!" Soran barked.

They spurred their horses forward just as the first volley hit the sand where they had been standing moments before. Brand twisted in the saddle, catching glimpses of figures cloaked in desert garb, faces obscured by masks. Their weapons were sleek, finely crafted—not the standard CABAL issue. He muttered under his breath, "Mercenaries."

Kaelen cursed under his breath. "They're not here to slow us down— they're here to kill us."

Brand ducked as another arrow whistled past his ear. The CABAL hadn't sent a horde after them—they had hired specialists.

Soran gritted his teeth, his voice tight with urgency. "We need to break their formation before they box us in."

Brand scanned the narrowing canyon ahead. An ambush, yes—but maybe also an opportunity.

"We push forward," Brand commanded. "Hard and fast. Get them off balance."

Kaelen's grin was sharp, even as chaos swirled around them. "So, we make them regret their paycheck?"

Brand's horse surged into a full sprint. The battle was on. And he was determined to win.

The canyon walls rose higher as they barreled through, their horses kicking up trails of dust. The mercenaries shifted with surgical precision, repositioning along the ridges, their eyes locked on their next strike.

Brand's gaze locked onto a figure ahead—an attacker, crouched on a ledge, drawing a bead on them. His teeth clenched. Without a second thought, he reached for his dagger, and with a flick of his wrist, sent it flying.

The mercenary barely reacted before the blade buried itself in his shoulder. He howled, stumbling backward, his bow falling from his grasp.

Soran and Kaelen flanked him, their faces grim. "We're not getting out of this unless we control the high ground," Soran shouted over the wind.

Kaelen ducked as another arrow sliced through the air. "Oh, perfect. Let's just scale the cliffs while we're at it."

Brand's mind raced. They needed a distraction—a decisive move to tip the scales.

Then he saw it: a natural rock overhang ahead, looming over the mercenaries. If they could bring it down...

"Kaelen, Soran!" Brand shouted, pointing toward the ledge. "We collapse it, we cut off their attack!"

Kaelen's eyes widened. "That's a big 'if,' Brand."

But Soran was already acting. He snatched a small explosive charge from his saddlebag—the last of their stock. "We just need to get close enough."

Brand nodded, his pulse quickening. Time to turn defense into offense.

"Cover me," Soran ordered, veering off toward the ledge, his horse charging straight into enemy fire. Kaelen pulled back, releasing a storm of crossbow bolts to pin the mercenaries down.

Brand followed, every muscle taut with anticipation. Timing was everything.

Soran reached the base of the ledge, hurled the explosive upward, and spurred his horse into a gallop, narrowly avoiding a volley of arrows as the charge detonated.

The explosion cracked through the rock face. A deafening roar echoed across the canyon as the overhang fractured and crumbled. Stone rained down, smashing into the mercenaries, cutting their line of fire.

Brand didn't hesitate. "Go! Now!"

With their attackers thrown into chaos, they surged forward, pushing past the wreckage. The canyon ahead narrowed—but beyond it, open ground awaited. And with it, freedom.

They'd made it.

For now.

The dust still hung thick in the canyon air, swirling in rolling clouds that obscured the wreckage of the ambush. The rumble of the rockslide echoed through the valley, fading into the vast emptiness of the desert.

Brand urged his horse forward, breaths sharp and fast. His body was coiled tight, waiting for the next attack that never came. Had they truly escaped?

Soran slowed, casting a quick glance over his shoulder. "No movement. No pursuit." The disbelief in his voice was unmistakable.

Kaelen exhaled heavily, wiping dust from his face. "Way too close." He shot Brand a pointed look. "You planned that gamble, right?"

Brand nodded sharply, though his grip on the reins remained vice-like. "Enough to know we had a chance. Not enough to guarantee survival."

Kaelen chuckled bitterly. "Let's not make a habit of that."

They moved away from the wreckage, the open desert stretching before them. Dunes and jagged rocks lay ahead—freedom, but with no cover. If another force came, they'd have nowhere to hide.

Soran reined in his horse, scanning the landscape. "We need to find somewhere to regroup. Figure out our next move."

Brand wiped sweat from his brow, squinting into the horizon. "There's a ridge to the east. We can rest there and see if we're still being followed."

For several minutes, they rode in silence, the adrenaline slowly wearing off. The weight of their near-miss hung heavy. The CABAL had known where they'd be. Someone had tracked them. Or worse, someone had betrayed them.

Kaelen broke the silence, his voice edged with suspicion. "How the hell did they know?"

Soran's jaw tightened. "We've been careful. No one outside of Rasha should've known we were headed here."

Brand didn't respond right away. Rasha. She had guided them here, urged them to uncover what was buried beneath the sands. But had she done so to help them—or to lead them into a trap?

"We don't know enough yet," Brand said at last. "But we need to assume it's not over."

When they reached the ridge, Brand dismounted and climbed to the high ground, scanning the horizon. No immediate threats. But safety was still a long way off.

Soran joined him, his expression grim. "What now?"

Brand exhaled, watching the sun sink lower. "Now we find out who's really hunting us."

Chapter 46:

Revelations in the Dark

The desert night settled over them, a vast void stretching beyond the ridge. The oppressive heat of the day had bled away, leaving a bone-deep chill that seemed to rise from the very sand.

Brand crouched near a small fire, the flickering flames casting twisted shadows on the jagged rocks. Soran and Kaelen sat nearby, their faces drawn with exhaustion, but neither seemed willing to sleep.

"We need answers," Soran broke the silence, his voice low but firm. "We need to know who sold us out."

Kaelen exhaled sharply, his eyes dark with suspicion. "Let's stop pretending. We're all thinking the same thing." He turned his gaze to Brand. "Rasha."

Brand didn't answer immediately. The same thought had been gnawing at him since the ambush—had Rasha led them into a trap, knowing the CABAL was waiting? Or had she been betrayed, just like them?

Soran's stare was unwavering. "You trust her?"

Brand's eyes remained fixed on the fire, his mind turning over the question. Trust. It was a luxury they couldn't afford.

"I don't know," he finally admitted. "But if she wanted us dead, she wouldn't need the CABAL to do it."

Kaelen's scowl deepened. "So that means someone else gave us up."

The wind shifted, carrying the faint, haunting howl of a distant predator—a sound too unnatural, too close.

Brand stiffened, his fingers brushing the hilt of his dagger. They weren't alone.

Soran rose, moving silently as he scanned the darkness. "Something's out there."

Kaelen muttered a curse. "Great. As if we needed more reasons to be paranoid."

Brand stood slowly, stretching his senses. The Flow pulsed through him, rippling through the sand like a distant heartbeat. There. Just beyond the firelight—a presence. Watching. Waiting.

Then, a voice. Low. A whisper. Carried by the wind.

"You took what was not yours to find."

Brand's blood froze. He whipped around, his eyes locking on the darkness. A figure emerged, cloaked in tattered robes, its face hidden beneath a hood. It moved without sound, gliding over the sand like some dark specter.

Kaelen drew his weapon, his tone dry. "Mysterious figures in the night. Just what I needed."

Brand ignored him, his attention fixed on the stranger. The Flow twisted unnaturally around them, warping, bending in ways that felt... wrong.

"Who are you?" Brand demanded.

The figure took a step closer, its voice colder than the desert night. "I am the consequence of your choices."

Soran's grip tightened on his blade. "That's not an answer."

The stranger tilted its head, the movement almost imperceptible. "No. But it is the truth."

The fire flickered wildly as the wind howled. Then, without warning, the figure was gone.

Only the echo of its words remained, lingering in the heavy air.

Brand's jaw tightened. This wasn't over.

The wind carried the fading remnants of the figure's voice into the void, leaving only silence. But the air felt charged. Brand's skin prickled. The way the Flow had bent around that figure—it wasn't right.

Soran exhaled sharply, his blade still half-drawn. "That wasn't an ordinary traveler."

Kaelen shook his head. "No kidding. Did you see how the sand barely moved when it... he... whatever it was, moved? Like it wasn't really here."

Brand stepped forward slowly, scanning the spot where the figure had stood. Nothing. No footprints. No sign of anyone.

Kaelen muttered under his breath. "This place is cursed. We should leave—now."

Brand ignored him, his gaze locked on the dark horizon. Something lingered here, a whisper beneath the fabric of reality. He pressed his hand to the sand, extending his senses into the Flow.

A sharp jolt shot through him—

Images crashed into his mind.

A battlefield—a wasteland of bodies scattered across the dunes. Warriors cloaked in blue light, standing resolute against a tide of crimson energy. Weapons infused with the Flow glowed faintly as they chanted words long lost to time. Then—

A figure stepping from the shadows. Red and blue light clashing, not balanced, but twisted—corrupted. The Flow recoiled, wounded. The warriors faltered. The battle was lost before it had even begun.

Then, the darkness swallowed everything.

Brand gasped, tearing his hand away from the sand. His heart thundered in his chest. His breath came in ragged bursts. The past had spoken to him.

Soran's eyes sharpened, his focus now fully on Brand. "What did you see?"

Brand swallowed hard, his voice tight. "A warning."

Kaelen's eyes darted between them. "Care to share with the rest of us?"

Brand steadied himself, fighting the overwhelming weight of what he'd glimpsed. "The war we're fighting—this isn't new. It began long before the CABAL. Someone twisted the Flow back then. Not just creating division... but something worse."

Soran's expression hardened. "And you think that figure—whoever they were—was connected to it?"

Brand nodded grimly. "They weren't just warning us. They were reminding me that the past... isn't finished with us yet."

A gust of wind stirred the sand, and for a brief moment, Brand thought he heard the whisper again—soft, almost inaudible.

"The Flow remembers."

And that meant the enemy knew too.

Brand stood motionless, his breaths ragged, still shaken by the vision. The past bled into the present, its weight pressing on him like a tangible force, suffocating.

Soran and Kaelen watched him, knowing this was a familiar reaction—Brand, when the Flow spoke, when something deeper than understanding tugged at him. But this time, the air was different.

Kaelen broke the silence first. "Alright, I hate to bring it up, but are we sure this isn't just another mind trick? We just fought our way out of a death trap. We could all be running on fumes."

Brand shook his head, his voice low and steady. "This wasn't the same." His gaze shifted to Soran. "I saw a battle. A war fought with the Flow itself. Before the CABAL. Before everything we know now."

Soran frowned, his brow furrowing. "And what does that mean for us, exactly?"

Brand exhaled slowly, his mind wrestling to piece together the fragments of what he'd witnessed. "It means... we're up against something older than we thought. The CABAL isn't just continuing a war. They're trying to finish what was started long before."

Kaelen crossed his arms, his expression dark. "And that's supposed to make me feel better?"

Brand's grip tightened around his dagger. It wasn't just the past haunting them. The Flow had been wounded once before—and the scar had never healed.

The wind kicked up, carrying the scent of sand and something colder, something forgotten and decayed, into the camp. It smelled like the ruins. Like death waiting to rise.

Soran's face darkened, a realization creeping in. "If that's true—if the CABAL is trying to reopen something from the past—we need to stop them. Now."

Brand nodded, his eyes scanning the horizon, the darkness stretching endlessly before them. The war wasn't just on the horizon. It had never ended.

The fire crackled, its warmth struggling to hold back the chill that was creeping up the ridge. Brand stood at the edge of their camp, staring into the night, his mind spinning with everything he had seen, everything he had learned.

The Flow had shown him glimpses of a distant past. But what it demanded of him now was unclear. Was he meant to stop the CABAL?

Or was there something deeper at work—something hidden even within the Flow itself?

Soran and Kaelen sat by the fire, the exhaustion of the battle, the chase, and the visions hanging heavy on them. Most men would have broken by now. But here they were—still fighting. Still standing.

Kaelen shifted, rubbing his hands together against the biting cold. "You're thinking too hard, Brand. I can hear it."

Brand smirked, his gaze still fixed on the horizon. "We're out in the middle of nowhere, hunted by people who either want us dead or want to use us. And you're worried about my thoughts?"

Kaelen stretched out, leaning back against a smooth rock. "I'd just rather know what's going on in that head of yours before it gets us all killed."

Soran tossed a stick into the fire, watching the embers rise and swirl. "We need to make a decision. The CABAL won't stop. And we don't have enough to go on to strike back yet." His eyes met Brand's. "Where do we go from here?"

The wind shifted, carrying with it a faint, eerie whisper—a sound only Brand seemed to hear. He closed his eyes, tuning into the pulse of the Flow beneath the earth. The past was still speaking.

Then, something tugged at him—a pull in his chest, a direction, a place. It wasn't instinct. It was the Flow itself, guiding him somewhere unknown.

Brand turned to face his companions, his expression hardening. "There's something waiting for us. Further east."

Soran raised a brow, a silent question in his eyes. "Waiting? Or calling?"

Brand hesitated, the weight of his words sinking in. "Both."

Kaelen groaned, shaking his head. "Of course it is. And what exactly do you think we're walking into this time?"

Brand didn't answer right away. He wasn't sure. But the feeling in his chest, the energy in his veins, was undeniable.

"We'll find out when we get there," he said finally. "But whatever it is, it's tied to everything. To all of this."

Soran stood, brushing dust from his cloak. "Then we ride at dawn."

Kaelen grumbled under his breath. "Was really hoping for 'after a full night's sleep.'"

Brand smirked. "You can sleep on your horse."

Kaelen muttered something about horses not being comfortable, but didn't argue further.

The fire crackled, the cold pressing in once more. The night felt endless, but the path ahead had never been clearer.

The Flow had spoken. And Brand would follow.

Chapter 47:

The Road to Ruin

Dawn broke in hues of deep violet and fiery orange, casting long, eerie shadows across the dunes as Brand, Soran, and Kaelen rode eastward. The desert's cool embrace would soon give way to the furnace-like heat of midday, but for now, it was a fleeting respite.

The ridge they had left behind was nothing more than a distant memory now, swallowed by the infinite expanse of sand and jagged rock. The CABAL wouldn't have abandoned the hunt, but for the moment, they had bought themselves time.

Soran rode quietly, eyes scanning the horizon. His mind, like Brand's, carried more than just fatigue. There was purpose in their journey, but no clear destination—only the pull of the Flow, urging them toward an uncertain end.

Kaelen, ever the skeptic, exhaled dramatically. "So, remind me again why we're riding deeper into what's literally the middle of nowhere?"

Brand glanced at him, his expression unreadable. "Because that's where we're meant to be."

Kaelen scoffed, rolling his eyes. "Great. Nothing like starting the day with another cryptic prophecy."

Soran shook his head, his voice calm but firm. "It's not just a feeling. The Flow led Brand to the ruins. It's leading him now. We trust it."

Kaelen muttered under his breath but didn't argue further. His faith in the Flow might have been thin, but his loyalty to Brand was what kept him riding forward.

By midday, the dunes gave way to cracked earth—parched, lifeless ground that seemed to whisper of things long forgotten.

Brand brought his horse to a stop, his gaze fixed on the horizon. "We're close."

Soran and Kaelen followed suit, scanning the desolate land. At first, it seemed empty—just barren wasteland stretching to infinity.

Then the wind shifted.

A low hum reverberated through the air—not heard, but felt. A pulse in the Flow—subtle but constant.

Kaelen stiffened, his eyes narrowing. "That's not right."

Soran dismounted, pressing a hand to the earth. The pulse was coming from beneath them.

Brand felt it too—an ancient force buried deep within the land.

This was the place. The Flow had guided them here.

And whatever lay buried beneath their feet, it was waiting to be uncovered.

Brand dismounted, his boots sinking into the cracked earth. The pulse wasn't just energy—it was something older, something woven into the very bones of the land. The Flow resonated with it, vibrating just beneath the surface like a memory of a time long past.

Soran knelt, fingers brushing the dry, brittle ground. "Whatever this is... it's close."

Kaelen crouched beside him, tapping a loose stone with his knuckle. The hollow echo that followed sent a chill through the air. "That's not right. Something's down there."

Brand's eyes narrowed. The earth beneath them wasn't solid—it was a thin veil, hiding something.

He closed his eyes and reached into the Flow. The hum deepened, swirling around him, offering glimpses—shadows of something massive buried beneath, something constructed, not born.

Then, the earth trembled.

A deep shudder that sent cracks racing out from beneath their feet. Something ancient was stirring.

Kaelen leapt back. "Tell me that's not about to collapse beneath us."

Soran stood fast, hand on his weapon. "We need to move. Now."

But Brand remained still. His hand pressed against the earth, his focus intense. This wasn't just crumbling—it was opening. The Flow was reacting to them, recognizing something buried deep within him, something tied to whatever lay beneath.

A sharp gust of wind howled through the air—

And then, the ground gave way.

Brand barely had time to react before the earth beneath him split apart, sending him plummeting into darkness. Soran and Kaelen's shouts faded as he fell, swallowed by the void.

Then, silence.

Brand landed hard, rolling across cold stone. Dust choked the air, and for a moment, all he saw was the dim flicker of the Flow's light.

He forced himself to his feet, coughing. The chamber stretched wide before him, its walls etched with faint symbols, their glow the dying embers of something once great.

In the center of the room, half-buried in sand, lay something massive.

A doorway—sealed by the weight of time.

A forgotten vault.

And whatever lay inside... had been waiting.

Brand rose slowly, brushing dust from his cloak. The air here was thick—not just with age, but with something unseen, something alive. The Flow didn't hum—it pulsed. It was waiting.

The vault before him was unlike anything he had encountered. No grand pillars, no intricate carvings celebrating an era long past. It was cold, sterile, its purpose not to honor history, but to contain something within.

Footsteps echoed from above. Soran and Kaelen descended, weapons drawn, their forms casting long shadows in the dim light.

"Brand?" Soran's voice held a note of caution. "What do you see?"

Brand took a deliberate step forward, his palm resting against the smooth stone of the sealed door. A shiver ran up his spine as a wave of energy rippled outward.

Kaelen's grip tightened. "I really don't like it when things start glowing. Never ends well."

The pulse of the Flow deepened, no longer pushing Brand away, but pulling him closer. The symbols on the vault began to shift, realigning, unlocking—like ancient locks undone by his touch.

Then, from the depths of the chamber, a voice—

"You should not be here."

The air thickened, pressing down like a heavy weight. The torches flickered violently, their flames twisting unnaturally, stretching shadows across the room. This wasn't an echo. This was something alive, something aware.

Brand stiffened, heart pounding. "I get that a lot. Who are you?"

Silence.

Then, the doorway split open with a harsh crack.

Darkness poured out, swallowing the chamber in a biting cold. The Flow recoiled, twisting away from the void like something afraid of what lay beyond.

From the shadows, a figure emerged.

It moved with unnerving slowness, wrapped in robes that defied age, its face obscured by a hood. But its eyes—

Brand's breath caught. The same eerie dual light he had seen in his vision. Blue and red, balanced yet unnaturally intense.

Soran took a step back, his voice quiet. "Brand…"

The figure tilted its head, regarding him with an unsettling calm. "You are one who hears the Flow. And yet, you do not understand it."

Brand swallowed hard, his voice steady despite the dread building in his chest. "Then teach me."

The figure's gaze bore into him. It lingered for what felt like an eternity before whispering, "No. You must choose."

A crushing pressure settled over Brand's chest. This wasn't about learning. It was about a decision.

And the weight of that decision would change everything.

Brand's heart raced as the figure's words reverberated in his mind. You must choose.

The air around him thickened, the Flow twisting and bending in response, as if holding its breath, waiting. Soran and Kaelen stood still, hands resting on their weapons, but neither moved. This trial was his alone.

Brand exhaled slowly, his footfall silent as he stepped forward. The figure didn't flinch. It didn't block his path. It merely observed, its dual-colored eyes piercing through him like an open wound.

"The Flow is not yours to control," the figure's voice rang out, a chorus of many speaking in unison. "It is not a tool. It is not a weapon.

It is a current, meant to be followed, not forced."

Brand straightened, his voice unwavering. "And yet, the CABAL seeks to bend it to their will. They seek to corrupt it. If I don't stop them, who will?"

The figure took a deliberate step forward, shadows twisting behind it, moving as though alive. "The Flow does not need control. It requires balance. The CABAL is not the first to seek dominion, and they will not be the last. Your task is not to conquer them. It is to understand the truth."

A surge of energy swept through the chamber like a storm. Brand's body tensed, fists clenched, as the force wrapped around him, lifting him off the ground. The Flow churned violently, pressing in from all sides.

Then, a vision struck—sharp and vivid.

Brand found himself standing on the edge of a battlefield, the air crackling with charged energy. Warriors clashed, blue light against red, the Flow itself shattering between them. The ground trembled beneath the weight of their conflict, cracking with the strain.

In the center of it all stood a man, draped in tattered robes, his hands outstretched as if commanding the chaos. His face was hidden, but his presence was undeniable. He was neither of the blue nor the red—he was something in between, something that blurred the lines.

Then, the battlefield buckled and collapsed.

Brand gasped, the vision tearing away like a storm ripping apart a fragile dream. He staggered, barely keeping himself upright as his body slammed back into reality.

The figure remained still, unwavering. "This is the choice you must make," it intoned, its voice a cold echo in the now-still air. "To fight is inevitable. But will you fight as they do, or will you break the cycle?"

Brand's heart thundered in his chest, his mind racing. The CABAL had to be stopped. He had sworn to stand against them, to fight for balance. But if he walked the same path they did, if he sought to control the Flow, was he any different?

A heavy silence fell.

And then, with a trembling exhale, Brand released his grip on the Flow.

The energy around him stilled, no longer a violent storm but a steady, pulsing presence. It did not fade—it simply existed, waiting for him, not as a weapon to be wielded, but as a guide to follow.

The figure's gaze softened, and it nodded once. "You are ready."

The vault behind it began to close, its massive stone doors sliding shut with an almost reverential slowness. The secret within had never been meant to be revealed. It had always been about Brand proving that he did not need what lay hidden.

The Flow, once again in harmony, surged around him, stronger than before. Brand turned to Soran and Kaelen, the weight of the moment pressing heavily on his chest.

"It's time to go," he said, his voice steady, but his eyes reflecting a new resolve.

No one spoke as they ascended from the chamber, the air lighter now, as if the very weight of the moment had been lifted.

Brand had made his choice.

And the world would never be the same again.

Chapter 48:

A New Path

The weight of the underground chamber lifted as Brand, Soran, and Kaelen emerged into the open desert. The sky above shifted from deep indigo to the first pale hues of dawn, casting elongated shadows across the dunes. Brand had never felt the Flow so distinctly, yet so gently, as if it no longer pressed against him but moved with him.

Kaelen exhaled a deep breath, shaking dust from his cloak. "So, I take it we're not all-powerful gods now?"

Brand shot him a look. "That was never the point."

Soran fell silent for a moment, his gaze fixed on Brand. "But something's changed, hasn't it?"

Brand nodded. The Flow had tested him. The Vault had challenged him. But instead of granting him power, it had forced him to understand what it truly meant to wield it.

"The CABAL will come looking," Soran said. "They'll want to know what we found."

"They'll assume we took something," Brand murmured. "But the truth is, we left something behind."

Kaelen raised an eyebrow. "Care to share with the rest of us?"

Brand exhaled, his eyes scanning the horizon. He had made his choice. And now, he had to live with it. "We're heading south," he said finally. "Away from the CABAL's reach for now."

Soran crossed his arms. "And then?"

Brand met his gaze. "Then we prepare for whatever comes next."

Kaelen groaned. "I knew you were going to say something vague and ominous."

Brand smirked, just slightly, but didn't respond. The world had shifted. Soon, the CABAL would feel it.

The desert wind carried them onward, toward a path uncertain, but undeniably theirs.

The sun had risen fully by the time Brand, Soran, and Kaelen crested a long ridge that overlooked the vast expanse of desert. The golden light stretched endlessly over the dunes, but something felt different. The air hummed with a charge, a subtle shift in the balance of things— as if the world itself had noticed Brand's decision.

Kaelen yawned, stretching his arms. "So, are we actually heading somewhere, or just wandering into another mystical crisis?"

Brand didn't answer right away. He could feel something tugging at the edge of his awareness, distant but unmistakable. A new current in the Flow, reaching outward like unseen threads weaving toward some unknown point.

Soran adjusted his saddle. "We can't just wander. The CABAL will regroup, and next time, they'll send more than mercenaries."

Brand nodded, his gaze still fixed on the horizon. There was something out there—an event unfolding, a shift already in motion. The CABAL had spent years trying to manipulate the Flow. What had happened in the Vault of Echoes had sent ripples through that manipulation, and now...

"They know," Brand murmured.

Kaelen frowned. "They know what?"

"That something's changed." Brand turned toward them. "They'll feel it, even if they don't understand it yet. And they'll move quickly to figure out what happened."

Soran tightened his grip on the reins. "Then we need to stay ahead of them."

Brand exhaled, his breath steady. "We head for the borderlands. The Outer Settlements."

Kaelen raised an eyebrow. "I was joking about wandering, but that's still not much of a plan."

Brand met his gaze, unwavering. "We're not going to hide. We're going to find the people who've been resisting the CABAL long before us."

A silence stretched between them.

Kaelen sighed, rubbing his temple. "And let me guess... they'll be thrilled to see us."

Brand gave him a small smirk. "Probably not."

Soran nodded. "But if we're going to fight back, we'll need allies."

Brand turned back to the horizon. For the first time in his life, he wasn't merely reacting. He was carving his own path. And the world had already begun shifting in response.

"We ride at dusk," he said. "By then, we'll know if we're truly alone out here."

The wind stirred around them, carrying the promise of what was to come.

Night fell swiftly as the three riders made their way into the open dunes, their path illuminated only by the twin moons overhead. The desert was silent, yet alive with unseen movements, shifting sands, and whispers carried on the wind.

Brand rode at the front, his senses attuned to the Flow. The energy around him was no longer turbulent—it had settled, like a great beast stirring from slumber.

Soran rode beside him. "We need to be cautious. The Outer Settlements are unpredictable. Some will help us. Others..." he trailed off, scanning the horizon. "They won't."

Kaelen scoffed. "Oh, good. I love wandering into places where half the population wants us dead."

Brand smirked slightly but kept his focus forward. This was different from their previous journeys. This wasn't about survival anymore.

This was about preparing for what came next.

Hours passed as they rode through the undulating dunes, their horses kicking up soft sprays of sand. Then, without warning, Brand felt something shift.

A pull. A ripple in the Flow.

He yanked his reins, bringing his horse to a halt. Soran and Kaelen followed instantly, their tension palpable.

"What is it?" Soran asked, his voice tight.

Brand closed his eyes, reaching outward. There. Not far. A presence. Many presences.

Kaelen sensed it a moment later. "Campfires."

On the distant ridge ahead, small flickering lights danced in the darkness. A settlement—or something else.

Soran's grip tightened around his weapon. "We're not alone out here."

Brand opened his eyes, exhaling slowly. This was the first step. The first real test.

"Let's find out who they are," he said, urging his horse forward.

Whatever awaited them, this was the path they had chosen.

As they approached the distant ridge, the flickering campfires sharpened into focus, revealing a small, fortified settlement nestled between the dunes. Its walls were built from salvaged stone and metal, a haphazard but sturdy defense against the desert's dangers.

Brand, Soran, and Kaelen slowed their approach, their horses kicking up soft sprays of sand. This was a place that had known war, a place that understood survival.

Soran lowered his voice. "They could be allies."

Kaelen scoffed. "Or they could be the kind of people who shoot first and ask questions later."

Brand studied the settlement, his instincts humming. The Flow here was restless, neither welcoming nor hostile—more like a wary watchfulness, as if the people inside were always on alert.

A sharp whistle split the night air. The sentries had spotted them.

From the walls, figures moved quickly, taking positions. The glint of drawn weapons caught in the firelight. Brand raised his hand in a silent signal, indicating they meant no harm.

A voice rang out, clear and cold. "State your purpose."

Brand nudged his horse forward, just enough to make himself clearly visible. "We're travelers seeking passage."

There was a pause, then the heavy creak of a gate swinging open.

"Enter slowly," the voice instructed. "And keep your hands where we can see them."

Brand exchanged a glance with Soran and Kaelen before guiding his horse forward. Whatever lay beyond the gate, they would face it together.

The gate slammed shut behind them with a final, echoing clang. The fire-lit eyes of the settlement turned upon them.

Chapter 49:

A City of Strangers

The moment they passed through the heavy gates, the settlement closed around them like a living thing. Eyes flickered from shadowed doorways, from behind market stalls draped in tattered cloth, from high perches where sentries kept their rifles trained on the newcomers.

The air was thick with the smells of sweat, cooked meat, and machine oil. This was not a peaceful village. It was a place carved from necessity, where survival was the law.

Kaelen muttered under his breath, "I don't suppose they have a welcome committee with drinks?"

Soran gave him a sharp look. "Stay sharp. This place reeks of desperation."

A woman stepped forward from the crowd, her posture straight, her eyes calculating. She was tall, with weathered skin and short-cropped hair, a rifle slung over her shoulder like an afterthought. She radiated the confidence of someone who had survived many battles and expected to survive many more.

"You're outsiders," she said, her voice even, but thick with suspicion.

Brand dismounted slowly, keeping his movements deliberate. "Travelers."

The woman's gaze flickered between them. "That's not an answer."

Soran crossed his arms. "We're looking for information. Maybe trade."

"Maybe," the woman said. "Or maybe you bring trouble."

Brand met her gaze. This wasn't the first time he'd had to prove himself in a place like this. It wouldn't be the last.

"I don't blame you for being cautious," he said. "But we're not the worst thing knocking at your door."

The woman studied him for a long moment, then gave a sharp nod toward the far end of the settlement. "You want to talk? Then you'll talk to the one who decides."

She turned on her heel and strode away, expecting them to follow.

Soran exhaled. "That went well."

Kaelen smirked. "Did it?"

Brand didn't answer. They had stepped into a city of strangers. Now, they had to figure out who among them were enemies.

The path through the settlement was uneven, lined with makeshift buildings constructed from salvaged metal and sun-bleached stone. The air hummed with quiet tension, conversations dropping to whispers as Brand and his companions followed the woman through the narrow streets.

The scent of roasting meat mingled with the sharp tang of oil and rust. Merchants hawked their wares from small stalls—scrap machinery, dried herbs, weapons of dubious origin. This was a place where survival came first, where trust was a commodity in short supply, and every transaction carried the weight of necessity.

Soran kept his hand near his weapon, eyes darting over the faces that watched them pass. "This place has seen its fair share of trouble."

Kaelen smirked. "I'm guessing we're about to make that worse."

Brand remained silent, his focus fixed on the woman leading them. She moved with the assuredness of someone who belonged here, someone who had earned their place.

They reached a large structure at the heart of the settlement—a repurposed building, half-ruined but reinforced with thick stone walls. The woman pushed the heavy door open and gestured for them to enter.

Inside, the air was cooler. A long table dominated the room, illuminated by flickering lamps. Maps and hand-drawn schematics covered the walls, detailing the surrounding desert, known CABAL movements, and potential safe routes.

At the far end of the table sat a man. His presence was quiet yet commanding, his gaze sharp as he appraised them. His skin was darkened by years under the sun, his gray-streaked hair tied back in a loose knot. A revolver rested beside his hand, its placement casual but deliberate.

The woman took a step forward, nodding toward Brand. "They say they're travelers. Looking for information."

The man studied them for a long moment before speaking. "Travelers tend to keep moving. You came here with purpose."

Brand met his gaze evenly. "We're looking for allies."

A beat of silence. Then the man leaned back slightly, tapping his fingers against the table. "And what makes you think we're looking for friends?"

Soran crossed his arms. "Because the CABAL isn't just our enemy. They're yours, too."

A flicker of something passed through the man's eyes. Not surprise—recognition.

Brand didn't relent. "You don't have to trust us. But we have information you might want to hear."

The man exhaled slowly, then nodded toward the empty seats. "Sit."

Brand complied. The real conversation was about to begin.

The tension in the room thickened as Brand and his companions took their seats. The settlement leader drummed his fingers against the table, his gaze unreadable.

"This city doesn't take in strays," he said finally. "We survive because we don't pick sides."

Brand leaned forward. "That's an illusion. You might not have chosen a side yet, but the CABAL won't give you the choice forever. When they come, it won't matter if you fought them or ignored them."

The man exhaled slowly, his expression unreadable. Then, glancing toward the woman who had led them here, he said, "Nia, tell them what happened last month."

The woman—Nia—crossed her arms. "A CABAL envoy came through, offering 'protection' in exchange for cooperation." Her voice was thick with disdain. "We turned them away."

Kaelen raised an eyebrow. "And they just... left?"

Nia's jaw tightened. "For now."

Soran nodded. "Which means they'll be back."

The leader leaned back, steepling his fingers. "And what exactly do you think you can do about that?"

Brand met his gaze. "We'll make sure they regret coming back."

Silence hung in the air for a long moment before the leader chuckled. "Bold words."

"They're more than words," Brand said. "We know how the CABAL operates. We know what they want—and we know how to disrupt them."

The leader studied him for a long moment, then nodded slightly. "You want allies? Prove it. We've got a problem that needs solving— something that will test whether you're as capable as you say."

Soran tensed. "What kind of problem?"

Nia spoke up. "There's a CABAL informant here in the settlement, feeding them information."

Kaelen sighed. "Of course there is."

Brand's expression hardened. This wasn't just a test—it was a risk. But if they wanted the settlement's trust, they had no choice but to take it.

"Then we find them," he said.

The leader smiled faintly. "Good. Let's see if you're worth keeping alive."

After the heavy door closed behind them, the cool night air washed over Brand, Soran, and Kaelen. The settlement had quieted, but an undercurrent of tension still pulsed through every whispered conversation. Somewhere among these people, a CABAL informant was hiding.

Kaelen exhaled sharply, rubbing his temple. "So now we're detectives? I'd prefer a straight-up fight over playing spy any day."

Soran shot him a look. "Killing the wrong person won't win us any favors."

Brand remained silent, scanning the streets. The informant wouldn't act like an outsider. They'd blend in—someone trusted enough to pass unnoticed.

Nia caught up to them, walking with measured steps. "We don't have much to go on," she said. "But there are a few people who've been asking the wrong kinds of questions lately."

Brand turned to her. "Names?"

She hesitated for a moment, then nodded. "A trader named Rellan, a healer called Meyla, and a former scavenger, Daro. All three have been seen talking to outsiders more than usual."

Kaelen smirked. "Great. Let's accuse the only people willing to talk to newcomers. That should win us some friends."

Brand ignored him, considering the options. A trader, a healer, and a scavenger—each with access to different parts of the settlement, each with the freedom to move between groups without raising suspicion.

Soran folded his arms. "We split up. Talk to them separately. See who flinches."

Nia shook her head. "Be too obvious, and the real informant will vanish."

Brand's gaze sharpened. She was right. This had to be handled with subtlety.

"We start with observation," Brand said. "We watch their movements before making a move."

Kaelen sighed. "So... we're spying?"

Brand smirked slightly. "Consider it laying a trap."

Soran nodded briskly. "Then let's spring it before the CABAL does."

The hunt was on.

Chapter 50:

Bargains in the Market

The market pulsed with life even under the cover of night. Flickering lanterns bathed makeshift stalls in a warm glow, the air heavy with the scent of grilled meat, spices, and the sharp tang of oil and metal. Vendors haggled in low voices, their eyes constantly darting, always alert.

The atmosphere was thick with voices—some raised in heated argument, others murmuring quiet deals in shadowed alcoves between stalls. A spice vendor waved a bundle of dried crimson leaves under a reluctant buyer's nose, boasting of its potency. Nearby, a weapons dealer displayed an array of crude but effective blades, their edges gleaming in the lantern light. The scent of cooked meats—spiced goat, roasted fowl, skewered fish—mingled with the musty aroma of old parchment and tanned leather.

A merchant shouted a price for rusted mechanical parts, while a cloaked figure exchanged small vials of shimmering liquid with a nervous buyer. The clatter of dice echoed from a nearby gambling stall, followed by a frustrated groan as someone lost their last coin.

Children dashed through the pathways, hands quick as shadows, snatching small trinkets before disappearing into the crowd.

Brand moved through the narrow pathways, blending seamlessly with the crowd, his hood drawn low. He wasn't waiting for a single act of betrayal—he was searching for patterns. The way people moved, how they reacted to the presence of outsiders, the subtle hesitations in their conversations. The market was a living, breathing entity, shifting with the moods of its inhabitants.

Soran had stationed himself at the far end of the market, keeping a watchful eye on Rellan, the trader. Known for dealing in rare goods, Rellan was an obvious suspect. He had access to valuable resources and a reason to make deals with outside forces.

Kaelen had drifted toward the healer's hut, observing Meyla as she treated patients. A healer could easily slip information—disguising messages as simple remedies, moving unnoticed among the people. Trust was freely given to those who healed.

Brand's focus remained on Daro, the former scavenger. The man sat alone at a worn table, sipping a drink with the kind of casual ease that came from knowing far more than he let on. No customers, no apparent trade—but Daro was here, watching.

Nia approached from the side, her voice barely a whisper. "Anything?"

Brand shook his head. "Not yet."

She sighed, her gaze scanning the crowd. "Whoever it is, they're careful."

Brand's eyes narrowed. Careful didn't mean perfect. There was always a slip—no matter how small.

Then he saw it.

A shadow flickered in the far alley, too quick to be casual. Someone had been watching them.

Brand's pulse quickened. The hunt wasn't just beginning. It had already started.

His muscles tensed as his gaze locked onto the fleeting figure vanishing into the alleyway. The air shifted, and the Flow pulsed in warning. Whoever had been watching them knew they'd been spotted.

Without hesitation, he moved. His steps were fast, precise, weaving through the dense crowd without breaking stride. A startled vendor almost dropped a stack of woven baskets as Brand slipped past him. The distant clang of metal rang out as a merchant slammed his counter shutter, closing shop for the night.

Soran and Kaelen reacted instantly. Soran took the long route, cutting off any possible escape. Kaelen, grinning despite himself, sprinted after Brand, matching his pace.

The alley ahead narrowed, the walls closing in on either side. The flickering light from the market barely reached this far, swallowed by the heavy shadows. Brand's boots pounded against uneven stone, the hurried footsteps ahead growing louder—the informant was fast, but fear made people reckless.

A sharp turn. A clatter of overturned crates. A flash of a cloak disappearing around another corner.

Brand surged forward. The Flow wrapped around him, sharpening his senses, mapping the movements ahead before his eyes could register them. He reached out with his instincts—

—and leaped.

His body twisted in midair, clearing a pile of discarded goods and landing just in time to see a figure dart into a side passage.

"Kaelen, left!" Brand barked.

Kaelen didn't hesitate, veering left to intercept. Soran was already ahead, cutting off other escape routes. The trap was closing.

The alley opened into a dead-end courtyard. A single lantern flickered above an abandoned well, casting jagged shadows across the walls.

Brand slowed, his senses alert. No sign of movement. No sound but the distant murmur of the market.

But he wasn't fooled.

He took a slow, steady breath and let the Flow guide him. There— just beyond the shadows, a heartbeat too steady for someone who had just been running.

Brand's fingers flexed at his sides. "Come out."

Silence.

Soran stepped forward, his hand on the hilt of his blade. "You can make this easy, or you can make it hurt."

A pause. Then, from the darkness, a voice—calm, composed, and far too confident.

"I was wondering when you'd notice me."

A figure stepped into the light.

The real game had begun.

The figure emerged into the dim lantern glow, their silhouette cutting sharply against the jagged walls of the alley. A loose cloak draped around their shoulders, worn and dusty, yet their posture was poised—too calculated to be an ordinary merchant or passerby.

Brand's gaze locked onto theirs, searching for a hint of fear, guilt, or arrogance. Instead, the stranger merely smirked.

Kaelen, ever impatient, scoffed. "You're awfully calm for someone who just ran for their life."

The figure tilted their head slightly, their voice smooth, edged with amusement. "Running was the polite thing to do. I thought I'd give you a bit of sport before we had this conversation."

Soran's blade gleamed in the lantern light. "Conversation? You're caught. You don't get to talk your way out of this."

The stranger sighed, shifting slightly. "Ah, but that's where you're wrong." A gloved hand reached for their belt—slow, deliberate—not for a weapon, but something small and metallic.

Brand's instincts flared. The Flow around them shifted, disturbed by an unseen force. He took a step forward, his voice low and commanding. "No sudden moves."

The stranger paused, their smirk widening. "You don't even know what I have, do you?"

Kaelen clenched his fists. "Do we look like we care?"

The informant ignored him, eyes fixed on Brand. "You feel it, don't you?"

Brand stiffened. He did. The object in their hand pulsed faintly in the Flow—not strong enough to be a full artifact, but attuned to it. Something meant to disrupt or manipulate.

Soran's patience snapped. He took a step closer, his voice low and dark. "Enough games. Who are you working for?"

The stranger exhaled slowly. "You already know."

Silence stretched. The CABAL.

Brand's jaw tightened. "Then why haven't they moved on this place yet? If you're feeding them information, why is this city still standing?"

The stranger's eyes gleamed with a knowing look. "Because I haven't told them to burn it. Yet."

A ripple of tension passed between them. This wasn't just an informant. This was someone with influence, someone playing a much longer game than simple betrayal.

Kaelen inhaled sharply, his voice thick with irritation. "I really hate smug bastards like you."

Brand didn't look away from the figure. They had the informant cornered, but something told him they weren't the ones holding the losing hand.

"Start talking," he said, his voice low and commanding. "Or you won't like what happens next."

The stranger chuckled, almost lazily. "Oh, I doubt that."

Then, with unnerving calm, they tossed the metal object onto the ground—

—and the alley exploded with light.

The burst of light was blinding, sending shockwaves through the alley. Brand shielded his eyes as searing energy crackled against the stone walls. A pulse rippled through the Flow, distorting reality for an instant before everything snapped back into place.

By the time the glare faded, the informant was gone.

Kaelen swore, stumbling back as the afterimage still burned his vision. "What in the hells was that?"

Soran coughed, steadying himself. "A diversion. And it worked."

Brand blinked rapidly, forcing his senses to realign. The Flow was still unsettled, rippling like water disturbed by a heavy stone. He reached out, trying to trace the residual energy—but it was already slipping through his grasp, fading like grains of sand.

"They knew we'd come," Brand muttered, voice tight with frustration. "This was all planned."

Nia skidded into the alley, weapon raised. "What happened?"

"The informant got away," Soran grumbled.

Brand turned, his frustration burning through his gaze. "They weren't some low-level spy. This one had direct ties to the CABAL. This wasn't just about feeding them information. This was about control."

Nia frowned, brow furrowed. "Control?"

Brand's jaw clenched as realization sank in. "They were manipulating the Flow. That device—it wasn't just a distraction. It was a message."

Kaelen exhaled sharply. "Great. And let me guess—whoever that message was for is already moving."

Brand nodded grimly. The CABAL wasn't coming. They were already here.

Soran gripped his blade tighter. "Then we move faster."

Nia's expression hardened, resolve settling in. "I need to warn the settlement leader. If the CABAL has infiltrated this deep, we have to prepare."

Brand took a step forward, his voice unwavering. "Not just prepare." His eyes locked onto theirs, a quiet certainty in his tone. "We strike first."

The weight of his words settled over them, the meaning clear. This wasn't just about rooting out a traitor anymore. This was war.

And war had just begun.

Chapter 51:

The Gathering Storm

The settlement buzzed with tension, whispers carrying through the crowd as the news spread—The CABAL was coming.

Brand stood in the meeting hall, arms crossed, while Darius, the settlement leader, paced before him. Nia leaned casually against the doorframe, her expression unreadable, and Soran and Kaelen sat nearby, their weapons within reach.

"We don't have the numbers to face them head-on," Darius said flatly. "Even with every able-bodied fighter standing with us, we're outmatched."

Brand's face remained impassive. "Then we don't fight them on their terms."

Darius scoffed. "You think we can outmaneuver them? They control the skies, the land routes—hell, they likely have eyes inside this very settlement."

Kaelen smirked, leaning back. "Oh, they do. We just chased one of their spies through the market."

Darius shot him a sharp glare. "And you let them escape?"

Soran stepped in, defusing the tension. "Not by choice. They were prepared for this."

Nia pushed off the doorframe, her voice steady. "Then we strike first. Take the fight to them before they can surround us."

Brand nodded. "We disrupt them. Hit their supply lines, take out their forward scouts, force them to hesitate before launching a full attack."

Darius rubbed his temple, exhaling sharply. "You're talking about guerrilla tactics."

Brand met his gaze unflinchingly. "I'm talking about survival."

The room fell silent, the weight of the coming battle settling over them. This wasn't just about holding the settlement. It was about making a stand—showing the CABAL they were not prey.

Darius sighed, nodding at last. "Then we move fast. Prepare the defenses, and send scouts to locate their forces."

Brand turned to Nia. "You said the CABAL envoy approached from the south before. Where did they come from?"

She folded her arms, her tone firm. "The southern ridge. That's where they'll come from again."

Brand's eyes darkened with resolve. "Then that's where we strike first."

The night was thick with tension as Brand, Soran, Kaelen, and a group of fighters crouched along the rocky ledge of the southern ridge.

Below them, the desert stretched endlessly, a dark sea of shifting sands under the pale glow of the moons.

Brand peered through a narrow gap in the rocks. Torchlight flickered in the distance—CABAL scouts moving with precision, their sharp eyes scanning the settlement's defenses. They weren't attacking yet. They were gathering intelligence.

Kaelen exhaled slowly. "Take them out now, and they won't be able to report back."

Soran nodded grimly. "But if even one escapes, they'll know we're expecting them."

Brand surveyed the terrain. The CABAL's force wasn't large—maybe ten scouts—but that meant a larger force was waiting just beyond sight. This was their chance to unbalance them.

Nia crouched beside Brand, her voice low and firm. "We need to be precise. Silent."

Brand exhaled, drawing in the Flow as it swirled around him, sharpening his instincts.

He signaled. Go.

The fighters moved like shadows, splitting into small teams. Brand led Soran and Kaelen down the left flank, navigating the rocky terrain with swift, silent steps. The CABAL scouts remained oblivious—until it was too late.

The first fell without a sound, Soran's blade cutting cleanly through his throat. Kaelen took down another, pinning him with brutal force before he could raise an alarm.

Brand struck next, slipping into the Flow as he lunged. His blade sank into the ribs of a CABAL soldier, the movement seamless, guided by something greater than instinct. For a heartbeat, he felt the soldier's energy slipping away, life draining into the stillness of the night.

Then, a sharp whistle split the air.

One of the CABAL scouts had spotted them.

"Move!" Brand hissed.

The quiet ambush shattered into chaos as the remaining scouts scrambled to react. The element of surprise was gone, but they had to finish this before word could reach the main force.

Nia's bowstring twanged, her arrow finding the throat of a retreating scout. Soran and Kaelen fought back-to-back, cutting through the last of the enemy as Brand sprinted after the final scout—a runner, fast, trying to flee over the ridge.

He can't get away.

Brand surged forward, the Flow bending around him. The scout leaped for higher ground—

—but Brand was faster. He tackled the man mid-stride, sending him crashing into the rocky earth. Before the scout could react, Brand's knife pressed against his throat.

The man froze, ragged breath escaping in shallow gasps. Fear radiated from him, but there was something else—a flicker of defiance.

Brand's grip tightened on the scout's collar as the ragged breaths grew more desperate. You're too late. They already know.

The words settled like a weight in Brand's chest. He didn't hesitate—slamming the hilt of his knife into the scout's temple, rendering him unconscious before rising to his feet.

Soran, Nia, and Kaelen sprinted toward him, their faces grim. The night's calm had shattered. Distant echoes of hurried voices and the clash of metal rang out from the direction of the settlement.

"They're moving," Soran muttered. "The CABAL's not waiting."

Brand turned toward the ridge, scanning the horizon. Then, he saw it.

A line of small fires flickered beyond the dunes. Torches. Dozens. Maybe more. Shadows moved in coordinated patterns between them. This wasn't a raiding party. This was an army.

Kaelen cursed under his breath. "We're about to be in a world of trouble."

Brand's mind raced. They were outnumbered. The settlement's walls were sturdy, but not designed for a siege. If the CABAL fully committed, they wouldn't stand a chance.

Nia's sharp gaze met his. "We can't win a straight fight."

Brand exhaled sharply. "No, but we can buy time."

Soran nodded, his expression hardening. "What's the plan?"

Brand's eyes fixed on the distant flames. They needed to delay the CABAL. Force them into a prolonged engagement, slow their momentum. If they could bleed their forces, the settlement might just survive.

"We split into small teams," Brand said. "Use the dunes for cover. Force them into smaller skirmishes. Take out their scouts, their runners. Confuse them. Make them think we have more forces than we do."

Kaelen cracked his knuckles, a dark smile tugging at his lips. "I like it. But if they get wise to it, they'll crush us like a sandstorm."

"That's why we don't fight to win," Brand replied, his voice steady. "We fight to survive."

Nia adjusted the grip on her bow. "Then let's make them bleed for every step they take."

Brand's gaze turned back to the distant torches. The battle had already begun. Now, it was about how long they could hold out.

The group moved swiftly toward the settlement, shadows in the dark. As they neared the gates, the mood had already shifted. People were gathering, weapons distributed, supplies rationed with cold efficiency. The air buzzed with tension.

Darius stood at the center of the camp, barking orders to a group of fighters. When his eyes landed on Brand and the others, he strode toward them, his expression tight with concern. "Tell me we have a plan."

"We've got a way to buy time," Brand said. "Hit-and-run tactics. Draw them into a fight they don't want, slow them down before they reach the walls."

Darius sighed heavily, rubbing his temple. "And if they push through anyway?"

Brand met his gaze, steady. "Then we make them pay for every inch they take."

Nearby, a group of rangers checked their weapons. One of them, a grizzled veteran named Orin, grunted. "I like this one," he said, nodding toward Brand. "Better to strike first than hide behind walls."

Kaelen smirked. "See? At least someone here's got a sense of adventure."

Orin snorted. "Adventure? Nah. Just experience. The CABAL doesn't play fair. They'll send shock troopers to break our morale, then the real killers will come."

Brand nodded. They weren't just fighting soldiers—they were facing an army built on fear.

Nia motioned to the supply carts. "We need to rig the perimeter. Traps, anything that slows them down."

Darius waved toward a group of engineers. "You heard her. Spikes, trenches, anything that forces them to break formation."

A younger fighter stepped forward, hesitating. "What about the civilians? Not everyone can fight."

Brand turned to him. This was the real burden of war—not just the fight itself, but the innocent lives caught in the middle.

"We get them underground," he said. "Reinforce the shelter under the supply depot. If it comes to that, they stay hidden."

Darius crossed his arms, looking uneasy. "And if we can't hold?"

Brand's jaw tightened. He wouldn't let it come to that. "Then we give them time to escape."

A heavy silence fell. They all knew what that meant. If the CABAL breached the settlement, they wouldn't just conquer—they'd burn it to the ground.

Soran exhaled, breaking the tension. "Then we make sure that doesn't happen."

Brand looked at each of them, the weight of leadership pressing down on him. This wasn't just about surviving anymore. It was about defying the CABAL's power.

And it started now.

The settlement hummed with urgency as the first light of dawn crept over the horizon. The sounds of preparation filled the air—hammers striking wood, blades being sharpened, whispered prayers from those who believed in something greater. The people were afraid, but they moved with purpose.

Brand stood atop one of the barricades, eyes scanning the dunes beyond the walls. The CABAL's torches had disappeared, but that only made their approach more perilous. They were coming—now in silence, moving through the shadows, waiting for the right moment to strike.

Darius joined him, arms crossed. "Think they'll try to breach the walls first?"

Brand shook his head. "No. They'll probe for weaknesses. Test our defenses. Stir panic."

Nia arrived next, her quiver full, her expression resolute. "Then we show them we're not weak."

A sharp whistle split the air—signal from the eastern watch. Brand turned sharply. On the crest of the dunes, a lone figure stood, something raised high.

A banner. CABAL colors. A challenge.

Kaelen scoffed. "That's a new move."

Brand narrowed his eyes. They weren't here just to attack—they were here to send a message.

Soran stepped forward. "We need to respond."

Brand nodded. If they wanted to speak before the bloodshed, they'd have to understand the message first.

"We ride out to meet them," Brand said, his voice steady. "But we ride ready for war."

Chapter 52:

First Blood

Brand rode at the head of a small group, descending the settlement's outer ridge. The sand still felt cool beneath the horses' hooves, while the sky shifted from violet to orange as the sun crept over the horizon.

The CABAL envoy stood motionless, their banner fluttering lightly in the morning breeze. Four figures flanked them, clad in dark, angular armor, their faces obscured by smooth, featureless helmets. They radiated control—disciplined, calculating.

The contrast between the two groups was stark. Brand and his people, rough and worn from years of survival, carried weapons that had seen countless battles, while the CABAL's warriors stood pristine, their armor reflecting no weakness, no hesitation. The air between them hummed with unspoken tension.

Soran pulled his horse alongside Brand's, voice low. "This is a show of force. They want us to see what we're up against."

Brand nodded. "Then we'll make sure they know what they're up against."

As they closed the distance, the CABAL envoy stepped forward. Unlike the armored guards, this one wore robes, their garments embroidered with intricate patterns resembling flowing currents—symbols of control over the Flow.

But it was their eyes that struck Brand most—cold, assessing, filled with the certainty of those who had never known true resistance.

"Who speaks for this settlement?" the envoy called, their voice carrying unnaturally through the open air.

Brand dismounted and stepped forward without hesitation. His boots pressed into the shifting sand, his stance unwavering. "I do."

The envoy studied him, tilting their head as if appraising him like an object. "Interesting."

Kaelen muttered behind him, "I hate when they say that."

The envoy ignored him. "Your defiance has been noted." They gestured toward the settlement. "This land is no longer yours. The CABAL has reclaimed it."

Brand's jaw tightened. Every muscle in his body screamed for him to strike first, to wipe the smug certainty from the envoy's face—but he held still. He needed to understand their intent.

"We have no intention of surrendering," Brand said, his voice calm but resolute.

The envoy exhaled softly, as if they had expected nothing else. "Then blood must be spilled."

For the first time, the envoy's expression shifted—not to anger, but to amusement—as if Brand's resistance was little more than a minor inconvenience in their path.

They raised a hand, and in an instant, one of the armored figures lunged forward.

The battle had begun.

The CABAL warrior moved with unnatural speed, closing the gap between them in the blink of an eye. Brand barely sidestepped, twisting as the curved blade sliced through the air where he had stood moments before.

Soran's sword flashed, meeting the CABAL's second strike mid-swing. The clash of metal rang out across the dunes, the force of the impact sending a tremor through the sand.

Brand pivoted, regaining his stance. The warrior's movements were unnervingly precise, almost mechanical—guided by something beyond training. It wasn't just skill; it was the Flow, weaponized into perfect lethality.

Kaelen cursed sharply as two more CABAL warriors surged forward. "Oh, this is going to be fun." He barely ducked in time as a second attacker swung at him, forcing him back toward the settlement's ridge.

The envoy stood motionless, watching with cold detachment. This wasn't negotiation—it had never been. This was an execution.

Brand blocked a downward strike, feeling the shock of the blow rattle through his arms. The CABAL fighter was stronger than him—stronger than he had any right to be. The Flow around him pulsed, disturbed by the unnatural energy feeding his movements.

Soran pressed forward, slashing at their attacker's exposed side. The warrior twisted at the last moment, deflecting the strike with reflexes that bordered on impossible. The CABAL weren't just enhanced—they were attuned, their bodies perfectly in sync with the energy that surrounded them.

Nia's arrow struck one of the attackers in the leg. The warrior staggered but didn't fall, showing no sign of pain—like the injury meant nothing. Brand's teeth ground together. They weren't fighting men—they were fighting weapons.

"Don't let them dictate the fight!" Brand called, adjusting his stance. They were faster, stronger—but they weren't invincible. The Flow wasn't theirs alone to command.

He took a deep breath, centering himself. Instead of forcing the battle, he let the currents flow around him—the shifting sand, the weight of his attacker's movements, the rhythm of each strike.

When the warrior lunged again, Brand didn't block. He moved with the Flow.

Ducking under the attack, he twisted behind his opponent, blade flashing as he struck.

The warrior staggered as Brand's knife found its mark—deep, but not lethal. Not yet.

Kaelen laughed, despite the danger. "That's more like it!"

The CABAL warrior growled—a rare slip of emotion—before surging forward again, but now, Brand was ready.

The fight was far from over.

The battle unfolded in chaotic bursts, shifting between precise strikes and raw survival. The CABAL warriors moved like a storm—unrelenting, disciplined, their attacks designed to provoke mistakes.

Brand ducked as another strike came dangerously close, feeling the sharp whisper of steel as it sliced through the air. Sweat drenched his back, muscles screaming as he deflected blow after blow. His opponent was relentless, moving with inhuman speed.

Kaelen's blade flashed beside him, intercepting a strike that would have landed clean on Brand's exposed flank. "You're welcome," Kaelen panted, his usual grin now strained.

Brand barely had time to nod before another strike came his way. He could feel the Flow stirring around him, urging him to move differently, to stop resisting, to guide his strikes like currents in the tide.

Soran was locked in combat with one of the taller CABAL warriors, his movements sharp, deliberate. The warrior fought with brutal efficiency, countering every move, reading Soran's attacks before they were fully executed. But Soran had something the CABAL didn't—instinct, unpredictability. With a sudden drop, he swept the enemy's legs, sending the armored fighter crashing into the sand.

From the ridge, Nia loosed another volley of arrows. One found its mark, embedding deep in a warrior's shoulder. The warrior barely flinched, their movements slowing but not stopping.

"This isn't working!" Nia shouted. "They're too resilient!"

Brand gritted his teeth. They were enhanced, but not invulnerable. There had to be a weakness. He let the Flow settle around him, tuning into the patterns in their movements, the controlled energy guiding their strikes. Then, in a flash, he saw it—a slight delay, a hesitation when recovering from a missed attack.

"Strike after they overextend!" Brand called. "They recover slower than they move!"

Kaelen reacted first, ducking beneath a deadly swing before twisting his dagger upward, catching the warrior under the arm where the armor was weakest. The warrior stumbled, visibly stunned.

Soran moved next, waiting for his opponent's lunge. With a fluid sidestep, he swung his sword in a precise arc. This time, the strike connected, slicing through dark plating, drawing a thin line of blood.

The tide of battle shifted. For the first time, the CABAL warriors faltered.

The envoy, who had been observing with detached amusement, raised a hand—a silent command.

Without hesitation, the CABAL warriors stopped, retreating several steps to form a tight line. Their breathing was controlled, but their postures were tense, alert.

Brand exhaled slowly, watching them carefully. They weren't fleeing—they were regrouping.

The envoy's voice sliced through the dust-filled air. "Interesting. You adapt faster than expected."

Brand's gaze narrowed. This wasn't over. Not by a long shot.

His fists clenched, his breathing steady. The CABAL warriors stood in formation, their envoy watching with quiet amusement. The battle had reached a lull—but only temporarily.

The air crackled with tension, like the calm before a storm.

The envoy took a slow step forward, their robes flowing with the movement, almost unruffled. "You surprise me," they said, their voice smooth, unhurried. "Few stand against us for long—fewer still push back."

Brand ignored the words, his focus razor-sharp. This was no longer just about survival. It was about showing they weren't prey.

Soran shifted beside him, his blade low, but ready. "They're stalling," he murmured.

Brand nodded, his mind racing. The envoy was waiting—waiting for something. Reinforcements? A change in tactics? He couldn't let them control the pace of this fight.

Brand stepped forward, his voice rising. "You came here expecting us to kneel." He took another step, eyes locked on the envoy. "You think that because you control the Flow, you control everything." His fingers curled at his sides, the energy swirling around him. But the Flow was never meant to be dominated—it was meant to be followed, guided.

For the first time, a flicker of emotion crossed the envoy's face— intrigue? Annoyance? "Control is inevitable," they said, their tone unwavering. "It is the only path to order."

Brand's breath slowed, a steady calm filling him. Then let's see how much control you really have.

He moved first. The Flow surged around him, propelling him forward faster than before. The envoy barely had time to react before Brand struck, his blade arcing toward their shoulder. In a single motion, the envoy raised a hand—and stopped the strike.

A shockwave pulsed outward, sending a blast of sand into the air as Brand was shoved back. It wasn't just strength that stopped him. He realized that was not Flux energy —it was the direct manipulation of the Flow.

The envoy smirked, their voice cold. "Now you understand."

But Brand wasn't done. He adjusted his stance, feeling the energy shift. The Flow wasn't theirs to control—it was something to be guided.

With a deep breath, he released his grip on the current—and flowed with it.

This time, when he struck, the envoy's attempt to block faltered. Brand slipped past their guard, his blade cutting a thin line across their arm. The envoy hissed in pain, stepping back, their expression unreadable.

The CABAL warriors moved at once, their formation breaking as they surged forward. The real battle had begun.

Kaelen let out a sharp laugh, already clashing with an attacker. "Well, that did it!"

Soran met another foe, steel ringing against steel. "No turning back now."

Brand tightened his grip, his stance unshaken. The Flow was with him. Now, it was time to break them.

Chapter 53:
The Siege Begins

The first wave of CABAL warriors surged forward, their ranks moving with eerie precision, as though they were one entity. Their approach was calculated—like an inevitable tide, unrelenting. Their black armor glinted in the rising sun, each warrior moving with mechanical perfection. No fear. No hesitation. Only purpose.

Before Brand could catch his breath, the settlement's defenses came alive. A hail of arrows arced through the air, their deadly points flashing in the morning light. The sharp whistle of their flight was followed by the sickening thud of steel sinking into flesh. Some CABAL soldiers faltered, stumbling to their knees, but most pressed forward as though the pain were irrelevant.

From the barricades, the defenders fought back desperately. Oil-soaked firepots flew, bursting into searing explosions upon impact. Smoke spiraled upward, blending with the stench of blood, charred flesh, and burning wood. The air was filled with the clash of steel, shouts of orders, and the panicked cries of the wounded.

From atop the main barricade, Darius shouted orders, his voice cutting through the chaos. "Hold your ground! Focus fire on the front line!"

Nia loosed another arrow, her fingers raw from the rapid fire. "They're pushing harder than expected!" she gasped between breaths.

Brand clenched his jaw. Of course they were. The CABAL never entered a fight without confidence in victory. He saw it in their movements—systematic, probing. The first wave wasn't meant to break through—it was a test.

Soran moved beside him, wiping blood from a fresh cut on his arm. "They're testing us."

Brand nodded grimly. "And once they find the weak points, they'll strike hard."

A sudden explosion rocked the barricade, sending debris flying. A section of the wall shuddered violently, splintering under the force of a CABAL shock trooper's energy-enhanced strike.

The Flow around Brand pulsed with warning. Something worse was coming.

Then, from the ridge, a new figure emerged—a towering CABAL commander, clad in segmented armor, energy flickering along the gauntlets. The warriors around him parted, stepping back as if in reverence. This wasn't just a soldier. This was a "warbringer."

The commander raised a single hand—and the battlefield shifted.

The sand trembled. The Flow twisted unnaturally, warping like a storm before the storm's arrival.

The next attack wouldn't be brute force.

It would be devastation.

The ground shuddered beneath the unrelenting assault. The air was thick with smoke, the acrid scent of scorched wood mixing with blood and sweat. The settlement's walls groaned under each impact, cracks spider-webbing through the wooden barricades. Screams of pain and the desperate cries of the wounded filled the air, drowning out the clash of steel.

Brand ducked as a spear slammed into the barricade beside him, splintering the wood on impact. His pulse roared in his ears, the weight of the battle pressing down on his chest. Blood—his or someone else's—smeared his cheek as he wiped it away, sword gripped tightly in hand.

"They're not letting up!" Nia shouted, loosing another arrow. Her arms trembled with exhaustion, but she didn't slow.

Brand's gaze snapped to the ridge. The CABAL commander stood motionless, watching, calculating. They weren't fighting with reckless aggression—they were waiting.

Darius stormed up to Brand, his face streaked with soot and sweat. "The eastern barricade won't hold another wave. We need to fall back!"

Brand's jaw clenched. If they retreated now, they'd be overrun.

Soran fought beside him, cutting down a CABAL soldier before turning to Brand. "We need to make a stand, or we're done."

Brand turned back to the commander, watching as the energy around his gauntlets flared brighter. It hit him—the commander wasn't just waiting. He was preparing.

The Flow around the battlefield shifted unnaturally. A low hum vibrated through the air, an ominous pull that raised the hairs on Brand's arms.

Then the CABAL commander raised a single hand.

The energy detonated outward.

A shockwave of pure force exploded from his palm, tearing through the battlefield like a storm unleashed. Defenders were tossed aside, their bodies flung through the air like ragdolls. The walls groaned, splintering apart as though struck by an unseen hammer. Sand whipped into the air in dense, blinding clouds, momentarily shrouding everything in a suffocating veil before Brand was slammed into the earth.

His vision swam. His lungs burned. The world tilted, spinning wildly out of control.

A muffled voice broke through the haze—Kaelen's. "Brand! Get up!"

Through the dust and chaos, the commander strode forward, his presence a weight that pressed down like the hand of fate itself. This was no longer a battle. It was a slaughter.

Brand gritted his teeth, fingers scraping the earth as he forced himself back to his feet. He wasn't done.

Not yet.

The battlefield had become a nightmare. Smoke churned into the sky in thick, choking plumes, suffocating the first light of dawn. The once-proud barricades lay in ruins, shattered wood and crumbled stone scattered across the sand. Blood pooled, darkening the ground beneath the defenders' feet.

Brand's head hammered with pain, but he fought to remain upright, anchoring himself to the earth as the world spun. The blast from the CABAL commander had sent bodies flying, leaving only the stubborn, the desperate, and the broken still standing.

Kaelen yanked Brand to his feet, his grip like iron around Brand's arm. "We can't hold this position!"

Darius stumbled toward them, his tunic torn, a deep gash slashing across his arm. "We're being overrun," he snarled, his voice ragged. "Fall back now, or there won't be anyone left to save."

Brand wiped blood from his mouth, his breath coming in harsh, uneven gasps. Retreat meant abandoning the settlement, the lives within it. But staying would mean death.

His gaze swept over the battlefield. Nia still fought from the high ground, her arrows finding their marks, but her quiver was nearly empty. Soran matched a CABAL warrior's speed, but fatigue was beginning to slow him.

Then the ground trembled again. Another shockwave, this time more powerful, rippled through the air as the CABAL commander advanced, his gauntlets crackling with raw energy. With every step, the sand quaked, and the Flow itself bent unnaturally, distorting with his power.

Brand's vision narrowed, locking onto the commander. This wasn't just another soldier. This was the executioner.

His teeth ground together. If they were going to die today, they wouldn't die running.

Kaelen cursed, but the fire in his eyes mirrored Brand's resolve. "Guess we're doing this, then!"

The commander raised his hand, his fingers flexing in preparation. Another pulse of energy exploded outward, sending shockwaves through the ground.

Brand twisted sharply at the last moment, the wave narrowly missing him but ripping the earth to shreds where he'd stood a heartbeat before. He felt the Flow shift, twisting violently around him. This time, he didn't fight it. He let it guide him, bending the energy to his will—not to control, but to move with it. His body surged forward, faster, sharper, more precise than before, his steps guided by the unseen currents.

Brand closed the distance with a fierce, measured step. His blade flashed, a blur of steel.

The CABAL commander blocked the strike with an effortless flick of his wrist, but there was a hesitation. A brief, telling delay where Brand felt the resistance shift, weakening.

A crack.

Soran saw it, too. Without missing a beat, he lunged from the opposite side, his blade aimed low. The commander twisted, but not fast enough.

The sound of steel cutting through flesh rang in the air. The commander staggered, his breath sharp.

The moment was fleeting—but it was enough. A flicker of hope, fragile but real.

Brand didn't waste it.

With a snarl, he struck again, his blade carving through the space between them.

The commander growled low in his throat, the wound on his side stark against his dark armor. For the first time, his movements faltered, his expression betraying a crack in his stoic facade. He looked... mortal. Vulnerable.

Brand surged forward, relentless. The Flow surged with him, guiding his steps and strikes with newfound precision. This time, he wasn't fighting against it. He was flowing with it, as if the energy had become an extension of himself.

Soran stayed in sync, circling wide, keeping the pressure on the commander's exposed side. Kaelen danced past another CABAL warrior, his twin daggers flashing, slashing at those trying to reinforce their leader. For the first time since the battle began, the defenders weren't just surviving—they were seizing the advantage.

The commander snarled, his features twisting with fury. He stepped back, energy crackling around him as he tried to regain his stance. But his power pulsed unevenly, jagged. His connection to the Flow had been disrupted, his once-impervious composure fractured. The true battle had only just begun.

From atop the ruined barricades, Nia spotted the opening. Without hesitation, she released her arrow. It flew true, sinking deep into the commander's shoulder.

The impact sent him stumbling back, his grip on the battle faltering.

Brand didn't wait for him to recover. He surged forward, twisting to avoid a desperate counterstrike, then brought his blade down with all his force. This time, the strike was deep.

The commander gasped, his knees giving way beneath him. The unnatural energy that had surrounded him flickered violently, then sputtered out. His soldiers, seeing their leader fall, faltered, their resolve splintering.

Darius seized the moment, his voice cutting through the chaos. "Now! Push them back!"

The defenders, fueled by a surge of adrenaline, threw themselves into the fray. Fatigue evaporated in the face of renewed purpose. The CABAL soldiers hesitated, their once-unshakable formation splintering.

Brand stood over the fallen commander, chest heaving. He could taste the victory, but knew it wasn't over. Not yet.

But as he looked around, he saw it in their eyes. The CABAL were no longer the relentless force they had been. For the first time, they knew fear.

Chapter 54:

Aftermath of Victory

The dust lingered in the air, thick with smoke and the acrid scent of blood and fire. The battlefield—once a chaotic struggle for survival—lay silent, unnervingly still.

Brand stood among the wreckage, sword loosely gripped in his hand, its weight heavy with the aftermath. Around him, the bodies of CABAL soldiers sprawled in the sand, broken and unmoving. Their once-feared force now lay in ruins.

But it wasn't just the enemy. The defenders—men and women who had given everything—now lay scattered among the corpses. The walls that had once stood as the last barrier against the desert's wrath were crumbled in places, jagged remnants of their final stand. Blood soaked the earth, and bodies littered the ground, some still clutching weapons they hadn't lived to use.

Kaelen wiped blood from his face, looking at Brand with a mix of exhaustion and disbelief. "We did it." His voice was hoarse, almost a whisper. "We actually did it."

But Brand didn't respond. His gaze drifted across the field—over the fallen, the wounded, the lost. They had won—but at what cost?

Darius stumbled toward them, clutching his side. "The CABAL's retreating. We broke them." His words carried the weight of victory, but his hollow eyes told another story. He, too, understood the price they had paid.

Soran knelt beside a fallen defender, checking for signs of life. Too many had fallen. Some were motionless, others gripped wounds that would soon claim them. The moans of the dying echoed through the stillness, a haunting contrast to the battle cries that had once filled the air.

Nia limped toward them, bow still in hand, her movements slow but determined. "We need to tend to the wounded. Gather what supplies we have left."

Brand barely heard her. His eyes were fixed on the spot where the CABAL commander had fallen. The body was gone.

A sickening twist tightened in his stomach. They had won the battle. But the war was far from over.

A cold wind stirred the dust, sweeping across the carnage like a whisper of things yet to come. Brand swallowed, forcing himself to breathe. This wasn't victory. It was survival—nothing more.

He had spent his life questioning what it truly meant to fight—to protect. But as he stared at the bodies of those who had believed in him, who had died by his side, he finally understood:

Victory was hollow if the ones you fought for were lost.

And somewhere beyond the horizon, the CABAL was still watching.

The fires burned low as the survivors gathered in the heart of the settlement. The celebration, if it could be called that, was a quiet affair—subdued, muted—a mere shadow of the triumph they had hoped for.

Brand sat alone, his back pressed against a shattered wall, the weight of exhaustion settling on him like an anchor. Around him, the settlement had become a place of mourning, not relief.

Kaelen approached, offering him a cup of water, his face drawn with weariness. "Drink. You look like you're already dead."

Brand accepted the cup but barely took a sip. His stomach churned at the sight before him—a group of villagers gathered around a hastily dug burial pit, laying the fallen to rest. There were too many.

Soran crouched beside him, rubbing a hand across his face. "We won, didn't we?" His laugh was dry, humorless. "Then why does it feel like we lost?"

Brand's breath left him in a sharp exhale. Because they had. Not in a way that could be counted on a map, but in the hearts of those still breathing.

Nia passed by, her arm bound in a sling, her bow slung across her back. Her sharp eyes were dulled, distant. She paused long enough to meet Brand's gaze before shaking her head. "Winning doesn't bring them back."

The silence that followed pressed down on him like a weight.

Darius approached, his face unreadable. "We need to figure out what comes next."

Brand glanced up at him, his body heavy with fatigue. "Next?"

Darius nodded, his voice grave. "The CABAL will come again. Maybe not tomorrow, maybe not next week—but they will return. Stronger." He exhaled deeply, folding his arms. "And we won't survive another siege."

Brand let the words sink in. The realization hit him like a blade to the gut—this wasn't over. It never would be.

He pushed himself to his feet, ignoring the dull ache in his muscles. The war wasn't about holding ground—it was about choosing where to fight.

"We move," Brand said, his voice firm. "Gather what we can. Find somewhere safer. Somewhere we can strike from."

Darius raised an eyebrow. "You're thinking of running?"

Brand's fingers tightened around his sword's hilt. Running wasn't the right word. He wasn't fleeing. He was shifting the battlefield.

"We can't wait for them to bring the fight to us," he said, his voice steady despite the weight pressing down on his chest. "It's time we take the fight to them."

The decision was made, but that didn't make it easier. Packing up what little was left wasn't just a logistical challenge—it was the severing of roots, the painful acceptance that the place they had fought for, bled for, was no longer theirs.

Brand stood at the settlement's edge, watching survivors scramble to gather supplies, loading carts with what little remained. Weapons were sharpened. Food rationed. Water stored carefully.

Nia approached again, her face drawn with exhaustion. "So, this is it?"

Brand turned to her, nodding. There was no other choice. Staying meant waiting for another siege. One they might not survive.

"We head for the deep canyons," Darius said, stepping up beside them. "The terrain will give us an advantage—harder to track, easier to defend."

Brand exhaled, knowing it was the right decision, yet feeling only the weight of defeat.

Nia slung her bow over her shoulder. "If we're doing this, we need to move before the CABAL regroups."

A silence settled over them. No one spoke the truth they all felt—leaving meant abandoning the dead. Abandoning the history of this place.

Brand turned toward the ruins of the barricades, his grip tightening around the hilt of his sword. They had fought—and they had won. But victory didn't always come with a place to call home.

He cast one last, lingering glance at the settlement, the echoes of what they had lost still heavy in the air. Then, with a deep, steadying breath, he turned away.

"Let's go."

The people, now refugees in their own land, followed him into the uncertainty of what lay ahead.

Chapter 55:

Into the Wild

The desert stretched endlessly before them, a vast, unyielding expanse of sand that seemed to swallow all hope. Beneath the brutal sun, the survivors trudged forward, their footsteps fading almost as soon as they were made—erased by the shifting dunes, like memories slipping through fingers.

Brand led the way, his gaze fixed on the distant horizon, eyes narrowed against the blinding glare. There was no telling how long they had before the CABAL regrouped, but one thing was certain: they weren't safe yet.

Darius stumbled beside him, his arm bound in a crude sling, wincing with every step. "The canyons are still days away. If we don't find water soon..." His voice trailed off, but the message was clear. They wouldn't survive without it.

Brand gave a short nod, his expression grim. They were already at their breaking point. The wounded dragged them down, and the desert offered no mercy.

A low voice cut through the oppressive silence. "Tracks behind us," Nia murmured from the rear, her words barely audible, meant only for Brand and Darius. "They're not ours."

Brand's grip on his sword tightened instinctively, the familiar weight of it offering little comfort. The CABAL was following them.

"We keep moving," he said, his voice cold with resolve. "And we make sure they don't catch us."

But inside, a darker thought flickered: the chase had already begun.

The desert's heat pressed on them like a suffocating shroud. Every breath was thick with the taste of dust and the stifling weight of the sun's fury. The survivors moved slower now, exhaustion dragging at their limbs, their supplies dwindling with each agonizing step.

Brand kept his eyes fixed on the dunes behind them, unease creeping up his spine like the tightening of a noose. The tracks Nia had spotted were no longer distant. The CABAL was closing in.

Kaelen caught up with him, wiping sweat from his brow, his expression strained. "We need to stop soon, Brand. People are collapsing."

Brand glanced at the villagers, their faces drawn, their bodies faltering. Some limped, others leaned on each other for support. The wounded—those who had survived the battle—were teetering on the edge of collapse.

"We push a little further," Brand said, though the words felt heavy on his tongue, thick with the weight of inevitability. He didn't need the Flow to sense the danger closing in around them. It was a suffocating presence, one that had settled deep in his bones.

Soran, who had been scouting ahead, came rushing back, his face tight with urgency. "We found something—an old ruin, partially buried up ahead. It could give us shelter."

Brand exchanged a glance with Darius. "Any signs of activity?"

Soran shook his head, his brow furrowed. "It looks abandoned. But..." He hesitated, his voice dropping to a near whisper. "There's something wrong with it. The air... it feels heavy."

Brand exhaled, his jaw tightening. A ruin meant shelter—but also the unknown. Still, with the CABAL on their heels and the survivors on the brink, they had no choice.

"Lead the way," Brand said, his voice as steady as he could make it.

As they moved toward the ruin, Brand cast a final glance over his shoulder. The dunes behind them lay still, unnervingly silent. Not a single gust of wind disturbed the sand.

The CABAL was closer. He could feel it in his bones.

The entrance to the ruins was half-buried, the stone doorway jagged and worn with the passage of time. Ancient symbols—crude yet intricate—were carved into the stone, their meanings lost to time. The structure seemed to defy the erosion of the desert, standing as a stubborn monument to a forgotten age.

Brand reached out, fingers brushing the cool surface of the stone. A faint pulse of energy passed through his hand, like a whisper in the Flow, ancient and distant. It was as though the ruin itself had a pulse, a faint, lingering memory of something long gone.

"This place is older than the settlement," Nia murmured, her voice soft, reverent. She ran her fingers over the symbols, tracing them like secrets lost in time. "Maybe older than the first cities."

Darius stepped closer, peering into the darkened doorway. "If it's abandoned, we should set up inside. At least it'll shield us from the sun."

Brand hesitated, his instincts whispering a warning. There was something about this place, something... unsettling. It wasn't danger, exactly. Not yet. But the air here felt thick with the weight of things forgotten, of memories that shouldn't be disturbed. The Flow wasn't right here; it was bent, twisted, like a reflection in broken glass.

Kaelen gave a short, weary laugh. "Whatever ghosts are haunting this place, they can't be worse than the CABAL. Let's move."

With no better options, the group pressed forward, stepping into the shadow of the ruins. The air immediately grew cooler, a stark contrast to the oppressive heat outside, but it carried with it the scent of damp stone and ancient dust. Shadows stretched long, curling and twisting along the walls, flickering in the dim torchlight as if they were alive, watching them.

Soran ran a hand along one of the towering pillars, his fingers brushing over its surface. "These weren't built for shelter," he said quietly, his voice low as though afraid of disturbing something older than the world itself. "This place... it was meant for something more."

Brand moved deeper into the ruin, his fingertips grazing over a shattered relief carved into the stone. A figure stood at the center, arms outstretched, surrounded by a swirling energy. The carving was so vivid it almost seemed alive. It felt eerily familiar, like a reflection of how the Flow moved through him when he summoned its power.

His pulse quickened, and for a fleeting moment, he imagined that the walls themselves were whispering. This place held answers—he was sure of it. But there was no time to investigate further.

A distant sound cut through the air, faint at first, but unmistakable. The rhythmic thudding of approaching footsteps—heavy, deliberate. Growing louder with each beat.

It was coming from outside.

And it was drawing nearer.

The sound of thudding intensified, as though a war drum was echoing from deep within the earth. The ruin trembled under its weight, and for a moment, Brand felt as though the stone itself had remembered the horrors it had once witnessed. It groaned in anticipation.

His chest tightened with urgency.

"We don't have much time," Brand said sharply, turning to face the group. His voice was steady, but a sense of dread pooled in his gut. "Get deeper into the ruins. If there's another way out, find it. Now."

Kaelen hesitated, but the urgency in Brand's tone left no room for argument. He nodded and motioned for the others to follow him into the depths of the ruin. Their shadows grew long, stretching across the stone like ghosts, swallowed by the darkness as they disappeared.

Darius and Soran remained, weapons drawn, their eyes scanning the dim entrance.

"They'll be here soon," Darius murmured, the words carrying the weight of an unspoken truth.

Brand nodded, stepping toward the entrance. Outside, the sands churned unnaturally, as though the desert itself was stirring in response to the coming danger. The CABAL was near.

Then, the first figure appeared—clad in black armor, the edges of his form flickering like a shadow in the dying light. His eyes glowed faint red, scanning the entrance with an unblinking, predatory stare. Behind him, more figures emerged, their footfalls soft and disciplined, like a storm creeping in.

They had found them. And they would not leave without blood.

Brand drew a slow breath, letting it steady the storm inside him. He couldn't fight them all. But he could buy time.

With a quiet step forward, just beyond the threshold, he let the moonlight gleam off his blade. It glinted like a promise of pain, the steel a cold extension of his resolve. "You came a long way to die," he said, his voice unwavering, the words cutting through the tension like a knife.

The CABAL warrior's head tilted, studying him with unnerving stillness. No words. Just cold, calculating eyes. Then, without a flicker of hesitation, he raised his weapon.

And with a primal roar, they charged.

Chapter 56:

A Mother's Final Act

The world spun into chaos as Brand collided with the first CABAL warrior. The clash of steel rang out, its impact jolting through his arms. He twisted, channeling the Flow to heighten his speed, slipping past the first attacker to strike at another.

Darius and Soran fought beside him, cutting down foes with ruthless precision, but the CABAL forces pressed on, their numbers overwhelming, their resolve unwavering.

Then, amid the din of battle, a new presence emerged—one Brand had dared not hope for. He had certainly never expected it.

A brilliant surge of energy erupted from the heart of the ruins, a force unlike anything Brand had ever felt. The CABAL warriors faltered as a wave of raw power crashed over them. The Flow responded, bending and shifting, and in that moment, Brand understood.

Oriana had arrived.

From the shadows, she emerged, her form radiant with the last remnants of her strength, her hands glowing with the energy of the

Flow and the glowing marks left by the Gauntlet now shining across her visible skin. Her once-worn face was now a mask of unwavering resolve, her eyes burning with an intensity Brand had never witnessed.

Tink and Belizar followed closely behind, their faces shifting from relief to dread as they took in the battle before them.

"Mother—" Brand began, but she raised a hand, silencing him. Her body was already fading, the energy draining her, yet she stood tall.

With a single, fluid motion, she extended her hands, and the air itself trembled.

The CABAL warriors screamed as their bodies were wrenched from the ground, their weapons torn from their grasps. The energy howled, sweeping through them like a purging fire. One by one, the warriors were hurled backward, vanishing into the swirling sands beyond the ruins.

The battle had ended.

But the price had yet to be paid.

Oriana's breath caught, and she staggered. Brand surged forward, catching her as she collapsed.

She met his gaze, her lips curving into a faint smile. "You've grown strong," she murmured. "But strength alone will not guide you."

Brand's hands shook. "Don't talk like that. We can—"

Oriana shook her head. Her time was ending, and they both knew it.

"The Flow brought me here for a reason," she murmured, brushing a trembling hand against his face. "And now, it will guide you forward."

Her body pulsed with light, the last remnants of her energy dissipating into the air. Then, as though she had never existed, Oriana faded into the wind.

Brand knelt there, silent, the weight of loss sinking deep into his chest. Around him, the survivors stood motionless, the enormity of what had just occurred settling in.

Tink stepped forward, her voice barely above a whisper. "She saved us..."

Brand swallowed hard, his hands tightening into fists. She had given everything, and now it was up to him to ensure it wasn't in vain.

He rose, his grief sharpening into something colder. Something more lethal.

The CABAL had come for him.

Now, it was time to turn the tables.

The silence after Oriana's passing was heavier than the battle itself. The Flow seemed to mourn her absence, the air thick with loss.

Brand remained kneeling, his hands still pressed to the ground where Oriana had vanished. She was gone, and nothing he could do would change that.

Tink stood a few feet away, her arms wrapped tightly around herself. Her face was pale, eyes rimmed red, yet there was something else in them—something unyielding.

She had related the story of how Oriana and Belizar had fended off more attacks by the CABAL after he had left and then how a Spirit

Fox told them to come here. She had known this was important based on Oriana's mood but had never suspected this was what they had been rushing towards.

"We should go," Darius said at last, breaking the silence. "The CABAL might regroup."

Brand didn't move.

Tink exhaled sharply, stepping closer. "Brand."

He met her gaze, and in that moment, he saw it—the fury beneath the grief, the storm barely contained.

"She saved you," Tink said, her voice trembling. "She saved all of us. And you—you're already thinking about the next fight, aren't you?"

Brand clenched his jaw. "The CABAL won't stop."

"And neither will you."

The accusation hung heavy between them. Beside her, Belizar let out a low, rumbling growl—not of hostility, but of discomfort.

"You don't get it, do you?" Tink's voice was rising now, her pain spilling over. "You're always chasing something. The next battle. The next fight. And every time, people die because of it."

Brand sprang to his feet, his grief twisting into something colder. "You think I wanted this? You think I asked for any of it?"

"I think you never stop to ask yourself if there's another way!" Tink shot back. Tears slid from the corners of her eyes, but her voice remained unwavering. "You could stay. We could rebuild. We could honor her by living, not by charging headfirst into another war."

Brand stared at her, his chest rising and falling. He wanted to stay. He wanted to take her hand, to promise her they could have something beyond all of this.

But he couldn't. The CABAL wouldn't let them. Not as long as he was here.

Tink saw it in his eyes before he spoke. She shook her head, turning away before he could utter the words.

"You're leaving," she whispered. "Aren't you?"

Brand swallowed hard. This was the moment. The choice that would define them.

And he had already made it.

"I have to," he said, the words tasting like ash. "But I'm leaving Brand behind. I need a new name, and since I'm going after the CABAL to strike back at them for...this" he gestured all around them, " I'll call myself Striker. Remember Brand for me—I cannot be him anymore."

Tink exhaled shakily. She didn't argue. Didn't try to stop him.

She simply nodded once, then turned and walked away.

Belizar hesitated, watching Brand for a long moment before following her. The weight of their footsteps echoed in his chest, heavier than the battle had ever been.

Brand—now Striker—was alone.

And the path before him was clear.

Chapter 57:

Arrival in the Free Cities

The first thing that hit Striker was the smell—a clash of machine oil, spice, and the sharp bite of ozone from the neon-lit streets. The Free Cities were nothing like the open desert. Gone was the vast emptiness of the dunes; in its place loomed towering megastructures, their walls pulsing with the hum of digital life.

He moved forward, boots clicking against the wet ferrocrete as a gust of hot, synthetic air washed over him. The scent of burnt circuits and street food mingled with the underlying metallic tang of pollution, an ever-present haze thick in the air. Above him, a skybridge flickered with malfunctioning neon lights, casting erratic pulses of red and blue into the streets below.

Striker adjusted the tattered cloak that concealed his blade, stepping from the transport hub onto a bustling street. The cacophony of the Free Cities was relentless. Voices in a dozen languages filled the air, blending with the bass-heavy thrum of club music spilling from underground dens and the distant wail of sirens.

Holo-ads projected along the city's glass facades, displaying sleek corporate products, cybernetic augmentations, and exotic narcotics, their hyperreal images occasionally glitching as power fluctuated. A towering holoscreen flashed above him, advertising underground fights, mercenary contracts, and illicit trades.

Everything in the Free Cities had a price, and if you weren't careful, you'd become the currency.

A group of heavily augmented citizens passed by, their synthetic limbs gleaming under the neon glow. One had a full ocular replacement, his eyes digitized into glowing green reticles. Another sported subdermal plating, his skin shimmering with a faint metallic sheen. Striker felt the weight of their glances as they moved past—assessing him, measuring his worth.

Drones hummed overhead, some belonging to the city's fragmented security forces, others to private syndicates or corporate enforcers. Every few meters, a black-market stall appeared—dealers peddling illegal software patches, weapon mods, or neurostim enhancers promising heightened reflexes.

Striker kept his head low, weaving through the crowd. He had no credits, no contacts, and no plan—only the name he had chosen for himself and the raw instinct to survive.

He paused outside a ramshackle cybernetics shop, its interior bathed in the sterile glow of bio-gel vats. Inside, a med-tech with chromed-out arms replaced a man's cybernetic limb, the whirring hum of servos filling the air. The patient winced as the new limb locked into place, his exposed nerve endings cauterized by a pulse of energy.

The city was ruthless. Striker had to be, too.

A sharp voice cut through the crowd behind him. "You look lost, desert boy."

Striker clenched his jaw, his body tensing. If he was going to carve out a place here, he needed to start somewhere.

Striker turned toward the voice, muscles coiled tight. A woman stood just beyond the neon haze, arms crossed, a smirk tugging at the corner of her lips. She was lean, wrapped in a synth-leather jacket lined with blinking circuitry, her eyes a deep amber glow—augments, scanning, analyzing.

"You new here?" she asked, not a question but a statement.

Striker said nothing, weighing her just as she weighed him. Her stance was loose but practiced—someone accustomed to trouble, or causing it.

She clicked her tongue. "Not much of a talker? That'll get you into trouble fast."

Behind her, the streets pulsed with activity—a fight had broken out in a nearby alley, the wet thud of fists against flesh barely drawing glances from passing citizens. A pair of enforcers stood at the edge of the chaos, placing bets rather than breaking it up.

Striker surveyed the scene. This city thrived on violence, and the only way to earn respect was to prove yourself.

"I know a place," the woman continued, eyeing him closely. "If you're looking to make creds. Fast."

Striker's jaw tightened. He had nothing—no money, no reputation. But he had his fists.

"Where?" he asked.

The woman grinned, tilting her head toward the alley. "The pits. You fight, you win, you get paid. If you're good enough, people start noticing."

Striker exhaled, steeling himself. He'd fought for survival before—but now, he'd fight for something more. A place in this world. A name.

"Take me there."

She laughed, turning on her heel. "Try to keep up, desert boy."

As he followed her deeper into the city, the neon lights flickered above him. Tonight, Striker would bleed. But if he survived, the Free Cities would know his name.

The underground fight pits were nothing like the disciplined combat Striker had known in the desert. This wasn't training. There were no rules—only pain, blood, and the law of the strongest.

The woman led him through a maze of back alleys, past neon-lit stalls hawking unlicensed augments and black-market stimulants. The deeper they went, the grimmer and more dangerous the streets grew. The air thickened with sweat, oil, and the low hum of malfunctioning tech.

At last, she stopped outside a rusted doorway, a holo-sign flickering erratically above it. The text glitched in and out, but the message was unmistakable: THE PIT.

She turned to him. "One rule: you don't die, you don't get paid."

Striker smirked. "Fair enough."

Inside, the pit was a cramped, circular space beneath a collapsed building, its walls reinforced with scrap metal and graffiti honoring past fighters—some victorious, others memorialized in death. The crowd erupted in cheers as a massive cyborg slammed his opponent to the ground, ending the fight with a sickening crunch.

A lanky man with glowing blue implants embedded in his temples stepped forward, sizing Striker up. "New meat?"

The woman nodded. "He's got potential."

The man sneered. "We'll see about that."

Striker barely had time to process before his name blared over the distorted speakers. His first fight.

The crowd parted as his opponent stepped into the ring—a heavily augmented brawler with metal-plated fists and a predator's grin.

Striker entered the pit, the lights flickering above him. This was his first step into the underworld. His first real test.

He took a deep breath, lowered his stance, and waited for the fight to begin.

The air in the pit was thick with sweat, blood, and the raw energy of the crowd. Metallic walls vibrated with the sound of boots pounding the grated floor, the roars of gamblers and spectators melding into a chaotic symphony of anticipation.

Striker locked eyes with his opponent—a towering brute with cybernetic arms that gleamed beneath the flickering lights, each knuckle encased in reinforced plating built to shatter bone.

A distorted voice crackled from the overhead speakers. "Fight!"

The brawler surged forward with alarming speed for his size. Striker barely sidestepped, the gust of the missed punch slicing past his cheek like a steel whip.

He countered with a quick jab, but his knuckles collided with a metal forearm, sending a jolt of pain up his wrist. The brute laughed—a deep, gravelly sound that made one thing clear: this was a fight Striker wasn't meant to win.

He rolled his shoulders and reset his stance. If brute force wouldn't cut it, he'd have to rely on speed—and precision.

The brawler came at him again, this time with a low swing aimed to sweep his legs. Striker sprang back, instincts from desert combat kicking in—reading the rhythm, dodging just before impact.

The crowd jeered, restless and bloodthirsty. But Striker didn't care about the show. He cared about survival.

Then he saw it—a stutter in the brute's step, a fractional delay when shifting weight between his augmented limbs.

Striker lunged, slamming a precise strike into the side of the man's knee—one of the few spots left untouched by cybernetics.

The brawler roared, staggering, his stance faltering.

Striker didn't hesitate. He followed with a flurry of calculated blows—ribs, throat, temple—each one driving his opponent further off balance.

Desperation fueled a wild counterpunch, but Striker ducked low and surged upward, driving his elbow into the man's jaw with brutal force.

The brawler stumbled back, crashing against the cage wall.

The crowd erupted—half in disbelief, half in fury. This wasn't the outcome they'd come to see.

The brawler snarled, shoving off the wall—but his movements were sluggish now, each step a fight against his own failing systems. Striker saw it—the hesitation, the misfires in coordination. The battle was over.

He had won.

With one final motion, Striker spun and delivered a brutal kick to the side of the head. The blow landed clean, sending the metal-plated brute crashing to the floor in a heap.

He didn't get back up.

For a heartbeat, the pit fell silent.

Then the distorted voice echoed overhead: "Winner: Striker."

The crowd erupted—cheers clashing with curses, the thrill of victory tangling with the sting of lost bets.

Striker stood over his fallen opponent, chest rising and falling with slow, steady breaths. His knuckles dripped blood, his muscles trembled, but he didn't waver.

He had survived.

And now, the Free Cities knew his name.

Epilogue:
The Multi-Verse

CODEX Verse:

The rain hadn't stopped since the final match. It washed away the blood and sweat of the underground arenas, leaving only whispers of the violence that had unfolded. In the heart of the Free Cities, beyond the neon glow and steel spires, a storm was brewing—but it wasn't the kind the weather could predict.

Brand stood at the edge of a rooftop, eyes fixed on the pulsing lights below. No longer just Brand. The name that had once been his, the name of a survivor, an exile, was gone.

Striker.

Not a title. Not a gift. A choice.

He had needed a name with purpose—something sharp, something that cut. A name that would strike back at the forces that had shaped his past, carving a place for himself in a world where he was no longer bound by the chains that had once held him. The CABAL had tried to erase him. They had tried to control him. Now, they would fear him.

But something lingered, something deeper gnawing at his thoughts. A hollow space where the Flow had once thrummed beneath his skin, guiding him, whispering possibilities. Now, there was only silence.

He flexed his fingers, staring at his hands—once instruments of precision, of balance. Now, they were weapons. Tools for a fight that had nothing to do with harmony and everything to do with power.

His victories in the arena had meant more than survival. They had meant dominance. The Free Cities had their own rules, their own masters, and he had surpassed them all. But the higher he rose, the clearer it became—the CABAL was still there, lurking, watching. Waiting.

They didn't see him as a threat—not yet. They saw him as a resource.

Striker exhaled sharply, letting his gaze sweep across the skyline. They would learn soon enough.

The weight of expectation had pressed down on him since the day he first fought back. In the desert, he had been shaped by training, honed into something sharper. But he had been told to seek harmony. That was before the desert and the CABAL took everything from him.

He no longer cared for harmony.

A distant siren wailed through the streets below, neon signs flickering as the city pulsed in its endless rhythm. Everything here was a game of control. The CABAL thought they controlled the Flow. The Free Cities believed they controlled fate. They were both wrong.

Striker exhaled slowly, turning away from the edge. There was no mentor left to guide him now. No one to offer wisdom. The Flow had gone silent, and he had no intention of ever seeking its voice again.

He would forge his own path.

The battles ahead wouldn't be fought in the arena.

They would be against the ones who believed they could own him.

And Striker did not belong to anyone.

Regis's Verse

Regis's thoughts drifted once again to his past adventures. Retirement looked more appealing with each passing day, yet every so often, a tug stirred in his mind—a low hum, almost like static, echoing the energy he'd felt the night he met Oriana.

And with it came the question.

The Prophecy.

Had he done the right thing?

He believed he had.

But how would he ever truly know?

CABAL Home Verse

The CABAL scientists were still reviewing the data, even years later. Their models had predicted the optimal conjunction between their Verse and the long-lost one, now only a whisper in theoretical archives. The disruptive energies should have long since faded.

Only one improbable factor could have caused the current

instability: sustained portal use from a third Verse.

A near impossibility.

And yet—it had happened.

This anomaly had to be understood.

Uncontrolled variables could not be allowed to threaten the plan.

So they continued their work, parsing data, probing records, and watching for signs.

Always watching.

The One

Beneath it all—

Beneath the quantum foam of probability and, some might even say, magic, upon which the Verses of the Multiverse floated—

there was The One.

Everywhere. Everywhen.

It sent energy and intent rippling through the frequencies of space and time, a subtle resonance meant to guide all things—

from the humblest of Spirit Animals to those destined for greatness—

forward.

But even The One could only offer support.

True destiny must be chosen.

CODE FOR A DIGITAL MONK
LORE GUIDE

I. The Multi-Verse

Reality - is not a singular world but a vast, intricate tapestry of interconnected Verses, each resonating with its own unique quantum energy signature.

Spirit Nodes - serve as natural anchors, enabling skilled individuals to traverse between them or transmit information much like a network within a Verse.

Folds - are naturally occurring anomalies, similar in nature to Spirit Nodes but far more dangerous and unstable.

Spirit Temples - with their connections to multiple Spirit Nodes, offer increased power, enabling travel between Verses.

Portals—extremely rare, natural phenomena that share properties with Spirit Temples. Some rare beings, such as Regis (Brand's father), are born outside their Verse but retain the signature of their origin, making them fundamentally different.

The Flow - The Flow originates from the One, the fundamental force underlying all time and space. It moves with purpose and intent, guiding events toward their destined course. Digital Monks attune themselves to the Flow, enabling them to act in harmony with reality rather than imposing their will upon it. Those aligned with the Flow experience greater ease and potency in their actions, supported by its guiding purpose.

The Flux - Pure, unbound energy—chaotic and brimming with potential, yet devoid of purpose. It can be shaped by willpower and force, making it the primary tool of the CABAL. Powerful users can channel the Flux to glimpse possible futures, though it lacks the stability and direction that the Flow provides. While the Digital Monks seek harmony with the Flow, the CABAL manipulates the Flux to impose control on the world, attempting to dominate even the Flow itself.

II. Organizations & Factions

The Digital Monks - Guardians of balance, devoting themselves to understanding and attuning to the Flow. Their training refines both mind and body, preparing them to serve as stabilizers in the world. They utilize Spirit Nodes and Spirit Temples to meditate, traverse Verses, and share knowledge. Some monks wield Artifacts to amplify their abilities, but only as extensions of their attunement to the Flow.

The CABAL - A secretive organization - is bent on control through the manipulation of the Flux. They aim to dominate and corrupt the Spirit Nodes, using them to expand their influence across all Verses. They believe that order must be imposed, seeing the Flow as an obstacle to be overcome rather than a guiding force. Their leaders are enhanced with cybernetic modifications, reinforcing their belief that destiny can be controlled through technology. The CABAL came to this Verse from another one eons ago but lost contact with the clash of forces from another Verse accessing this realm at the same time – creating Emberglass as a byproduct of the collision of forces.

III. Key Characters & Roles

Regis - The Verse-traveling seeker who carries the glyph of the CODEX. Regis is guided by the Flow to fulfill a prophecy and becomes the father of Brand.

Oriana - A desert healer with latent spiritual attunement. She provides sanctuary to Regis and becomes the mother of Brand, forming a powerful harmonic link with him.

Brand - The child of prophecy, born of two Verses. As he grows, he begins to resonate with the Flow and shows both instinctive courage and moments of overwhelming potential. His journey from innocent to chosen begins in Book 1.

Soren - A seasoned warrior and mentor. Stoic, strategic, and quietly protective, Doren helps guide Brand's early growth and serves as a bridge between martial strength and moral clarity.

Kaelen - A fierce and loyal fighter, Kaelen blends pragmatism with heart. He acts as a stabilizing force for Brand and the group, often the first to defend or act.

Vaelin - The mystic of the group. Introspective and deeply connected to the early understanding of Flow, Vaelin offers wisdom, spiritual insight, and guidance to Brand beyond tactics.

Revik – a former companion of Oriana's who is now a member of the Desert Rangers.

Tink - A youthful and brilliant tinkerer. Inventive and full of clever contraptions, Tink brings humor, improvisation, and unexpected utility to the team. She is Brand's childhood friend and first love interest.

Belizar - The cybernetic Spirit Lizard and ancient guardian. Sometimes cryptic, often comical, Belizar is much older than he lets on — and much more important. He understands the Flow, the CABAL, and the CODEX better than any mortal.

Desert Rangers - A nomadic defense force aligned with the guardians of sacred sites. They ride the edge of civilization and mysticism, working to protect Spirit Nodes from tampering — especially by forces like the CABAL.

The Crystalline Voice - The disembodied resonance that speaks to Regis in the Threshold cave. Possibly a manifestation of the CODEX itself or message from the One via the Flow.

The One - The infinite source beneath all Verses, the very foundation of all existence. The Flow emanates from the One, guiding reality toward its inherent balance. Those who attune to the One through the Flow gain insight beyond the constraints of time and space, perceiving what is meant to be rather than what merely is. Corruption arises when forces seek to control or divert this natural state, as seen in the CABAL's attempts to dominate the Flow. An omnipresent but silent force — normally referenced in tone and spirit, rather than dialogue.

IV. Locations of Power

Spirit Nodes - Concentrated points where energy aligns, where the Flow and Flux converge. Used by Digital Monks for meditation, communication, and traversal across Verses. The CABAL seeks to corrupt these Nodes, twisting their energies into instruments of control.

Spirit Temples - Structures built at key intersections of the Flow, serving as both training grounds and sanctuaries for the Digital Monks. Act as havens, shielding those within from the destabilizing effects of corrupted Flux. Atemiwaza taps into the ancient knowledge of the CODEX within these sacred spaces.

Ashara - The desert village where Oriana lives. It serves as the emotional and cultural core of the early story, and the setting for the Festival of Emberlights

Festival Grounds of Emberlights - The glowing heart of Ashara's annual celebration, where Oriana and Regis first meet. Emberglass lanterns and dancing rituals provide spiritual symbolism for Flow and resonance

Threshold Caves - Located near Ashara. These crystal-filled caves are where Regis encounters visions and crosses Verses. The setting features deeply spiritual moments, glyphs, and metaphysical resonance

Ancient Ruins of Ashara and Kal'Shara– Trials for Oriana during her journey helping her fight the CABAL and learn about Flux and

Flow.

Ancient Runs/The Forgotten Depths - A haunting, whisper-filled site that Brand explores, connected to echoes of past civilizations. He has a powerful vision here involving a glowing city under twin suns. The ruins are spiritually and narratively significant

The Vault / Temple Doors - Described as a structure that responds to Oriana and the Flow. Guarded by symbolic carvings and tied to ancient power, this becomes a transitional site leading into deeper lore connected to the Flow

Ashara Outpost - A trading hub of makeshift tents and battered structures. It sits on the edge of civilization and law, representing danger and the influence of outside forces like the CABAL. Rasha, a fixer-like figure, operates here

Circular Building of Rasha's Authority - A place of information exchange and negotiation at the heart of Ashara Outpost. This space is neutral territory, watched over by Rasha and filled with mercenaries and travelers

Market at Night (Ashara Outpost) - A vivid, living space filled with traders, informants, and suspicion. Brand conducts a covert investigation here alongside Tink, Kaelen, and Soran

Desert Ridge / Cliff Region - The rocky terrain where Oriana uses the Flow to collapse dunes and bury CABAL beasts. This is also the lead-up to the temple-like structure she later enters

V. The CODEX & Destiny

The CODEX - A living repository of lost wisdom. Preserves ancient techniques and truths about the very nature of energy. Serves as a bridge between Verses.

Brand's Unique Role - As the offspring of two distinct energy signatures, only he can harmonize the Flow and Flux. He must decide whether to impose his will like the CABAL or move within the Flow like the Digital Monks.

ABOUT THE AUTHOR

Victor Newsom (aka LordElvic), a long-time book lover, gamer, and avid fan of art and science. He has four grown children and lives on a mountain with his wife and "grand kitten."

Victor holds multiple patents, a Black Belt in Taekwondo, a multitude of tattoos, has appeared in Bodybuilding (Iron Man), FinTech, and Gaming magazines, and is known to present at conferences where he will talk at length about technology innovations in payments and crypto (whether you ask him about it or not, you have been warned). This trilogy (CODE FOR A DIGITAL MONK), like the first book (RISE OF THE WAR TWINS) was inspired by the NFT collections, artwork, community, and goals of the SYNTHTOPIA project and the DESTABILIZERS.

Find out more at www.synthtopia.world

As LordElvic – the author explores music, video, and art creation. You can catch more of his work below:

YouTube: https://www.youtube.com/channel/
UCh2KrYB85mbzVo2jGS0fw_w

Spotify: https://open.spotify.com/
artist/0VlRXdEwuhpW2boauRdFR4

Apple Music: https://music.apple.com/us/artist/
lordelvic/1790304810

And you can always find his books available at most online book sellers around the world!